Enter a world of vibrant passion and intrigue as chronicled by one of the most beloved and bestselling authors of historical romance writing today, the incomparable Jane Feather.

In this pair of linked novels, two unforgettable sisters joined by family and destiny are each caught up in deceit, desire, and an adventure where they find love beyond their wildest dreams . . . with the men of their dreams.

Sensible Pen . . .
No one believed her—
but for once in her life she would follow her heart to discover the truth about the past.

Flirtatious Pippa . . .
She'd always led a charmed life—
until she became unknowingly caught in a treacherous web.

This is her story. . . .

Also by Jane Feather

Kissed by
Shadows

Jane
Feather

BANTAM BOOKS

KISSED BY SHADOWS

A Bantam Book/February 2003

ISBN 0-553-58308-5

Published simultaneously in the United States and Canada

Bantam Books are published by Bantam Books, a division of Random
House, Inc. Its trademark, consisting of the words "Bantam Books" and
the portrayal of a rooster, is Registered in U.S. Patent and Trademark Office and in other countries. Marca Registrada. Bantam Books, New York,
New York.

PRINTED IN THE UNITED STATES OF AMERICA

OPM   10 9 8 7 6 5 4 3 2 1

Kissed by Shadows

Prologue

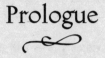

THE PANELED CHAMBER WAS IN SHADOWS, THE ONLY light thrown from a branched candelabrum on a side table that caught the deep fire of ruby, the golden glow of topaz, the rich flash of emerald adorning the heavy silks and velvets of the six men in the chamber.

The tall windows were shuttered, closing out the warm summer night, and the air in the chamber was stifling. The men were sweating, dark patches staining the thickly embroidered brocade of their doublets, rivulets trickling down the back of their necks where their hair clung wet beneath jeweled velvet caps.

As a group they approached the daybed that stood in deepest shadow against the wall. The bed was draped with a white sheet and the still figure upon it looked as if she lay upon her bier. One arm hung down, the fingertips brushing the rich Turkey carpet. Her hair, the color of cinnamon, was loose on the pillow, her thin frame clad only in a linen nightshift. Freckles were visible even in the shadowed gloom, standing out harshly against the extreme pallor of her countenance. Paper-thin eyelids fluttered as if she were dreaming, and then were still again.

"You are certain she is aware of nothing?" The question was startling as it broke the almost reverent silence in the chamber. The voice, although barely more than a whisper, was a thickly accented rasp.

"She is unconscious, Your Majesty. She will not come to herself for many hours." One of his companions moved up to stand beside him as he looked down upon the woman.

"Indeed, Your Majesty, this will not even invade her dreams."

The king turned his head towards this last speaker. He gave a short sardonic laugh. "In general, Ruy, my companions in the games of love are honored and pleasured by my attentions."

"This is no game of love, Philip, 'tis insurance," the other said quietly, with the familiarity of an old and intimate friend.

The king touched his fingers to his lips, stroked his short beard. "I have no need of the reminder, Ruy."

Ruy Gomez merely nodded. "Shall we withdraw, sir?"

"Or, if Your Majesty prefers, we could move the screen to give you privacy." One of the others gestured to a tall screen that stood in front of the empty hearth.

The king looked at the circle of solemn faces around him. His eye fell on one man, who stood isolated from the rest, in the far corner of the chamber. His face was shuttered, averted from the daybed, every line of his body indicating the most acute discomfort.

"There is no need for the husband to remain," the king stated. "My lord Nielson, you may wait in the antechamber."

The man bowed jerkily and hurried from the chamber without once glancing towards the daybed.

"Bring forward the screen and the rest of you may withdraw beyond it." The king's voice was harsh and determined, as if he had resolved finally upon executing a distasteful duty.

His orders were obeyed.

"A single candle at the head," the king instructed.

Ruy Gomez removed a lit candle from the candelabrum and placed it in the sconce on the wall above the daybed, then he bowed and withdrew.

The light shone down on the pale countenance, the still, white figure. The king stood in shadow at the foot of the bed. He unlaced his hose of white doeskin, loosened his doublet of cloth of gold, and brusquely moved aside the woman's linen shift. He looked down at her as she lay in the pool of golden light, then he leaned forward to part the milky thighs, to run his hands over the pale skin of her belly.

Beyond the screen the four men waited. The silence in the chamber was profound; it was almost as if it were inhabited only by statues. When the king emerged from behind the screen, they seemed to exhale as one.

"It is done," he stated. "Take her to her husband."

The man who now approached the daybed was dressed with more simplicity than his companions. His only jewel was a curious brooch at his throat, a serpent of blackest jet with two brilliant emeralds for eyes and a forked tongue tipped with a blue-white diamond. The man's face was impassive as he bent over the woman, swiftly adjusting the shift so that she was once again completely covered. He touched her cheek, moving aside a lock of reddish-brown hair that had fallen over her eyes.

The woman's eyes suddenly opened. She stared up at him. She tried to raise her arm but when he placed a hand over her eyes, drawing down the lids again, she was once more still, her breathing deep and slow.

He lifted her, wrapping her in the white sheet that had draped the bed. None of the other men looked at him as he passed into the antechamber, where he placed his burden without speaking into the outstretched arms of her husband. Immediately he strode away from the chamber, disappearing into the shadows of the long corridor.

Within the paneled chamber Ruy Gomez went to the window and threw back the shutters.

A light breeze wafted into the room, bringing the scent of roses and the sweet song of a nightingale.

One

PIPPA WAS AWARE OF THE BRIGHT SUNLIGHT BEFORE she opened her eyes. She lay still until she was fully awake. She knew almost without waiting for the sensations to make themselves apparent that her mouth would be dry, her limbs heavy, a faint dull ache in her joints. Whenever she slept past daybreak, it was always thus.

It was so unusual for her to sleep late. She had always awoken at cockcrow, ready for whatever the new day might hold. But in the last weeks, since the queen's wedding to Philip of Spain, there had been these mornings when she'd awoken feeling leaden and listless, a pain behind her eyes that took half the day to dissipate.

She moved her body carefully on the deep feather mattress. Stuart was beside her. He had not come to bed with her the previous evening, but that was generally the case. Wine still lingered on his breath and she guessed it had been dawn before he had left his friends and the cards and dice to which he was addicted.

She turned onto her side away from him, unwilling

as yet to ring the handbell for her maid and begin the tedious process of dressing for the day.

As she moved her legs apart she noticed the slight discomfort, the dried stickiness on her thighs. *Why?* she thought with exasperation. Just why did Stuart only make love to her when she was asleep? She had never shown herself an unwilling partner. Indeed, in the early weeks after their marriage she had done everything she could to make their bedplay inviting and exciting. His enthusiasm had been distinctly muted, she reflected, but at least she'd been awake on each occasion.

Her husband stirred beside her, and with renewed energy Pippa rolled over, propping herself on an elbow to face him. Even in sleep, even with wine-soured breath, he was utterly beautiful. Fair curls clustered on a broad alabaster brow, thick brown eyelashes were crescent moons on his high cheekbones, his complexion tinged with gold from the sun. Lord Nielson was an avid hunter, a man who loved all outdoor pursuits as much as he loved the card tables. A man who could burn the candle at both ends without any apparent ill effects.

As if aware of his wife's scrutiny, he opened his eyes. Eyes the color of pure aquamarine, the whites as clear as a baby's.

Pippa's voice had an edge to it. "Why didn't you wake me, Stuart? If you wished to couple last night, why didn't you wake me?"

He looked discomfited, reached out a hand to touch her arm. "You were sleeping so soundly, Pippa. I had a great need for you but I didn't wish to disturb you."

Pippa sat up, brushing his hand away. "Why would you keep the pleasure to yourself? This is the fourth or fifth time this month. Do you enjoy making love to a corpse?"

Hot color flooded Stuart's fair complexion. He flung aside the covers and almost jumped to the floor, keeping his back to her. "That is a vile thing to say."

"Maybe so," Pippa said, sitting up. "But you must forgive me if I find it an equally vile thing to be used for your pleasure in my sleep."

Pippa knew the sharpness of her tongue and in general tried to moderate it with her husband. He became hurt so easily, and then as swiftly sullen. When he was in good spirits he was an amusing, pleasant companion, quick-witted and energetic. He suited her own temperament very well, which was why, she reflected now, she had agreed to marry him. That and his undeniable beauty.

She nibbled at a loose fingernail, frowning as she watched him thrust his arms into the wide sleeves of a chamber robe, still with his back averted. She didn't think she was shallow enough to find beauty sufficient in a husband, but Stuart Nielson had also charmed her with his physical prowess, his ability to make her laugh, and not least his devout admiration.

"I'll be in my dressing chamber," he said to the door frame. "Do you wish me to summon Martha?"

"If you please," Pippa responded, falling back against the pillows, closing her eyes once again. The bright sunlight exacerbated the dull thudding in her head.

There had been more to it than that, of course. At twenty-five she had been suddenly surprised by the sense that something was missing in her life. Until that revelation she had stoutly maintained that marriage was an irrelevancy, that she was having far too much amusement among the young players at court to settle into domesticity and the inevitable childbearing. But then her sister Pen had married Owen d'Arcy, and Pippa had realized that her own life seemed very empty. It was amusing to dance, to flirt with passionate encounters, but it was no longer enough.

A soft tap at the door heralded the arrival of Martha, bearing hot water in a covered jug. She greeted her mistress cheerfully. "Good morrow, madam. 'Tis a beautiful day."

"Yes," Pippa agreed but with so little enthusiasm that her maid regarded her with some concern.

"Is it your head again, madam?"

Pippa sighed and passed a hand over her eyes. "Aye. 'Tis the very devil, Martha. I've never suffered from headaches before."

"Mayhap your ladyship is with child," Martha observed shrewdly. "After seven months of marriage, 'tis quite possible."

"It's not truly been seven months, Martha," Pippa reminded the maid. She sat on the edge of the bed, gazing down at the richly waxed oak floor. She and Stuart had been married in January. They had had six weeks of marriage before the Lady Elizabeth, the queen's half sister, had been accused of treason in the aftermath of Thomas Wyatt's rebellion and imprisoned in the Tower. Pippa, as her closest companion, had been one of the few women permitted to share her imprisonment.

On Elizabeth's release at the end of May, Pippa had been reunited with her husband, and separated by the queen's order from her friend. Mary saw sedition everywhere and insisted that her half sister have only strangers as her companion/guards during her house arrest at the palace of Woodstock in Oxfordshire.

Pippa had been ordered with her husband to attend at court, Stuart had been active in the negotiations for the queen's marriage to Philip of Spain, and they had resumed married life.

" 'Tis been over two months since you returned to court, my lady," Martha observed, setting her jug of water on the dresser.

"Two months," Pippa muttered. There were times when it seemed much longer, longer even than the three months of terror in the Tower, when the scaffold on which Lady Jane Grey had died stood on the green beneath their windows, an ever-present reminder of the penalty for treason.

Stuart had hardly been an ardent lover since his wife's return. She tried now to remember how it had been in the few weeks after their wedding night, before her imprisonment. He had been diffident on their wedding night but she had thought little of it. The passionate flirtation of their courtship had died a sudden death, but again she had thought little of it. Indeed she had had no time to think of anything amid the bloody turmoil of Wyatt's rebellion, the mass executions that followed it, and the terrifying danger in which Elizabeth and her friends had stood.

And now her husband only coupled with her when she was sound asleep.

Did the act disgust him? Did he see it simply as a distasteful duty best accomplished swiftly and with minimal contact?

The thought was so startling her head jerked up of its own volition and she winced at the renewed pain behind her eyes.

Perhaps it wasn't the act itself that disgusted him, but his wife. He no longer found his wife appealing. Perhaps in her absence in the Tower he had taken a mistress, a woman more to his taste.

Pippa stood up and slowly pulled her nightshift over

her head. "Fetch a bath, Martha. I would bathe this morning."

"Yes, madam." Martha hurried from the chamber.

Pippa went to the glass of finely beaten silver and surveyed her body with clear-eyed criticism. She was thin. Bony. Scrawny. Now, the Lady Elizabeth was thin, but elegantly so. Slender was the word one might use.

Pippa thought caustically that there was nothing elegant about the wavery image of the bag of bones in the mirror.

Strange how she had never questioned her physical appearance before. She peered closer, wondering if it would be possible to count the freckles that thickly scattered her very white complexion. Not a hope in hell. Her eyes were not unattractive though. They were more gold than green in the sunlight and slightly slanted. Her hair was thick, at least, even if it was an unruly mass. But the color was quite pretty.

"Madam, will you retire behind the screen, the men are bringing up the bath."

"Oh, yes. I didn't hear you come in." Pippa abandoned her inventory and slipped behind the worked screen to wait until the bustle in the bedchamber had ceased and the sound of the door closing on the burly servitors ensured privacy once more.

She emerged and stepped into the copper tub with a sigh of relief. Her body felt used and that wash of distaste made her lip curl. *Why?* Just what had gone wrong with this marriage? She took up the washcloth and scrubbed at her inner thighs with rough vigor.

On Queen Mary's accession, Pippa had joined the household of the Lady Elizabeth, the queen's half sister. With all the excitement of the queen's disputed accession and Mary's final triumph over the machinations of the Duke of Northumberland, Pippa had thought life beside the clever and vibrant Lady Elizabeth could only provide stimulation and adventure. And indeed it had, in the first six months after the queen's coronation.

Stuart Nielson, a distant relative of Elizabeth's on her mother Boleyn's side, had joined the court. And from the very first, it seemed, he had singled out Pippa for attentions that went far beyond the skillful flirting that she enjoyed so much.

Pippa closed her eyes as the warm water soothed her. She remembered the first time she had laid eyes upon him. It was at a joust at Whitehall, part of the coronation celebrations. Stuart had unhorsed his opponent in one try of the lance. At the banquet and dancing that night he had been made much of for his skill, both on the dance floor and in the lists, and the women of the court, both attached and single, had openly admired his beauty.

Pippa soaped a foot in leisurely fashion. Had she been flattered by the way he declared his preference for Lady Philippa Hadlow? On reflection, she didn't think so. She'd played in the fields of courtly gallantry for six years; she was immune to flattery unless it amused her.

It had been a whirlwind courtship. Her mother and stepfather had encouraged it, probably because they had despaired of her ever marrying; her sister Pen had almost thrust her into Stuart's arms; even her stepbrother, Robin, usually overly critical of her flirtatious activities, had made a friend of Stuart and had pronounced himself perfectly satisfied with his sister's choice.

Pippa pulled a face that was half smile, half grimace as she thought of Robin's firmly stated approval. It wasn't that she discounted his opinions, quite the reverse, but sometimes he could be very pompous.

"Madam, will you dress now?" Martha's discreet tones brought Pippa's reminiscing to an end.

She rose in a shower of drops and wrapped herself in the towel Martha handed her. "I think I'll wear the peacock-blue gown with the rose-pink underskirt," she announced. She needed something to lift her spirits. It was so unusual for her to feel depressed and out of sorts that it took considerable effort to force herself to think of what pleasures the day ahead might hold.

"Should I prepare a powder for your head, my lady?"

"If you please, and I'll break my fast. Just ale and some bread and cheese." Pippa dropped the towel and went to the domed window that looked down upon the park. Brightly clad figures were already strolling along the graveled walks. A party of Spaniards crossed the lawns to the terrace beneath her windows. They walked close together, hands always at the ready on their sword hilts. They were much disliked by the English court, and were subject to assault in the streets if they were unlucky enough to meet a group of rowdy Londoners. Their melodious yet incomprehensible speech rose on the air.

Pippa's lip curled, her long nose twitched slightly. She found them as a whole arrogant, pompous, and totally lacking in humor. But these days she had little choice but to smile courteously, dance when asked, applaud at their entertainments.

House arrest in Elizabeth's company at Woodstock would be infinitely preferable, she decided, as she turned to take her undergarments from the waiting Martha.

Half an hour later, a hunk of bread and cheese in

hand, she examined her reflection once more in the mirror. Clothes were a distinct improvement. The vibrant colors and rich flowing materials disguised her prominent bones and gave a degree of luster to her white skin so that the freckles weren't quite so conspicuous. She had tamed her rebellious hair with a caul of delicate gold netting and the glint of the gold set off her tawny eyes.

Yes, dressed she presented a rather attractive appearance, although far from conventional beauty. But then, of course, when her husband sought her company in bed she had only her bare bones to offer him.

Her head throbbed anew and she dabbed a little lavender water on her handkerchief and pressed it to her temples. The headache powder was taking longer than usual to bring relief.

She turned as the door opened behind her. Stuart entered smiling. "Ah, how well we complement each other," he said approvingly as he took in her costume. "I tried to guess what gown you would choose and I see I guessed right."

The smile was a facade, Pippa thought. Both the smile and the charming tone. She couldn't tell whether it was simply anger at their earlier argument that lay beneath the surface or something deeper.

However, she offered a responding smile. Their shared pleasure in the luxurious materials and colors of dress had been another factor in their early attraction for each other. Stuart had always gone to great pains to ensure that his own garments complemented hers. This morning was no exception. His doublet of topaz velvet, the sleeves slashed to reveal the lining of dark blue satin that matched his striped hose, was a perfect foil for her own turquoise and rose.

He came over to her and delicately brushed a crumb from her lip before taking her hand and lightly kissing the corner of her mouth. He whispered, mindful of Martha's presence in the chamber, "Forgive me for last night, Pippa dearest. I was overdrunk and careless of your needs."

She could allow herself to believe him; it was so much easier than dealing with her own doubts and questions. His smile now seemed warm and genuine, and she knew well how fond he was of wine and how much he and his cronies could drink over the card table.

"I would not care for it to happen again," she said, her own voice low.

He bent his head to kiss her again, and she didn't see the shadow that passed across his eyes.

He said brightly, "Come, madam wife, we are bidden to the queen's presence chamber. I understand the Spaniards are to arrange a tourney of canes later this morning and we are all to take part. Poor sport, I think it, but we must be courteous to our guests."

There was a brittle edge to his voice that Pippa found a little puzzling, but then she dismissed it. The Spaniards' preference for the tame jousting with canes rather than lances was a matter of ridicule and scorn among the Englishmen at the court and an athlete of Stuart's standard would be particularly contemptuous. But, of course, Philip of Spain was the queen's husband and the vagaries of his retinue must be smiled upon.

They left the chamber arm in arm. The wide corridor outside was thronged with servants and courtiers. The antechamber to the queen's presence chamber was even more closely crowded, but way was made for Lord and Lady Nielson. They passed into the queen's presence and the double doors closed behind them.

Simon Renard, the Spanish ambassador, stood beside the queen's chair under the cloth of estate. Philip of Spain, however, was absent from the chamber, although the chattering of his retinue resembled to Pippa's ears the sound of starlings giving forth in foreign tongue.

The queen did not immediately deign to recognize the newcomers. Pippa knew that this galled Stuart, however he had no choice but to bite his tongue since his wife was no longer in Mary's favor. Pippa's family had stood by Mary during her troubles and the queen remained certain of their loyalty, but when Pippa had chosen to enter Elizabeth's service it had been seen, however unreasonably, as a defection. She was no longer trusted by the queen or the Privy Council, tolerated only because of her husband and her family.

Pippa was not a whit put out by this withdrawal of favor, although she was sorry that it pained her husband. She looked around the small group in the chamber.

"Oh, there's Robin." She dropped her husband's arm and made a move towards her stepbrother, who stood to one side of the chamber, slightly apart from the main group.

Stuart seized her forearm and spoke in an urgent undertone. "Pippa, you have not yet been acknowledged by Her Highness. You cannot greet anyone else first."

It was true and Pippa yielded with a sigh. They stood ignored for what seemed a very long time before a chamberlain approached and indicated that the queen's grace would receive them.

Mary smiled upon Lord Nielson and frowned upon his wife. "You are in good health, Lady Nielson?" Her tone was distant.

"Yes, indeed, I thank you, Your Grace." Pippa remained in a deep curtsy, head bowed in submission.

"You may rise."

Pippa rose, her skirts settling in graceful folds around her. She thought that Mary was regarding her with a closer scrutiny than ordinarily.

"Do you have any correspondence with the Lady Elizabeth?"

"It has not been sanctioned by Your Grace," Pippa responded in a tone that carefully expressed puzzlement at the question.

Mary glanced sideways at Renard, one eyebrow slightly lifted. "No," she said with a dismissive gesture. "And neither will it be."

Pippa curtsied again and moved backwards out of the royal presence. Her husband, however, did not accompany her. Mary had retained his presence with a lifted finger.

"You will take part in the cane play this afternoon, Lord Nielson. The king is most anxious to try his skills against such a lauded opponent."

"It will be my honor to match canes with His Majesty, madam."

Mary nodded, and hesitated for a moment before saying, "You will ensure, I trust, that His Majesty's opponents understand the intricacies and skill required in the Spanish joust."

A game of breaking sticks, Stuart reflected even as he covertly assured his queen that no hint of English contempt would mar the Spaniards' pleasure.

Pippa, now free, hurried to where her stepbrother stood with the French ambassador, the disgruntled and now disfavored Antoine de Noailles. But even as she reached her quarry her eye was caught by a man standing alone against the narrow door behind the queen's chair. The door that led to the queen's privy chamber.

He was leaning his shoulders against the door. He wore a short cloak of dark gray silk over a plain white shirt and dove-colored doublet. His shirt was open at the neck, strangely casual in this formal setting. She gazed at his bare throat, and her skin prickled. Her gaze moved up, and then she was aware only of his eyes. Wide, deep-set, clearest gray.

Her step faltered. Where had she seen those eyes before? How could a stranger's throat seem so familiar? A curious dread crept up her spine, tendrils of fearful confusion tangled her mind, as if she were fighting her way up from a nightmare.

She had never seen him before. She *knew* she had never seen him before. His face, quite apart from the piercing clarity of his eyes, would be impossible to forget. It was strangely crumpled, the features haphazardly put together, and yet there was the oddest symmetry to it.

He didn't stir from his negligent pose against the door, but he looked at her and then he smiled. It was a smile of such surpassing sweetness, of such compassion, of such complete reassurance, that Pippa had to restrain herself from rushing across the chamber to his side.

She stood, her feet refusing to resume their path towards Robin. Bewilderment swamped her. His smile and the dread that had settled upon her shoulders like an almost palpable cloud were connected in some way, and yet how could they be?

"Pippa?" Robin's voice snapped her free. She glanced with relief at the familiar, beloved, untidy figure of her stepbrother.

"I was coming to find you." Her voice sounded squeaky.

"You looked like Lot's wife," he observed. "Turned

to a pillar of salt. What did you see over your shoulder?"

"Nothing," she said, shrugging as if she could cast off the shadow. "I just find Mary's disfavor so uncomfortable. And I know it distresses Stuart."

Robin looked at her closely. It was a reasonable enough explanation for anyone but Pippa. But he knew full well that Pippa did not find her present disfavor in the least uncomfortable, it merely confirmed her in her loyalty to Elizabeth.

"You look peaky," he observed with some concern. "Are you unwell?"

"No . . . no, not in the least," she returned firmly.

Experience told Robin that he'd get nowhere by pressing. "I have news from Pen," he said. "Or at least, the ambassador has a dispatch from Owen and Pen has added a few sentences."

"Oh, show me at once." Pippa turned herself away from the man by the door. She found she needed to turn her whole body away, and felt her movements to be stilted, like the articulated limbs of one of her nephew's toy soldiers. And even with her back to him as she approached the French ambassador in the window embrasure, she could feel his eyes upon her.

"Lady Pippa." Antoine de Noailles addressed her with the casual familiarity of an old friend. "I have here a dispatch from Chevalier d'Arcy. Your sister encloses a few words for you."

"My thanks." Pippa almost snatched the parchment from his hands in her eagerness. And then involuntarily she glanced once more over her shoulder before immediately unfolding the sheet.

"Who is that man by the door, Robin?" Her voice

was satisfactorily casual, she thought, as she perused her sister's words, for the moment not taking them in.

Robin looked across the chamber. "You mean Ashton?"

"I'd hardly ask you his name if I knew it already," she retorted in the sparring manner customary between brother and sister. "The man in the dark gray cloak, over by the door to the privy chamber. He just seems familiar, but I don't recall seeing him before."

"Oh, that's Lionel Ashton, Lady Pippa." The French ambassador supplied the information. "He has close ties to the queen's husband, although he's by birth an Englishman. He's known for his subtlety, a man who works best from the sidelines. He does not in general frequent the court so it's not surprising that you have not seen him before."

The ambassador scratched his nose as he continued to look across the chamber. "I wonder what has brought him out in the open now. I believe his task has been to smooth discreetly the path between the English and Spanish courts. But perhaps the ill-feeling has grown so strong it requires more direct mediation." This last was said in sardonic tones. There was no love lost between the French and Spanish embassies.

"I see."

An Englishman allied with the Spaniards. How could he possibly be familiar? She must be imagining things, Pippa decided. She was not in general subject to extravagant flights of fancy. It probably had something to do with the headache powder, which, thank God, was beginning to work.

Pippa determinedly reread her sister's letter. "Oh, this is wonderful. Pen says that they are hoping to be in England by Christmas."

Robin's face split into a beam of delight. "We must send word to Lady Guinevere and my father."

"Right away," Pippa said. "I'll do it now." She looked towards the queen's chair, wondering if she could slip discreetly from the presence chamber. She had, after all, been dismissed from the queen's immediate presence.

Stuart was in conversation with Ruy Gomez, Philip of Spain's closest friend and advisor. Pippa thought that her husband seemed ill at ease, his full mouth unusually taut, a sheen of sweat on his upper lip. As if aware of her regard he turned to look at her. His expression was strained and he didn't acknowledge her smile. Ruy Gomez did not even glance in her direction. His handsome angular and swarthy countenance remained calm, cool as if he were in an ice house instead of this sweltering crowded chamber on an August morning.

As Pippa watched, Stuart left Ruy Gomez and crossed the chamber to where Lionel Ashton stood. He seemed no more comfortable in the Englishman's company than he had in the Spaniard's, Pippa thought, a puzzled frown creasing her brow. Without conscious intention she strolled around the chamber towards the two men standing behind the queen's chair.

She acknowledged acquaintances as she passed, paused for a word or a greeting when appropriate, aware of a fixed smile upon her face. To her annoyance Stuart moved away from Ashton before she could reach them and the opportunity for an introduction was lost.

Lionel Ashton, however, remained in his place. He did not move as she reached him, indeed seemed unaware of her. Then, as she made to pass him, he laid a hand on her arm. It was as quickly removed. He murmured, "Your pardon," and resumed his calm appraisal of the chamber.

Pippa felt the warm, light touch of his hand through the fine silk of her tight sleeve.

It was a touch her skin knew.

Two

"You have talked with Lord Kendal?" Noailles asked Robin in an undertone. He was obliged to repeat the question when his companion did not immediately respond.

Robin was watching his stepsister's roundabout departure from the presence chamber. She looked strained, heavy-eyed. He saw her pause by Lionel Ashton, saw the light brushing touch of the man's hand on Pippa's sleeve.

Strange that she should have been so interested in a man whose attendance at court was more of a shadow than a substantial presence. Robin had seen Ashton only three times since the man had arrived with Philip in July and he knew nothing of his personal circumstances. Of his business here he knew only what the French ambassador had just told him.

"Your pardon, sir." He became aware of the ambassador's question and turned his full attention to Noailles.

"Your father," the ambassador said, moving farther

back into the window embrasure. "Did you talk with him as yet?"

"Yes," Robin replied in the same undertone. "But he will make no move against the queen, although he mislikes the Spanish marriage as much as anyone. He says he supports Elizabeth as heir to the throne, but in the event that the queen has a child then he will support the queen's offspring."

The French ambassador pursed his lips. "There are too many honorable men of your father's thinking," he muttered. "Integrity and loyalty are fair enough in their place, but do Englishmen really wish to become a dependency of Spain? Colonized like the Netherlands? Ruled by the Inquisition?"

Robin shrugged slightly. "They do not like it, but they saw what happened to those who would oppose it. Even now the skeletons of those who supported Wyatt in his rebellion hang upon the gibbets in reminder."

"Surely 'tis not fear that keeps the Earl of Kendal from open opposition?" Noailles muttered.

Robin's color rose. "You would not question my father's courage!"

"No . . . no," the ambassador said hastily. "Hardly. But without the support of men like Lord Kendal, Lady Elizabeth's situation is perilous."

"I know it." Robin's dour gaze roamed the chamber thronged with the Spaniards, haughty and arrogant in their rich plumage. Their English counterparts seemed dull in comparison. His eye fell on Stuart Nielson. He stood now to one side of Ruy Gomez and Simon Renard, and to Robin it seemed that Stuart was in attendance on the two Spaniards, awaiting their pleasure in some way.

He was aware of a flash of anger that a man of Stuart

Nielson's lineage, courtly charms, and prowess at arms should appear as a supplicant, somehow subservient to the interlopers. Forgetting Noailles, he took a step forward, intent on disrupting the disagreeable scene by drawing Pippa's husband into conversation.

"So, Robin, have you given thought to what we discussed?" The ambassador laid a detaining hand on Robin's brocade sleeve.

Reluctantly Robin turned back to Noailles. "Aye," he said, his expression grave, his vivid blue eyes holding the other's gaze steadily. "I will act as your courier to the Lady Elizabeth."

Noailles nodded briefly. "Then we should not be seen overlong in conversation. I bid you good day, Lord Robin." He bowed and moved away.

Robin looked again for his brother-in-law but he was no longer in the chamber. The heat was oppressive and there was a heavy scent of perfume in the air, although it did little to combat the odor of flesh perspiring in heavy velvets and brocaded satins.

Robin leaned out of the window and took a deep breath of the summer air. It was not as fresh as it might be either. There had been no rain for days and from the city arose a reeking miasma of rotting garbage. The sluggish river stank of decaying mud and refuse, and the green slime coating its banks. It would be a pleasure to leave London and take Noailles's letters to Elizabeth at Woodstock. Robin turned back to the presence chamber and saw Simon Renard making his way purposefully towards him. He pretended not to notice his approach and with the air of one on important and urgent business made for the door before Renard could reach him.

His errand to Elizabeth would carry considerable risk, as the lady was forbidden to send or receive any communications, or to receive visitors who were not approved by her custodian, Sir Henry Bedingfield. However, Robin knew of several ways to circumvent the gaoler's precautions.

Pippa would be glad of the opportunity to write privately to Elizabeth, he reflected as he strode down the great staircase of the palace. Once he'd arranged the details of his departure he'd tell her. She would have to keep her correspondence a secret from her husband, but Robin didn't think that that scruple would trouble Pippa unduly. Stuart knew where her loyalties lay, she had after all, when only a bride, shared Elizabeth's imprisonment in the Tower.

He stepped out onto the wide terrace that ran the length of the palace, facing the river. The sweep of weeping willows along the bank offered the promise of a cool green shade and a degree of peace from the crowded gardens and chambers of the palace.

Robin made his way across the lawn, his head down as he debated the best way to make his approach to Elizabeth. But his clear thinking was disturbed by a sense of unease. He worried at it for a while, like a terrier with a rat, until he identified it.

Pippa. Pippa was not herself. She hadn't been for the last three or four weeks, now he came to think of it. Perhaps she was pregnant. But she wouldn't keep that to herself. She certainly wouldn't keep it from her husband and Stuart showed no signs of a joyful father-to-be.

The sunless ground beneath the willows was damp and smelled loamy. It was a pleasant smell, only faintly corrupted by the river mud. A bed of pink marsh mallows clustered thickly along the edge of the riverbank and Robin was suddenly reminded of a day long ago when he and Pen had walked through the meadows of her mother's house in Derbyshire and he had picked a bouquet of marsh mallows for her.

He had been twelve years old, Pen ten. They had held hands sticky with heat and emotion and had walked in tongue-tied silence all afternoon.

He smiled now at the memory. He adored all three of his sisters; Anna, his little half sister, and Pen and Pippa, his stepsisters. But Pen's place in his heart was very special. That childhood infatuation had given way after their parents' marriage to the deep abiding love of unbreakable friendship, and he missed her now. She had been in France with her husband and their four children of assorted parentage for almost a year.

But in December, by Christmas, they would be back. He bent to pick one of the pink flowers at his feet.

There came a sudden shout of alarm and then the desperate flapping of a flock of mallards as they rose as one body from the river and skimmed over its surface with hoarse cries.

"Madre de dios!" The exclamation was followed by a string of Spanish that was beyond Robin's comprehension. The voice, however, was distinctly female.

He stepped to the edge of the bank and peered down at the river some three feet below. A flat-bottomed punt had driven itself, or been driven, prow first into the soft mud of the bank. The punt's occupant was struggling with the pole to push the craft free but with little success.

"How did that happen?" Robin inquired, squatting on the bank.

To his surprise the young woman spoke in perfect English with just the faintest accent. "I don't know. I was trying to steer it into the shallows and a big barge went by and then a great wave came behind and . . . well, see for yourself."

She gave an expressive shrug as she leaned forward again in renewed effort to free her boat from the mud. The pole in her hand stuck in the mud. She yanked on it with another string of Spanish. It came loose with a great sucking sound and with such sudden violence that she toppled backwards and lay in an ungainly tangle of stockinged legs and rather dirty petticoats.

Robin couldn't help laughing although he knew it was unkind. The unlucky sailor scrambled to her knees and glared at him. "You think it is funny, you? I tell you it is not funny. Why can you not be gallant and help me?"

Robin looked down at his finely tooled leather boots, his cranberry-colored kidskin hose. He regarded the muddy river with disfavor. He looked at the young woman as she knelt in the punt.

A tangle of black hair roughly bound in a kerchief that was already coming loose, eyes the color of midnight, creamy skin smeared with mud and tinged pink with annoyance and frustration.

He jumped down into the mud, resignedly hearing the squelch of his boots as he sank to his midcalves. He leaned on the prow of the punt and heaved it backwards.

"Harder . . . harder!" the girl in the punt exhorted.

She *was* a girl, not a woman, Robin thought from the distance of his own thirty years, as he put his shoulder into the work. "I can do this without your encouragement," he declared acidly. "And sit still. Every time you move, the balance shifts."

"Oh, I beg your pardon," she said, all contrition, and sat on the thwart, hands folded demurely in her lap.

Robin paused, panting slightly. " 'Tis no good," he said. " 'Tis stuck fast. When the tide comes in it will float free."

"But when will that be?" The girl sounded shocked. "I cannot sit here and wait. Someone will find me."

"I'd have thought that an outcome to be desired," Robin observed, wiping his sweating brow with his handkerchief.

"Well, it's not," she said. "I must return home before Dona Bernardina wakes from her siesta. I just wished to go out by myself for an hour."

She sounded so distressed Robin lost his desire to tease. "Perhaps if you get out of the punt it'll be easier for me to free it," he suggested. "I could lift you onto the bank."

"I did not think I was *so* heavy," the girl said with a frown. "But if you think it will make a difference . . ." She stood up, holding out her hands.

Robin caught her around the waist and lifted her unceremoniously onto the bank. She was actually no light weight, but he had spent too much time in the company of his sisters to venture a comment on the normality of puppy fat.

"So, where does your duenna lay her head?" he inquired, leaning on the pole, regarding the girl quizzically.

"Up the river a little way." The girl gestured in the direction of the Savoy Palace. "I found the boat moored along the bank while I was walking and thought to take it just for half an hour. But now . . . Oh, can you not free it?" Her voice rose with sudden agitation.

"Yes, I'm certain I can," Robin reassured. "But tell me your name. Where are your parents?"

It was clear to him that she must have arrived in England as part of the contingent of Spaniards. It was clear she was not a servant. Spanish servants didn't have duennas, and neither did they speak near-perfect English. But he had never seen her at court, and he thought, despite her present disarray, that he would have remembered such a face.

"You will not tell anyone?" She regarded him closely.

He shook his head. "No, but I will see you safely home."

She seemed to consider, then said with a touch of the Spanish arrogance that so annoyed him among the courtiers, "I am Dona Luisa de los Velez of the house of Mendoza."

"Ah," Robin said. The house of Mendoza was one of the oldest and greatest in Spain. He frowned suddenly. "There are no members of the Mendoza family here at court."

"No," she agreed.

Something in her expression made him drop the pole and join her on the bank. He sat beside her. "How old are you, Dona Luisa?"

"I have eighteen summers."

A woman then, he thought. Not really a girl. "You have a husband?"

She shook her head. "I was betrothed to the Duke of Vasquez, but then he died of the pox when he was thirteen. Then they would have me wed the Marques de Perez, but I refused."

Restlessly her fingers trawled through the bright pink flowers at her side. "I said I would rather take the veil. He is an old man, past fifty. I would not let him touch me."

Robin said nothing. He picked marsh mallows,

threading them together in a chain as he remembered seeing Pen and Pippa do.

"My father died a few months ago. He left me to the guardianship of Don Lionel Ashton."

At the name Robin's fingers stilled. "An Englishman?" he queried softly.

"An old and trusted friend of my father's. I have known him all my life. My mother relies on him absolutely. It was decided that he would bring me to England when he came with Philip and that I would thus be diverted." A note of irony entered her voice but Robin noticed that her fingers quivered slightly among the flowers.

"And are you?"

"How can I be diverted when I am kept immured in a stone mansion on the river, constantly under the eye of Bernardina. I *have* no diversions."

"Why does your guardian not bring you to court? You are of an age."

Luisa did not immediately reply. After a minute she said, " 'Tis not that Don Ashton is neglectful or unkind, indeed he is not, but I think he's too busy to think of me. He is not often at court himself, and whenever I ask him if I might not meet some of the young ladies there he says he does not know any."

She raised her dark gaze to Robin. "Could that be so?"

Robin thought of Lionel Ashton. He had never seen him in the company of others. In any gathering almost always he stood alone. It was clear that his business for Philip of Spain did not lie in the public corridors of diplomacy.

"I do not know your guardian," he said. "He does

not usually take part in court diversions, so it is possible."

"Well, he cannot then blame me for seeking my *own*," declared Luisa.

"Stealing punts and getting stuck in the mud is a strange diversion for a Mendoza," Robin said dryly.

"Ah, what right have you to criticize?" she demanded.

Robin lay back on the bank, linking his muddy hands behind his head. "None at all. It was merely an observation."

"Well, what am I to do?"

"I think as a start it might be wise to return you to your slumbering duenna," he suggested.

Luisa flung herself on her back beside him and gazed up into the sun-tinged tendrils of the willow above her. "Is that all you can think of?"

"For now."

She sighed. "I wish I were not so sensible."

Robin gave a shout of laughter and a starling scolded him from way above in the leafy fronds.

"You may well laugh," she said bitterly. "But if I were not sensible, and not a Mendoza, I would run away, seek my fortune on the high seas."

"The high seas seem rather ambitious for one defeated by the River Thames."

For answer she threw a handful of marsh mallows into his face. Laughing, Robin sat up, brushing the flowers from his doublet. "For a Spanish lady, I have to say that you are remarkably ill-schooled," he declared, grinning at her.

"High-spirited is the term," she returned, lifting her chin with an air of great dignity.

He laughed again and got to his feet. He reached

down his hands to pull her up. "You remind me of my sisters."

Her astounded expression told him he had made a grave error. "Only in that you're so unconventional," he said hastily.

There was a moment's silence. Luisa smoothed down her muddy skirts with an air of decorum that was so ludicrous Robin had to fight to keep a straight face.

"You think me not womanly," she stated finally.

"No . . . no, of course not. Indeed you are . . . are most womanly," he amended quickly.

"But I am like a sister . . . a baby sister." With downcast eyes she smoothed the creases from her bodice, adjusted the lace at the neck.

Robin regarded her. He had the strangest sense that he was being manipulated in some way. Now, where he'd seen the plumpness of emerging womanhood, he saw voluptuous curves. Tangled and begrimed though she was, Dona Luisa aroused in him none of the feelings of a brother.

"I think you had better return home," he stated. "Wait here while I free the punt."

She made no demur as he jumped down into the mud and pushed the craft free of the bank. When it was once more afloat he reached up and lifted her into the boat. He tried to keep his hands beneath her breasts but there was no way to avoid their soft upward swell. She smelled of mud and flowers, a young sweetness that took his breath away.

"No, wait," he said as she immediately took up the pole with a businesslike air, standing feet braced on the bottom of the punt. "Let me do it. You might not find a knight in shining armor the next time you run aground."

Luisa raised an eyebrow, just the most delicate twitch of a most delicate arch, and handed him the pole as he jumped aboard. She sat on the thwart, observing after a while as they reached midstream, "I see I am in the hands of a master."

Flirtatious little minx!

She was worse than Pippa had ever been, Robin reflected, grimly driving the pole into the shallow river bottom close to the bank.

"Tell me which water steps," he instructed after fifteen minutes of silence, during which the punt moved steadily.

"Over there is where I found the punt." Luisa pointed to a narrow wooden pier jutting out from the bank. "I don't know who the punt belongs to, but I should return it there, and then I can walk to the house along the bank."

"Very well." Robin steered the punt to the pier. He jumped out with the painter and tied it securely. "Come." He held out his hand and helped her up beside him.

"My thanks." She looked at him without a smidgeon of her earlier flirtatious mischief. "I don't know whom I'm thanking."

"Robin of Beaucaire, at your service, Dona Luisa." He executed a formal bow and with the utmost solemnity she curtsied, her bedraggled skirts falling around her in perfect folds.

He offered her his arm and they walked along the bank until they reached the lower sweep of lawn leading up to one of the new stone mansions on the Strand.

"Whose house is this?"

"My guardian's. Don Ashton's," she replied. "I believe

he bought it through a steward before we landed at Southampton."

"I see."

Lionel Ashton grew ever more intriguing. A man who owned one of the palatial mansions on the Strand, and yet did not live in England.

"My thanks again, Robin of Beaucaire," Luisa said now with an almost shy smile. "I don't suppose I will see you again." Suddenly she stood on tiptoe and quickly kissed his cheek. Then she hurried away, gathering her skirts high as she ran up the slope towards the house.

Robin shook his head. They would certainly meet again. He glanced down ruefully at his ruined boots and hose. He'd been particularly fond of the cranberry hose, but then he recalled that Pippa had told him that when he wore them he looked as if he'd been treading grapes.

Perhaps she was right. Pippa had style, not that he'd ever taken any notice of her opinions before. But maybe the cranberry hose weren't that great a loss.

He walked back along the riverbank to Whitehall. It was a long walk and mud squelched in his boots, but he whistled softly to himself.

Three

THE TOURNAMENT GROUND BAKED BENEATH THE LATE-afternoon sun. The contestants sweated atop their gaily caparisoned horses; the spectators languidly fanned themselves on the padded benches beneath striped awnings. The queen wearily closed her eyes, retreating farther into the shadow cast by the canopy of state over her chair.

The imperative summons of a herald's trumpet signaled the start of the fourth joust of this interminable afternoon and the queen leaned forward again, an expression of alert interest now on her face as she watched her husband enter the ground, his milk-white destrier caracoling in obedience to its rider's commands. It was an impressive display of horsemanship and Mary's smile became fond and proud as she glanced around at her companions to make sure they too appreciated her husband's expertise.

Another tucket from the herald and Lord Nielson entered the lists from the opposite end. It was a much less spectacular entrance although Stuart was every bit as accomplished a horseman as Philip of Spain. But

Pippa, watching from one of the lower benches, guessed that her husband was governed by discretion.

She glanced up at Robin, who stood beside her. He had no part to play in the present tournament and having changed his river-muddied garments was content to be a mere spectator. His mind until Stuart's appearance had been most pleasantly occupied elsewhere.

"It wouldn't do for Stuart to outshine His Majesty before his wife and the entire court," Pippa murmured sardonically, her derision barely concealed.

Robin frowned, his eyes on the bout. Stuart made a very clumsy pass with his cane and Philip wheeled his horse and brought his own stick to crack against his opponent's. Stuart's weapon split in two.

"I think your husband carries his diplomacy too far," Robin declared. "He's not even trying to give Philip a match."

"No," agreed Pippa, frowning now in her turn. "He seems to spend more time in the company of the Spaniards these days than that of his own people. Have you noticed?"

"Aye." Robin nodded. He was about to say how he'd also noticed that Stuart was curiously and distastefully deferential and ill at ease even with the most peacocking of the Spanish courtiers, but decided to hold his tongue. He would not criticize Pippa's husband to her.

The two jousters clashed again and this time Stuart's cane hit true and the king's flew to the ground. Robin drew a deep breath. He glanced up to where the queen sat. She was still leaning forward on her chair, her eyes now concerned as they rested on her husband. He could not be made to look bad among this already hostile crowd.

But there was no fear of that. Stuart lost the next two

bouts, his cane split resoundingly on both occasions. There was wild cheering from the Spaniards and a sullen silence from the English as the two contestants rode over to the stands to make their bows to the queen.

Pippa scrutinized her husband's countenance. It was expressionless, pale, his eyes hooded, his full mouth set. He looked at her just once and she could feel the embarrassment and anger radiating from him in great waves. And she felt too that some of that anger was directed at her. But how could she be to blame for his deliberate decision to allow Philip of Spain to humiliate him? She gave him a consoling smile and he turned his shoulder to her.

"I don't understand it," Robin said. "He could let Philip win if he felt he *had* to, but not so completely."

"You forget how very good at jousting Stuart is," Pippa said thoughtfully. "I suspect it's harder to lose by a hair if you're very good."

Robin didn't agree but once again kept his reflections to himself.

"I think I've had enough," Pippa said. "Having seen my husband soundly defeated by the king, I should think I would be permitted to leave, don't you?" Irony laced her voice as she glanced back up at the queen.

"I'll escort you," Robin said. "You're very pale, more so than usual. All your freckles are standing out."

"I can always rely on you to tell me the most unflattering truths, brother dear," Pippa stated, rising to her feet. "But have no fear, 'tis just the heat. Stay and enjoy the next spectacle. Two teams are to match canes, as I understand it. Such excitement!"

She gave him a smile that held a smidgeon of her usual mischievous spirit and he was sufficiently reassured not to insist on escorting her. He waved in acknowledgment and took her vacated seat on the bench.

Pippa, realizing that Mary was watching her departure, curtsied deeply and received a haughty nod of dismissal in response. Relieved, she slid past the rows of spectators and made her escape. Heralds' trumpets sounded behind her as she walked through the narrow entrance to the lists and into the relative quiet of a sun-filled cloistered courtyard.

A man stood in the center of the courtyard, leaning against the sundial, idly cleaning his fingernails with the tip of his dagger.

Lionel Ashton.

Pippa's step quite uncharacteristically faltered. Then she moved backwards into the shadows of the cloister and stood motionless, trying to untangle the skein of conflicting emotions that held her fast as a fly in a spider's web. She couldn't take her eyes off the man. He had discarded his cloak and wore only doublet and shirt open at the neck as it had been that morning, with plain black silk hose. He was bareheaded and she saw how the sun turned the strands of gray among the dark hair into silver threads.

What was he doing alone out here? He seemed unaware of the servants crisscrossing the courtyard, of pages scurrying in and out of doorways, or even of a pair of wolfhounds prowling the cobbles, pausing every now and again to sniff at his ankles. He had the quality of utter stillness, utter detachment from his surroundings.

She had seen him before. She *knew* she had.

Pippa was not one to let a mystery stand. She pushed aside the odd feeling that had kept her in motionless retreat, moved briskly out of the shadows, and crossed the courtyard. Her jeweled silk slippers made no sound on the cobbles but her turquoise and rose damask skirts swished with her step.

He looked up when she was a few paces away and his clear gray eyes met hers. There was no mistaking their message. It declared a connection between them, one that was both complicit and open.

"Mr. Ashton." Pippa addressed the problem in her customarily straightforward fashion. "I find myself very puzzled. I know we have not been introduced but I am certain we have met before. Can you enlighten me?"

He slid his dagger into its sheath and bowed. "No, madam, we have not. I would not have forgotten such a meeting." His voice was deep and rich, and his smile was as she remembered from that morning, as sweet and tender as the first snowdrop. "You have the advantage of me, it would seem." He raised an eyebrow.

"Lady Nielson," Pippa supplied, nonplussed. How could he possibly deny that they had met before? The message in his gaze was an open admission. And yet she couldn't remember herself. Once again she felt the cold prickle of fear on the back of her neck.

"Ah, yes. You are married to Viscount Nielson," he observed, not altering his position against the sundial. "Now I think about it, we did come across each other this morning in the queen's presence chamber. Perhaps that is the memory you seek."

"No, 'tis not." Pippa shook her head. "I felt the same recognition then."

"My apologies, my lady, but I cannot enlighten you." He sounded amused.

Doubt assailed her. She couldn't be the only one to have the memory if it was correct. Perhaps she was simply mistaken. But there was no mistaking the strange flutter of excitement that blended seamlessly with the confused sense of dread, filling her head so that she couldn't think clearly.

"You have abandoned the tourney?" he said, smiling still.

"I have little stomach for contrived outcomes," Pippa declared, an edge to her voice as she struggled to master her confusion.

Lionel Ashton nodded. "From what I saw of the match, your husband's loss to Philip was somewhat spectacular and one can't help wondering if it was truly necessary. It does indeed seem a pity that our Spanish friends won't rely on their own skills for success."

"*Your* Spanish friends, as I understand it, sir," she returned with asperity. "Not mine, I assure you."

His smile changed. It lost its sweetness and his eyes became cold. Then almost as suddenly, almost before she could register the change, he was once more smiling gently at her. "They are not all bad," he said, his tone mollifying.

"The king's reputation preceded him," she stated, aware that this was dangerous talk, but that had never stopped her from speaking her mind in the past and wasn't about to now. "You would deny that reputation?"

Lionel Ashton stroked his beard that he wore in the Spanish fashion, small and triangular, and once again Pippa was struck by the curiously haphazard arrangement of his features. His nose was prominent and crooked, his mouth slightly twisted, his chin large and deeply cleft, his eyebrows thick as bushes and speckled with gray like his beard. A man more unlike Stuart in his appearance would be impossible to find. Stuart was beautiful, his features perfectly composed. Lionel Ashton was not even handsome. Indeed, not to put too fine a point upon it, he was ugly. And yet there was something about him that stirred Pippa in a way that she knew in her blood she must not attempt to explore or understand.

"Well, sir, would you?" she challenged.

"You refer to the king's reputation for womanizing?"

Pippa made no answer and after a minute he continued in a detached tone, "Philip is no saint. But your queen was well aware of that fact. I would suggest her husband's reputation is for her and her alone to worry about."

It was, Pippa decided, a snub. However, snubs rarely troubled her. "On the contrary, sir, it is a matter for all loyal Englishmen." She dropped him a curtsy and turned away.

He moved from the sundial and took her hand, tucking it neatly into his arm. "Since we've now become acquainted, madam, pray allow me to walk a little with you. The pleasaunce is particularly agreeable at this time of day."

Pippa experienced a sudden flash of panic. There was nothing wrong with her accepting the escort of a gentleman of the court. Nothing for anyone to object to. Stuart wouldn't give it a second thought. And yet with the same instinct as before she knew she must not walk with Lionel Ashton. In the pleasaunce or anywhere else.

"Forgive me," she murmured, pulling her hand free. "I have the headache . . . the heat . . . I have no wish to walk. . . ." Breathlessly she hurried away towards the arched entrance to the courtyard.

Lionel Ashton watched her go, his hands resting lightly on his hips where hung his sheathed rapier and dagger. Pippa didn't look back but if she had done she would have been frightened by his expression. His eyes were now iron-hard, filled with anger and contempt, and something else. Something very like dismay.

He turned on his heel and made his way to the lists where two lines of dismounted courtiers, one line wearing the colors of Spain, the other Tudor green and white, advanced and retreated amid the thud and splintering of their canes.

Stuart Nielson was standing at the far side of the ground, still in the leather padded doublet he had worn for the joust. Full armor was not considered necessary when one played only with sticks. He stood alone, and Lionel wondered if it was through choice or because his usual companions were too embarrassed for him after his mortifying loss. Not that the reason interested Lionel in the least.

He made his way towards Stuart, who saw him coming and turned hastily back to the tented enclosure where the participants prepared themselves for their bouts. Lionel increased his pace.

"Lord Nielson, a word with you."

Stuart seemed to hesitate, and then he stopped. He waited for the other man to reach him. "Well?" There was no invitation in the sharp question.

"A hard loss, I gather," Lionel offered, his voice soft. "Perhaps you have no need to immolate yourself quite so thoroughly."

Stuart stared at him, his aquamarine eyes both hostile and frightened. "What do you mean?"

"Why, only that you could give Philip a little more challenge while achieving your objective." Lionel was looking out over the lists rather than at Stuart. His tone was remote.

"What difference does it make?" Stuart demanded harshly. "I accept and obey my orders. *All* of them."

"Yes . . . yes, so you do, most admirably," Lionel said in the same remote tone.

Stuart flushed angrily. The dismissive contempt in the other's manner was unmistakable even though they had still not exchanged a glance.

"There are no signs as yet?" Lionel asked.

Stuart's flush deepened. "Not that I'm aware." He paused, then continued on a note almost of bluster, "But it would be wise to desist for a few days."

Lionel swung his head slowly towards him. "Why so?"

Stuart's hand rested unconsciously on his sword hilt and his face now was as pale as it had been suffused before. "There are difficulties," he said. "Objections."

"Objections to what? She is aware of nothing." Lionel was speaking very softly but his gaze was intent as it rested on the other man's countenance.

"She is aware of some things," Stuart said with difficulty. "How can she not be?"

Lionel continued to regard him closely. The hardness of his expression diminished some. The man was in agony. And so he should be, Lionel reflected with a resurgence of contempt, but then he softened again. Stuart Nielson was in an impossible position. And even if Lionel Ashton believed that he himself would have died rather than accept such a position he was not going to throw the first stone.

"I will tell them that it would be wise to desist from now until we have some definite sign one way or the other," he said, and saw the naked relief shine forth from Lord Nielson's blue eyes. "Soon there should be something . . . or nothing. You understand me?"

"Aye." Stuart nodded. "I will keep a close eye."

"Yes, I imagine you will," the other said dryly. "I give you good afternoon, Lord Nielson."

He bowed and Stuart returned the courtesy briefly. He remained where he was however, in the stifling heat beneath the tent, amid the bustle of competitors, the scurry of pages and varlets and grooms, the heavy odor of horseflesh, leather, and manure. Then when he became acutely aware of the glances cast in his direction, sympathetic some of them, curious some of them, one or two directly hostile, he left the tent by a rear exit, looking neither to right nor left.

Behind the tent, horses stamped, tossed their heads, as the heavy jeweled saddles and bridles were lifted from them. They were huge, magnificent creatures, dangerous, fearless, willful, bred to go into battle bearing the weight of a fully armored man.

Stuart paused beside his own charger, who stood relatively quietly at the water trough in the hands of a pair of grooms. The animal raised his head as Stuart approached and his eyes rolled. Stuart could almost see reproach there. The horse had been badly managed that afternoon and knew it. He was used to winning, used to the applause, the cheers, the acclaim, certainly not accustomed to slinking off the field in disgrace.

The horse, lips pulled back from his teeth, was clearly not in the mood to be stroked. But he was not a domesticated beast at the best of times and Stuart made no attempt to touch him.

"Check his fetlocks and give him a warm mash," he instructed the grooms, then made his way through the press of horseflesh and along a beaten path that ran behind the stands that lined the lists. The path brought him to a gate into the pleasaunce. Here fountains plashed and the sweet scents of roses, lavender, and lilac filled the air.

He could hear the sound of instruments and followed the music to the center of the pleasaunce where a small group of courtiers lounged on tapestries spread upon the grass. Pages moved among them with flagons of fine rhenish and silver platters of sweetmeats and savory tarts.

The musicians were seated to one side under the spreading arms of a copper beech. Stuart listened, his eyes on the lyre player. He took a goblet from a page, absently selected a tart of goose liver and bacon, and then, accepting a waved invitation from one of his friends, took a seat on a tapestry beside the fountain.

"A bad afternoon," his friend observed without inflection.

"Aye," Stuart said curtly.

"We must not offend our Spanish guests," the other murmured, casting a sidelong glance at his companion.

"No."

"No doubt there'll be some unpleasantness at first, but it will pass . . . a nine days' wonder."

As long as it didn't happen again. Stuart kept this reflection to himself. One defection would eventually be forgiven by the anti-Spanish contingent, but no more. Neither would any overt appearance of friendship, of *supplication.* His skin crawled in revulsion.

He looked across at the musicians. At the lyre player, whose black head was bent over his instrument, his eyes riveted to his plucking fingers. If he was aware of Stuart's intent regard he gave no indication, but it was always thus when Gabriel was playing, lost in his music.

Stuart abruptly cast aside the remnants of the tart he'd been eating as revulsion again rose bitter as bile in his throat. He got to his feet, upending the contents of his goblet on the grass, heedless of the splatters on the tapestry.

What choice did he have? The alternative was unthinkable.

"What ails you, Stuart?" His friend looked up at him in alarm.

"Nothing. I have just remembered I promised to meet with my wife at this hour."

"Ah, the spirited Lady Pippa," the other said with a somewhat lascivious grin. "There's many a man would enjoy being in your shoes, my friend." *In your bed* was left unspoken but the implication was clear.

Stuart forced a flicker of the gratified smile that he knew was expected, then left with a murmur of farewell.

Gabriel, the lyre player, raised his eyes momentarily from his instrument as Lord Nielson departed.

PIPPA SAT AT THE OPEN WINDOW OF HER BEDCHAMber, her tambour frame idle in her lap. Afternoon was giving way to evening but the sun was still warm on her back and her unquiet mind was lulled by the continuous, indolent buzzing of a bee. Her body was filled with languor, as if she'd been drugged, her eyelids drooped.

The door opened, jerking her awake. She blinked in surprise, as much at the idea that she'd been about to take an unprecedented nap as at her husband's unexpected appearance.

"I thought you were still at the tourney," she said.

"I saw you leave," he returned. "Unable to stomach your husband's defeat, I imagine?" His voice was bitter. He began to unfasten the heavy clips of his padded doublet.

"Why did you have to humiliate yourself so?" Pippa demanded. "I understand it was politic to lose, but in such fashion?"

She knew Stuart was upset and angry but she had again the sense that he was holding her to blame for something. Still dismayed at their quarrel of the morning, hurt and troubled at its cause, she was in no mood to offer soft words of consolation. That she was also disturbed, thrown off course, by her encounter with Lionel Ashton, Pippa chose to ignore.

"What could you possibly know about it?" Stuart demanded, throwing his doublet to the floor. He flexed his shoulders, working the tired muscles. Losing a joust was every bit as tiring as winning one, and the sour aftermath of defeat made normal aches and pains even worse.

Pippa leaned her head against the high back of her chair. *Why was she so tired!* She made an effort to keep her voice reasonable. "I don't see why you would attack me, Stuart. What have I done? It seems to me after last night that I have the right to be angry, not you." Despite her best efforts the note of recrimination was loud and clear.

His face flushed. "You are my wife, madam, 'tis your duty to give yourself to me whenever I wish it."

Pippa rose to her feet, her tambour frame falling to the floor. She was flushed herself now, her hazel eyes burning. "And when have I ever refused you?" she demanded. "I object merely to being taken, used like some household chattel. God's bones, why wouldn't you wake me!"

He put his hands to his face and his fingers trembled violently. When he spoke his voice was barely above a whisper. "I asked your forgiveness this morning, Pippa.

Can you not be more generous? I explained that I was overdrunk. I didn't think about what I was doing."

Pippa turned her back on him, clasping her hands tightly as she fought down her anger and resentment. "It was not the first time, Stuart. Something is wrong between us. I would know what it is. Have I done something to offend you? I cannot put it right if I don't know what it is."

Stuart stared at her averted back. *Sweet Jesus!* She talked of offending him!

Shame, guilt, horror swamped him. Denial tumbled from his lips. "Of course you haven't. Of course there's nothing wrong between us. You talk nonsense, Pippa."

"Nonsense!" She spun around to face him. "It is not nonsense, Stuart! Ever since Mary and Philip were married, you have been behaving strangely. Distant with me ... except when I'm asleep," she added acidly. "You're always in the company of the Spanish, always obsequious, always deferential. And this afternoon was the last straw! You will lose all your friends and—"

"Hold your tongue, woman!" He flung the words at her, in a tone she had never heard him use before. Now he was ashen, his eyes filled with a wild desperation.

He took a step towards her and Pippa shrank back involuntarily, afraid that he was going to strike her. Something she would never have believed possible until this minute.

But her sudden movement gave him pause and he stopped some feet from her. "You have a scold's tongue," he said more moderately. "Oblige me by bridling it."

Pippa set her lips. "I am only trying to understand, my lord," she said, her face taut. "I know there's something amiss and I would put it right."

"And I tell you there is nothing, *nothing*, amiss except your refusal to accept that," he declared. "Now cease your shrewishness, Pippa."

Without knowing quite why she did so Pippa walked up to him, placed her hands on his shoulders, and stood on tiptoe to kiss him full on the mouth. His physical recoil was as obvious as the clash of cymbals, then he put his arms around her, but his hold was halfhearted, and she could feel his reluctance in every muscle.

Slowly she stepped back. "Your pardon, husband," she said deliberately, and he knew she was not apologizing for her shrewishness. That flinch had been instinctive, uncontrollable.

"Let us forget it, my dear," he said, hearing how awkward he sounded. "A trifling quarrel. Let us put it behind us."

"Yes," she said, regarding him now with a dawning comprehension. "Yes, by all means, let us put it behind us."

"I must go," he said. "An engagement . . . I am already late. I'll join you at the banquet."

"I think perhaps I shall keep to my chamber this evening," Pippa said. "I have not felt well all day. My head . . ." She brushed her temples with fleeting fingertips. "I shall retire early."

"Very well." He went to the door, then hesitated, his hand on the latch. "Perhaps you have some . . . some womanly affliction?" he suggested, not turning to look at her.

Pippa frowned. Stuart had never evinced anything but the most delicate reticence about her monthly cycle. He left her bed when asked and returned six days later, not a word spoken.

"I don't believe so," she stated.

"But should it not soon . . . soon be the time . . ." he stammered, still without turning.

"You wish for a child, Stuart?" she asked directly.

"Of course. How could I not?" Abruptly, without waiting for her answer, he left the chamber, the door closing with a snap on his heels.

Pippa remained standing in the middle of the chamber. They had not kissed since . . . no, during their marriage they had never kissed, she realized. Oh, he gave her the occasional peck on the cheek or the brow, but a full passionate kiss of the kind she had just initiated, *never*. Once or twice in their courtship, but never since their marriage.

And she had simply accepted his lack of ardor as a fact of their life together. Nothing else had been wanting and she had been so taken up with her own and Elizabeth's peril in the weeks immediately following her wedding, there had been no time to think of anything else. Then, on her release from prison, Stuart had been so deeply involved with the preparations and negotiations for Mary's wedding Pippa had barely seen him except in public. And his lovemaking had been of the solitary kind, as she knew to her cost.

He had recoiled from her mouth, shrank from her body.

If she no longer pleased him, then who did? He must have a mistress. There was no other explanation. During the weeks of her imprisonment in the Tower, Stuart had taken a mistress.

Pippa returned to her seat at the window. It could not be a superficial relationship, one entered into purely for mutual bodily pleasure during a time when he had no other sexual outlet. Otherwise he would not recoil from his wife.

His wife repulsed him.

It was a dreadful thought. Pippa believed she could accept and forgive a casual liaison. Men had needs after all, and through her own choice she had not been there to satisfy Stuart's. But a passionate love affair, one so all-consuming that he could not endure to touch his wife. No, that was a very different matter.

He needed a child, as all men did, so he possessed his wife in the dark, in her sleep, when he could be done with it without any real connection between them.

God's bones! What other explanation could there be?

Who was it? She racked her brain trying to think of some woman with whom Stuart seemed often in company, but she could come up with no one. Her brain seemed numb.

Robin. Robin would be able to discover.

Her languor disappeared, her headache with it. On a burst of energy, Pippa jumped to her feet and went in search of her stepbrother.

Four

LUISA GAZED DOWN AT HER EMBROIDERY, REALIZING that she hadn't set a stitch for half an hour or more. At the same moment she realized that Dona Bernardina was still solemnly reading aloud an account of the life of Saint Catherine, in her halting English.

"Aye, how clumsy this language is!" Bernardina exclaimed. "How do you pronounce this word, *hija*?"

Luisa blinked to rid her mind's eye of a strong face, a well-shaped curving mouth, a pair of startling blue eyes, and a thatch of unruly curls. She leaned over to look at the page where Bernardina's finger jabbed at the letters.

"Wheel," she said.

Bernardina grimaced, then firmly closed the book. She considered it her duty to master English and since Luisa spoke the language with some fluency had hoped to divert the girl by using her as a teacher. But Luisa was not to be diverted by the lives of the saints or anything else, it seemed, this evening.

"Are you fatigued, *querida*?"

"No," Luisa replied with a quick smile. Bernardina was always so watchful, so overly protective.

"You would not be so if you would take a siesta." Bernardina ignored Luisa's answer since it didn't fit with her own diagnosis. "A siesta at midday, out of the heat of the sun, is necessary if one is not to be fatigued in the evening."

Luisa cast aside her embroidery and rose to her feet. "Bernardina . . . dear Bernardina . . . what possible difference does it make if I am fatigued in the evening. There is nothing to do in the evening!" She flung her arms wide as if to indicate the great vacuum in which she lived.

There was the sound of the massive front door opening, hurried feet in the hall, then the voice of her guardian and the steward of the household. Luisa stood still, listening. Would he come in? She couldn't remember when she'd last had the chance to speak with him. And she most definitely wished to speak with him now.

Lionel finished giving his orders to the steward and hurried to the stairs, intent on changing his dress for something more suitable for a ceremonial evening at Whitehall. There was to be an elaborate musical entertainment. Lionel was not interested in the entertainment itself but Simon Renard and Ruy Gomez would be in attendance, not to mention Philip himself. They would be expecting to conduct business as usual tonight and he had to explain that after his conversation with Stuart Nielson there had been a change of plan.

He set one foot on the stair, then hesitated, glancing towards the closed oak door to the parlor. He was guiltily aware that it had been several days since he'd inquired after his ward's health and welfare. He could spare five minutes now.

Luisa turned to the parlor door as it opened, a tinge

of color now in her cheeks, her dark eyes bright as she prepared to do battle with Don Ashton.

Lionel smiled at the two women. "I give you good even, Dona Bernardina, Luisa. All is well, I trust. Have you passed a pleasant day?"

"A day of the utmost tedium," Luisa declared firmly. "A day just like every other."

"Oh, now, *querida*," Bernardina protested. "How can you say such things. Don Ashton doesn't wish to hear such a complaining."

"But he must hear it," Luisa insisted. "Don Ashton, when will you take me to court?"

Lionel was somewhat taken aback. Luisa in general preserved the demeanor of a well-schooled Spanish maiden in his company. She had murmured once or twice about going to court but had seemed to accept with docility his explanation that he was too busy to arrange anything. He had had a niggling awareness that she had been promised more out of this journey than to be left isolated, however luxuriously, in a mansion on the river. But he had so much to concern him at present that finding companionship and entertainment for his ward was a very low priority.

In the face of this determined insistence he was at something of a loss. "I have to find a sponsor for you, some lady of the court who will take you under her wing," he attempted in excuse. "There is so much you do not know about the ways of the English court. You would not wish to make mistakes and look foolish, I am sure."

Luisa did not reply with the expected agreement. She tilted her chin in challenging fashion, saying, "There are Spanish ladies at the English court. The

Duchess of Alva is there now. She would be honored to sponsor me? I am a Mendoza, Don Ashton."

She was indeed, Lionel thought, half amused, half annoyed by this confrontation. He knew Luisa had a mind of her own, she had refused the marriage arranged for her after all, but he had not expected her to cause him any trouble during this sojourn on English soil. He'd known her since she was a child, but she had always been chaperoned, silent in the company of her elders, decorous and docile.

It seemed he had not *really* known her at all, Lionel reflected, regarding her set face and the haughty angle of her chin.

He caught that tilted chin on his forefinger, and looked down into her upturned face. He offered her a smile that was both rueful and cajoling. "*Hija*, be patient. As soon as I have time away from Philip's concerns I will do something for you. Until then, can you not enjoy the landscape . . . so different from Seville. And the river . . ."

He gestured towards the windows, open to the soft evening air, and the lawn that swept down to the Thames, aware as he did so that such assets were no substitute for the music, dancing, feasting in the company of other young people that Luisa was entitled to enjoy.

Luisa had half expected this and had a second string to her bow. "If I may not go to court, then may I have a boat to go on the river?" she asked. "How can I enjoy the river and the countryside from within the house and garden? If I have a boat for the river and a horse to ride in the parks and forests, then I will be able to enjoy these things."

"Oh, but Luisa, child, I cannot bear to be on the

water, and I cannot ride, you know I cannot," bewailed Bernardina, who, as duenna, would be obliged to accompany her charge on her expeditions.

"You need not come," Luisa declared. "I will have a boatman and a groom. And besides," she added, "you are always saying that I need to be more in the air."

She fixed her challenging gaze once more upon her guardian. "English ladies do not have duennas, they have boatmen and grooms. I know this for a fact. I would have the same."

"And just how do you know this?" Lionel inquired, now definitely more amused than annoyed.

"I listen to the servants," she told him. "I ask them questions. I wish to find out about this country and its customs."

"Ay!" Bernardina flung up her hands. "You should not be talking with servants, English servants, no less! I said to your mother that we should have a Spanish household."

"There was no room on the ships for them," Luisa pointed out. "And if English servants are good enough for the English then why should they not be good enough for us?"

Lionel stroked his chin in thought. To permit such freedom would be against the wishes of Luisa's mother, he knew well. But Dona Maria, grief-stricken at the death of her husband and overwhelmed by her daughter's refusal to marry her elderly suitor, had jumped at his charitable offer to take Luisa to England with him. She would not question his authority to make what decisions he chose about the girl's welfare.

And what harm could there be in a little of the freedom extended to an English girl of Luisa's background? On their return to Spain the girl would marry some

Spanish grandee and settle into the conventional life of an aristocratic lady, dutifully presenting her husband with a child at regular intervals. But there was no reason why a little unusual license should damage her reputation, no reason indeed that it should ever be known in her homeland. Besides, he found he approved of her interest in the country in which she found herself. It showed a lively mind.

"I will make the necessary arrangements," he said. "Now, if you will excuse me, I must change my dress for I must return to Whitehall." He bowed to the duenna, lightly chucked Luisa's chin, and left them, his mind already turning to the evening ahead, domestic concerns forgotten before he had set foot on the stair.

Luisa resumed her seat, and with an air of satisfaction picked up her embroidery again and set a stitch. It wasn't the court, but it was something. With a horse and a boat she would be free to explore. The boatman and the groom could be managed. She had never had the least difficulty persuading servants to keep her counsel and do her bidding.

And maybe, she thought, just maybe, if she took a boat up the river to Whitehall, or rode along the lanes and through the parks around the palace she might run into Robin of Beaucaire again.

A little smile curved her mouth as she leaned sideways to move the lamp closer to her work.

"YOU THINK STUART HAS A MISTRESS?" ROBIN demanded, shaking his head at the thought. "You must be mistaken, Pippa. It would be known. I would have heard a whisper, no one can keep these matters secret."

"I can think of no other explanation," Pippa said,

glancing around to make sure they were not overheard. The long gallery where they walked was empty of courtiers, however. A herald in the Duke of Norfolk's livery carrying a message from his master hastened past on his way to the water steps. He didn't give them a second glance.

She leaned against one of the tall pillars, her fingers restlessly plaiting the ribbons of her sleeves. "Perhaps it is not a woman of the court. Perhaps 'tis someone he met somewhere else, someone he keeps separate in some love nest."

"Pippa, you have no evidence for such a suspicion," Robin pointed out.

"I told you, he wants nothing to do with me," Pippa said in a fierce undertone. "I tried to kiss him and he drew back. He has no interest in our bed . . . or at least . . ." She stopped, finding that while she could talk of most things with her stepbrother, revealing the humiliation of Stuart's preferred sexual congress was too intimate.

Robin shuffled his feet awkwardly. He coughed behind his hand and if he could have done so he would have brought this uncomfortable discussion to a swift conclusion. But Pippa was so clearly distressed, *angry* and distressed, he amended, and had no one else to turn to with Pen away. She needed him to act her confidant and offer what support and help he could.

"Did you see much of him while I was in the Tower?" Pippa asked, knotting a rose silk ribbon with one hand. "What was he doing while I was in prison?"

"Very much the same as the rest of us, watching his step and taking a care for his head," Robin informed her. "No one was safe then. The queen saw treachery at every turn, and with good reason."

"So he was in no particular woman's company?"

"Not to my knowledge."

"Did he seem worried about me?" She dropped the ribbon and looked up at him, tilting her head back against the pillar.

"As worried as we all were. Your mother, my father, me . . . yes, of course he was worried. He came often to the house at Holborn to talk with my father and Lady Guinevere about what could be done to gain your release."

"I wonder if he was angry with me for making such a choice so soon after we were married," Pippa mused, frowning. "He didn't seem to be, but maybe he was. Maybe he decided to take a mistress because of that."

"I think you're making too much of this, Pippa." Robin spoke briskly. "Stuart is not a complicated person at all. And he certainly wouldn't be revenged upon you just because you were loyal to Elizabeth. He's too good-natured for that. Too sure of himself, of his popularity, his skills, his courtly talents. Of course he wouldn't do something so petty."

Pippa was silent for a minute. What Robin said was true, fitted with what she knew of her husband, or, at least, with what she had thought she knew of him. He was not petty.

"I think he must be in love," she said finally, her voice rather small. "A wild passion that he cannot help but indulge."

"Oh, now you're talking romantic nonsense," Robin declared. "And that's not in the least like you, Pippa."

"Well, there has to be some explanation," she snapped. "He's changed. Why does he lick Spanish hands like a lapdog?"

"I don't see how a passionate love affair could explain that!" Robin responded as acerbically as Pippa.

"Unless it's all he can think about and he doesn't care what he does."

Robin held steepled fingers to his mouth. It was true that Stuart was behaving in some puzzling ways. "I don't think it's got anything to do with a mistress," he said. "But if you like I'll do some digging, see what I can come up with. But I think the simplest thing is just to ask him."

"Ask him what?" Pippa cried. "You can't ask him why he doesn't seem to want to be with me anymore. I've already asked him myself, and if he won't tell me he's not going to tell you."

"No, perhaps not. Anyway I wouldn't interfere in such a matter. It's between you and Stuart. But I can ask him what's going on with the Spanish."

"And you could make a few discreet inquiries about the other matter," she said.

"Yes, I will do that." He looked at her anxiously. Pippa had always been so vibrant and mercurial, now she seemed weighed down with the burdens of Atlas. He remembered how gravely her mother and then her elder sister had responded in their own difficulties when the world with its injustices and threats had pressed close upon them. But they had always seemed somehow deeper, more complex characters than Pippa. They had always embraced the serious side of life.

He would have expected Pippa to shrug off her troubles and go her merry way, but apparently her personality and reactions were more akin to her mother's and sister's than anyone would have guessed from the tempestuous child and the lighthearted, flirtatious young woman of the court who had preceded this incarnation.

"Is there anything else that troubles you?" he asked, searching her face. He saw a pulse jump suddenly in her temple, a flash cross the hazel eyes, then she shrugged.

"No, nothing else. It is enough, I believe."

"Aye," he agreed, but he knew she was lying. There *was* something else. Her usually open countenance was now shuttered and it seemed that she had withdrawn into herself, leaving him conversing in this empty corridor with a cipher.

"Do you attend the musical entertainment this evening?"

Pippa shook her head. "No, I have no stomach for it. I feel as if I haven't slept properly in weeks. I shall ask Martha to bring me a cup of hippocras and sleep until daybreak."

"You look as if you could do with it," Robin said, bending to kiss her cheek. "Leave the rest to me."

She smiled, a wan smile but it was an attempt, returned the kiss, and they parted. Pippa made her way to her chamber. Martha should bring her a cup of hippocras and a dish of coddled eggs with manchet bread. Nursery fare. And she would sleep. No strange tangled dreamworld tonight, just sweet oblivion. Stuart, she knew, would not touch her in her sleep this night.

QUEEN MARY NODDED GENTLY TO THE STRAINS OF music plucked from the musicians' instruments. They were playing "Greensleeves," an air composed by her father, Henry VIII, and a tune particularly close to her heart. Her father had ill-treated her in her adolescence and earlier womanhood, but as a child he had adored her and she had never ceased to adore him, to long for his love and approval even during their worst estrangements. She had longed for it, but for many years she had refused to do the one thing that would have given it to her: agree to accept her own illegitimacy and disavow the pope's authority as head of the church in England.

Finally she had yielded and had been restored to the succession. After her brother Edward's death, she had fought for and won the throne. And now here she sat under the canopy of estate, married to a Catholic king, for the moment undisputed queen of England, her enemies confounded.

But for how long? The question was ever-present, lurking on a good day just below the surface of her mind. On a bad day all she could think of.

A child, most especially a son, would ensure her throne. The son of Philip of Spain would return England to the Catholic fold forever, link this country to the Holy Roman Empire through Philip's father and Mary's cousin, the emperor Charles V.

Mary leaned back on her throne, the jewels set into the chair above her head blazing in the brightly lit chamber. She laid a hand fleetingly on her belly, wondering if Philip's seed had yet taken root.

In her womb?

Or the other?

Her gaze roamed the chamber, glanced off the courtiers standing in knots or sitting in little groups on stools or thick cushions. Simon Renard, the Spanish ambassador and her longtime ally and conspirator, stood with Philip's most trusted councillor, Ruy Gomez. Their heads were together as they murmured to each other.

Mary glanced at her husband, who sat beside her. He seemed uninterested in the music, his chin resting on his palm, his elbow propped on his knee clad in hose of gilded doeskin. His eyes were on the two men by the window as if he was trying to read their lips.

Another man joined the two. Lionel Ashton, elegant in doublet and hose of emerald green, with a short cloak of ivory velvet studded with jet, seemed, Mary thought, to materialize from the air. An unconscious frown deepened on her brow. Unlike her husband she found the Englishman a puzzle. Philip considered him a useful asset, a cultivated Englishman who had embraced Spain. A man who knew both sides, who could offer useful insights into both camps. A man who was vital to the business that concerned them both.

A distasteful business, Mary would be the first to acknowledge, but in general she refused to allow herself to dwell upon it, and certainly not upon the details. But there was something about Lionel Ashton that made her uneasy. Nothing she could put her finger upon, but something about his remoteness, his seeming detachment, that gave her a prickle of uncertainty.

Her husband leaned over to her. "You will excuse me, madam."

She smiled at him. "Of course, my lord."

Philip rose from his throne, causing a flurry of activity as pages and attendants gathered to assist him. The musicians, accustomed to a distracted audience, continued to play.

Philip joined the three by the long window. They bowed to the king. "Gentlemen," he murmured. "Is all in order for later?" His eyes flickered without volition to the young lyre player.

"It would be advisable, sire, to leave the lady undisturbed for the next few nights," Lionel said quietly.

"Why so? Has she her terms?" The question was sharp.

"Not to my knowledge, sire, but it would not do to arouse suspicions at this juncture," Lionel replied. Absently he touched the curiously shaped brooch nestled in the lace at his throat.

"The husband is proving difficult?" Again Philip's eyes flickered to the musicians.

"No, but his wife is no fool, sire."

Philip drew back slightly at Ashton's blunt, almost dismissive tone. "I fail to understand, Don Ashton. The woman is aware of nothing."

Lionel bowed. "At the time, sire ... only at the time."

Simon Renard shot him a sharp glance. Had he been the only one to hear the edge of contempt beneath the seemingly calm correction? Neither of his companions appeared to have noticed anything amiss; they both nodded as comprehension dawned.

"I wonder the husband could not handle that issue," Ruy Gomez said with a fastidious curl of his lip.

"A short interruption will matter little," Philip said with a shrug. He looked over at his wife. "I will devote my energies to but one woman for a night or so."

His laugh was coarse, reminding his companions of Philip's true character. In general, he played to perfection the courteous, devoted husband of a woman eleven years his senior.

"The queen, sire, is most attentive to her husband," Ruy Gomez pointed out. "She accords you every honor."

"Aye," Philip muttered with a grimace of distaste.

"But 'tis hard, gentlemen, to bed each night with a woman who knows only how to endure."

"The queen knows her duty, sire, both to her husband and her country," declared Renard in instant defense of a woman he considered a friend as much as a useful political tool.

"Yes . . . yes . . ." Philip said soothingly. "But 'tis still no easy duty to lie nightly with a woman who prays beforehand with all the fervency of a saint going to her martyrdom, Renard."

Lionel stepped away from this conversation. It no longer concerned him. Stuart Nielson had just entered the chamber and Lionel wondered why his wife was not with him. And he realized then that he had been waiting for her. Of course, he had been waiting for her to appear every night for the last month. Waiting for the moment when she took the goblet of wine her husband gave her. Waiting for the moment when an hour or so later, already heavy-eyed, she would excuse herself and retire for the night.

He had waited for her with a cold dispassion. A deliberate detachment. She was merely an object. To be used to further the interests of Philip and Mary, the grand design of a kingdom, and she was purely incidental to the deep black river of hatred that informed Lionel Ashton's every move.

And yet tonight, when he had no need to await her, he had waited with anticipation and was disappointed by her absence.

The realization startled him.

Why?

As he pondered the question he understood the answer and it was a hard acknowledgment. He had wanted to see her as she was.

As a woman who interested him.

Tonight when she was not wanted, when neither he nor she had any part to play in the loathsome strands of the royal plot, he could see her simply as a woman, just as he had seen her that afternoon in the courtyard. *A woman who interested him.*

But he had forsworn all interest in women. Only thus could he follow his path. There was but one driving force to his life, one single compulsion, and if he admitted concern or feelings of any kind for Pippa he would lose his focus.

He strode towards the door. His work here was done for the night.

Stuart Nielson was standing with uncharacteristic irresolution just inside the doorway. For the moment he made no attempt to join any of the groups made up of his acquaintances, friends, and closest cronies. His eyes were on the musicians.

Lionel paused beside him, a frown in his eye. Stuart was a poor dissembler and soon his obvious distress would cause questions and remark. He said cheerfully, "Lady Nielson is not joining the court this evening?"

A muscle twitched in Stuart's cheek. His eyes darted to where the king with his councillors stood across the chamber. "I thought it was agreed—"

"Yes . . . yes, it is agreed," Lionel interrupted, lowering his voice even as he kept a congenial smile on his face. "I merely made polite inquiry."

He lightly patted the other's arm, saying with deceptive gentleness, "Take my advice, my lord, and strive for a little more relaxation. After this afternoon's debacle you would not wish to draw any more unwelcome attention."

He paused, then continued in more pointed tones, "I

would suggest you have a care where you direct your eyes also."

Stuart heard only the deepest contempt in Ashton's voice. He knew it was deserved and the knowledge made it all the more unbearable. His hand went to his sword hilt.

"No . . . no, my friend." Lionel shook his head, laying a hand once more on Stuart's arm. "The advice is good, heed it. Had you had more of a care in the past, I doubt you would be in your present situation. You, or your wife." He dropped his hand and left the chamber.

Stuart fought the surge of helpless rage that threatened to consume him. Ashton was right. Somewhere, somehow he had made the mistake that had him now caught in the teeth of the most vicious mantrap. He had been careless, slipped with a word or a look. He would never know how Simon Renard had learned his secret, but those who watched him as they watched everyone in this treacherous court had seen what they could use to their advantage.

With effortful determination he looked around the chamber, selected a group, and went to join them. He managed to smile, to offer the occasional contribution to the conversation, but as he lounged seemingly at his ease on a thick cushion his mind struggled with possible solutions to an impossible situation.

They would not let him go now, he knew that. If he had made a stand at the very beginning, defied them to do their worst, then perhaps it would have been different. But the consequences would have been hideous and he had chosen to believe that they would have done what they said. He had ample reason to believe that they would. And now whether they achieved their objective or not, he knew too much. He was far too dangerous for them to let him alone, to let him go his way after he'd helped them. They would either find some other use for him, or they would kill him.

But what about Pippa? If she failed them would they give up and let her alone? Turn their attention to some other young wife? She knew nothing, she was no threat to them. But if their plan succeeded, would they leave her unmolested when it was all over? They had promised they would, but what price the promises of such men?

And Gabriel? Was he safe? He knew nothing. As long as Stuart kept his end of the bargain, continued to be compliant, then surely Gabriel was safe.

He looked up then and across at the musicians. For a moment, the lyre player raised his own eyes as if drawn by Stuart's gaze. Their eyes met, then Gabriel lowered his to his instrument, and Stuart, sick and trembling with an overpowering terror for what he'd done, for what he'd not done, for what was going to happen, for the whole viper's nest in which he thrashed around, got to his feet and left the chamber trying not to run.

He had to get out of the palace. If he were dead, would everyone else be safe? It was not the first time the thought had come to him, but it was stronger this time than ever before.

The dagger to his throat, poison, the dark swift currents of the River Thames. There were many ways to end his existence.

But he didn't want to die. And maybe his death would be futile. Alive perhaps, just perhaps, he could find a way to protect those he loved from the consequences of his own cowardice.

His love for Gabriel was greater than the sum of all his emotions, it tore at him, it filled him, it made him weep and shout aloud for joy. But he loved Pippa too, in a different way. His affection for his wife had grown over the months they'd been together. It had always been edged with guilt. She did not know, how could she, that she was a protective foil. He had tried to be a good and loving husband, careful and considerate. But when the fabric of his elaborate construction had been ripped asunder, he could hardly bear to be in the same chamber with her. His shame was unendurable, the hideous shame of those dreadful nights in the antechamber before they brought her out to him. . . .

A cold sweat broke out on his brow and he staggered sideways against the wall. In the shadow of a pillar he retched miserably. He could not go on with this. To behave with his wife as if all was as it should be. He could no longer endure to talk with her, smile at her, be close to her. He could not endure to lie beside her, hearing her sleeping innocent breath as he writhed in the torment of his betrayal.

He had to find a way out of this. Out of this marriage that so wronged his wife. A way to be with Gabriel in truth and honesty.

Five

"I THINK YOU WILL FIND THE MARE A SUITABLE mount, Luisa." Lionel regarded his purchase with a touch of complacency. The animal was a graceful beast, well-mannered, a perfect lady's horse.

Luisa's smile was radiant. "Oh, she's beautiful, Don Ashton. I don't know how to thank you."

"You may thank me by enjoying her and not badgering me to take you to court," he suggested dryly.

Luisa flushed a little. "I do not mean to badger you, sir, indeed I don't. I know that you're busy with affairs of state. And yet you found time to buy me this lovely horse. I am very grateful." She turned her smile on him and Lionel was startled by its effect. Luisa was no longer the little girl he had persisted in thinking her.

He shook his head in an unconscious gesture to dispel the charm of a smile that had no place between guardian and ward. "This is Malcolm, your groom," he said, gesturing to the muscular man of middle age who held the horse's bridle.

Malcolm touched his forelock. "My lady," he said gruffly.

Luisa treated him to the full force of her smile, hiding her slight dismay. Malcolm did not look as if he could be easily managed. He was no ordinary groom. There was something about his carriage, his air of watchfulness, the rough-and-ready cutlass he wore at his belt, that spoke more of a bodyguard than a groom.

"I'm sure we shall deal very well together, Malcolm," she said brightly.

"Aye, m'lady."

"What are you going to call the mare?" inquired Lionel.

"Crema," she said without hesitation. "Does she not have that color?"

Lionel agreed that she did. "I have acquired a small barge for you. It has no housing and can be handled by only two oarsmen, so 'tis nothing very elaborate, but it will be quite adequate for short river journeys under fair skies. It will be brought to the water steps tomorrow."

"You are very kind, sir."

He raised a quizzical eyebrow. "But you would still prefer to be at court?"

"I will not plague you any further, Don Ashton," Luisa replied demurely.

He laughed, not fooled for a minute. "Well, I have an engagement so I must leave you now, but enjoy your ride on Crema."

Luisa walked all around the mare, examining her from every angle. "She is lovely, isn't she, Malcolm?"

"Aye, m'lady. And very good-tempered."

"High-spirited?" inquired Luisa, gazing thoughtfully at the horse.

"Well-schooled."

"I like a degree of spirit in my mounts," she declared, laying a hand on Crema's neck.

"That so, m'lady?" Malcolm sounded indifferent.

Luisa shot him a sideways assessing glance. "Did Don Ashton give you any instructions as to how we were to ride . . . or where?"

He shook his head. "Reckon 'tis up to you, m'lady. My job's to keep you safe."

"I see." Luisa continued her perambulation around the horse. "Then I would like to ride towards Whitehall Palace. There's a park there?"

"Aye, m'lady, a small one."

"Then I will change my dress at once. I will be but ten minutes." She hurried away to the house.

Malcolm whistled between his teeth. In his experience a lady's ten minutes would stretch easily to a half hour. He led the mare towards the tack room and gestured to a groom to saddle the animal while he went to fetch his own mount.

It was closer to an hour before Luisa, accompanied by Bernardina, reappeared. She had tried and cast aside three gowns before settling on her present costume. She had decided that the Spanish gown of dark blue velvet with turquoise fastenings to the center of the skirt complemented her eyes very nicely. The collar of her turquoise silk *ropa* rose high at the back of her neck outside the small lace ruff that encircled her throat. She was particularly pleased with the mantilla of figured silk that was pinned to the dark braids looped over her ears, to fall in graceful folds down her back. She could use it to veil her face against rising dust . . . or interested eyes. A very useful article, as the most discreet of Spanish ladies well knew.

It would be a great shame, she reflected, if she did not contrive to run into Robin of Beaucaire this morning. He had only ever seen her in a muddy tangle on the bottom of a punt. This was a very different presentation. However, should she fail to encounter him, then she had another plan in mind.

Her eyes darted speculatively to the waiting Malcolm. How easy would it be to distract him for a few minutes? She had not yet taken his full measure but the morning's ride would give her some clues.

"Bernardina, this is Malcolm. He is to look after me on my ride," Luisa stated as they reached the groom and the horses.

"Malcolm, you must tell Dona Bernardina that I am quite safe with your escort. If Don Ashton considers it to be so, then it must be so." She directed this last to her duenna in the tone of one stating an irrefutable truth.

"You would not question Don Ashton's judgment, Bernardina, would you?" She stroked the mare's nose and the horse whickered into her palm.

"No . . . no, of course not," Bernardina said with an unhappy sigh. "But I should come with you, *querida*. I'm sure I should. Your dear mother would not wish you to ride out accompanied only by a groom."

"You hate to ride, dear one," Luisa pointed out, laying a hand on the other woman's arm. "This is England. The customs are different." Her voice was cajoling, her smile teasing.

"I suppose so." Bernardina fixed Malcolm with a piercing stare. "This is Dona Luisa de los Velez of the house of Mendoza," she announced. "A lady of one of the greatest families of Spain. You understand that."

"Aye, madam." Malcolm returned the regard blandly. "Mr. Ashton made all clear. I have my orders."

Bernardina pursed her lips. "You must ride at her

side at all times. Have a hand to her bridle at all times . . . you understand this."

"Bernardina, no!" cried Luisa. "I will not have my bridle held. There is not the slightest need. I ride well. You know I do. My father himself taught me."

This last reminder was sufficient to silence Bernardina, who held the memory of Luisa's father in great reverence.

"Madam, have no fear for the lady's safety," Malcolm said, taking advantage of the duenna's moment of reflection. "I assure you she will be always in my sight."

He turned to Luisa. "Let me help you mount, m'lady." He knelt on the cobbles and offered his cupped hands as a step.

Luisa managed to mount with creditable agility despite the mass of material hampering her movements. Once correctly positioned on the sidesaddle she settled her skirts around her and took up her reins. Already she felt a lifting of her spirits, a sense of freedom as she surveyed the world from atop the mare, who moved beneath her as if eager to be stepping out.

"Oh, we shall gallop," Luisa promised, leaning sideways to pat Crema's neck. "Indeed we shall."

"Oh, no . . . no, you must do no such thing!" exclaimed Bernardina, reluctant acceptance banished. *"Madre de dios, hija!* You cannot gallop. Think how unseemly, how unsafe!"

" 'Tis neither, Bernardina," Luisa said, laughing. "Is it, Malcolm?"

"Depends how you ride, m'lady," he said with a grunt. "Let's wait and see, shall we?"

Luisa held her peace. She could see that Bernardina, despite her protestations, was actually somewhat reassured by the groom's burly physique and matter-of-fact manner, and for herself, if he expected her to prove her skill then she would.

"Let us go, then," she said. "Dearest Bernardina, don't look so tragic. Nothing is going to happen and we'll be back before you know it . . . and if you wish, I will take a siesta after our *merienda* at noon." She threw the sop and was rewarded by a mollified if anxious smile.

They rode out of the stable yard, down the driveway, through the gates, and into a narrow lane.

"We'll go this-a-way, m'lady. There'll be some traffic, so keep a tight hold on the horse." Malcolm was watching her closely although his voice was casual.

Luisa nodded and took a firmer hold of the reins. She frowned in concentration. She had ridden often around the family estates outside Seville but never along crowded, narrow lanes full of people, barking dogs, tumbling urchins, amid the high cries of street vendors and the rank odors of a city sweltering in a dry summer heat.

Crema seemed unperturbed, however, and picked her way delicately, following Malcolm's dun gelding. After a few turns they reached a broader thoroughfare that ran parallel with the river. It was as busy as the lanes, but there was more room for maneuver and Luisa could take time to savor the freedom, the sense of anticipation she felt for the first time since they'd arrived at Don Ashton's grand house on the river and she'd realized that this was simply another form of domestic imprisonment, differing only in landscape from the circumscribed life she had endured at home.

She inhaled the smells, was bombarded by the noise, her eyes drank in every sight, her mind, like drenched sand, absorbed everything.

When the road widened Malcolm fell back to ride beside her. He offered no conversation but Luisa was aware that he was watching her closely although it often seemed that his attention was elsewhere. After a while, she asked directly, "Did my guardian hire you as a groom or as a bodyguard, Malcolm?"

"Depends on the situation, m'lady. One or the other, or both . . . depending."

Luisa wondered if she had really seen the flicker of a smile at the corner of his impassive mouth before he'd answered her. She decided she had. "But whom I talk to, or where I go, if there's no danger . . . then that's not your concern?"

He stared straight ahead. "That's for me to judge, m'lady."

"Ah." Luisa thought for a minute. "But are you obliged to report every detail of our rides to my guardian?"

He continued to stare ahead. "That's for me to judge, m'lady," he repeated stolidly.

"That is not very helpful, Malcolm," Luisa stated.

Now he glanced sideways at her and she knew she had been right about the smile. "You have a duenna," he said. "Seems to me you don't need another one."

Luisa smiled at him. "I promise you I will do nothing on our rides that will put you in a difficult position as long as you don't feel you have to be a duenna."

"Good enough for me, m'lady." He returned his eyes to the middle distance.

They rode in companionable silence until they reached the small wooded park that stretched up from the river to surround Whitehall Palace on three sides. Luisa was surprised that the park was open to the public. The great royal palaces in Spain were walled, with guarded gates. Here the ordinary folk of London wandered at will among the flower gardens, along the graveled paths, in the green shade of the woods, mingling with the richly clad courtiers, each group ignoring the other as if they lived on separate planes.

Luisa's eyes were only on the courtiers. And only on the men.

"I would like to ride towards the river," she said.

"As you wish, m'lady." Malcolm took a path through the trees.

A group of men came towards them, talking earnestly among themselves. They moved aside as the two riders approached. Luisa decided to take the opportunity offered her. She glanced at Malcolm and drew rein. Malcolm checked his horse, then without further acknowledgment moved forward at a slow walk.

"My lords?" Luisa smiled at the group, who halted immediately.

"Madam?" One spoke to her, they all bowed simultaneously.

"I wonder if you're acquainted with Lord Robin of Beaucaire."

"Indeed, madam." The one who had spoken stepped forward. "Lord Robin is known to us all."

"Could I trouble you to give him this?" Luisa took a folded sheet of parchment from the pocket of her *ropa*. It was sealed with wax. She held it out.

The spokesman of the group stepped forward and took it from her. "It will be my pleasure, madam. May I tell him who sent it?"

His gaze was both curious and predatory and Luisa with a swift movement that bespoke all the arrogance of a Mendoza flipped the mantilla over her face. "It will be apparent if you deliver my message, sir," she said, her tone frigid.

The courtier bowed and stepped back, a slightly ironical smile on his lips. "Well, well," he murmured, tapping the letter into his palm as the lady and her escort rode on. "What is Robin up to? He's never been one for the ladies. And a Spanish lady at that. Do we know her?"

"Never seen her before," one of his companions declared. "And that's not a face to be forgotten. Robin must enlighten us."

There was a unanimous chuckle and they continued on their way to the palace.

"Are you ready to turn back, m'lady?" Malcolm inquired after a few minutes. "I assume your business is completed?"

"I haven't had a gallop yet," she replied, lifting the mantilla from her face. "I promised myself and Crema that we would gallop."

"There's a meadow along the riverbank," he said placidly.

Luisa nodded. "Lead on, Malcolm."

PIPPA STOOD AT THE WINDOW IN HER BEDCHAMBER, looking out over the gardens bathed in midday heat. A film of sweat gathered on her brow and she was aware of a faint but nagging nausea.

She clasped her throat with one hand, idly stroking with her thumb and forefinger. It seemed she was pregnant. Her terms were only a week overdue but she had always been able to rely on their regularity. Her breasts felt full and tender as if the bleeding were about to start, but she knew in her body's core that she had conceived.

One of those nights of Stuart's secret lovemaking had borne fruit.

He would be pleased, of course. She glanced over her shoulder at the bed with its carved and gilded posts, its rich tapestried hangings. Since their quarrel after the joust he had not shared that bed with her. She had slept chaste and alone, and awoken untouched and alone.

Martha came in with an armful of clean linen. She cast her mistress a shrewdly assessing glance. "Something amiss, madam?"

"No," Pippa said, moving away from the window. "Nothing at all."

Martha pursed her lips but kept a skeptical silence. She knew a great deal more about Lady Nielson's state of health than her ladyship gave her credit for.

There was a knock at the door and Martha set her burden on the bed and went to open it. " 'Tis Lord Robin, madam." She stood aside to let him in.

"Thank you, Martha. You may go," Pippa said.

The maid curtsied and left. Robin turned the key in the door. "Have you written your letter to the Lady Elizabeth?"

"Yes, 'tis here." She went to an iron-bound chest on a table against the wall and unlocked it with a key hanging on her girdle. "When will you go?"

"I leave this evening. I have several stops to make in Buckinghamshire. I carry dispatches for Lord Russell, who is so strong in Elizabeth's support, and also for William of Thame at Rycote. He's more ambivalent in his support, but I hope to work upon him a little. I expect to be gone no more than a week." He took Pippa's letter and tucked it into the inner pocket of his doublet.

"Will you take wine?" Pippa lifted the flagon that always awaited Stuart on the side table.

Robin nodded and she poured burgundy into two pewter cups. She handed him one and took a sip of the other. It tasted metallic on her tongue and with a grimace she put it down. "Did you discover anything?"

"No," he said flatly. "Stuart is always surrounded by his Spanish friends, I have not been able to talk with him alone. I have inquired discreetly and no one has had anything to offer on the subject of a mistress."

He shrugged. "I don't know what to say, Pippa."

"Neither do I," she said bleakly. "I barely see him except in public. He doesn't sleep here anymore . . . not since we quarreled."

"Perhaps he's just angry. He'll recover his good temper in time," Robin suggested, but aware that it was a lame attempt at encouragement.

Pippa shook her head with a short, dismissive laugh. "I doubt that, Robin." She fetched the flagon and refilled his cup. "But tell me, will you see Lady Elizabeth?"

"Not on this occasion. I don't wish to draw attention to myself." Robin embraced the change of topic. "This time I shall merely act as courier and talk with Parry how best to organize the chain of information."

He sipped his wine. "You've heard that Thomas Parry has set up house at the Bull in Woodstock?"

"I knew the council wanted to get him away from Elizabeth," Pippa said, trying to concentrate on a subject that a few days ago would have absorbed her completely. "But the village is almost in the grounds of the palace. How could that separate him from Elizabeth?"

Robin chuckled. "Well, it doesn't. The council thought Bedingfield would be willing to manage Elizabeth's finances himself as well as acting her gaoler, but he won't touch her household management with a barge pole, so he had to leave Thomas in charge. But he threw him out of the palace itself, as a compromise measure. Of course, what it means is that Thomas can set up his own camp in the town and plot for Elizabeth without any interference from Bedingfield."

Pippa sat down on the bed, her eyes now alive with interest and amusement. "Poor Bedingfield. He's not a bad person, but he's not made to be a gaoler and he's certainly no match for either Elizabeth or Thomas."

Robin laughed with rich enjoyment. "No, and now, while he's watching Elizabeth in the palace Thomas is playing his own games in town, and if he turns his attention to Thomas, Elizabeth gets on with her own plots."

"And you'll communicate with Thomas, who'll arrange to get information into the palace for Elizabeth," Pippa stated.

"Precisely."

"I wish I could see her," Pippa said with a sigh. "I miss talking to her, Robin."

Robin regarded her shrewdly. "About anything in particular?"

Pippa shook her head. "No, I just miss her."

"Mmm. It always surprised me how well you two got on. Lady Elizabeth is such a scholar and you—"

"Are not," Pippa interrupted before he could say anything less complimentary. "I'm not stupid, however. You don't have to be a scholar to be good company. Look at yourself."

Robin grinned. "Touché." Pippa seemed much more herself now and he felt somewhat reassured as he set down his cup before bending to kiss her. "I'll be on my way. I'll be back in a week."

"God go with you." She rose from the bed and accompanied him to the door.

"Don't fret about Stuart, Pippa. He'll get over whatever's troubling him."

"Yes, of course he will." She smiled, and waved him away.

Robin glanced back before rounding the corner of the corridor. Pippa still stood in the doorway of her chamber and he saw that the smile had disappeared. With it went his reassurance.

His step heavier, he continued on his way, frowning down at the floor. He was brought up short as he nearly ran headlong into a man coming towards him.

He looked up with an exclamation. "I beg your pardon!"

"Dreaming of a fair maid, Robin?" Lord Kimbolten teased.

"Not exactly, Peter." Robin shrugged with an assumption of ease.

"Well, that surprises me, since a fair maid is dreaming of you," Peter said with a significant leer.

"And what's that supposed to mean?" Robin looked at him suspiciously. Peter Kimbolten was known for his jests and practical jokes.

"Only that the fairest maiden I've ever seen is writing you *billets doux*." Peter removed the letter from the breast pocket of his doublet and wafted it in the air.

"What in the devil's name are you talking about, Peter?"

"Why, just that while I was strolling in the woods with a few friends I was accosted by a damsel on a rather magnificent mare. She wished me to play love's messenger." He sniffed the letter with an exaggerated twitch of his nose. "No perfume, how strange."

"I've no time for games," Robin said impatiently. He turned to go but Peter seized his arm.

"I jest a little, Robin. But the story still stands. A lady on a horse gave me a letter to give to you. As simple as that."

"What lady?" Robin stared at him.

"I asked her the same thing, but she said you would discover that when you opened her message . . . I'd lay odds she was Spanish, though," he added, watching his friend with narrowed eyes.

Robin's sudden change of color, a shift of his eyes told Lord Kimbolten that there was indeed mischief afoot. He chortled. "Oh, a secret mistress, Robin? What a dark horse you are!"

" 'Tis no such thing!" Robin snatched the letter from his loosened grasp. "And I'll thank you, Peter, not to go spreading rumors."

"As if I would!" He laid a hand to his heart. "You wound me, Robin, indeed you do."

"You, my friend, are a foolish sot!" Robin declared roundly with all the privilege of long-standing friendship. "And I know your meddlesome tongue!"

He thrust the letter into his pocket, where it joined Pippa's to Elizabeth, and went on his way, leaving his friend grinning as he planned how best to circulate this amusing little tidbit of gossip.

Robin didn't open Luisa's letter until he was outside in the relative privacy of a rose garden. He sat down on a stone bench beneath a trellised arbor and slit the wafer.

If Lord Robin of Beaucaire has any interest in furthering the acquaintance of a certain lady of the most lamentable skill with a punt he should know that she likes to walk in the moonlight in the orchard of her house at eleven o'clock every evening.

Robin threw back his head and laughed. *Minx!* Even Pippa in her flirtatious heyday had not been so brazen. But since he could not keep the suggested assignation until he'd returned from Woodstock, Dona Luisa would have to cool her heels for a week's worth of moonlit evenings.

He folded the letter and replaced it in his pocket. So she had a horse now. She must have prevailed upon Ashton to grant her some liberty. But just what would that silent, observant, remote gentleman think of his gently bred and sheltered ward's amusing herself in a clandestine flirtation with an English courtier?

His smile died abruptly. Just what part did Lionel Ashton actually play in the plots and contrivances that engaged the Spaniards at the English court? He seemed always to be on the outside looking in. He took no part in any of the competitive activities; he was a distant presence at formal court functions; he was clearly in the king's intimate circle. But why he was here was a mystery. Robin didn't think he'd actually seen him *do* anything. He'd barely heard him speak.

Pippa had expressed some interest in him, though. But then, Pippa was interested in everyone and everything. It was one of her greatest charms, and always had been. At least until recently. These days it was hard to get her to show interest in anything, she seemed totally absorbed with her own marital troubles.

Frowning now, Robin left the arbor, his mind moving from speculation about Lionel Ashton to the puzzle of Stuart and his subservient behavior with the Spaniards. Stuart, of all people! A man who had been negotiating on an equal footing with the Spaniards for months on the details of the wedding. His privileged status as one of Mary's council was unimpeachable. He knew the Spanish. He drank with them. He bargained and he argued with them. Until now.

When had it changed?

Robin stopped suddenly in the middle of a gravel pathway as a picture formed in his mind. Lionel Ashton talking with Stuart. On several occasions.

He prodded his memory, trying to clarify the image. Always the two of them, standing apart. Ashton, as usual, apparently detached, his eyes on nothing as he spoke, almost as if he was not acknowledging the man he was talking to. Not so Stuart. Stuart had been intent on whatever was being said. Intent and radiating discomfort.

In fact, Robin thought now, it was more than discomfort. He had seemed to be as embarrassed and wretched as a subordinate being rebuked by his superior. But he only had this manner with Lionel Ashton. With the Spaniards themselves, Stuart was irritatingly placatory, bending over backwards to accommodate their wishes, but it was something more with the English Ashton.

Did Lionel Ashton have anything to do with Stuart's volte-face? Was he indeed some kind of superior? Some kind of handler? Robin was aware that he was thinking like a spy now, but he'd practiced that trade for close to five years, so that was hardly surprising.

Ashton would bear some investigation. And where better to start than with the man's ward on a moonlit summer evening?

Six

Pippa leaned back against the broad trunk of the spreading beech tree. Sunlight filtered through the leaves above, casting dappled light on the group of men and women sitting on rugs and cushions on the mossy ground.

Mary had discovered the delights of alfresco dining and rarely a week passed without some meal enjoyed in the open air. Not everyone found sitting upon the ground particularly comfortable or the presence of flying insects a welcome addition to the fare, but the court, as it must, acquiesced to the queen's pleasure with every appearance of enjoyment.

Pippa held a lavender-soaked handkerchief against the pulse in her throat; it seemed to cool her. She listened with a polite smile to the chatter around her, nodding every now and again, murmuring some agreeable comment at judicious intervals. It was a trick she had perfected in the last weeks. It gave her a pleasant and attentive air while freeing her mind to pursue its own course.

She was to all intents and purposes a prisoner at

Mary's court. She could not leave it without the queen's permission and where she went was strictly circumscribed. She would be permitted in her husband's company to visit her family in their house in Holborn, but not to go farther afield. And at present her mother, stepfather, and half sister, Anna, were spending the summer at Mallory Hall in Derbyshire.

Behind her bland exterior she was dreaming now of long-ago summers spent in the soft verdant Dove valley surrounded by the heather-topped peaks of the surrounding mountains. In her memory Mallory Hall was a golden house of warm glowing stone, filled with the scents of dried lavender, roses from the garden, and the lingering tang of woodsmoke. Her reverie was peopled with the household servants of her childhood: her nurse, Tilly; Master Crowder, the steward; Magister Howard, gone to his grave the previous winter; and the huntsman Master Greene. She had lived an idyll during those long childhood summers, until Hugh of Beaucaire had come knocking at their gates and plunged the quiet, orderly pace of their lives into chaos.

She could not regret that disruption since it had brought her mother so much joy in Hugh's love, but she could not help feeling now that all else had stemmed from it. If they had not been compelled to come to London all those years ago, she would not now be wed to Stuart Nielson, carrying his child, a virtual prisoner in the palace of Whitehall.

And Pen would not, after her own trials and tribulations, be deliriously happy with her Owen d'Arcy and their brood.

No, she could not regret that disruption.

A wave of the now familiar nausea crept over her. She fought it down, breathing deeply. God's bones, how she needed her mother's counsel. What would she not give to be in her mother's arms, in the peace of the Derbyshire countryside at this moment?

The nausea grew stronger, refused to be tamed. The smell of roasting meat was suddenly unbearable. She scrambled hastily to her feet, toppling her untouched goblet of wine, accidentally kicking a silver serving platter on the ground as she looked for an escape.

She murmured a word of excuse and tried not to run as she left the circle, plunging deeper into the grove of trees. She was going to be sick. It was unstoppable and she could not possibly get back to her chamber in time.

She fell to her knees among the thick corded roots of an ancient oak tree. The smell of damp moss and fungus rose up, pungent on the air. Why was it that these days every smell was so pronounced? Smells she would not ordinarily even have noticed?

She leaned forward, retching miserably, trying at the same time to hold back her unbound hair as it swung over her face. Then the swatch of hair was lifted and held away from her. The air was wonderfully cool on the back of her neck, and as the paroxysm passed, the relief it always brought filled her with an albeit temporary sense of well-being.

Except that someone was standing over her, holding her hair clear of her face and neck.

"Is it over?" The voice behind her was Lionel Ashton's. A handkerchief appeared in front of her face as she still knelt among the tree roots.

Dear God! How long had he been standing there? Numbly, overwhelmed with embarrassment, Pippa took the handkerchief. It was bad enough that anyone should have seen her vomit like that, but the idea that it was a man, no, *this* man, filled her with dismay.

She pushed herself off her knees and stood up, the handkerchief pressed to her mouth. Awkwardly she stepped away from the tree roots. He still held her hair and she stumbled against him. Amid the welter of emotions she could distinguish no single sensation. She was aware of mortification, of a shocking sensual thrill at the press of his body, and then of the familiar strange, unfocused dread in his presence.

She tried to move away from him but he held on to her, her hair still twisted around his hand. "Steady," he said calmly. "Steady. You're still shaking."

Pippa didn't know why she was shaking. But she did know it wasn't something to be explained as the simple aftermath of her wrenching nausea. But she felt his hold as unbreakable and for a moment remained quietly against him, aware again of the sharpness of her sense of smell. She could detect musk, sweat, leather, dried lavender, and the ethereal scent of sunshine.

Then he released her and the swatch of hair he held. His hands were on her elbows steadying her as she stepped away from him. Her heart was hammering against her ribs, the little grove wavered around her, and for a ghastly moment she thought she was going to be sick again. Then everything settled down. The trees became their usual still and sturdy shapes and her heart slowed.

Pippa shook her hair back, wishing that she had something with which to tie it. Unbound hair had seemed so right for the day's casual entertainment, and it went so well with her simple low-necked gown of primrose yellow silk that she had fancied had a milkmaid look to it with its puffed and banded sleeves and lace ruching. But when she had dressed that morning she had not given a thought to the difficulties of alfresco nausea. *What price vanity?* she thought with a grim internal smile.

"Can I get you something?" Lionel asked, his gaze searching her face. She was still very pale, and her nose seemed pinched, longer and thinner than it actually was. Her freckles stood out as if they were on stalks, and her eyes looked bruised. Despite the elegant gown and the perfect circlet of pearls at her throat she looked as scrawny and pathetic as a half-starved waif.

Pippa finally looked up at him. His smile was as sweet and his gaze as compassionate as ever it had been. It drew her to him, seemed to enfold her, offering safety, and something else . . . something paradoxically dangerous.

She found that she was no longer embarrassed. "Bread helps," she said. "Plain bread."

"I'll bring you some right away. Rest over here." He took her arm and led her to a fallen tree trunk. "Sit there, I'll be back in a minute."

Pippa obeyed without a murmur. There was something about Lionel Ashton that made the idea of withstanding him quite impossible to imagine. But she was feeling a little weak, she told herself, so it was hardly surprising.

She looked down at his handkerchief that she held scrunched in her hand and thought vaguely that she must give it to Martha to launder before she gave it back to him. Her skin felt clammy and she took her own lavender-scented handkerchief from her sleeve and pressed it to her temples.

Lionel returned with a thick slice of barley bread and a leather flagon. He sat beside her on the tree trunk and gave her the bread.

Pippa broke off a piece of crust and ate it slowly. The

effect was instant. Her color came back as the hollow residue of nausea disappeared. She ate the rest of the bread slowly, savoring each crumb and not questioning the intimacy of the companionable silence that had settled over them. A ray of sunlight pierced the leaves above and struck the back of her neck, its warmth sending waves of relaxation down her spine.

"Drink some of this." He held the flagon out to her.

Pippa was startled by the sound of his voice. It seemed an eternity since she had heard anything but the rustle of a squirrel and the twitter of a bird.

She shook her head. "No . . . no, I thank you. I find I don't care for wine at the moment."

"This is mead. I think you will find it strengthening." He continued to hold out the flagon.

Pippa took it, wondering at her newfound docility. It was not that she was ordinarily stubborn or unreasonable, but she tended to have a mind of her own. Now she seemed to have become as wobbly and unformed as an unset quince jelly. The comparison brought an involuntary chuckle to her lips.

"That's a delightful sound," her companion approved. "Take a drink now."

Pippa put the flagon to her lips and swallowed. He was right. Where wine these days had an acid metallic taste that turned her stomach, the mead was pure honey, soothing her belly, flowing warm to the tips of her fingers.

"I never thought to try mead," she said, handing him back the flagon.

"I have some experience of pregnant women," he offered, putting the stopper back into the neck of the flagon.

Pippa stared at him, shocked at the casual statement. "Your wife . . . you have children?"

"No." It was a flat negative and she realized that it didn't encourage further probing. However, she was unable to help herself.

"No, you have no wife? Or no, you have no children?"

"I have neither wife nor child."

"But you have had experience of pregnant women?"

"That is what I said." *Why in hell had he invited this catechism?* Lionel wondered, furious with himself for such a slip. He never *ever* revealed personal details. Never *ever* let down his guard.

Pippa crumbled the last morsel of bread between her fingers and accepted that she had gone as far as she could. She didn't like the cold flatness of his tone. It didn't go with the sweetness of his smile or the warmth and compassion in his eyes.

She said with a casual shrug, "As yet I have barely acknowledged my pregnancy myself, sir. 'Tis hardly a topic for discussion between strangers."

"Are we strangers, Lady Pippa?" He laughed softly and he was once more himself. "I do not feel that to be the case."

"No," she said frankly. "Neither do I, although I don't know why not. However, Mr. Ashton, I am a married woman, and, as you so rightly assume, I appear to be carrying my husband's child."

"Quite," he murmured, stretching his long legs in front of him on the grass. "And those facts should keep us strangers?"

Pippa glanced at him. "You don't think so?"

He shook his head. "No, madam, I do not. One may be friends without impropriety, I believe."

"Yes," she agreed slowly. "But I do not choose my friends from among Spaniards and those committed to their cause."

"Ah." He nodded solemnly. "You are, of course, loyal to the Lady Elizabeth."

"That is no secret."

"No, indeed." He stood up. "But I fail to see why that should impede our friendship, my dear lady. If I do not question your affiliations, then why would you question mine?" He reached down to take her hands and pull her to her feet. "Friends can agree to differ, I believe."

Pippa again felt she was being swept along on a tide not of her own harnessing. His hands were warm and strong on her own. The mead was powerful honey in her belly.

"Perhaps so," she said, and firmly removed her hands from his. "I thank you for your kindness, Mr. Ashton, but pray excuse me now." She turned from him and flitted, a primrose butterfly, through the trees towards the palace.

Lionel remained in the grove for a few more minutes. So Philip's seed was well sown in the womb of a young, fertile, healthy woman. There was every reason to expect the pregnancy to go full term and produce a sound child.

A child that Spain must not claim.

If there was no child of the English/Spanish alliance, then on Mary's death Elizabeth would inherit the throne, and the hell that was the Inquisition would not consume England's heart and soul as it had devoured the Netherlands' and every other territory where the dread hand of Spain had fallen.

He raised his head and gazed unseeing into the green

canopy above. He could still smell it, the smoke of the unseasoned wood that fueled her pyre. He would always smell it, as he would always hear the sullen yet terrified silence of the crowd amid the pious recitations of the priests and the staccato orders of the soldiers.

One piercing scream had escaped her, and then not another sound as the flames from the damp wood crept with agonizing reluctance around her broken body.

And he had had to stand and watch, helplessly bearing silent witness to the horror, swearing vengeance as hatred devoured him with the flames that finally consumed Margaret.

There would be burnings here, too, soon enough, if Philip was able to consolidate his position. But Mary was frail, weakened by a lifetime's ill health, years of deprivation, and her desperate struggle for survival. She was nearly forty, she could not live for many more years. England's agony would be short-lived as long as there was no child that Philip could claim as his own.

Lionel's face was a mask as he continued to stare sightlessly up through the leaves. Behind the mask his mind moved rapidly along well-traveled routes.

It was not possible alone to take on the might that was the Holy Roman Empire and its vile confederates, but there were others who shared his loathing, the devouring force of vengeance. Together they could send Philip of Spain, one arm of that empire, slinking home, driven out by a hostile people, his appetite for England unsatisfied, his emperor father's grand design in ruins.

As long as the marriage produced no child.

Even if Mary conceived, no one expected her to carry a child to term. If she did, then there were those in place who knew how to deal with it. His own task lay with the other strand to the royal plot: Lady Nielson and the child she carried. And what better way to over-turn a plot than to be intimately involved in its execu-tion?

The acknowledgment brought a bitter derisory smile to his lips. His plans were already in place. He needed only to gain Pippa's confidence, and he believed he was well on the way to doing that.

One woman's peace of mind was a tiny price to pay for the many thousands of lives that would be saved.

And for the satisfaction of vengeance.

Or so he told himself as he left the grove, directing his steps back towards the voices and music under the beech trees.

"TELL ME, MARTHA, IS YOUR MISTRESS QUITE WELL, do you think?"

The maid turned from the armoire at the sound of Lord Nielson's voice. "Oh, sir, you startled me. I didn't hear you come in."

"You were busy," Stuart observed with an engaging smile. "You are most diligent in caring for my wife."

Martha, with a gratified air, smoothed the folds of the velvet gown she had been about to hang up in the armoire. "I do my best, my lord."

"Yes, indeed you do." He closed the door behind him with a snap, and stood leaning against it with a decep-tively casual air. He had no desire to be surprised by Pippa's sudden return to her bedchamber.

"So, Martha, have you noticed anything amiss with my wife? Does she appear to be in good health?"

Martha hesitated. She was not in her mistress's confi-dence, a fact that she resented as much as it puzzled her. Lady Pippa could not possibly imagine that her maid, the woman who served her in the most intimate fashion, would not notice the absence of her terms, the morning's greenish pallor, the fluctuations in her appetite, and yet she had said nothing. It had occurred to Martha that perhaps her mistress didn't recognize the signs, but she had dismissed the thought. Lady Pippa was no naive girl.

But why would she keep her pregnancy a secret? It was advanced enough now to be confirmed. Martha pursed her lips in thought.

"Well, girl?" Stuart's prompting was sharp, his eyes narrowed in impatience.

Martha decided she needed to keep in his lordship's good graces. It wasn't as if Lady Pippa had taken her into her confidence and asked her not to disclose the information.

"My lady hasn't said anything to me, sir, but I think it likely that she's with child," she said, her eyes downcast, her hands demurely clasped against her skirts.

Stuart felt a great wash of relief. It was over then. Never again would he have to deliver her unconscious to the antechamber. He would have no further part to play. His wife would become now the concern, *the property*, of the Spanish.

Revulsion and the old fear followed close on the heels of relief. What would happen to them all now? Pippa was safe while she carried Philip's child. Her husband was a necessary prop as the proud father-to-be. But once the child was delivered . . .

But perhaps he could use the pregnancy as a bargaining counter. Perhaps he could now negotiate Gabriel's freedom from persecution. It didn't matter for himself, he deserved whatever Fate, or Philip and his cohorts, had in store, but Gabriel was an innocent. He knew nothing of this.

As innocent as Pippa.

Stewart nodded at Martha and left the chamber hurriedly. There were some things it was not useful to contemplate. What was done was done. Now he would take the glad tidings and try to gain some advantage from being the bearer of good news.

The guards outside the council chamber came to attention as Lord Nielson approached. "Is His Majesty within?" Stuart's tone was haughty.

"Aye, my lord. With Her Majesty, the queen, and the king's close councillors."

"Good. Pray tell them that Lord Nielson craves an audience."

"Aye, my lord." The guard bowed and knocked with his stave of office on the oak door. It was opened by another guard. Whispers were exchanged, then the door closed again.

Stuart waited, pacing the narrow antechamber between the window and the door.

"Their Majesties will see you now, Lord Nielson."

He spun from the window and without acknowledging the guard's bow strode into the paneled chamber. Philip and Mary sat together under the canopy of state on a raised dais. Below them at the long council table sat the members of Philip's council and, of course, Simon Renard. They regarded Stuart expectantly but no one offered him a seat.

He stood at the foot of the table and bowed low to Their Majesties, before offering a more moderate courtesy to the council. "I have news, madam, sire, my lords."

"Good news, I trust," Ruy Gomez said in a lazy drawl.

"I believe Lady Nielson to be with child," he responded, and the words now stuck in his craw. The contempt directed at him in the chamber was thick enough to cut, but it was no greater than what he felt for himself, crawling to them with what was now a humiliating confession.

"Has this been confirmed by a physician?" inquired the queen, leaning forward slightly.

"No, madam. But by her maid."

"And by Lady Nielson, of course."

"Not as yet, madam." His discomfort increased and he could feel the sweat gathering in the hollow of his throat beneath his ruff. "I have but just now had the information from her maid. I have not yet discussed it with my wife."

"Well, I trust you were not in too much of a hurry to bring us this news," Simon Renard declared, tapping his beringed fingers on the table.

"Maids are usually the first to know," Ruy Gomez said. "But I suggest, my lord, that you make haste to have a physician's confirmation as well as your wife's. We will hold back our celebration until such time as you do." He gazed with cold eyes at the man before him.

Stuart stood straighter, and for the first time when confronted with the insolence of his tormentors he fought back. "You need have no doubts, sir," he snapped. "And I would ask assurances now that Gabriel be released from his duties in Her Majesty's service and permitted to leave the palace, as it was agreed."

Simon Renard raised an eyebrow. "Ah . . . your bauble, of course. But where would he go? An indigent lyre player would be eaten alive in the streets of London."

Stuart was very white, his eyes brilliant as gems. "I would make provision," he stated.

Renard's mouth curved in a narrow smile and he nodded slowly. "But of course you would." He turned to his fellows at the table. "However, we believe your friend would be safer under *our* protection. Is that not so, my lords?"

"For a while longer," agreed Ruy Gomez with a smooth smile.

"My lords, I demand—"

"You *demand*, sir?" Philip exclaimed, half rising from his chair. "Bear in mind that there are witnesses to the man's crimes of perversion . . . sodomy . . . and heresy." His voice shook slightly with the depth of his emotion.

"Crimes against God," he declared with sudden force, his eyes burning with the fires of conviction. "It wants only my signature to send him to the hangman by way of those who would most assuredly succeed in persuading him to repent his sins."

"And any of his partners in these acts of bestiality," put in Ruy Gomez, leaning across the table now, his gaze steady, with a politician's coldness rather than the fanatical burn of the king's.

Stuart knew that once more he was defeated. He stood silent, awaiting dismissal from Their Majesties. It was Mary who released him with a curt word. He bowed and backed from the chamber.

Outside, he wiped his brow with his handkerchief. He needed Gabriel. He needed to see him whole, smiling his wonderful soft smile as he plucked sweetness from his lyre; he needed to hold him, eager and loving. Only then could he banish the dreadful images that had

been conjured in the council chamber. Gabriel screaming on the rack, broken on the wheel, burning in the
fire. They could do that. They *would* do that.

But he dared not go to the minstrels' dormitory,
where Gabriel would be resting before the evening's
duties. They only ever met outside the palace, in the little tavern where bedsport of all kinds was tolerated with
an indifferent shrug, so long as the indifference was well
paid for. Stuart hated it, the hole-in-the-corner sordid-
ness of it all. But now he would give a king's ransom for
five minutes there alone in Gabriel's company.

Tonight, he promised himself. Tonight they would
meet.

THERE WAS A SHORT SILENCE IN THE COUNCIL CHAM-
ber after Lord Nielson's departure. Then the queen
spoke with a certain intensity in her voice, her eyes unusually bright.

"My lords, I am assured by my physicians that I am
carrying a child."

Renard was the first to respond. "You are to be congratulated, madam. That is indeed wonderful news."
He turned to Philip. "Sire, the people will rally to you
now, their disaffection will vanish under this news. An
heir to the throne, a child for their beloved queen.
There will be no more mutterings, no more popular re-
bellions."

"My people . . . *our* people . . . will indeed be glad of
the news, my dear sir," Mary said, smiling at her husband. "It has been so long since they have had a healthy
infant heir to the throne." She touched her stomacher
fleetingly. "A healthy boy child."

Philip rose from his chair and bowed low before his

wife. He took her hand and carried it to his lips. "Most honored lady, you fill my heart with such joy, and with undying gratitude. But I would talk with your physicians. We must be certain that all the signs are favorable and that they know how to take care of you."

Basking in her husband's anxious attention, the queen rose and left the council chamber with stately if complacent tread.

"Nevertheless we must not lose our insurance," Ruy Gomez said softly. "Sufficient care must be taken there also."

"Don Ashton will see to it," Renard said with quiet confidence. "We can safely leave Lady Nielson's welfare in his hands."

"Indeed." Gomez nodded. "Shall you discuss it with him, or shall I?"

Seven

~❦~

"THE KING MUST BE FEELING VERY SATISFIED," LIONEL observed from the deep stone windowsill where he was perched to catch any stray breeze wafting up from the river.

His tone was pleasant enough, dispassionate almost, and yet Simon Renard wondered if he heard a slightly sardonic edge to it, as if Ashton was amused, and not in a kindly fashion. He remembered that once or twice in the past he had fancied hearing such a note in his voice. Of course, the idea of a man's impregnating two women in the same month could be cause for a raised eyebrow in ordinary circles, but this was a matter of state, a matter of the highest importance. It was not something to be treated as a prurient jest.

He examined Ashton with a frown but could tell nothing from the man's customarily impassive expression. Perhaps he had been mistaken. Lionel Ashton had never been anything but a committed supporter of Philip's affairs since he had accompanied the king from the Netherlands on his wedding journey. Renard had developed a great respect for his shrewd intelligence, his calm, detached manner, and the efficient ease with which he manipulated people and affairs around him. He was a man who got things done. He was also a man who kept himself to himself and minded his own business; however, that personal reticence had no impact on the enterprise they shared, and, indeed, was a quality that Renard cultivated himself and much admired.

"We are all satisfied with the outcome," he said a little stiffly. "The king has—"

"Been most diligent," Lionel interrupted with a soft laugh. "And achieved his just reward. Let us hope the queen's pregnancy is uneventful and brings forth a healthy prince."

"That is in God's hands," Renard stated. "You seem amused, Ashton."

"No . . . not in the least. Merely delighted," Lionel declared. " 'Tis a matter for felicitations not gloom, Renard."

"Well, yes, indeed," the ambassador agreed with a degree of hesitation. He still felt that there was something not quite correct about Ashton's response to his news. "But 'tis also a matter of grave importance to the state."

"That is understood," Lionel said, still smiling. "When does the queen intend to make a formal announcement?"

"Within the week. It will be cried in every town square and the following Sunday thanks will be given from every pulpit in the land. It will be an occasion for celebration from coast to coast." Renard's usually dour and solemn expression lightened considerably and Lionel thought he almost looked joyful.

Lionel contented himself with the quiet statement that such news would certainly please the people.

"And 'tis to be hoped they will finally be reconciled to the marriage."

"Yes," Lionel agreed. "And what of Lady Nielson? Is the world to know of her happy condition at once?"

"That is not an issue that concerns us," Renard said. "That is for her and her husband to decide. What does concern us, however, is the lady's health and welfare. Of course we all hope and pray that the queen will be safely delivered, but . . ." He shrugged. "Lady Nielson must be watched over with the greatest attention. No danger must come to her and she must be prevented from doing anything that might endanger the child."

Lionel nodded. "That had occurred to me." He regarded Renard with apparent indifference while he waited to see if the other man would play into his hand.

"It is the king's wish that you take on this charge," Renard continued, carefully examining his long, soft white hands. "Ensure that the lady and her child remain well."

"I would have thought that to be a task more suited to her husband," Lionel said, casually turning his head aside to look down onto the bowling green below. A spirited game was taking place and the subject of their discussion was at that moment lifting her bowl to take her turn. She looked better than the other day, Lionel thought, wondering if hefting bowling balls, even the lighter lady's variety, was an activity to be discouraged in a pregnant woman.

"Maybe, but the husband's cooperation cannot be relied upon. He is acting under duress and his wife's pregnancy is not one to bring him joy," Renard pointed out dryly. "We would prefer to have one of our own taking charge of the lady."

Oh, how sweetly they had swum into his net, Lionel thought with a hidden smile.

"I will be happy to do so," he said easily, getting up from the windowsill. "Would you consider bowling to be a dangerous activity, Renard? Because if so, I should go and distract the lady from her present game."

"I am no physician, but I would think lifting anything heavy is unwise, particularly in these early weeks," Renard declared with an air of distaste. He was not comfortable discussing such intimately female topics, although he thought nothing of writing about them in the baldest terms in his dispatches to the emperor.

"Then I will go to my charge." Lionel bowed and left the ambassador to his own thoughts.

Renard riffled through the papers on his desk but his mind was not on them. He was thinking of how little he knew of Lionel Ashton. He had detailed knowledge of most of the members of Philip's entourage but they were for the most part Spanish and their lives and family histories were an open book easily read by Renard's spies. But Lionel Ashton was an Englishman, although it appeared that he had not lived in England for many years. He had close ties to the Mendozas; it was said he had once saved Don Antonio's life when the Spaniard had been attacked by bandits on the road to Seville. But despite that connection he had not been a regular habitue of the Spanish court until he had joined Philip in Flanders, where the king had been spending a few last weeks of freedom before setting sail for his wedding to Mary.

A few weeks of debauchery, knowing Philip, Renard reflected with a twitch of his aristocratic nose. Ashton did not strike him as a companion in such games, though. There was something of the ascetic about the man. It would explain his friendship with the Mendozas, who were renowned for their Castilian arrogance, their strict piety and rigorous decorum.

One had to assume Ashton was a good and practicing Catholic. He attended mass, of course, but then so did everyone else, including the deceitful, tricky Lady Elizabeth, who, despite her protestations to the contrary, was no loyal follower of the one true religion.

Renard pushed aside his papers and rose to his feet. Elizabeth. That was another pressing problem. Somehow she was getting information from the outside. She was supposed to receive no visitors, but they were getting through. She was corresponding with France; Renard's spies had intercepted a messenger only last week carrying a letter from Elizabeth to the French ambassador. For the life of him, he couldn't think how to stop the gap, plug the leak.

For as long as Elizabeth was alive she presented a very real threat to Mary's throne. Her death would solve all his problems, but he could not persuade Mary to agree to it. Despite all the evidence she had of her sister's plottings, she refused to order her execution. She had had every opportunity when Elizabeth had been imprisoned, every opportunity and every excuse, and she had refused out of some misplaced sense of sisterly obligation.

An assassination would only bring down the wrath of the already disgruntled populace onto the royal heads. And Renard could think of no other way to deal with the menace.

He went to the window, shaking his head gloomily. He looked down at the bowling green and saw Lionel Ashton approach Lady Pippa where she stood in the shade of a poplar awaiting her turn.

There, and only there, lay the Spanish hope for the kingdom. Renard loved Mary with much more than ordinary friendship but he was not blind to reality. Maybe she would carry this child to a successful delivery, but the chances were slight. The healthy young woman on the bowling green had a much better chance of ensuring England fell under Spanish dominion.

PIPPA WAS AWARE OF LIONEL ASHTON'S PRESENCE ON the bowling green many minutes before he approached her. She watched him covertly. What was so different about him? What made him stand out from everyone around him? He was unprepossessing by any conventional standards, he dressed without ostentation, he seemed to make no particular attempt to make himself agreeable. And he appeared to have no special talents; he was inclined neither to sports nor to music, and she had never seen him dance.

Yet he made her shiver when she was in his vicinity. A strange shiver of apprehension and pleasure. She knew that somehow she knew him, that his touch was familiar on her skin. And she knew that she yearned for that touch. Sometimes she could almost feel his lips upon hers.

Pippa shook her head briskly, trying to dispel the images, the sensations she was conjuring. The extraordinary thought occurred that perhaps she was in love. She had never been in love. She had had many flirtations in her giddy youth when she had put off marriage way beyond the usual age, thanks to her indulgent parents. She felt deep affection for Stuart, appreciation of his many talents; she enjoyed his company . . . or had done until recently. But she was not in love with him.

This was no surprising revelation. She had always known it. But she had not hankered after romantic passion. It had always struck her as slightly foolish in a grown and experienced woman.

Her mother and sister loved their husbands with a single-minded devotion, but Pippa could not imagine either of them throwing caution to the winds just for love, in the way so many of her acquaintances sighed, whimpered, and swooned their way through romantic devastations. And Pippa felt not the slightest inclination to follow suit whenever Lionel Ashton appeared in her sights.

No, of course she was not in love with the man. She was simply puzzled, intrigued, confused by this strange sense of foreknowledge. Perhaps she'd met him in a previous existence. It was such a nonsensical, not to mention heretical, thought that she couldn't help chuckling.

"Something amuses you?"

Lionel was smiling too as he came up to her. "What could possibly make you laugh all alone under a tree watching the most boring, staid game ever invented?"

"My own thoughts," Pippa replied.

"Care to share them?"

"No."

"Then I shall have to speculate. I warn you I have a very free and lively imagination." He leaned against the tree, thrusting his hands into the pockets of his short gray cloak.

She laughed up at him. "Give your imagination free rein, sir. I doubt you'll come anywhere close." At this moment they were so easy together, it was like joking with Robin . . . except that it wasn't in the least like it.

She changed the subject, sharpening her tone a little.

"I don't think bowls is boring and staid. I quite enjoy the competition. But I have noticed, sir, that you hold yourself above our little amusements. Your mind is presumably occupied with higher matters."

"Probably," he agreed equably. "I have never been amused by trivialities."

Pippa drew a swift breath. "Would you match wits and tongues, sir? I'll wager mine are as sharp as yours."

He smiled down at her. "One day you shall prove it," he said.

The gray eyes seemed to be laughing at her but the promise they held was as tangible as a tangle of limbs on a feather bed. And then the cold gray threads of that confused dread began to wreathe around her, banishing the promise, and Pippa trembled deep in her belly. *Who was he?*

Lionel read the question in the forest depths of her eyes. And he read her fear. He moved swiftly to dispel the moment. "So, how are you feeling today? You look rather less like a half-drowned kitten."

"A half-drowned kitten!" Pippa exclaimed, shaken out of her intensity by such an unflattering description. "I did *not* look like that. It's most ungallant of you to remind me of my mortification . . . of what you saw."

"Yes, it is, I ask your pardon. But actually you did look rather pathetic. . . ." He held up a hand to forestall her irritated protest. "Only to be expected, of course, in the circumstances."

"Maybe that was so, but 'tis still unchivalrous of you to bring it up."

"An apt phrase." He grinned at her and she couldn't help her own reluctant response.

"That's better." Casually he brushed her cheek with a

fingertip. "You haven't answered my question. How do you feel today?"

Her cheek seemed to come alive beneath the brushing touch. And yet it was nothing out of the ordinary, no more than a punctuation mark. She flicked at her cheek with the back of her hand as if a fly had settled there, and answered calmly, "I have good days and bad ones. Today, thank God, is a good one."

"The nausea will pass around the twelfth week," he informed her.

Pippa decided she'd had enough prevarication. Lionel Ashton had had the upper hand for too long. "You have neither wife nor child, and yet you know such things. Are you a physician under that cloak, Mr. Ashton?" Her steady gaze challenged him to answer her as he had refused to do in the grove.

This time he showed no signs of snubbing her with a coldly distant negative. "No, but I was my mother's last born, and the only boy," he replied cheerfully. "For some reason the women in my family showed no discretion when discussing such things."

"Oh, I see." That answered her question most satisfactorily. "How many sisters do you have?"

"I had five."

She heard the minute hesitation, then the tiny emphasis on the past tense and understood that this she did not probe. The air around them had suddenly become sensitized and she had the sense that another step would take her into quicksand. She wondered if perhaps he had lost all of his sisters. It happened sometimes, when disease would take an entire family. But she would probe no further.

"My knowledge tells me that you should perhaps

avoid lifting heavy things," he suggested, indicating the bowling ball at her feet.

"Oh, but 'tis a light one!" Pippa protested.

He shrugged. "As you wish. I merely pass on what I've heard." He glanced around as if in search. "You have no female relatives with you?"

"My sister is in France. My mother and her family are in Derbyshire." Pippa tried to conceal the ache of her loneliness. "The Lady Elizabeth I may not see. Even letters between us are banned."

He glanced at her sharply, his attuned ear picking up a false note. He guessed that Robin of Beaucaire was combining his mission for the French ambassador with a personal one for his sister. He had a great deal of respect for Lord Robin and would have enjoyed joining forces with him in the business they both shared, but Lionel could not risk breaking his cover. Not even Noailles knew the identity of the spy who provided him with the deepest secrets of Philip's council. Lionel, on the other hand, knew the identities of all the principal clandestine players in Elizabeth's court, and he'd been aware of Robin's mission almost at its inception.

Of course, Pippa, close as she was with her brother, might know something that he did not, but it would not be wise to probe, however casually, at this juncture. Pippa was too clever and had lived too long in the atmosphere of danger to give anything away by accident. Most particularly not to someone she considered a sworn enemy to her own loyalties. Once this promising new confidence between them had grown stronger perhaps he could introduce the subject. But slowly, slowly. Lionel had always believed in the tortoise rather than the hare.

Pippa's gaze returned to the game in progress on the

green. "I believe it's my turn." She bent to pick up the ball and balanced it in the palm of her free hand. "See, Mr. Ashton, 'tis not in the least heavy." She laughed at him.

He shrugged again and said once more: "I pass on only what I've been told, madam."

Pippa heard the faintest note of reproach in his tone. For some reason it gave her pause. "Perhaps you're right," she said. "But I must continue to play this round or my team will forfeit the game."

She left him with a quick and apologetic smile that puzzled her. Why did she feel she should have taken his advice? He was a man who meant nothing to her, someone who had no right to dictate to her or direct her in any way. And yet she felt she had been disobliging. It was most disconcerting.

She forced herself to concentrate, taking in the position of the bowls on the green. If she could knock those two together and spin the one into the lonely bowl on its left, then she would have won and need play no more.

She frowned, trying to block out the heedless chatter around her. No one took anything seriously, she thought crossly. If they would just be quiet for one moment. And then miraculously the moment came. The voices died down all at once as sometimes happens when a large group seems to take a collective breath. Pippa sent the ball in a perfect roll, heard the satisfying clunk as it hit its intended targets, and watched with a broad grin as the right one spun off into the other target.

A babble of voices arose again around her, congratulations and a smattering of applause. She turned in triumph to look at the poplar tree but Lionel Ashton had gone. He hadn't even waited to see her play.

She could not hide her disappointment from herself. She had wanted him to see her win. It struck her as a thoroughly childish response.

It was all very irksome. Pippa shook her head as if to clear it and strolled over to the spectators to receive her husband's congratulations as was expected of her.

Stuart greeted her with a kiss on the cheek and gracefully pinned a rose to the neck of her gown. "Well played, my dear. I could not have bettered that shot."

"Praise indeed from such a master," Pippa murmured, aware that she sounded churlish. But she found his public attentions intolerable these days when he never came near her in private. She was convinced now that his attentions were a sham designed to cover him while he played in some other woman's bed.

Stuart took her arm. "Let us walk a little, if you're not fatigued."

"Fatigued? How should I be?" she said, forcing a smile, no more willing than Stuart to draw unwelcome attention. "Bowls is not an exhausting game. Mostly one just stands around."

"Then let us walk down by the river. It will be cooler."

"As you will, husband." She was puzzled. The make-believe had been attended to, he had no need to embellish upon it. He must want something from her. Well, it could only be interesting to discover.

He tucked her hand into his arm and smiling benignly at those around them led her away from the green with the air of one bearing off a prize.

"Your gown is not one I've seen before," he observed. "I like that particular shade of green."

"Pen sent me the material, a bolt of the finest damask, from France, and several yards of Valenciennes lace," Pippa said, beginning to wonder whether her husband had indeed sought her private company just to discuss a new gown. "The color is so delicate, like apple blossom."

"Beautifully set off by the dark red underskirt," Stuart said seriously. "A most pleasing combination."

"*I* thought so," Pippa agreed. They had reached the riverbank now. The wide path was crowded with courtiers, but the late-afternoon air had no freshness to it, it hung heavy and stale with the day's odors.

"Will this weather ever break?" Pippa murmured almost to herself as she fanned herself vigorously. "'Tis already September."

Stuart did not immediately respond. He struck off down a side path that led into the cooler shade of the weeping willows that lined the riverbank.

"So why are we taking this cozy little walk?" Pippa asked. "After all, 'tis unlike you these days to seek out my company. You could just as easily have complimented me on my gown at the bowling green."

Her voice was sharp but she made no attempt to moderate it. She was sick to death of the charade and maybe now she could drag some explanation out of him. At this point she didn't care whether he would confess to an undying passion that made his wife repulsive to him. Whatever the truth was, she would find it easier to endure than this limbo.

"You must forgive me, Pippa, but I have had much on my mind," Stuart said in a low voice.

"Then why would you not share these things with me?" She stopped on the path, looking up at him. She saw the conscious flash in his eyes, the way his gaze shifted abruptly, and two red spots that flared high on his cheekbones.

"That is a question I might ask of you, madam," he stated harshly. "I believe there is something you should tell me."

Pippa stared at him. "Like what, Stuart?"

"You should know."

"What are you asking me, Stuart?" she demanded directly. He could not possibly have guessed at her pregnancy. She hadn't decided when she would tell him, but for the moment it was something precious to herself, and, deep down, she knew she harbored the unworthy thought that he wasn't entitled to the triumphant satisfaction of the prospective father. He had done nothing to deserve it. She was punishing him, but why shouldn't she deny him just a few extra weeks of complacency?

He stopped on the path. "I believe you to be with child."

"Oh." Pippa continued to stare at him. "And why would you believe that, Stuart? You have not shared my bed for close on four weeks," she pointed out bitterly.

His color deepened. He coughed, stumbled over his words. "Your maid . . . Martha . . . she said—"

"You questioned my *maid*!" Pippa exclaimed in outrage. "You would not discuss this with *me*! Indeed, you come nowhere near me except when you must. And then you go behind my back, asking my maid for—" She stopped with a gesture of disgust, turning her back to him.

"No . . . no, Pippa, it's not like that." He laid a hand

on her shoulder. It quivered beneath his hand but she did not turn back to him.

"So what *is* it like, Stuart? You find your pleasure in some other bed, and now you have a nicely impregnated wife to make everything look perfect. That's what it's like, isn't it?" Her voice was low and bitter as aloes.

"No," he protested. "No, 'tis not like that. I love you, Pippa."

"Oh, don't give me such lame protestations, Stuart. I thought better of you," she said tiredly. "At least do me the courtesy of honesty. You take your pleasure in another woman's bed, while you fulfill your marital duty by getting an heir on your wife's body. My felicitations, my lord." She shook off his hand, spun around, and stalked off back to the riverbank and the palace.

Stuart took a step after her and then stopped. What good would it do? There was nothing he could say to change any of this. He could swear with absolute truth that there was no other woman. He could swear with absolute truth that he had not got an heir on his wife's sleeping body.

But then he would have to tell the truth, and that could not be told.

He followed Pippa back to the riverbank. Once again he thought how simple it would be just to slip beneath the brown water, let the slimy tangle of weeds trap him, hold him down. Then it would all be over.

Over for him. Not for Gabriel. He had to protect Gabriel. Renard's spies watched the musician as they watched Stuart. He could not spirit him out of London, they would be on them within a day. His only hope was to see this through, and then beg for Gabriel's freedom when Philip and Renard and Gomez had what they wanted . . . when they had Pippa's child.

Stuart thought of last night, in the South Bank tavern. They had talked, Gabriel had played for him, and they had slept in each other's arms. He had woken with the dawn chorus and for a moment had had the illusion that all was well with the world. But only for a moment.

Eight

"I FEAR RENARD INTERCEPTED THE LAST MESSENGER we sent to Noailles," Sir Thomas Parry said as he stood in the midafternoon sunshine in the stable yard of the Bull Inn at Woodstock, bidding farewell to his visitor. "You will have a care, Lord Robin?" He gestured significantly to the oiled leather package Robin was stowing in his saddlebag.

"Of course, Sir Thomas." Robin sounded a touch impatient. Parry had kept him overlong that morning repeating information, asking yet again for details of Mary's court, and gathering together the letters he wished Robin to carry to Noailles and to his other agents in London. "And you will be sure that the Lady Elizabeth gets my sister's letter."

" 'Tis on its way now," Parry declared. "With a present of game from a local squire." His pronounced Welsh accents were plummy with satisfaction.

"We have found that Bedingfield shows no inclination to suspect presents of food. I imagine some of it finds its way to his own table." Parry chuckled, his several chins shaking. "Such gifts provide an excellent conduit for passing messages to Lady Elizabeth. Of course, we have a friend in the kitchens who knows what to look for."

"Of course. You are to be congratulated on such a smooth and devious operation," Robin said dryly. It was not surprising Bedingfield couldn't keep control of his prisoner and her affairs. There were more holes in his palace-gaol than a sieve and Thomas Parry was a master at exploiting them.

"We do our best, my dear sir, we do our best," Thomas declared, thrusting out his barrel chest.

"I must be on my way. I would be back in London by nightfall." Robin held out his hand in farewell. His page had been instructed to wait for him with a spare horse in the village of High Wycombe so that he could be back in London by late evening if he rode fast.

Back in time to make a delayed moonlight rendezvous with a young lady on the banks of the River Thames.

Farewells completed, he swung onto his horse and rode out of the Bull's stable yard.

Robin reflected that the greatest fear for Elizabeth was of an assassination attempt by Mary's supporters. Mary intended to keep her warehoused in that draughty ill-kempt palace, out of sight and out of mind, but Elizabeth with her pleas and her plots to circumvent her imprisonment was making absolutely certain that she was never out of her sister's mind or the minds of her councillors.

There was much muttering in the country now about how England would be better off with a queen who practiced her father's and brother's religion instead of one who would take the country back to the old and mostly forgotten ways. Elizabeth was very much a threat to her sister's secure hold on the throne and it would not take much for someone to decide to get rid of the threat she posed altogether.

Robin, together with the rest of his family, had supported Mary's accession on her brother Edward's death. But Mary's harsh treatment of Elizabeth, followed by the Spanish marriage and the increasing threat of the Inquisition, had turned many of her supporters against her. Robin, fiercely protective of his stepsister who had suffered so unjustly with Elizabeth, had joined their number.

Robin encouraged his horse into a spirited trot. He had pleasanter matters to contemplate. He reached the inn in High Wycombe in three hours and found his page awaiting him.

"Hal's been saddled and ready to go this last hour, my lord," the boy said, scrambling up from the ale bench outside the inn door. "You're later than expected."

"Aye, I was kept overlong at Woodstock." Robin swung down. "Any news in the last week?" He stuck his head around the inn door and called for a mug of ale.

Jem looked sly. "There's a rumor going about, sir."

"Oh?" Robin took the foaming pitcher brought to him and drank it down in one long draught. He set the pitcher on the bench and regarded his page. "What kind of rumor?"

"I heard tell, my lord, that the queen is with child." Jem delivered his information with a smug grin. "Thought you'd like to know. 'Tis on every tongue."

Robin whistled under his breath. "And how did that get about so quickly?" But he knew the answer. A piece of news of that importance would fly on the air the minute anyone put it into words.

He mounted his fresh horse and set off again, leaving Jem to care for the tired gelding his master had ridden from Oxford. He dismissed Elizabeth and her sister from his thoughts, looking up into the darkening sky where a great yellow harvest moon was rising over the treetops. A beautiful night for a romantic rendezvous.

Would Luisa be walking in the garden as she'd promised? Eagerness now put spur to his horse.

It was past curfew when he reached Aldgate, but he carried a carte blanche signed by the queen herself. It was an honor Mary had given to Robin's father for his loyal help in securing her throne and it had naturally devolved upon his son. Robin ensured that he did nothing to jeopardize this useful document. There were times when the ability to enter and leave the city, at times forbidden to the general public, was very useful.

The guards waved him through the wicket gate and he rode swiftly down to the menacing edifice of the Tower. There, after transferring the precious packet of letters from his saddlebags to his doublet, he stabled his horse at an inn where he was well known and walked to the water steps at the Lion Gate.

"Ho! You there!" he called softly to a boatman leaning on the oars of a small skiff.

The man pulled swiftly to the steps. "Where to, sir?"

"I want your boat," Robin said, taking a leather purse from his doublet pocket. "I'll pay you a sovereign for the use of it for three hours." He thunked the purse into the palm of his other hand so that the substantial chink of coin was easily heard.

The man jumped readily to the quay, holding the skiff's painter. "I'll 'ave an evenin' in the Black Dog, I reckon." He gestured to the light that spilled from the open door of a tavern set just back from the quay and offered Robin a toothless grin.

"Then I'll find you there." Robin handed him the agreed sum, then jumped into the boat and the man threw the painter in after him.

Robin settled into the rhythm of the oars, pulling strongly. He should have been fatigued after a day's hard riding but he found anticipation lent strength to his arms. It was a beautiful night, with a slight breeze to lift the lingering oppression of the day's heat.

The yellow moon was high in the sky when he reached what he thought were the water steps of Lionel Ashton's mansion. Robin sat in the skiff in midstream and gazed up through the moonlight towards the house. He had seen it only once, and that in broad daylight, but he could remember no distinguishing features. It was just another of the imposing stone piles built by the newly rich along the river. In the moonlight it looked large and unremarkable. The quay appeared like any other.

He noticed a small barge tied to the quay and remembered that Luisa had said her guardian kept no craft. There were no boatmen around that he could see, so it was unlikely that it belonged to a visitor.

He began to wonder if he was in the right place, everything looked so very different from the water. However, he wasn't going to find out hanging around ten yards from shore, so with a half shrug Robin pulled the boat close to the quay.

A sudden blaze of light dazzled him for a moment. He put up a hand to shield his eyes.

"Oh, you've come," a soft voice cried jubilantly. "I have been waiting for days and days. I thought you had decided you didn't like me after all."

"For God's sake, Luisa, lower that lamp!" he demanded in a fierce whisper. "I'm blind as a bat."

"Oh, I do beg your pardon." The light disappeared altogether. "It was just that I needed to be certain it was you."

"And are you now certain?" He blinked once or twice to get rid of the after-dazzle.

"Oh, yes. But I really had given up expecting you. Why did you not come before?"

Robin shipped his oars and looked up at her where she stood on the quay. She had extinguished the lamp and was visible now only in the moonlight. Her black hair hung loose to shoulders that were covered by a film of silvery gossamer. Her gown was of some very pale material that seemed to shimmer. Whether that was an effect of the light Robin didn't know. He did know that it made her look insubstantial, a mere figment of the moonlight.

Her voice, however, was robust as she stepped closer to the edge of the quay and leaned out. "Throw me the rope and I'll tie it to this ring here. I think that's what it's for."

"It is," Robin agreed. "But let me get a little closer. If you lean out any farther you'll fall headlong into the river."

"I have excellent balance," Luisa informed him cheerfully. She straightened, however, and waited for him to pull the few strokes necessary to bring him alongside the quay.

He could very easily have tied up himself but Luisa was standing expectantly holding out her hand and it seemed a shame to disappoint her. He handed her up the painter and watched as she looped it through the ring and tied it securely.

"There," she said. "I don't think it will come un-done."

"No," he agreed, stepping out onto the steps. He climbed up to her.

She stepped away from the quay and Robin followed until they were on the sweep of grass that led up to the house. There were a few lamps burning in the upstairs windows of the house, but the garden itself was well shadowed by tall trees.

Luisa glanced over her shoulder towards the house. "Good, Bernardina has extinguished her lamp. She'll sleep like the dead until morning."

"And what of your guardian?"

Luisa shrugged. "He is not in at present, but he would not look to see if I was in my chamber. It would not occur to him. I doubt he thinks of me more than once a week."

Robin wondered if he could detect a slight note of resentment in her voice. "That is all to the good, surely," he observed. "If you're making midnight assig-nations."

Her laugh was a little uncertain. "That's what I'm doing, I suppose."

"I can think of no more accurate way of describing it."

"Why did you not come before?"

"I had to leave London for a few days . . . some busi-ness."

"Oh, I see." She began to play with the fringe of the gossamer shawl she wore around her shoulders. " 'Tis very brazen, is it not?"

"Absolutely," he agreed with a grin. "But why should that concern you now?"

"Does it concern you?" Her dark eyes carried a look of uncertainty as she gazed up at him.

"Not in the least," Robin said. "I am accustomed to unconventional women."

"Oh." She smiled, showing the whitest teeth. "I would not wish to give you a disgust of me."

That made him laugh. "Were that likely, I would not be here now."

"No, I imagine you would not," Luisa said, sounding much more at ease. Deliberately she drew backwards into the deeper shadow of a shrubbery, obliging Robin to follow her.

She stood in the secluded center of the shrubbery and for the first time wondered what she was doing, alone here in the middle of the night with a strange Englishman. If she were ever discovered they would shut her up in a convent run by one of the strictest orders.

"Is something amiss?" Robin inquired, absently realizing that two buttons of his doublet were undone. He must have forgotten to button up after he'd pocketed the package of letters. Its weight was still reassuringly heavy and warm against his chest.

Luisa's eyes had followed his and before he could rectify the sartorial negligence she stepped forward and with seemingly businesslike efficiency did up the buttons herself. It brought her very close to him and in his surprise Robin was caught off guard. He felt his body stir at the warm softness of Luisa's.

He stepped backwards hastily, holding her at arm's length. Had that been deliberate, or was it simply the ingenuous gesture of an innocent?

But when he looked at her eyes, he dismissed the latter explanation. Dona Luisa de los Velez of the house of

Mendoza might well be an innocent in practice but she was definitely not in intention.

"Forgive me," she said. "I wished only to help."

"Quite," Robin returned with a dry smile. "My thanks. And what is it that you wish in return, Dona Luisa?"

She looked at him suspiciously. "Why should you imagine that I want anything, Lord Robin?"

He smiled. "Don't prevaricate. I'm willing to indulge you within reason."

It seemed to him that this young Mendoza was unstoppable and he had somehow landed the task of satisfying her quest for excitement and experience while keeping her safe for whatever her Spanish destiny held for her. There were too many predators in the streets of London for an ingenue to try her wings under anything but the strictest protection.

It was a task best undertaken by Lionel Ashton, of course, but that gentleman seemed to have little interest in his ward. Robin found the prospect of doing Ashton's work for him curiously appealing.

He would play the guardian and the teacher. A safe enough role, surely. "So," he said, still smiling. "What do you want of me, Dona Luisa?"

She hesitated, then said with an eloquent shrug, "Nothing out of the ordinary, sir."

He gave a short crack of laughter. "Don't expect me to believe that. In my experience out-of-the-ordinary women tend to want similar favors. Come, tell me." He beckoned her to a stone bench set into a neatly carved arbor in a privet hedge. "Let us sit down and discuss this."

Luisa sat beside him. It was a small bench and their thighs touched. Luisa's nose wrinkled. "You smell very rank, Lord Robin," she stated with distressing frankness. "In my country it is not customary for a man to visit a lady with the sweat of the day upon him."

Robin turned to stare at her, for an instant completely dumbstruck. He stood up and put several feet between them before he found his voice.

"I would have you know, madam, that I have ridden fifty miles today, and then rowed from the Tower. All to see you. If you are so nice in your notions that you cannot accept the help of a man with the sweat of honest toil upon him, then I will take my leave."

Luisa jumped up. "Oh, no . . . no, please do not go. Please don't take offense. I have the most . . . most dreadful habit of speaking my mind. I do not mind that you smell . . . indeed I don't."

Robin wasn't at all sure that this declaration improved matters. And now that it had been pointed out, he could smell his own rankness on the somnolent air. He never gave a second thought to his appearance, he was always untidy, a matter for gentle teasing among his family. But now he began to wonder if he was less than scrupulous about matters of personal hygiene. When had he last changed his shirt and linen?

His father had chided him often for neglecting to do so when they had traveled together during Robin's youth.

"I have had a hard day's travel and came to you as soon as possible," he said stiffly. "You must forgive me for offending." He left the shrubbery with an anger that was rooted as much in discomfort as in annoyance.

Luisa flew after him. She seized his arm. "Oh, please . . . 'twas so thoughtless of me. Forgive me. I never ride far, so how can I know what it's like? And I do not mean to sound ungrateful that you came to me with all speed. Please, forgive me."

She gazed up at him with bright eyes full of conviction. She stood on tiptoe and kissed his cheek. She stroked and patted his hand as if it were a lost kitten.

Robin felt his discomfort and annoyance slip from him. So he reeked of sweat and horseflesh. So he had offended the tender nose of this sheltered child. But this excitement-inclined young woman had more on her mind than a less than fragrant tutor in London's entertainments.

"What do you want of me, Luisa?" he asked again.

She regarded him anxiously as if to be sure everything had returned to an even keel, then said, "Well, now that I have a boat and a horse I can leave the house more freely. I was thinking that if you would bring me man's clothes next time, we could go quite safely into the city at night, when Bernardina is asleep."

"Man's clothes?" Robin scrutinized her, then gave her her own again. "My dear girl, you don't have the figure to get away with it."

She gazed down at herself. "Whyever not?"

"You have too many roundnesses," he said bluntly, hands passing through the air to indicate breasts and bottom.

Luisa was undeterred by what she considered a compliment. "Then I will wear a long cloak. It will cover all roundnesses."

Robin considered. His little attempt at minor insult had fallen short because Luisa's particular plumpness was a fashionable advantage among the Spaniards. Trading barbs of a personal nature with a mere miss was beyond the dignity of a man who had a considerable reputation in his chosen and very dangerous profession.

"I'll decide for myself what you should wear," he said firmly. "I will bring you what I consider suitable. Stand still and let me take a look at you to assess the fit."

"I cannot see the point if I'm to be shrouded in a cloak," Luisa observed, although she stood still for him, and then turned as he twirled an imperative finger. "I can't imagine how you can guess at what's beneath this farthingale," she said.

Robin heard the mischief in her voice. Dona Luisa was not to be easily managed. But then neither was he.

"I will return in two nights, he said without responding to her mischief. "At eleven, if that's the safest time for you."

"Bernardina retires at ten. She keeps such early hours in England, but I expect 'tis because she's bored," Luisa said. She sighed. "Poor Bernardina. She has no friends here . . . no one to pass the evenings with in gossip as she used to."

"Perhaps I should bring a disguise for her and she can join us on this little expedition," Robin suggested, jumping into the skiff. He was rewarded with a peal of laughter. Such a wondrously joyous sound he couldn't prevent his own delighted smile.

He untied the painter and took up the oars again. Luisa stood on the quay waving him away in the moonlight until she had disappeared into the midnight darkness.

He found the skiff's owner in the Black Dog waxing maudlin over what was clearly one of a long line of tankards of strong ale. The man blinked up at him, not recognizing him.

"Your skiff's at the steps," Robin said. "You'd best keep an eye on it, lest someone decide to borrow it."

The man grunted and his head sank into his tankard.

Robin shrugged. His obligation was done. He left the tavern and went for his horse.

It was close to three o'clock when he arrived at Whitehall Palace. It was not too late for the hardened carousers of the court. They would be at cards or dice, listening to music, drinking deep. Philip of Spain, now released from the necessity of serving his wife's bed, would probably be among them.

Robin's grimace of distaste was involuntary. His dislike of the queen's husband was so powerful that only training enabled him to maintain the superficial courtesies. Philip was a debaucher, but even his sternest critics had to admit that he worked on affairs of state with the same dedication he showed to pleasure. He would sleep two hours and be at his desk at dawn, after attending early mass.

Robin had lodgings in the palace, a small chamber in a wing occupied for the most part by the lowlier members of the court. He rarely used the room, preferring the more spacious accommodations of his father's house in Holborn, but he was too tired tonight to ride any farther.

His route took him along the corridor that led past the apartments of Lord and Lady Nielson. A large suite of rooms for a favored courtier, a man who had been intimately involved in the negotiations for the queen's marriage.

A light shone beneath the door to Pippa's bedchamber. Robin paused. He had no desire to interrupt some marital intimacy but after what Pippa had confided it was probably unlikely that Stuart was visiting his wife at this hour of the night. It was more likely that Pippa was wakeful and unhappy.

He tapped on the door.

"Who is it?" Pippa's voice did not sound sleepy.

"Robin."

"Just a minute." Pippa slid out of bed and padded barefoot to open the door. She pushed her loosened hair away from her face and looked at him in surprise and concern. " 'Tis so late, Robin. Is something the matter?"

"No. I've just returned from Woodstock. I was going to bed and saw your light. You should be asleep."

Pippa stepped back, pulling the door wide in invitation. "I find it hard to sleep these nights." She climbed back into bed, propping the pillows behind her. "Tell me of your visit. Did you see Elizabeth?"

Robin helped himself to wine from the flagon on the sideboard before perching on the end of the bed. "No, but your letter was delivered. I expect an answer on my next visit. But Jem had some news for me." He sipped his wine and raised an eyebrow.

Pippa nodded. "The queen is with child."

" 'Tis not yet public knowledge?"

"No. At the end of the week, I understand, amid great fanfare."

Robin took another sip of his wine, regarding his stepsister over the lip of the goblet. She had something else to say, he was sure of it. "And . . . ?"

Pippa leaned back against the pillows. "And it seems that I too am with child. The queen and I will bear our pregnancies together."

"My felicitations." Robin leaned over to kiss her cheek. "It pleases you, doesn't it, Pippa?"

"Yes," she answered slowly. "Yes, in one way it does. But to carry the child of a man who finds no pleasure in his wife is hard, Robin."

"Stuart must be pleased!" Robin protested.

"Oh, yes, he's delighted. His wife is with child, he will have an heir. He receives everyone's congratulations with all the complacency of a man who deserves them."

Robin winced at the bitterness of her voice. "Pippa, dearest Pippa, be happy. The child is yours as much as Stuart's. You will have joy in *your* child."

Pippa was silent for a minute, then she said, "Yes, of course you're right. I will concentrate on the child and think nothing of my husband's infidelities. How many other women have done the same?"

She was thinking of her mother now. Her mother had married twice after the husband of her daughters had been killed. Bad marriages both of them. But Guinevere had concentrated all her love and spirit on her daughters. Pippa could do the same.

But her mother's world had turned when Hugh of Beaucaire had ridden into her life.

"Pippa, I hate to see you so melancholy," Robin said as her expression remained as bleak as ever. It was so unlike Pippa to be sad and depressed, she was always so vibrant, always the one to bring anyone out of the doldrums.

She shook her head. " 'Tis probably the pregnancy. It makes me feel very strange; when I'm not wanting to puke, I either want to cry like a baby or laugh like a maniac."

"Ah." Robin nodded, relieved at such a simple explanation, and willing to accept it even though he knew it was far from the whole story.

He changed the subject, asking with a frown, "Do I reek, Pippa?"

She looked at him in surprise. Sniffed, then said, "No more than usual, why?"

"No more than usual?" Robin looked pained. "I thought it was just because I've been traveling all day."

Pippa laughed, the first sound of pure amusement he had heard from her in several weeks. "Oh, Robin, you're always untidy and a bit sweaty. It's the way you are. No one minds."

"Perhaps you're just used to it?" he suggested glumly.

Pippa considered this. "Perhaps," she agreed. "But why bring it up now?" Her eyes gleamed suddenly and she sat up straighter in the bed. "Robin, you have a secret."

Robin felt himself blushing. "I do not," he denied.

"Oh, yes, you do," she crowed delightedly. "And I'll wager it's a lover."

Robin got off the bed. "You should be asleep," he said. "I'll see you in the morning." He blew her a kiss and left her still laughing against the pillows.

Nine

PIPPA SLEPT FITFULLY AND AWOKE TO THE ECSTATIC music of the dawn chorus beyond her open windows. She lay still, knowing that the minute she sat up the surge of nausea would overwhelm her.

It would go on for twelve weeks, Lionel had said. As far as she could calculate she was close to eight weeks pregnant now and the prospect of another month of this was depressing. She touched her belly, trying to connect with the life she carried, and wondered if she would find the sickness less troublesome if all was well with her marriage.

Of course, she'd never had any patience with illness, however trivial, so probably she would find this frailty as irksome as she did even if she and Stuart were dwelling in the blissful realms of a fulfilled and happy union.

She closed her eyes again and tried to concentrate on Stuart, on some way of making sense of his estrangement without simply assuming that there was another woman. It was such an obvious explanation, but maybe there was something else. Maybe he was troubled and she had refused to see it, jumping to conclusions and thinking only of herself.

She tried to force herself to picture Stuart, but she saw Lionel Ashton. The gray eyes filled with understanding, sympathy, and humor, quite at odds with the curiously detached air he had when in the company of others. He was not detached when he was with her though. It was as if he was presenting a very different side of himself.

She tried again to picture Stuart, to force her mind to examine the situation with her husband, to look for explanations from which maybe there would come a solution. But it wouldn't work. Lionel's face was the only one she could summon, and she found herself contemplating the puzzles he presented with a single-minded concentration.

And there were plenty of puzzles, not least how and why an Englishman was traveling in Philip's retinue. His position there had to be a powerful one, even though he stood so often apart. But his air of remote authority was unmistakable. He seemed to expect deference, and from what Pippa had seen he received it. Even from Philip's councillors.

And what of those five sisters? Some sadness there . . . no, more than sadness, she had felt it. And why had he slammed the door so vehemently on her initial questions about a wife? Particularly when it was a door he himself had half opened. No wife, no child. Did that mean he had never been married? Where had he spent his childhood? England, Spain . . . His command of Spanish, from the little Pippa had heard, would lend credence to a life spent in that country.

It was a much pleasanter mental exercise than worrying about Stuart, Pippa realized. When she thought of

Lionel she felt less alone, as if she had an ally. And that was a puzzle, because she knew she had Robin, who would stand by her through thick and thin. He was her ally, he was her friend and her brother. So why when she thought of needing support did Lionel Ashton pop into her head before Robin?

Pippa sat up gingerly. Miraculously nothing happened. She reached sideways for the basket of dry bread that Martha now left for her every night. Martha who had betrayed Pippa's secret to Stuart without consulting her mistress.

Pippa nibbled the bread. She was not really annoyed with the maid, whose position was not an easy one in such a matter. The fault lay only with Stuart. But that bone was picked clean now and nothing useful could come of storing up her resentment.

Slowly she swung her feet to the floor. She felt fine. As slowly she stood up, nibbling the bread. Still no problems. Perhaps today was going to be one of the good ones.

The prospect cheered her and she went to the window, leaning out to draw deep breaths of a fresh air that would soon be heavy and stale as the sun rose. The sounds of the waking city drifted up from the river. Calls of boatmen and street vendors. From below rose the sounds of the palace springing to life and the smells of morning cooking fires drifted upward. That didn't seem to disturb her accentuated sense of smell either this morning.

It reminded her of her conversation with Robin, and Pippa grinned to herself. None of Robin's family could understand why he had not found himself a good wife by now. He had had his adventures, as Pippa knew, but no woman had captured his heart as well as his eye. But perhaps that had changed. Something out of the ordinary had happened for Robin to be suddenly concerned about the freshness of his linen.

She rested her elbows on the windowsill and gazed down into the garden, feeling at peace, indeed almost happy. And the sense of contentment was abruptly sharpened when she saw Lionel Ashton step out onto the terrace beneath her window. Her breath caught, her blood stirred. It was ridiculous, Pippa told herself. She was a respectable married woman pregnant with her husband's child. And yet she caught herself willing him to look up.

And he did.

Lionel stepped back a little so that he had a clearer view of Pippa's bedchamber. He raised a hand and she waved back at him.

"You're up betimes, Mr. Ashton," she called down to him.

She was leaning perilously far out of the window, Lionel reflected. It was clearly his duty to encourage her to withdraw to safety before she and the king of Spain's child came tumbling to the paving at his feet.

He cupped his hands around his mouth and called back without seeming to raise his voice. "So it seems are you, madam. If you care to walk in the morning air, I will await you here."

Pippa waved in acknowledgment and withdrew her head. A burst of energy seemed to bring color to the world. It would be lovely to take a morning walk while the air was still fresh, before the chattering, gossiping scrutiny of courtiers destroyed the peace.

She reached for the handbell that would summon Martha and then decided it would take too long. The girl would still be asleep. It was awkward to manage the laces of a stomacher herself, but why bother with the cumbersome garment? Why bother with a farthingale? It was too early for anyone to see her. Although if they did it would certainly scandalize. But Pippa found that she was in no mood to care, and the very fact of her carelessness made her feel more like herself than she had done in weeks.

She found a simple silk gown of a particularly flattering shade of topaz that she would ordinarily wear only in the privacy of her boudoir or in the country with her intimate family. It went over a plain white linen chemise. She decided to do without hose and thrust her feet into a pair of kidskin sandals. She tugged a comb through the cinnamon tangle of curls and pulled her hair to the back of her neck, tying it roughly with a white scarf. A quick glance at her image in the mirror of beaten silver made her hesitate. Was it too scandalous to appear here, in public, in such dishabille?

Then Pippa reminded herself that she had never danced in the court of public opinion. Let the tongues of scandal wag as they may.

She left her chamber and hastened through the long corridors, down a little-used staircase, and through a small door that gave onto the terrace.

Lionel was still standing where she had last seen him. He seemed again to have separated himself from his surroundings and for an instant Pippa regretted her impulse. It seemed impossible to intrude upon him. He held himself loosely in his clothes, almost as if they weren't part of him. And yet, unlike Pippa, he was dressed for the court day. A short crimson cloak hung from his shoulders, his black doublet and hose were slashed with the same crimson. A ruby gleamed in the turned-up brim of his black velvet hat.

Pippa was wondering whether to run back to her chamber and summon Martha to dress her properly when Lionel turned his head towards her. He didn't move any other part of his body, she noticed. But it was as if he had sensed her presence hovering beneath the stone arch of the narrow doorway.

He came towards her then, smiling. "You have an indefinable sense of what suits both you and the occasion," he observed, taking her hand, raising it to his lips as he bowed.

Pippa felt a deep pleasure at the compliment. "I thought to escape formality for once," she said.

"I wish I had had the same thought." He tucked her hand in his arm and turned towards the river.

"And what would you have worn to achieve the same effect?" Pippa asked, genuinely interested in this sartorial question.

"Shirt and hose," he responded promptly.

Pippa drew a swift breath. Why was that image so dangerous? It was a rhetorical question.

Lionel too realized that he was playing in dangerous fields. He had had no intention of doing so but she had drawn him in, with her lighthearted dress, her smile, the sense he felt that she had shed some burden. It was as if he was seeing the real Pippa instead of the troubled, sad, and confused woman who had been put in his charge.

"You're not feeling sick this morning?" he asked, deliberately prosaic.

"No," Pippa said cheerfully. "This will be a good day, I am determined." She slipped her hand from beneath his arm and stepped quickly onto the riverbank. Without thought, she kicked her feet free of her sandals and dug her toes into the still dew-wet grass. "Oh, it reminds me of my childhood! Whenever I could I would go barefoot in the summer."

She walked to the river's edge. The traffic on the river was busy now and the palace quay was abuzz with official barges.

"There's a river that runs through the valley at Mallory Hall. Pen and I would paddle in the mud. Have you ever felt mud between your toes, Lionel?"

It was the first time she had used his given name. Lionel noticed, Pippa did not.

"It's a barely retrievable memory," he replied. "Why don't you do it now?"

She laughed at him over her shoulder. "I cannot!"

"Would you have said that a year ago?" He looked at her shrewdly.

Pippa shook her head. "No. But since then I've been imprisoned in the Tower, discovered that my husband . . . discovered that I carry my husband's child. There comes a time, Mr. Ashton, when one must grow up." She pushed her toes into the damp grass again. "My family would probably laugh to hear me say that."

He wanted to enfold her. To kiss the top of her head. To run his hands down her back. To span her waist, find its curves beneath the loose gown.

"You do not have to forget to laugh in order to grow up," he said, aware of the sour taste of his own betrayal thickening his tongue, acid in his throat.

Pippa turned back to him. "No, I suppose that's true." She found her sandals and slid her wet feet into them with a grimace. "I must go back. It wouldn't do for the world to see me in such dishabille. But I thank you for your company." Her tone was both formal and awkward.

"And I thank you for yours," Lionel said, offering her his arm.

Pippa hesitated. "Perhaps you should go back alone, sir. There will be many more people up and about. It might appear that . . ." She gave him a halfhearted smile.

"It might," he agreed. He touched her cheek as he had done once before. "I could almost wish that appearance was truth, Pippa."

Pippa met his gaze steadily. For a moment they looked at each other. Then Lionel came to himself. "Forgive me." He bowed over her hand and left her.

Pippa stared after him. He had voiced a desire that she had been doing everything possible to ignore.

The scarf that bound her hair had become loosened and she reached behind her to retie it. This was a situation in which many people found themselves, she told herself. Most marriages had some degree of convenience about them so it was always possible that a rogue emotion could kidnap a respectably married woman . . . or man. It seemed to have happened to Stuart, after all.

She touched her belly. A rogue emotion was acceptable as long as no one knew of it. She started back to the palace.

As far as she knew, no one saw her as she returned to her bedchamber. Martha, with a reproachful air, was already there pouring hot water into the basin on the dresser. She looked askance at Pippa's dress. "You rose without me, m'lady."

"Yes, I didn't wish to disturb you so early." Pippa loosened her hair from the ribbon. "I wished to walk alone before the world was up and about."

"I didn't know whether you'd wish for meat or cheese this morning, m'lady."

Pippa surveyed the tray of fresh bread and butter. "A dish of coddled eggs and ham if you please. Oh, and a tankard of mead. I find I'm not sick this morning, Martha, and have a great appetite."

"Very well, my lady." Martha was still not certain of where she stood in her mistress's graces, but was thankful that so far she had received no indications of ill favor. "Should I help you remove your gown?"

"No, I can manage myself, thank you." Pippa smiled to soften the blow but was aware that Martha was put out. The maid left and Pippa stripped off her clothes and sponged herself with the hot water in the basin.

Once again she thought of Robin. Once again she chuckled to herself. Pen would love the story.

But Pen was not here. No one was here to appreciate the possibility of Robin's falling victim to romance. No one was here to . . .

Pippa pulled herself up short. Self-pity was about the most useless response to her situation that she could imagine.

She would dress and go in search of Robin, see if she could tease his secret out of him. It would certainly distract her from self-pity.

She ate breakfast with an appetite that had eluded her for the last weeks. The taste of the food on her tongue seemed particularly savory, and the mead, now her favorite drink, filled her with a sense of well-being.

Martha had just laced her stomacher and was adjusting the small round ruff at Pippa's neck when there was a knock at the door. Martha went to open it.

A page in the queen's livery stepped into the chamber. He intoned his message into the air. "Her Majesty requests the presence of Lady Nielson at an audience at nine of the clock."

"Lady Nielson will be honored to attend," Pippa responded automatically. "I assume you bear the same message to Lord Nielson."

"No, madam. I have not been so instructed." The page bowed and withdrew.

That was strange, Pippa thought. And then immediately felt the clutch of the old fear. Was it a sinister summons? She was never singled out for the queen's attention, merely treated as a necessary if unwelcome adjunct of her husband. Had Mary discovered that she was corresponding with Elizabeth? Was she going to confront her in this private audience? Would Stuart have an explanation for the summons?

She selected an emerald breast jewel from the silver casket on the dresser and matched it with emerald and turquoise rings. Her fingers had the tiniest tremor as she slid the rings over her knuckles.

She stood in front of the mirror, trying to control her fear with a scrupulous inventory of her appearance. Her gown of forest green edged with silver lace and opening over a primrose yellow underskirt was perfectly suitable for the morning's audience. As was the black velvet hood with its emerald-studded horseshoe frontlet.

The inventory restored her confidence a little. She reasoned that if Robin was still at large then Mary could not possibly know of the letter he had carried to Woodstock. Pippa knew that Robin had safely delivered the letter, so it had not been intercepted . . . unless one of Bedingfield's men had intercepted it within the palace walls before it reached Elizabeth.

Her heart thumped uncomfortably and she had half a mind to ask Martha to loosen her laces. She touched lavender water to her temples and breathed slowly until her heart had settled into its normal rhythm. There was no point anticipating trouble.

Pippa glanced at the enameled watch that hung from the girdle of fine gold chain at her waist. It was barely eight o'clock. More than enough time to seek out Stuart, to see if he could throw any light on the summons, and then Robin. Maybe he would know something.

A door connected her bedchamber with her husband's. It was a door that was rarely opened these days. Pippa tapped lightly, waited a few minutes, then lifted the latch. She stood on the threshold, reluctant to enter without invitation. The chamber was in shuttered darkness but was empty. The bed was undisturbed.

Stuart kept late nights, but he usually sought his bed by dawn. And he was never an early riser. He had not said he was traveling anywhere, and he would have told her. There were some pieces of information that had to be shared if they were to preserve the public appearance of harmony. So where had he laid his head last night?

She pushed the question from her, stepped back into her own chamber, and closed the door. She glanced quickly at Martha, but the woman seemed busy piling the breakfast dishes onto a tray and didn't look up. Pippa knew, however, that the maid kept close company with Stuart's manservant. Martha was probably well aware of when his lordship failed to sleep in his own bed.

Pippa left the bedchamber and made her way through the maze of corridors to Robin's small chamber. Single men not of Mary's household were not treated with much deference by the queen's chancellor when it came to allotting accommodation, and the corridors grew narrower, the doors more closely spaced, the wall hangings frayed and lusterless as Pippa entered the north wing of the palace.

There were few people about and it was very quiet, dust motes thick in the sun's rays penetrating the gloom from the very few narrow windows. Pippa barely noticed her surroundings, so intent was she on the queen's summons. She passed a door that stood very slightly ajar. Voices whispered from the chamber behind.

She had gone five paces past when recognition penetrated her reverie. She stopped, frowning. What could Stuart be doing in this remote and unfavored part of the palace? She retraced her steps and stood unashamedly eavesdropping at the gap in the door.

Two men whispering. Stuart and one other. At first she couldn't understand what she was hearing, it made no sense. It was love talk, soft endearments, little murmurs, then a sound that chilled her. The unmistakable sound of flesh moving on flesh.

No, it wasn't possible!

She swallowed, hearing the sound loud in the quiet still corridor. She was losing her mind. Hearing things. Some strange fantasy trance induced by pregnancy.

Pippa stepped closer to the door. She touched with her fingertips and it opened a few more inches. She could see the bed, a narrow cot in a meager chamber.

This was no fantasy. She was not hearing things. She was not losing her mind. It was Stuart on the bed. She could not see who was with him but she didn't need to.

Softly she stepped back into the corridor. Leaving the door as it was, Pippa flew back the way she had come, her skirts swinging around her, her jeweled satin slippers making no sound on the oak floor.

Within the chamber Gabriel moved away from Stuart. "Did you hear something?" His voice was fearful.

Stuart shook his head. "No, nothing. A mouse maybe." He laughed softly. "We're quite safe here, Gabriel. No one occupies this chamber, I made sure of it."

"But the door . . . 'tis open." Gabriel pointed, his face ashen.

Stuart rose to his feet. He crossed the narrow space to the door. He peered into the corridor. It was deserted. He closed the door again, but as he turned back to the chamber the latch clicked open again and the door swung ajar about an inch.

"The latch doesn't hold properly," he said. "That's all. I'll make sure it closes properly next time."

Gabriel ran a hand over his waxen countenance. " 'Tis too dangerous here, Stuart. I prefer the tavern."

Stuart grimaced with distaste. "I loathe it there, love. 'Tis so sordid." He came back to the bed, sitting on the edge, reaching down for a leather flagon of wine at his feet. He lifted it to his lips then held it to Gabriel's. "You worry too much."

It wasn't as if they had anything to hide anymore. There was no safety anywhere.

The bitter reflection turned the wine to gall on his tongue. But Gabriel did not know this truth and must never know it.

Gabriel drank deep, then wiped his mouth with the back of his hand. "I must play for the card games this afternoon, in the great salon. Will you be there?"

"Aye. I never pass up the opportunity for a game," Stuart said with a laugh that was supposed to reassure the musician.

Gabriel tried a smile but it was a weak attempt. "I'll go now."

Stuart made no attempt to stop him. If Gabriel was jumpy then it was only kindness to let him hurry to where he felt safe.

But there was nowhere safe. Stuart sat on the bed, the flagon of wine held loosely between his hands. He stared down at the floor. A mouse scurried out from beneath the cot. He watched it disappear into a hole in the floorboards.

He had made a decision. He was being blackmailed so why should they still scurry around in holes and corners? Hiding themselves in the squalid chambers of a tavern? It wasn't as if they were hiding anyway. Renard's spies watched their every move. They probably knew he had found this unoccupied chamber. And if they didn't now, they soon would. But there was no reason why anyone else should know of it.

They couldn't be open about their love, but if they practiced reasonable security they could keep this private chamber to themselves. It lacked much in the way of comfort, but it was safe, well away from the social areas of the palace. It gave some dignity to their love. And using it gave Stuart some sense of control. Lessened the dreadful sense of being manipulated like a marionette, of having no say in what happened to him, or how he conducted his life. It was illusion, of course, but he could pretend that it wasn't. For Gabriel's sake.

He glanced up at the door. Gabriel had closed it behind him but again the latch had not held. Well, that was easily mended. He would have a strong lock put upon it. That should reassure Gabriel and keep out a spy's prying eye.

Stuart rose and carefully adjusted his dress. He

glanced around the chamber wondering how to make it more inviting. A coverlet for the straw mattress at the very least.

He strolled in studied leisurely manner to his own bedchamber. He glanced towards the connecting door to Pippa's chamber. He had heard her vomiting in the mornings and the revulsion he had felt had had nothing to do with her sickness, but everything to do with what had caused it. Hating himself he had cowered in his bed, burying his head beneath his pillow to drown out the sound.

There were no such sounds from the next-door chamber this morning. With a wash of relief he flung open the shutters, threw off his clothes, and climbed into bed. An hour's sleep would refresh him and he would find Pippa later in the morning. They should present themselves together at the queen's public audience. They could not talk to each other anymore except in broadest generalities, but the public form of their marriage must be preserved, and Pippa had proved herself as adept as he at maintaining the pretence.

PIPPA SAT IN A SECLUDED CORNER OF THE PLEAS-aunce. It was still too early to attract visitors and apart from gardeners she had it to herself. A faint mist rose from the fountains as the water rose and fell in rhythmic arcs.

She was numb. So strong was the sensation that she wriggled her toes and fingers and was surprised to find that she could feel them. She couldn't think, she could only sit in this strange cold place isolated from the warm and sensate world.

She had never been so alone.

"Your pardon, madam . . ." A gardener's apologetic voice intruded and she realized with a start that he had spoken before.

"Yes?"

He gestured with his rake. "The gravel, madam. Beneath the bench." He looked at her curiously. "You quite well, madam? Should I send for someone?"

"No . . . no, thank you." She rose, sweeping her skirts aside. She glanced at her watch. It was almost nine. If she didn't hurry she would commit the unthinkable and be late for an audience with the queen.

Her head felt stuffed with fog and somehow it seemed quite unimportant that she might be late. She could summon no interest in the point of this audience. What could happen? An accusation of treason. Imprisonment in the Tower? It didn't matter.

She walked quickly back through the gardens, along the terrace, into the palace. People spoke to her, smiled, waved a greeting. She saw none of them. At the doors to the presence chamber she stopped.

"Madam." The herald bowed, knocked with his stave. The doors were opened and she was ushered into the great room. It was deserted. Even this failed to make an impact. The herald walked ahead of her to the door that led into the queen's private audience chamber.

He flung open the doors. "Lady Nielson, Your Majesty."

Pippa walked into the chamber. Mary was alone with her ladies, sitting at her desk on which were scattered various papers of state. She subjected Pippa to a close scrutiny.

"Good morning, Lady Nielson."

"Madam." Pippa swept a low curtsy, falling to one

knee. It had been a long time since their relationship had been warm enough for Mary to use her first name.

Mary gestured that she should rise, and indicated a cushion. "Pray be seated. Pregnant women must have a care for themselves." A thin smile flickered. "Your husband spilled your secret."

" 'Tis no secret, madam." Pippa sank down onto the cushion, her skirts spreading around her. Her body performed the correct maneuvers, her tongue said all the right things, but her mind seemed to play no part in any of it. She offered Mary a smile of her own that contained a slight question.

Mary nodded. "You have heard the whispers."

"Indeed, madam. Pray accept my felicitations."

Mary nodded. "So, it seems we shall carry our children together. Suffer the pains of childbirth . . ." Again the smile flickered.

Pippa was aware on some periphery of recognition that the smile was unpleasant and that something lay behind it. But she still moved in the cool, foggy space that enclosed her, and her polite answering smile was blank.

"You are well?" Mary leaned forward, her hands clasped on the desk.

"Except for nausea, madam," Pippa responded. "But I am told that will pass after the twelfth week."

Mary sat back. "Yes, so I understand. I am fortunate. I have not experienced it."

Pippa inclined her head in acknowledgment but made no comment.

"Ah, we must have a care for the Lady Pippa, my dear madam."

Pippa blinked at the new voice that seemed to have come from nowhere. Philip had appeared suddenly at his wife's side and the curtain behind her desk swayed slightly.

"Yes," Mary agreed, her voice flat. "She must stay close at court. My own physicians shall attend her."

"There is no need, madam. I have my own and—"

"No, no," Philip interrupted. "We shall not hear of it. You shall have the same care as the queen of England, madam. We insist upon it. Do we not?" He turned for corroboration to Mary, who merely smiled her assent.

"My husband, sir, will be most grateful," Pippa said, surprised to hear that her voice sounded both cold and ironic.

There was a short silence, an element of chill in the air. Then Mary said, "We will send our physicians to you this afternoon, Lady Nielson. You will find them skilled."

It was a dismissal. Pippa rose with the ease of experience from the low cushion. She curtsied to both king and queen and backed out of the privy chamber.

Lionel stepped out from behind the curtain where he had remained after the king had revealed himself. He bowed to Their Majesties and moved swiftly after Pippa.

What had happened to her since they'd walked together earlier? A few short hours ago? She appeared to be inhabiting some half world. Her eyes were blank, her expression carved in stone. It had seemed that she was completely unaware of her surroundings.

She had reached the end of the outer chamber when he spoke her name.

Slowly Pippa stopped and turned towards him.

Ten

"I WAS COMING TO FIND YOU," PIPPA SAID, STAR-
tling herself with the admission. She had not formed
the intention consciously but now that she saw him she
knew quite simply that there was no one else she could
turn to.

Lionel strode towards her. "What's the matter,
Pippa? Something's happened. What is it?" His voice
was urgent.

Pippa felt the last of her defenses crumbling under
the piercing warmth of his eyes, the insistent concern in
his voice. She gazed back at him, for the moment unable to find the right words. "Where can we go?" she
asked finally.

Lionel glanced around. There were servants in the
presence chamber now, readying it for the public audience later that morning. They were casting curious
looks at himself and Pippa and he couldn't blame them.
Pippa's distress and tension were almost palpable.

"Outside." He took her hand in a firm warm clasp.
"Whatever it is it will be better aired in the open."

"Yes," Pippa said. Sunlight, air, open spaces. She

needed all of those to throw light on this dreadful dark bewilderment that was draining her of all sense of herself, of who and what she was . . . of the person she thought she *had* been.

They left the presence chamber. The corridor beyond was thronged with people chatting in excited knots, hurrying importantly about their business, or simply lounging against the walls observing the scene.

Lionel moved Pippa's hand to his arm so that their progress had a more natural appearance. He felt her hand quiver on his sleeve but she walked quickly beside him, looking neither to right nor left, hastening towards the doors at the end of the corridor.

Outside Lionel directed their steps to a little-frequented path that circled the kitchen gardens at the rear of the palace.

"Now, tell me what has happened."

Pippa took her hand from his arm. She crossed her arms over her breast and looked up at the sky for a minute. "Will you hold me?"

He took her in his arms. A gentle almost tentative hold but she clung to him fiercely, turning her face up to him. "Kiss me."

He kissed her, again gently. He had no idea what was behind this but he could no more have refused her than he could have cut off his own hand. He had wanted to hold her, to kiss her. Wanted it for weeks now.

He ran his hands over the narrow back, feeling the sharp shoulder blades, the knobs of her spine beneath the casing of her gown. She was deepening the kiss, pressing his mouth open with her tongue, delving within. There was something desperate about her, about her need for him, and finally, reluctantly, Lionel drew back, his hands clasping her narrow waist.

He smiled down at her ruefully. "Pippa, I don't mean to sound ungrateful for such invitations, but I would like to know why they've been issued."

She put her steepled fingers to her tingling mouth, and the words came out in a flood of anguish. "I am five and twenty and I do not know how I am to live the rest of my life like this . . . like an empty . . . a discarded shell. He has condemned me to live without love, without touching . . . to live with a man who is repulsed by the very sight of me. How can I spend the rest of my life like that?"

She took a deep shuddering breath as if she had forgotten how to breathe, and the words poured forth anew. "He deemed me worthless . . . worthy only of being used as a cloak to cover his real desires. How could he take everything that is *me*, my needs, my *self*, and cast it all aside in favor of his own? He has used me as a shield, hidden behind our marriage. And I'm to endure that. Live until one of us dies, forever untouched, unloved. Forever without . . . without being held or kissed in the ways of passion because he must indulge his own.

"Why? Why did he choose me?" Now she was angry, her voice tight with tears she would not shed.

"Why did he choose me for such a monstrous deception? Why did he think I was worth so little?" she repeated, punching the words at Lionel as if he were to blame, her eyes bright with tears of fury and a hurt that ran so deep it stabbed him to the heart.

For a dreadful moment his mind would not work. It seemed impossible that her husband had told her the truth about himself. And yet what else could it be? Cold terror swamped his belly. She could not possibly . . . not *possibly* . . . know what had been done to her.

He took her hands, said urgently, "I don't understand, Pippa. What is it that you mean?" His clear gray gaze held hers until some of the wildness left her countenance.

"I mean that I came upon my husband in bed with another man," she articulated slowly and emphatically. "That is what I mean. I mean that my marriage is a sham, a deceit, so that my husband can safely follow his own inclinations. And I'm carrying *his* child to make it even more convincing." Her voice caught.

"Now he will never have any reason to come to my bed, to do with me what so clearly revolts him. That is what I mean." She fell silent, her breathing rapid and shallow, her color ebbing and flowing, the bright sheen of tears still glazing her eyes.

Lionel exhaled slowly. Beneath her outrage and her bewilderment he could hear the fear . . . fear that she was diminished in some essential fashion by her husband's hideous deception. He understood that fear, he had felt it once himself when he had been forced to accept his own powerlessness. It was a crippling terror that struck at the very soul and spirit of humanity.

A terror that still filled him sometimes, stirred by the scent of green wood smoldering, or the crackle of flames.

Lionel accepted that he shared responsibility for much that had been done to this woman, but he could not hold himself responsible for her marriage or for Stuart Nielson's betrayal of his wife, and he could help her now with that terror that he understood so well. He could restore her knowledge of herself, give her back her humanity, the dignity of self-worth.

He cupped her cheek in the palm of one hand. He bent and kissed her eyes, the tip of her nose, the corners of her mouth. She didn't move, her eyes remained open, but a shiver ran through her taut frame.

He moved his mouth to beneath her ear, to the side of her neck, to the tender skin beneath her chin. Her head fell back, exposing the white column of her throat, the now wildly jumping pulse; the swell of her uplifted breasts rose above the low, square neckline of her gown.

Desire rushed him, took his breath away, obscured reason and rational thought. He needed no excuse. This was no mission of healing and renewal. He wanted this woman. From the very first moment he had been drawn to her. He had pretended to deny it, to deny the magnet that attracted them each to the other, but he would do so no longer.

"I want you," he said softly, his breath whispering over her skin. "I want to hold you, love you, possess you utterly, every inch of your skin, every fiber of your being. I would touch you in ways that will make your body sing, bury my tongue in your most secret places, drink deep of your sweetness, drown my senses in your fragrance."

He kissed her mouth even as he whispered his passion and his longing. Pippa pressed into him, as if she could lose herself in the boundaries of the body that held her. She could not, would not, think. She tasted his tongue, the salt of his skin, put her arms tight around him to encompass him with her body as she was held in his.

His words, rustling still in the hot air around them, brought a rushing warmth in her belly, a tingling across her skin, a tremor in the taut muscles of her thighs. When he lifted her in his arms she curled sideways, her arms around his neck, her mouth pressed to his. Her eyes were still wide open as if she could not bear to lose a single thread of sensation.

He carried her. Pippa could never remember anyone carrying her since childhood and the idea amused her, breaking for a moment the trance of desire as it brought a little bubble of a giggle to her lips even as she kept her mouth on his.

They were in a shady place now, fragrant with the scent of cut grass. Pippa had no interest in their surroundings. Lionel knelt with her, laid her down on a thick sweet bed of grass.

She stirred, murmured, as he unfastened her bodice. She gave him her breasts, holding them for his caressing mouth, her nipples hard, prickling, sending a jolt deep in her loins as if there were some line connecting the two parts of her body.

He licked the little pool of sweat from the hollow of her throat, licked away the dampness that glistened between her breasts. His hands moved beneath her skirts, sliding up her thighs.

She lay back on the bed of new-cut grass, her eyes still on his rapt countenance. His fingers moved on her flesh, unfurling the tight complex folds of her sex. Touching, stroking, opening. Pippa stirred, a soft murmur of delight spilling from her lips. She had not known this was possible.

Lionel smiled at her, knowing what she was feeling, knowing that it was new for her. He kissed her again, his cupped palm holding her sex, warm and strong. She felt her own dampness and a sensation that was almost painful in its intensity. She bit his lower lip and tasted blood.

He knelt up as she lay awash in her own pleasure. He loosened his hose, pushed aside her skirts with sudden roughness. His hands cupped her bottom as he lifted her hips and slid into her wet and welcoming body as easily as a hand into a kid glove.

And now it was a different sensation. Pippa, her hazel eyes fixed on his as they hung over her, held her breath as she absorbed the newness of this. She had coupled with Stuart many times, but this was something quite different. Her whole being seemed to have a part in it. Every tiny piece of her body was intimately involved in this loving.

And the delight was different from a minute ago. Now Lionel's pleasure was a part of her own. She gloried in the feel of him inside her, the strong vibrant throbs of his penis against the sheath that held him. She tried to curl her legs around him, to hold him more tightly within her, but the tangled mass of her clothes got in the way, snaring her feet, trapping her knees.

"Damnable clothes!" she gasped. "This should not be done with clothes."

He smiled lazily down at her. "Not always," he agreed. "But sometimes it adds another dimension."

He drew back a little and she felt him leaving her. A little breath of disappointment escaped her. Then he was back, slowly, so very slowly, and she lifted her hips, the cleft of her body smacking hard against his belly; her eyes finally snapped shut and she was aware only of her own body, of this amazing, astounding delight that made her curl her toes, tighten every inch of her legs, her belly, did strange and wonderful things to her ears, and made her scalp tight. Then it let go and she was soft and unformed as melted candlewax lying on her bed of new-cut grass.

Pippa lay with her eyes closed. She wanted to sleep, to roll onto her side and sleep, her body curled over the

wonderful thing that had happened to it, a wonderful
thing that was slowly slipping away from her.

Lionel knelt up, laced his hose, gazing down at the
still figure, her skirts rucked up around her. There was
something endearing about the thinness of her ankles,
her calves and thighs. He thought she was asleep. Her
sandy eyelashes were crescents against the pale freckled
countenance that retained the glow of lovemaking. Her
headdress was awry, the black velvet and emeralds glowing against the grass beneath her. Her beringed fingers
lay hapless beside her still form.

He rearranged the tangle of skirts and petticoats and
as he did so her eyes opened. "I think I fell asleep."

"I think you did," he agreed, leaning over to brush a
straying lock of cinnamon hair away from her eyes. "Are
you ready to get up?"

Pippa sat up. She glanced around and saw that they
were under some kind of shelter. No sides, just a tin
roof, and she was lying on a mountain of grass cuttings.

"Is this a compost heap?"

"Not yet," Lionel said with a chuckle. "Simply the
makings of one."

Pippa straightened her hood and the emerald-
studded frontlet. She observed, "I have never been
made love to on a compost heap before, but then again
I now realize that I have never been made love to before." Her smile was quizzical as she held up her hands.

He took them and pulled her to her feet. Her observation required no response except the private pleasure
it gave him.

"I must look quite disarrayed," Pippa said, brushing
grass off her skirt. "I have grass in my hair, don't I?"

"Yes . . . perhaps if you take off the hood . . . ?"

"Without a mirror I could never put the pins back

again," she said. "More importantly, my hose is twisted, and that, I should tell you, sir, is very uncomfortable." Without blinking, she hauled up the layers of skirts and petticoats and straightened her white silk hose, twisting and turning so that he glimpsed the length of thigh, the curve of a buttock.

His body stirred anew.

Pippa settled her skirts around her again. She glanced at him, suddenly unsure of herself again as an unpleasant thought assailed her. Had he pitied her? She had poured out her soul. Had pity led him to succor her in that way?

"What is it?"

She shook her head. "Nothing. Will I pass muster if I make all haste to my chamber?"

"What is it, Pippa?"

His voice was steady, determined.

She walked out from beneath the shelter of the tin roof. The midday sun beat down on her head. She tried to put words to the morass of feelings, intuitions, hurts. Lionel had not hurt her, but the fact that he had tried to assuage her hurt seemed in itself paradoxically painful.

"I am very grateful," she said, hearing the stiffness in her voice. "You did what you could to make me feel better. My husband considers me less than the dust beneath his feet. You gave me back my pride. I am very grateful."

Lionel leaned against one of the wooden posts that supported the tin roof. Pippa was right. It had started like that, but that reason had not lasted beyond the first touch.

"Pippa, I don't love women just to make them feel better," he stated. "Sadly I'm not so selfless." He rested his head against the post at his back and continued with the detached dispassionate air he used in most situations. "I've found you desirable from the first moment I saw you.

"Now, maybe that's an aberration on my part." Here he shrugged. "But who am I to say? I will only say that I have never made love to a woman out of pity. And you insult us both by such a presumption."

Pippa touched her breast jewel and found the cold smoothness of the gem beneath her clutching fingers oddly comforting. She looked at him, comforted too by the calm remote air that was Lionel Ashton at his ordinary self.

She was desirable, many men had found her so. Unconventional in her looks and her manner, maybe, but she had had enough urgent sighs, enough compliments, enough bold offers to confirm her in the knowledge that her womanhood was appreciated.

Between her legs was the absolute confirmation of that desire. Not a sticky residue of a hasty and unwanted but necessary coupling, but of a wonderful shared explosion of pleasure. They had loved, she and Lionel. And she knew herself to be lovable, to be desirable.

"Forgive me," she said, stepping close to him. "I didn't mean to look a gift horse in the mouth." She reached up to kiss him. "You are a gift, Mr. Ashton. And I thank you."

"I believe we had an exchange of gifts, Lady Pippa," he said, raising her hand to his mouth. His eyes laughed at this absurd game they were playing. "The next exchange should be a little more designed, I believe."

"No clothes," Pippa said with a grin. She was lighthearted, unable now to recapture the gloom, the dreadful depression of her spirits that had dogged her.

"I would love you naked, Mr. Ashton."

"And I you, madam." He bowed.

"You carried me in here, sir, perhaps you should carry me out." Pippa was laughing, remembering the novel sensation of being held against him, his arms so strong around her.

But his expression changed, darkened. "No, I don't think so. Go quickly. I will wait here for ten minutes."

Pippa left him, made her way back to the path that encircled the kitchen garden. He had carried her. No one had carried her in that way since she was a child. Why had he snubbed her?

She was not watching where she was going and found herself in the orchard, deserted except for gardeners. She straightened her hood again, aware that such adjustments would do little to conceal the grass that seemed to have clung to every fiber of her dress. There was dirt beneath her fingernails.

She walked steadily, head held high, looking neither to right nor left as she proceeded down the aisles between the trees. It didn't really matter what gardeners thought of her disheveled appearance, but ignoring them seemed the most dignified way of managing the situation.

When she emerged from the orchard she took a pathway that led into the blacksmiths' courtyard of the palace. Amid the clang of hammer on anvil, the smell of hot coals and sweating horseflesh, the hurry and bustle of busy people, her appearance was barely noticed. She ducked through an arched entrance into the palace and took a series of servants' staircases that eventually deposited her in the corridor where her own chamber was to be found.

Martha was not in the chamber, and Pippa, after a glance at her image in the mirror, could only be thankful. She kicked off her grass-stained slippers, unpinned her hood, and shook out her hair. Grass cuttings littered the floor. She nudged them under the bed and the tapestry rug with her bare feet. Then she laughed at herself for such a childishly guilty maneuver. She was not accountable to anyone . . . not even to Stuart. No longer.

The thought gave her pause. She examined her conscience and could find not a smidgeon of remorse for her infidelity. She was still bitterly angry with Stuart, and the hurt remained if she probed at it. He had treated her as less than human. But should she confront him? Or should she let matters drift, take their course, enjoy her own life, and leave her husband to enjoy his? He would not be hurt by his wife's clandestine liaison as long as it remained clandestine. Yes, for the moment she would do just that. She would maintain the public facade and take refuge in her adventure of love with Lionel Ashton.

Of course, that would not last forever. . . . But, no, she would not think like that. She would live in and for this moment. And she would share it with no one, not Robin, not even Pen.

Pippa stripped off her clothes and shook them out of the window. Bits of grass drifted down to the terrace beneath but none of the languid walkers seemed to find anything strange in the green rain. It was so hot it was probably too much effort to look up.

She felt wonderfully sleepy, her limbs heavy, and the thick feather bed sang a siren's song. She lay down under the light coverlet and closed her eyes, feeling the sun warm on her lids, as her mind lazily revisited the glorious hour with Lionel. She remembered how it had felt when he had lifted her in his arms. How she, who was not in the habit of playing the helpless miss, had not only allowed herself to be carried, but had found it an arousing experience. She smiled to herself again, and turned on her side to sleep.

But sleep strangely would not come. A shadow hovered at the edges of her memory. She couldn't see it clearly to identify it, but it kept her on the edge of sleep. She tried to recapture the glorious relaxation engendered by lovemaking, but something had spoiled it. Unease clouded recollection.

She sat up impatiently and hugged her knees, worrying at the shadow, trying to give it some shape. Lionel had carried her. It had made her laugh at the time. So why now did the recollection produce this unnameable discomfort?

Nothing became clear. Pippa lay down again, idly gazing up at the scene embroidered on the tester. A pair of lovers by a stream, surrounded by peacocks and swans; in the background a stag on a distant hill. A very pretty idealized scene, and one that held no clues to her present mood.

After a while, though, the scene soothed her with its familiarity. She decided that it was not surprising that she should feel upset, off-kilter by the events of the morning. In the few short hours since dawn she'd experienced enough upheaval to unhinge the most placid of temperaments. And hers these days was far from placid thanks to the peculiarities of pregnancy. Most of the time she didn't know whether she was going to laugh or cry in response to the most mundane event or remark.

Calmer now, she turned on her side and this time sleep embraced her.

Eleven

ROBIN PEERED AT THE CONTENTS OF THE LINEN PRESS in his chamber in the family house at Holborn. The house was quiet, his parents and half sister were still in Derbyshire and there was only a skeleton staff left in London.

His page stood beside the bed holding a pair of gold embroidered hose and a linen shirt, regarding his master with curiosity. It was most unlike Lord Robin to spend such an inordinate length of time on choosing his wardrobe. A wooden tub of rapidly cooling, scummy water stood in the middle of the chamber, evidence of Lord Robin's sudden interest in personal hygiene.

"There are grease spots on this doublet," Robin said in disgust, tossing the green velvet to the floor. "I would think, Jem, that you would have more of a care for my clothes than to put them away soiled."

Jem said nothing, and kept to himself the reflection that this had never been mentioned before as part of his duties.

"You had best take out every garment and examine it carefully. They are to be sponged and pressed where necessary," Robin instructed, burrowing deeper in the press, his voice muffled by dusty cloth. "Ah, perhaps this will do."

He backed out with a doublet of russet silk. "There was an ochre velvet cloak that went with this, I'm sure of it." He tossed the doublet onto the bed and burrowed into the press again.

"Here!" Triumphantly he emerged with the cloak, holding it up to the lamplight. " 'Tis somewhat creased, but that is easily remedied." He tossed it to Jem, who just managed to catch it.

"Take it to the stillroom maid and ask her to press it . . . and the doublet. Hurry now." He clapped his hands imperatively.

Jem relinquished the hose and shirt, gathered up the doublet and cloak, and hastened from the chamber.

Robin examined the fresh linen on the bed, white linen underbritches, white shirt. They looked clean but he seemed to remember that his father's underwear smelled of lavender from the little sachets of dried herbs that were always scattered among the garments in the armoire and linen press.

Robin could detect no delicate hint of fragrance coming from his own undergarments as he put them on, but they were certainly clean, and the shirt had received the attentions of the flat iron.

His skin was most certainly scrubbed and sweet. He glanced complacently at the tub, and the square of scented soap that the stillroom maid had supplied. He had even soaped his hair. He ran his hands through the still-damp curls and stroked his beard, wondering if he should trim it. It was a little straggly, he decided.

He sat down at the table and drew the mirror towards him. His image wavered in the beaten copper. He drew the lamp closer and leaned forward, the small scissors in his hand. He snipped away at the uneven strands and then wondered if he'd gone too far. Perhaps he should shave it off altogether.

That was an overly radical solution, he decided, taking up an ivory comb and tidying his beard. Hearing Jem coming back to the chamber, Robin glanced over his shoulder. "Tell me, lad, is this even?" He pulled at both sides of the beard.

Jem peered closely. " 'Tis a mite longer on the left, I think, sir."

"God's bones!" Robin muttered. "The more I snip the more uneven it seems to get. Here . . . you do it." He handed the scissors to the page.

Jem took them uneasily. "I'm no barber, sir."

"No, well, neither am I," Robin said impatiently. "You can't do worse than I have done."

"Right, sir." Bending close, Jem took a few tentative snips. He stood back and surveyed his handiwork. "Looks even now, sir."

Robin turned back to the mirror. He tugged at the ends of the beard. They seemed to be roughly of the same length. "Well, it'll have to do," he said, getting to his feet. "Pass me the hose."

Jem did so, watching as his master insinuated his stocky but muscular legs into the tight-fitting netherstocks. Robin tucked the shirt into the waist of the gold embroidered panes that formed the upper part of the hose, and laced up the waistband. He put on the doublet and adjusted the set of the small ruff at his neck with fussy little pats that astonished his page.

"That should do it," Robin muttered, more to himself than his companion. He slung the short cloak around his shoulders, and turned to face Jem. "So, what do you think?"

"About what, sir?"

"Oh, don't be obtuse, lad! How do I look?"

Jem put his head on one side. "Like someone going a-courting, sir," he observed.

"Impertinence!" Robin said, but without rancor. He had invited an opinion and he never expected Jem to hold his tongue in such instances.

He buckled on his sword and dagger, took up a pair of lace-edged jeweled gloves that had been a present from Pen, and set a flat, dark green velvet hat on his still-disordered curls.

"Get you to bed, Jem . . . or to the tavern if you've a mind. I'll not be needing you again until morning."

"Thank you, Lord Robin." Jem grinned. "I wish you good success, sir."

Robin shook his head and left the chamber. The tall case clock on the stairs was striking ten o'clock. He paused in the hall to collect a neatly wrapped parcel from the side bench and let himself out of the house. The air was close, the sky for once clouded, and he could smell thunder in the air.

He stood on the driveway sniffing the wind. He had intended to take Luisa on the river but if a storm was brewing then he couldn't expose her to the elements.

He strode to the stables to fetch his horse. "Set a pillion pad behind the saddle," he instructed his groom. Luisa had her own mount but Robin guessed that she had not considered the difficulties of liberating it from the stables in the middle of the night under the eyes, sleepy or not, of Ashton's grooms. He was also not sure how well she rode and had decided he would feel safer if she was mounted behind him. They could explore the city streets, and always take shelter in a tavern if the weather broke.

He rode to Lionel Ashton's mansion. From the front it was even more imposing than from the river approach. Stone lions guarded the gates, and lamplight spilled from cressets set over the great oak front doors. A wall enclosed the property but Robin in an earlier reconnaissance had discovered the narrow lane that ran around the wall and gave access to the river.

He dismounted and led his horse into the lane, where he tethered him to a sapling. Placidly the animal began to crop the tired grass at his feet.

Robin trod softly towards the river. The heat was oppressive and sweat gathered on his forehead. The wall ended just before the riverbank, where the bushes from the mansion's garden offered a thick protective barrier to the property itself.

Robin drew his sword and slashed his way through the bushes, cursing as branches snagged his clothes. He stepped out onto the lawn, dark now under the moonless sky. A magnificent oak tree stood in the middle of the lawn, a circular bench around its massive trunk.

A white-clad figure glimmered faintly in the darkness, sitting on the bench.

"Luisa?"

She jumped up at the whisper, looked around, then saw him. "Oh, I was so afraid you would not come. I believe it is going to storm."

"Yes, I think so, too."

She was standing very close to him, looking up at him, her eyes glowing black ovals against the darkness around them.

"Perhaps we should postpone our adventure

tonight," he said. "It would not do to get caught in the storm."

"But there are places we can shelter, are there not? I would visit a tavern. Drink some wine, listen to the talk." Her voice was eager, cajoling.

Robin laughed softly. He could not possibly disappoint her. "Aye, we can do those things."

"Did you bring me clothes?"

He handed her the parcel.

"I'll be but a minute." She plunged into the shrubbery.

"Oh, what are these?" The disconcerted tones floated out from the shrubbery. "I thought I was to dress as a boy."

"I told you I would bring what I considered suitable," Robin replied. "Can you manage the hooks at the back, or would you like some help?"

"I can manage." She didn't sound too happy about it and Robin smiled to himself as he waited.

"This is not at all what I had had in mind." Luisa spoke as she emerged from concealment, brushing at the simple dull brown holland gown she now wore. "There is not even a touch of lace at the neck."

"The less conspicuous you look, the more exploring we can do," Robin pointed out. "My idea was that you should not be noticed at all. Fade into the background . . . if you understand me."

Luisa turned up her aristocratic nose. "I am a Mendoza. I would have you know, Lord Robin, that Mendozas do not fade into the background."

"No, I'm sure they don't," he agreed with a grin. "But tonight you are not a Mendoza, you're a young servant girl. One who will draw no remark."

Luisa considered for an instant, then shook her head

as if casting aside her disgruntlement. "I suppose you know best. But this is a very ugly cap. I think I will not wear it." She turned over in her hands the plain, coarse linen cap Robin had provided. "I will leave my hair unbound."

Robin decided not to press the point. He picked up her cloak from the bench under the oak tree and handed it to her. "At least you won't need to wear this to cover the roundnesses," he observed with another grin.

Luisa took the folded garment over her arm. " 'Tis certainly too hot for it."

"Aye." Robin nodded. "But bring it in case of rain. Come now, my horse is saddled in the lane."

"But I have to fetch Crema."

"No, you ride with me. We don't want to risk raising the entire stable block."

Luisa pursed her lips. "Yes, I think that is good," she said with a judicious nod. "Malcolm might be awake."

"Malcolm?"

"Don Ashton hired him as my groom, but I think he's more of a bodyguard."

"Then we most certainly don't wish to waken him," Robin declared. He led the way to the thick screen of bushes at the rear of the property. "Take hold of my cloak and keep close to my back while I forge a path through," he instructed. "I'd not return you to your duenna with a scratched face."

Luisa did as she was told, burying her face in the folds of the ochre velvet cloak, stumbling on his heels as he cut his way through the sharp tangle of twigs and thorns to the lane beyond.

Once there she shook out her hair, picking out leaves and twigs. "Did you not get scratched?" Her voice was concerned as she came close to him, peering up into his face. "Oh, there is blood on your cheek." She licked a finger and dabbed at his cheek.

It was a gesture so artlessly intimate that Robin's breath caught. Once again he couldn't decide whether she acted out of pure innocence, but whatever the motive she was stepping close to a very dangerous brink. She was safe enough with him, but she couldn't assume that all men were as honorable as he was.

He took her wrist and pulled her hand away from his face. "For God's sake, Luisa! Be more discreet."

Luisa glanced around. "But why? There's no one here." Her tone was all innocence, her eyes all anticipation.

"Don't play games."

Luisa laughed. "Why not? It amuses me, Lord Robin. Come, let us start our adventure."

Robin found it very easy to accept defeat. He was no duenna, Luisa's social indiscretions were not his responsibility. He had no authority over her and desired none. He had simply promised to show her something of the world, and if by amusing her he amused himself, all well and good.

He lifted her onto the pillion pad briskly, trying to ignore the soft warmth of the curvaceous waist between his hands. Then he mounted in front of her.

Luisa settled onto the pillion and clasped his waist. "I should hold on to you, should I not?"

"It would perhaps be advisable."

"Yes, so I thought." There was more than a hint of complacency in her voice.

Robin ignored it. "So where shall we go first?"

"To see a cockfight or a bearbaiting," his companion responded promptly. "They have them in Spain but ladies never watch them. I would see them for myself."

Robin shrugged. "So be it."

If Luisa had strong nerves perhaps she would enjoy such spectacles, but he seriously doubted it. He remembered Pippa when she was about ten begging her stepfather to allow her to go to a bearbaiting. Lord Hugh had overridden his wife's objections and taken her himself. He had brought her home long before it was over, a sickened and wretched child who had been miserable for days. Robin was inclined to follow his father's example. Pippa always needed to find things out for herself and Luisa seemed to him to be struck from the same mold.

Luisa gazed around her, entranced, as they passed through the nighttime streets of London. There were many people around, drunks tumbling out of taverns, groups of young courtiers exchanging half-serious sword passes on street corners. Watchmen carried lanterns to illuminate the wider thoroughfares and Robin avoided the dark narrow alleys that ran off them.

He pointed out the landmarks as they went. Luisa showed little interest in St. Paul's at the top of Ludgate Hill, but she was fascinated by London Bridge, still decorated with the hideous remnants of Wyatt's rebellion, scraps of flesh clinging to the skulls, strands of dried hair hanging limp, eyeless sockets gazing into infinity. The massive edifice of the Tower of London hulked in the darkness farther along the river.

The ghastly frieze did not however disconcert her. She had seen that and worse at an auto-da-fé in her native land. "I would like to come to the bridge when the shops are open," she observed. " 'Tis like a town in itself. All those houses and shops."

"Our way lies across it," Robin said. "If your heart

remains set on a cockfight?" He glanced over his shoulder at her, eyebrows raised.

Luisa slipped a hand into the bodice of her maid's gown and pulled out a purse. "I would have a wager," she said. "The Mendozas are known for their skill at gambling, but I have not yet had the opportunity to see if 'tis in my blood."

"Ah." Robin nodded. "Maybe you shouldn't try to find out. Gaming can be the very devil if it gets its hooks into you."

"Oh, I don't think so," she replied with an insouciant shrug. "We Mendozas have very deep pockets. More than one fortune has been won and lost in my family."

Robin said no more. He dismounted outside an insalubrious house so crookedly crammed between its neighbors that it looked as if they were holding it up. He lifted Luisa down and gave his reins to one of the eager crowd of urchins who pressed close in upon them.

Luisa felt the first faint tremor of doubt. The smells were powerfully unpleasant and the boys were too close to her, their hands touching and pulling at her gown and apron, feeling her all over, she realized with a shock. She slapped out at them in a flash of outrage. Two of them danced closer, dodging her hands, chanting something at her that she couldn't understand but guessed from their expressions was obscene.

Robin caught them both and with rough justice knocked their heads together. They collapsed, wailing, to their knees on the mired cobbles and the others fell back as the lord's angry gaze swept over them.

"I thought you said I wouldn't draw unwelcome attention," Luisa demanded as he hurried her through an ill-fitting door and into a malodorous passage.

"I was wrong," he said grimly. "But if you'd been dressed as yourself they would have slit your throat."

"But you would have protected me!" she exclaimed.

"I would have *tried*," Robin agreed. He continued rather brusquely, "But I don't have an inflated sense of my own powers, and neither should you. I'm no guardian angel, Luisa. You too need to keep your eyes and wits about you and behave with circumspection."

"But they were just children. No match for you, surely!"

"There are children, and children," he pointed out. "And there were quite a number of them, a number that would have grown in the blink of an eye."

Luisa, somewhat chastened, allowed him to take her arm and lead her down the passage to where the sounds of shouting and cheering bellowed from behind a closed door. When Robin opened the door she thought she would faint. The stench of blood, ale, filthy bodies, made her head reel.

She stared, sickened at the circle of red, greedy, glistening faces; their mouths all seemed to be open, shouting at once, as they leaned forward towards the makeshift ring where at first she couldn't see what was on the blood-clotted sawdust and then couldn't bear to.

She turned her head into Robin's broad chest, her stomach heaving.

His father was always right, Robin reflected, merely turning away, holding her head against his chest as he ushered her back outside where the vile air in contrast seemed to Luisa to be as fresh as a meadow of daisies.

"Bearbaiting now?" he questioned calmly, retrieving his horse from the urchin who still held him.

Luisa shook her head. "No, I don't think so. I think you should not have brought me here."

"No, quite possibly not," Robin agreed. "But had I not done so, your curiosity would never have been satisfied, and you most probably would have accused me of acting like a duenna."

"I expect I would."

Her voice was very small and Robin, without thought, bent and kissed the corner of her mouth. "We all make mistakes," he said. "I cannot count the number I've made in my time." He lifted her onto the pillion pad.

Luisa touched the corner of her mouth where his lips had brushed. "You have the advantage of experience."

"Yes, you could say that." He laughed up at her. "Don't look so disconsolate, Luisa. Take advantage of my experience, it is entirely at your disposal."

He swung up in front of her just as a great rumble of thunder rolled across the river. His horse threw up his head and sniffed the wind, shifting uneasily on the wooden bridge.

"Let's get the hell out of here." Robin nudged the animal's flanks with his booted heels.

Luisa clung on tight as the horse broke into a canter. The bridge was suddenly very quiet, the crowds of urchins melted into the darkness of doorways. Lightning forked into the river.

"Where are we going?"

"Somewhere dry and warm, where I can drink some porter and you can try your hand at dice," he called against the rushing wind, the sound of the river throwing itself against the high banks.

The rain came. Great sheets of it, falling straight from the black sky. Lightning flashed, thunder bellowed, and the horse galloped as if frenzied, through the rapidly clearing thoroughfares of the city.

Robin turned into a cobbled courtyard surrounded on three sides by a galleried tavern. Rain pelted, hitting the cobbles and springing up in a ceaseless fountain. He rode under the protection of the gallery; the rain fell behind them like a waterfall from the edge of the gallery. Light poured from the doors that stood open on the ground floor and the sounds of merriment warred with the thunder and the rain beyond.

Robin rode his horse straight through one of the doors and into a stone-flagged passageway from which a wooden staircase rose to the upper floor. Pitch torches were sconced along the smoke-blackened lime-washed walls and the huge shadow of the horse with its two riders struck Luisa as an image out of Dante's *Inferno*.

She shivered in her soaked gown, the coarse material clinging unpleasantly. Her unbound hair dripped down her back.

"Take yer 'orse, m'lord?" a small voice piped from somewhere around the animal's nether regions.

"Aye, rub him down and there'll be a farthing in it for you," Robin said as he swung down in the narrow space.

Luisa slid down unaided. " 'Tis so cold," she said. "I didn't think I would ever be cold again."

"We'll soon warm you up." He propelled her ahead of him into a low-ceilinged taproom where a massive fire burned what seemed like a whole tree trunk. At long deal tables and benches men and women sat in various stages of intoxication amid the click and clack of dice.

Luisa sniffed. There was a wonderful smell coming from somewhere that set her juices running. She was hungry. Famished. She obeyed the pressure on her shoulder that pushed her towards the fire, and then into the inglenook, so that she was sitting on a brick bench almost inside the fire. The heat was intense but for the moment she was only grateful as her gown steamed and she stretched her wet boots and stockings towards the blaze.

"You won't be able to stand more than five minutes," Robin said with a chuckle. He was drying his head with a piece of rough and none-too-clean toweling that he'd found somewhere. His clothes were ruined, he reflected, but without too much dismay.

"Something smells wonderful."

"Oh, Goodwife Margery makes the best hot pot this side of Lancashire," Robin told her. "I'll fetch you a bowl when you come out of the fire." He turned aside to take two mugs of porter from a potboy. He held one out to Luisa. "Here. This'll put heart in you."

Luisa took a tentative sip, and then another. "Oh, 'tis good!" She beamed at him in her haze of steam. "I *am* enjoying myself, Lord Robin."

He nodded, a smile on his lips and his eyes. He thought how radiant she looked in her bedraggled state. As if she'd come alive suddenly. He thought of his sisters, of the variety and interest that had always informed their lives, and he thought what a wretched existence this cloistered Spanish aristocrat had led thus far.

Luisa felt her body still under his intent gaze. She couldn't read his thoughts but she could read his interest, his sympathy, and something else that her woman's intuition translated accurately as rather more than liking. She felt herself opening under that look, blossoming in some way. It filled her with warmth and anticipation, as if she was about to discover things about herself that she had not yet even guessed at.

"Come out now," he said. "You're beginning to look like a boiled lobster." He held out his hand to her.

She took it, despite the unflattering comparison, and allowed him to pull her out of the inglenook. Her fingers closed tightly over his, but instantly he dropped her hand.

He called, "Goodwife, bring us a bowl of hot pot."

Luisa decided not to press her advantage. She sensed that Robin was not sure at all about what was going on here, whereas she was absolutely certain. But she didn't wish to scare him off. He needed gentle handling.

She sat down at the long bench in front of a large bowl of meat and vegetables in a rich broth. They shared the bowl, ladling it onto bread trenchers with the common spoon. She toyed with a second mug of porter but had no desire to feel any more light-headed than she did already. Her companion drank deep but seemed unaffected by it. Around them the noise rose, competing with the beating of the rain against the thatched roof. The fire was hot at her back.

"So, are you ready to try your hand at the dice?"

Robin's voice startled her out of the warm, satisfied trance that enveloped her. "Oh, yes. Yes, please." She scrambled off the bench and followed him to the table where the dice were being rolled.

A few curious glances were thrown at her, but when Robin merely indicated her with a careless inclusive nod as she straddled the bench beside him, whatever explanation the nod contained was accepted. She watched for a few throws, observing how the wagering went. Robin offered her no advice, indeed didn't even look at her, and it dawned on her that as far as the men at the table were concerned she was Lord Robin's doxy for the evening. A lady of the night.

Laughter bubbled in her throat. This was so much better a disguise than men's clothes. She could play this part to perfection.

She pouted at him. "A few pennies, my lord? I would try my hand."

"I thought you had your own money," he retorted, his eyes narrowing.

"Oh, but 'tis for you to entertain me, my lord. In exchange . . ." she added meaningfully.

Robin kept a straight face with some difficulty. He tossed her a small pile of pennies. "See what you can do with those."

Luisa propped an elbow on the table, picked up the dice in her free hand, shook, and rolled with an expert twist of her wrist that surprised her, it was so natural.

Two hours later she had cleared the table, sending her fellow players grumbling out of the door. She gathered up the little pile of coins and dropped them into the pouch in her bosom. "A profit, I think?"

"Aye, except that it was my stake."

"Oh, should I repay you?" She reached again into her bosom.

Robin shook his head hastily. The neck of the gown seemed to be lower, slightly out of alignment, probably as a result of its wetting, but her breasts as a result rose in quite unashamed plump curves of a startling creaminess.

"The storm has abated," he said. " 'Tis time we went home."

"But we can do this again?" she asked urgently, laying a hand on his arm. "I would like to try the cards next time."

"Yes, I'm sure that can be arranged." He hurried her out of the taproom, calling for his horse.

The air was clearer and fresher although the sky was still dark with cloud as they rode back to Lionel Ashton's mansion. All the lights were extinguished when they broke through the soaked screen of bushes onto the lawn.

"Your guardian is at home?" It was half question, half statement.

"He must be. They don't extinguish the lamps until he's returned."

"How will you get in?"

Luisa dug once more into her bosom and came up with a small key. "There is a servants' door at the side. I locked it after me and took the key this evening. 'Tis very rarely used, so I hope no one noticed." She shrugged and Robin averted his eyes from the effect this had on her décolletage. "If they did, it will be forgotten soon enough."

"I hope so."

She stepped very close to him so that he could smell the rain in her hair and the lingering tang of woodsmoke from the inglenook. "Will you come when Bernardina is taking her siesta? We could walk a little, talk . . . there's so much I would like to know. So much you could tell me."

She smiled at him, and unconsciously brushed her still-damp hair away from her face. "You said your experience was at my disposal, Lord Robin."

"You are a flirtatious baggage, Dona Luisa," Robin stated forcefully. "You don't fool me for a minute."

She laughed at that. "I'm not trying to, sir." She reached up and kissed his cheek. "You will come . . . say you will come."

"If I can," he said, stepping back. "But I cannot promise when. I have duties at court, Luisa." He tried to make his voice strong and authoritative, as if he were talking to an importunate child. It didn't work, however.

"Oh, yes, I understand that," she said, nodding her head firmly. "Of course I do. Men's work is so important. But I will walk by the river every fine day at noon, since I have little else to do. 'Tis woman's lot to watch and wait, after all." A smile of surpassing innocence and mischief accompanied the declaration.

Robin was momentarily at a loss for words. It occurred to him that his sisters had often had the same effect on him.

Luisa dropped him a curtsy. "I give you good night, Lord Robin. And my thanks for a most entertaining evening." She blew him a kiss as she flitted away towards the house.

Robin, feeling rather as if the wind had been taken from his sails, waited for some sign that she was safe inside. It came in a few minutes when a casement opened on the second floor and a glimmer of candlelight passed across it.

He left the garden determined that on their next encounter Dona Luisa would not have the last word. And once again he thought how often he'd made the same determination with one or another of his stepsisters. Perhaps it was Luisa's resemblance to Pen and Pippa that drew him to her so powerfully.

It was a startling thought.

Twelve

THE LONG HEAT WAVE HAD BROKEN. PIPPA KNELT ON the window seat of her bedchamber taking deep breaths of the rain-washed air. The grass on the sweep of lawn was bright green again, the flowers had lifted their drought-stricken heads, and the leaves on the trees had a shine to them once more.

The terrace below her window was thronged with courtiers taking their morning gossipy constitutional. Very few had ventured onto the puddle-strewn gravel paths or the drenched lawns.

Pippa was still in her nightshift although it was already midmorning. She had slept late and awoken feeling sluggish and nauseated. She had slept late but not well, indeed she felt as if she had not really closed her eyes at all. A vague unease, a sense of apprehension dogged her. She had had a dream but in the bright light of day she couldn't remember anything about it, and yet she knew that it was the source of her unease.

Nausea rose unstoppable. "God's blood, Eve has something to answer for," she muttered as she ran for the commode.

Martha tutted sympathetically and was ready with a dampened lavender-scented towel and a cup of water flavored with spearmint when her mistress finally rose from her knees.

Pippa rinsed out her mouth and washed her face. She felt better. She took the mug of warmed mead that Martha next gave her together with a piece of buttered barley bread and returned to the window seat.

She didn't hear the door to Stuart's chamber open until he spoke hesitantly from the doorway. Her body went rigid. She had not seen him even in public since she had discovered him with his lover two days earlier. She had not questioned his absence, merely been thankful for it.

"I give you good morning, Pippa."

Pippa didn't turn from the window. She didn't think she could bear to look at him and still be silent . . . still manage not to hurl her agonized outrage at him. Lionel's lovemaking had given her back herself, but had done nothing to assuage her hurt and fury at the man who had so used her. And yet she knew she must say nothing. She couldn't imagine what would happen if she confronted Stuart. What would he do, what *could* he do? It was quite simply an unimaginable situation. She knew that Stuart would never forgive her; guilt would not let him forgive her for discovering his secret. And since she would never be able to forgive him for such a betrayal whether she confronted him or not, she was trapped into silence. The charade of this marriage had to be preserved for public consumption.

"You have been away from court these last two days?" she asked distantly.

"The queen asked me to visit her estates in Essex," he said. "She has a mind to visit Woodham Walter with the king next month. Philip expressed an interest in hunting the forest down there."

"I see. Is the entire court to remove there?" Still she did not turn from her view of the terrace below her window although her eyes took in nothing.

"That has not as yet been decided."

Stuart stood awkwardly in the door. He felt a flash of anger as if Pippa were to blame for making him feel awkward and ill at ease in her company. "Why are you not yet dressed? The morning audience will take place in less than an hour."

"I am not feeling well this morning," she returned. "The queen I'm sure will excuse me since she is in the same happy condition . . . although she informs me that she doesn't suffer from my particular symptom."

Stuart had heard her earlier vomiting and winced at the sarcasm he sensed in her voice. She was accusing him of causing the miseries of her pregnancy, where surely she should be rejoicing in a condition that a normal woman would embrace with satisfaction. In the circumstances he was helpless either to challenge or sympathize.

"You wish me to make your excuses?"

"If you please."

"Very well, madam." He bowed to her back and retreated into his own chamber.

Pippa gazed down at the terrace below waiting for the definitive click of the latch that told her Stuart had truly left her.

"Will you return to bed, madam, or will you dress?"

She realized that Martha had been a silent audience to that encounter. "I will dress," she said, turning away from the window. "But I will keep my chamber this morning."

*   *   *

STUART LEFT HIS OWN CHAMBER HALF AN HOUR LATER, dressed with subdued elegance, an air of determined good humor on his handsome countenance, the coldness of his encounter with his wife resolutely dismissed. He had told Pippa the truth about his absence over the last two days, and the respite, brief though it had been, from the dreadful tension and humiliation of his deception had strengthened him.

Or so he thought until he came face-to-face with Lionel Ashton in the royal antechamber. One look at the man, when he turned and regarded Stuart with his air of contemptuous detachment, was sufficient to reduce Lord Nielson to the miserable wretch who had taken over his person.

"Lord Nielson, welcome back to court." Ashton bowed, smiled. "Your errand was successful, I trust."

"I bore the queen's messages, yes," Stuart said stiffly. "If the king chooses to hunt in Essex he will find all prepared."

Ashton nodded. His gaze roamed around the antechamber. "And your wife? Does she not accompany you this morning?"

Stuart felt himself flush; his fingers curled, the nails biting into his palms. "She keeps her chamber this morning."

Ashton nodded again. He inspected his own hands with a slight frown as if he found something amiss, and said without looking up, "Pregnancy is hard on a woman. I don't believe I have congratulated you as yet, Nielson."

Stuart's hand went to his sword hilt in an involuntary movement. He didn't think he could bear the contempt.

And then his hand fell to his side. He had no choice but to endure.

"I have been asked to keep a close eye on your wife. You will not object, I trust, if I visit her in her chamber?" Ashton inclined his head in question.

"If my wife has no objection, how could I?" Stuart said through stiff lips.

"Indeed," Ashton agreed with a faint smile. "I give you good morning, my lord." He bowed and strolled away, leaving Stuart to gather the shreds of his dignity around him and enter the competitive, malicious, dangerous fray that was Queen Mary's presence chamber.

LIONEL MADE HIS WAY SWIFTLY TO THE NIELSONS' apartments. No one would find anything untoward in his visiting Lady Nielson in her private chamber in the middle of the morning. Such ease of visiting among acquaintances was an accepted part of the court rituals. And besides, he had the husband's permission to pay his respects to the ailing wife.

He knocked on the door and the maid opened it.

"Is Lady Nielson receiving visitors?"

"One minute, sir. Who shall I say?"

"Mr. Ashton."

Martha left the door open a fraction. She returned in a second saying, "My lady will receive you, sir." She held the door wide.

"My thanks." He stepped into the chamber.

"That will be all, Martha," Pippa said, rising from a low chair by the empty hearth where she had been composing a letter to her sister.

"Mr. Ashton, this is an unexpected pleasure." She smiled at him, trying to keep the warmth, the rush of excitement from her expression, until the maid had left the chamber.

He took her hands. They had not been alone since the morning among the grass cuttings. "This is not one of your good days," he observed, assessing her washed-out countenance.

"It wasn't," she replied. "Not so far. But it might be improving."

Lightly he brushed the corner of her mouth with his own. " 'Tis a beautiful morning. Not one to be spent within doors."

"No," she agreed, tightening her fingers around his. "What do you suggest?"

"A few hours on the river. Come to the kitchen water steps in a half hour." He twisted a strand of her hair around his index finger and released it, smiling at the way the curl sprang tight again. "You will not be missed for a few hours."

A slight frown crossed her eyes. "You sound very certain."

He shrugged easily. "I met your husband. He said you were keeping to your chamber. No one will be looking for you."

The frown deepened but she said, "No, I suppose that is so." It was unlikely that Stuart would return after their earlier unsatisfactory meeting. And, besides, she thought, he had abdicated all rights to information about her movements, let alone to a say in them. The defiant anger was pointless, she knew, but it made her feel better.

Lionel regretted bringing Stuart's presence between them since it so clearly distressed her, and yet he could see no way to avoid it. Pippa's husband could not be ignored. "In half an hour," he repeated, touching her lips with his finger. "Bring a cloak. The air is cooler this morning."

The door closed behind him and Pippa ran both hands through her hair, pushing it away from her face, compulsively tucking unruly strands behind her ears as if it would order her world. But her world, reality, seemed to have broken the bounds of order. She was going to spend the next few hours with her lover. On the river, making love, losing herself in the immediacy of desire and passion and lust. She wanted nothing else. Her heart skipped, her thighs tightened, her loins ached at the knowledge.

But she couldn't ignore the other present, the other reality. She carried her husband's child. At some point there would have to be an accounting.

But in the meantime there was to be a morning on the river, and the chamber robe she was wearing would not do at all.

"Martha, bring me the red damask with the gold embroidered underskirt, if you please."

Pippa took up her hairbrush and pulled it through her hair, enjoying the way it sprang in luxuriant glossy curls from beneath the bristles. Pregnancy had some good effects it seemed. Her hair color was deeper, its texture thicker and richer. Her ordinarily minuscule bosom was growing more noticeable too. Maybe, when the nausea had passed, she could begin to enjoy her condition. The thought lifted her spirits even further.

Dressed to her satisfaction, her hair looped at her neck in a caul of fine silver filigree, a cloak of black taffeta cast carelessly around her shoulders, she left the chamber with her customary quick, light step.

Lionel waited at the kitchen water steps among the bustle of servants unloading barges laden with produce, game, sides of beef and mutton from the royal estates. The smell of blood and rotting vegetables crushed in the bottom of panniers and crates tinged the freshness of the morning air. Feeding the court was a massive and complex operation. The royal cellarman was screaming, red-faced, at a man who had brought him a cask of malmsey instead of the port he had ordered.

Lionel's stillness, his air of detachment in the midst of this near-chaos, seemed to render him invisible. He saw Pippa when she was some yards away and covertly watched her approach. She seemed almost to be skipping, her cloak flying out behind her with the speed of her progress.

He realized that it had been many weeks since he'd seen the lighthearted side of Lady Nielson. He'd first met her when he'd arrived at Southampton with the king on his wedding journey. Pippa and her husband had been part of the welcoming party who were to accompany the Spanish king and his court to Canterbury for the ceremony.

She had made little impression on him then, because she was not important to his own purposes. He knew only what was common knowledge, that she remained utterly loyal to Elizabeth and that the queen as a result held her at court as a virtual prisoner, regarding her with grave disfavor. But he had noticed how quick she was, both in speech and movements, and he'd guessed at the streak of rebellion lurking beneath the apparently compliant facade.

It was this, he decided, that earned her Mary's continued lack of favor. Mary was generally generous with her forgiveness and, since Stuart Nielson was one of her most devoted courtiers, it would have been quite natural for the queen to embrace the penitent Pippa on her release. But Pippa was not penitent. Oh, she was courteous, docile, but there was a look in those hazel eyes, a set to the mouth and jaw, even a quality to her thin angular nose that radiated defiance. And her tongue was swift and sharp, her wit laced with irony.

It was not surprising therefore that when Ruy Gomez and Simon Renard had hatched their little plot for ensuring the Spanish succession, Mary, after a long day spent on her knees in prayer, had not only agreed to the plan but had acquiesced almost with enthusiasm in their choice of the woman who was to receive the king's dubious gift.

The gift came with considerable penalty, a fact that Lionel suspected had sweetened the pill for the queen. A woman she suspected of disloyalty would be the only real sufferer. The husband's sins against the church were so heinous that he was entitled to no consideration, indeed in Mary's eyes he could consider himself fortunate that his punishment was not ultimate. She embraced her husband's game and played it with the consummate skill at deception that had kept her alive for close to forty years, and that had eventually brought her the throne.

Lionel walked to meet Pippa before her lively, colorful arrival could draw attention. He was unaware of the darkness of his expression. He didn't know how to prevent her suffering, and until the first night he had carried her unconscious body back to her husband he had not given it a second thought. He had seen only his task. He must thwart Philip's plans and he would do that by being a trusted partner in those plans. If the woman conceived and was brought to bed he would see to it that the baby did not fulfill the role Philip and his advisors intended. Its mother was merely incidental, to be dealt with in whatever way was necessary. The future of his country depended upon it.

But Lionel knew now that he had overestimated his ability to distance himself from the grim truths behind his actions. When he had held Pippa's slight, almost weightless frame in his arms he had been forced to accept his own part, even as a mere bystander, in her violation. She had become real to him, her humanity as strong as the pulse he could see beating in her throat beneath the white skin.

He had watched the bystanders at Margaret's burning, and he had cried out loud in anguish at their dumb, blind acceptance of what they were seeing.

He would not have Pippa hurt further, and yet he could see no way to avoid it. Philip would not get the child. He would make certain of that. But Pippa would have to be hidden, live a life of exile, and in order for her to agree to that she would have to know the truth. And Lionel could not bear that.

"Oh, you look angry!" Pippa exclaimed as they met. "Has something troubled you?"

"This damnable court troubles me," he said. It was time to start hinting at the truth if he was to gain her full confidence.

Pippa looked at him with sudden intensity. "And what does that mean? I thought you a stout supporter of our present court."

"Appearances can be deceiving." He offered her his arm.

She didn't immediately take it. "That is certainly true. But would you have me believe that you are not what you seem?" Her expression was troubled, the sunny aspect of a minute ago vanished.

"Not in anything of importance," he stated. "Not in any way that should distress you, Pippa."

She swallowed, stared at him fixedly. "I have had one betrayal, Lionel, almost more than I can endure, I cannot bear another one." With a slight gesture she half turned to leave.

Lionel took her arm. "I swear to you, love, that I will not betray you."

She turned back, said simply, "Then I will believe you."

Pippa didn't know why she accepted his declaration without question. She had no reason to do so, and every reason that experience dictated not to. And yet she did. She accepted his word as she would accept that of Robin, or Pen, or her parents.

Lionel drew her away from the water steps. Beneath his calm, smiling exterior, a worm of self-disgust turned. He would keep his oath. He would not betray her.

Not again.

"Where are we going? I thought we were to take a boat on the river."

"We are. But there's a rather more secluded mooring spot just a little way along the river. I have a penchant for privacy."

Pippa inclined her head in slightly ironic agreement. "I had certainly noticed that you're never the life and soul of the party, Mr. Ashton."

"Alas," he agreed with a mournful sigh. "I have no talent for small talk."

Pippa merely smiled in response and said nothing further. He had offered her a chink in his armor of reticence. Just why did he find this court *damnable*? Damnable enough to bring that forbidding set to his mouth, the darkness to his eyes, that she'd surprised when he came to meet her. Whatever his thoughts, they had not been pleasant.

If he was in fact *not* loyal to Philip and Mary, then what deep game was he playing? Could he be an ally, a fellow conspirator in the plans to secure Elizabeth's succession?

She stumbled against a protruding tree root, so deep was she in her reflections. Lionel caught her against him and Pippa realized that they were alone under the trees. The residue of the night's storm still dripped from the leaves and a spot fell onto the bridge of her nose when she turned her face up to his.

She forgot all questions, all speculation. There was just this moment when the crushed grass at her feet smelled sweetly of rain, a ray of sunlight pierced the dripping leaves above her and fell across her face, and with a swift dart his tongue licked the drop of rain from her nose. Then his mouth took hers and she leaned into him, her lips parting beneath his, their tongues fencing, curling around each other in a playful dance. It was a deep and passionate kiss that made her knees tremble and brought an urgent surging need to her loins.

Breathless, they drew apart again. Lionel smiled at her. "Good morning," he said. "We omitted the courtesies earlier."

"So we did. I give you good morning, sir," she replied.

He took her hand and led her along the narrow path to a point where the trees thinned and there was a natural break in the riverbank, forming a small cove. A rowing boat was tethered to the trunk of a weeping willow.

" 'Tis hard to believe the palace is only a few steps away," Pippa said in wonder. It was so quiet here, the overhanging willow trees forming a living canopy over the little cove.

"The riverbank holds many such secrets," Lionel said, bending to take the painter and haul the little boat up to the bank. He jumped lightly into the boat and held up his hands to her. "Can you step down?"

"Easily." She took his hands and with an agile leap landed beside him. "I don't suppose I shall be able to do that when I become fat."

He made no response and she wondered if perhaps he considered it tactless to refer to her pregnancy when they were about to embark on a morning of love. But then she decided that since it was now an essential part of her and certainly couldn't be ignored, it must become a part of this love.

"Make yourself comfortable on the cushions." Lionel indicated the thick silken pile in the stern.

"Oh, a love nest!" Pippa exclaimed, flopping down on the cushions, arranging her skirts around her. "How delightful."

"Do you always say just what comes into your head?" Lionel inquired, busying himself with the painter.

"Generally, when I feel comfortable." She leaned back, watching him as he untied the boat. He was dressed very plainly in workmanlike leather hose and doublet with a plain linen shirt that he wore unlaced at the neck, without a ruff. The simplicity of his garb suited him; it seemed to accentuate the power and competence of his movements, and for some reason it made her toes curl with anticipation.

"Does my free speech bother you?" she asked, hearing a husky rasp in her voice that was not normally there.

"Not in the least. It pleases me that you feel

comfortable enough in my company to be yourself." He glanced over his shoulder at her, his eyes gleaming. "And it is indeed intended as a love nest."

Pippa's toes curled ever tighter in her thin slippers, and she shifted slightly on her silken bed. "Why do we have to go anywhere? Why can't we just stay here?"

Lionel seemed to consider. Then he retied the boat. "I don't mind doing without the exercise," he observed amenably.

"You refer to rowing exercise, I trust?" Pippa's raised eyebrow belied her innocent smile.

"Is there another kind?" He dropped down on the cushions beside her and unclasped the cloak at her throat. It slipped away from her and he ran a fingertip up the side of her neck to trace the curve of her ear.

She turned on her side to face him, her own fingertips exploring his features as if she would learn every contour, every plane of his countenance. She leaned forward and kissed his eyelids, then fluttered her eyelashes against his cheeks in a delicate butterfly of a kiss.

"I know you wished to make love without the impediment of cloth," he murmured against her ear. "But I don't see how that can be managed here." He nibbled her earlobe, before dipping his tongue within, tracing the delicate whorls, making her squirm with ticklish delight.

"One should always have something to look forward to," Pippa whispered, lying back on the cushions, reaching her arms around his neck, pulling him down to her. She moved her thighs apart so that he could lie along her length, his elbows propped on either side of her head, his legs within her own.

He kissed her slowly, savoring her mouth as if enjoying a particularly fine wine. He moved his tongue over her lips, and traced the contours of her face in a moist caress. He lowered his head to the swell of her breasts above the low neckline of her gown. The delicate fragrance of her skin sent his senses reeling.

She twisted her fingers into his hair, feeling it slightly coarse and thick to the touch. She tugged at it playfully and scratched his scalp with her nails. His breath was warm on her skin as his tongue stroked into the cleft of her breasts.

He rolled sideways onto the cushions beside her. Propped on one elbow he slowly, leisurely, lifted her skirts, up over her silk-stockinged legs to her waist.

Pippa felt the air cool on her bared skin where his caressing hand was warm as it smoothed over her thighs and belly. He kissed her belly, dipping his tongue into her navel. He slid a hand between her thighs, a finger tracing little circles on the soft inner skin.

Her body dissolved the instant he put his mouth to her sex. She cried out, pressing her hands to her lips to silence herself.

He raised his head and laughed softly. "You're gratifyingly easy to please, my love. I had barely begun."

"It's you," she said, when she had breath enough to speak. "I think you could make that happen just by looking at me."

"I must try it one day," he said with a grin. "In the queen's presence chamber, perhaps?"

Pippa's eyes widened. "You wouldn't?"

"Wait and see."

He knelt up between her thighs and Pippa brushed his hands aside as he moved to unlace his britches. She did the job herself swiftly, eagerly, then held him, rolling his penis between her hands, marveling at its hard, pulsating power. She sat up and delicately kissed the tip, tasting the salty moisture that gathered there.

"I never realized before what a beautiful part of a man this is," she said, examining his flesh as thoughtfully as if she were assessing the virtues of an object in a curio store. She kissed it again, smiling up at him as she did so. "Are women as beautiful?"

"I would say more so," Lionel responded, finding himself aroused almost beyond bearing by this strangely matter-of-fact discussion that so belied the knowingness of her touch. "But then I'm biased."

"Ah, I suppose you are." She held his penis against her cheek, rubbing it with quick yet soft movements.

Lionel gave a short exclamation and stilled her hand. "Enough, Pippa!"

She smiled again. "As you say." She lay down on the cushions again, sliding her body down, raising her hips in invitation. "Is this more to your liking, sir?"

"You are a wicked woman!"

"I do seem to be," she agreed smugly. "But I didn't know I was until I met you." She gave a little sigh as he slid into her body. "Why does this feel so right, Lionel? As if it was always meant to be." Her eyes closed and he understood the question to be purely rhetorical, which was fortunate since he was incapable of answering.

When they drew apart finally they lay in a tangle of limbs and creased clothes. Pippa kept her eyes closed, inhaling the earthy scent of sex that seemed to mingle with the loamy river smells and the rain-damp grass. It was right, this that was between them. Pure and right. Once again she could find no scruple of conscience. Sleep claimed her, inexorable.

Lionel lay watching her. He had never felt so in tune with anyone before, so absolutely perfectly matched.

And yet this wonderful thing had grown in the soil of a grievous violation, a hideous betrayal. And Pippa knew none of that. How could he possibly keep the purity of this that they had when it had sprung from such corrupt roots?

Pippa awoke with a start, for a moment disoriented. She had dipped deep into sleep but only for a brief interval. Lionel's face was bent over her and her dream of the night before came back to her, startlingly vivid. She had been lying somewhere, on something, she didn't know what, and a bird, some giant bird with a massive wingspan had hovered over her, its talons spread to seize her and carry her off. She had been helpless, unable to move, or to cry out.

She stared up at Lionel's countenance and saw there the same darkness of expression that she had surprised earlier. Still in the tangle of dream memory she was suddenly frightened and confused, and then he smiled the sweet, compassionate smile that had first drawn her to him, that now filled her with such comfort and reassurance.

He said quietly, "You look troubled, love."

"No." She sat up, pushing down her skirt. "I think I was asleep, and I woke up too quickly. I felt sick for an instant." Pippa didn't know why she was lying to him about something so insignificant. How difficult could it be to tell him she'd remembered a strange dream? It happened to people all the time. But the lie had just spilled from her lips.

Lionel didn't believe her. She was too transparent a soul to be an effective liar, but he could see no reason why she should dissemble on the heels of such a perfect union. He chose not to question.

He stood up in the boat and it rocked in the little

cove. Swiftly he laced his hose as Pippa tidied herself, keeping her eyes down, seemingly intent on her task of smoothing out the creases in the fine damask.

"I did bring some dry bread, if you think that will help?" he observed, bending to pull a wicker hamper from beneath the thwart. He opened the hamper. The scent of ripe strawberries was heady on the air.

"Strawberries!" Pippa exclaimed, welcoming the distraction that broke the strange stilted atmosphere that had fallen so abruptly between them. "How did you get strawberries in September?"

"They're hothouse grown," he said, taking out a wooden box where a layer of deep red, glistening fruit lay on a bed of soft green moss. "I thought you might enjoy them."

He set the box on the thwart and brought out a flagon of wine, and another of mead. "Unless you prefer plain bread." A loaf of wheaten bread joined the strawberries.

"I adore strawberries!" Pippa declared, her eyes bright. "I am so tired of plain fare."

He couldn't help but laugh at her greedy expression and the moment of tension dissipated. He sat beside her on the cushions again. He held a strawberry to her lips and she opened her mouth wide. He laughed again and lay back watching her expression.

"Delicious." She lay down again, resting her head in his lap. "Feed me!"

Lionel smiled at the importunate demand that so adroitly returned the sensual dimension to their morning on the river. He took a deep draught of crisp rhenish from the flagon of wine, then set about his task in earnest, painting her lips with strawberry juice that she licked off with quick darts of her tongue, teasing her tongue with the fruit, letting her suck it before relinquishing it between her red and eager lips.

"Aren't you going to have any?" she asked with a lazily resurgent conscience.

"I brought them for you." He bent over her, holding a piece of fruit just above her mouth.

The clear gray eyes held her own.

And she saw it again. The giant bird, the predatory beak, sharp gray eyes.

"No . . . no thank you," she said, pushing his hand aside. "You eat the rest. I think I've had sufficient." She sat up, moving sideways so that she was once more resting on the cushions, but she kept a space between their bodies.

Lionel popped the berry into his own mouth. He leaned sideways for the flagon again, took another draught, making his movements casual, matter-of-fact, as if he could not feel the tension radiating from her, as if he was unaware of the dreadful anxiety that emanated from her like an aura.

"I have mead." He stretched sideways for the other flagon. He pulled the top with his teeth and passed it to her.

"My thanks." Pippa took a sip. "Forgive me . . . I . . . I had a strange dream last night that I couldn't remember. But for some reason I'm remembering bits of it now, and 'tis making me uncomfortable. I don't know why."

She laughed, a nervous and unconvincing laugh. "Pregnancy probably. Everything can be explained away by pregnancy."

Lionel slid an arm beneath her and drew her against him. Her head rested in the hollow of his shoulder.

"Bad dreams come at any time," he said. "Try to sleep now. I'll hold you safe."

His voice soothed her. She trusted him. It was hardly surprising that her dreams these days reflected confused images of cruelty and helplessness. After what Stuart had done to her . . .

But in Lionel's arms she could sleep in safety. He was her perfect match. She would trust him with her life.

Thirteen

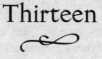

DONA BERNARDINA AWOKE FROM HER SIESTA RATHER earlier than usual. She lay in her darkened bedchamber with the now familiar sense that something felt awry, as if the calm routine of her daily life had been disturbed. She sat up, gathering her chamber robe around her, and rose from the bed.

She peered in the half-light at the face of the little clock on the mantel. It told her it was barely three in the afternoon. She always slept until four, when she took a light *merienda* to tide her over until she and Luisa sat down for their evening meal at eight.

She drew aside the curtains. It was an overcast afternoon, with a hint of autumn in the air, now that the heat wave had broken. She looked down at the garden. There was only a gardener to be seen, pruning the roses that still bloomed vigorously in the bed that bordered the terrace. At the end of the garden the strip of the river showed as a dull gray.

Bernardina drew her robe tighter around her. The cloudy skies and the dull river made her cold and she wished she was back in her native Seville under the brassy skies and the heat of the midafternoon sun that hammered itself into the white cobbles of the interior patio of the Mendoza residence. There she would sit with Luisa's mother, feeling the heat in her bones, lazily fanning herself, sipping a cooling drink amid the scents of jasmine, oranges, and roses, while the fountain plashed and Luisa practiced her harp in the shade of the colonnaded cloister.

Luisa was such a good child. She never gave her duenna a moment's anxiety. She was always sweetly obedient to her mother's dictates . . . until the unfortunate marriage proposal.

Bernardina turned from the window, shaking her head. Then they had seen a different side of their girl. She had been obdurate. Polite, quiet, but utterly determined in her refusal to accept the Marques de Perez as her husband. She had insisted that her father would not have compelled her to accept a marriage distasteful to her, and her dear mother had had to agree.

Dona Maria had appealed to Don Ashton as her late husband's confidant and family friend. He had supported Luisa in the private discussions he had had with her mother, and then had offered to take her to England with him. It had seemed like salvation to Luisa's distraught mother, and Dona Bernardina had shouldered the burden of accompanying the child without a word of complaint.

Now, however, she deeply regretted her sacrifice. Nothing was right, nothing was as it was supposed to be. Luisa was not the sweet girl she had known. She couldn't put her finger on it, but something was different. And Don Ashton was not fulfilling his promised duties as guardian.

Bernardina's mouth pursed and she nodded her head

in vigorous agreement with her reflections. Grasping her robe ever more tightly around her as if to shield herself from the evil influences this dreadful land contained, she left her bedchamber and went along the corridor to Luisa's.

She tapped on the door. There was no answer. Luisa had dutifully gone for her siesta after their midday meal. Perhaps she was still asleep? Dona Bernardina softly opened the door.

The chamber was in full light, the windows unshuttered, the curtains drawn back. The bed was empty, no indentation of a head on the pillow.

Bernardina closed the door at her back. She looked around. Every instinct rebelled at the idea of snooping among Luisa's possessions but surely she had a responsibility. If the lax moral climate in this wretched country was corrupting her charge, then Bernardina had a duty to Luisa's mother to put a stop to it.

She opened drawers in the chest, peered into the armoire, but her heart was not in it. She saw nothing to confirm her suspicions and was not prepared to dig and delve.

Her unease unabated, Bernardina returned to her own chamber and rang the handbell for her maid.

"I will dress, Ana."

Ana was one of the few servants they had been able to bring from Seville; room on the boats that had transported the party had been hard to come by. Ana had served Bernardina for twenty years and despite her years was still spry and still had an ear to servants' gossip.

She helped her mistress into the formal gown without which Bernardina would not show her face downstairs, even if there was no one in the house but herself.

"Have you seen Dona Luisa this afternoon?" Bernardina inquired casually, adjusting her mantilla.

"No, madam. Is she not in her chamber?"

"I expect she went for a walk," Bernardina said. "Or perhaps for a ride with that Malcolm."

"Malcolm has gone into the city, madam. He had some errands to run for Don Ashton."

"I see." Bernardina offered a smile that she hoped was casual enough to deflect Ana's curiosity. "I don't care for this mantilla, Ana. Bring me the black one with the gold embroidery."

Bernardina made her stately progress downstairs just as the master of the house came in through the front door.

Lionel cast aside his cloak, tossed his riding whip onto the bench by the door, and stripped off his gloves. He saw Bernardina standing both hesitant and expectant on the bottom step of the staircase.

"Dona Bernardina." He bowed, trying to conceal his impatience. Everything about the woman shouted a need to unburden herself about something. And that something had to be Luisa. He was already feeling guilty about his neglect of his ward, but he couldn't seem to find the time to devote his energies to her concerns.

"I must beg a few minutes of your time, Don Ashton." Bernardina stepped down as she spoke and offered him a hurried curtsy.

Lionel sighed inaudibly. "Indeed, madam. I am at your disposal." He gestured towards the parlor. It was on the tip of his tongue to ask where Luisa was, but prescience bit his tongue.

"Don Ashton, I am very concerned about Luisa," Bernardina began.

Prescience could not be faulted. He nodded, perching on the carved arm of a gilt chair. "What is the trouble, madam?"

"I don't know exactly," Bernardina said. "But she is not in the house at the moment, and I believe it is not the first time."

Lionel frowned. "She is not a prisoner, Dona Bernardina."

The woman's faded complexion took on a pinkish hue. "That may be so, but it would be only courteous of her to inform me, her duenna, of where she is going. Instead she slips out when I am asleep. That is not right, Don Ashton."

"You have no idea where she is?"

The woman shook her head. "She has become very secretive, that is another thing. She always confided in me before, but now she has secrets, I *know* it."

Lionel's frown deepened. "She is a young woman now, madam. 'Tis only natural that she should wish for some privacy."

Bernardina shook her head vigorously. "No, that is not the way a young Spanish maiden should behave."

"Well, tell me exactly what you suspect."

"I do not *know*," Bernardina declared. "That is why I am so worried."

"If you do not know, I cannot see what I can do." Lionel's impatience crept into his voice. He couldn't imagine what harm Luisa could come to. If she went out riding she had Malcolm with her, if she went on the river she had the boatmen.

"You have allowed her too much freedom, Don Ashton," Bernardina said, her color growing higher. "If you had not encouraged her to ride out by herself, she would not have taken strange notions into her head."

"But what *are* these strange notions?"

Bernardina's mouth pursed. Again she could put no words to her suspicions because apart from her present absence Luisa had said or done nothing apparently out of the ordinary. And yet her duenna *knew* that something was going on.

"Would you like me to talk to her?" Lionel offered, seeing the woman's wordless distress.

"Yes, and you must tell her that she may no longer leave the house without my permission, and you must dismiss that Malcolm."

It was a social taboo for Bernardina to give the master of the house orders or to use such a peremptory tone and it told Lionel that Bernardina was even more upset than he'd thought.

He said gently, "Let's not overreact, madam. There can be no harm in her going out with Malcolm's escort. I will talk with her this evening."

Bernardina shook her head and dabbed at her eyes with a corner of her mantilla. "If harm should befall her, Don Ashton, I will have to answer to her mother."

"No harm will befall her. What possibly could happen to her?" He was once more impatient.

Bernardina turned her head aside and whispered, "Men," as if the word was almost too evil to be spoken aloud.

Lionel might have laughed, except that he understood the seriousness of such a fear for an aristocratic Spanish matron in charge of an aristocratic Spanish maiden. "Oh, come now, madam, Luisa hasn't met any men," he pointed out. "She's not been to court, she has no society."

"Nevertheless, she has come under some evil influence." Bernardina nodded vigorously.

This struck Lionel as overstating the case, but he made no attempt to argue with her. She was clearly distraught. "Very well, I will talk with her this evening," he repeated. "Now you must excuse me, Dona Bernardina, I have an audience with the king in an hour." He bowed and turned to the door.

It opened and Luisa stood there, her cheeks flushed, her eyes bright. "Why, Don Ashton, we don't usually see you at this hour."

He regarded her closely. "I understand you've been out of the house, Luisa. Dona Bernardina was concerned."

"Oh, Bernardina, why would you be concerned? You know I cannot sleep in the daytime. I went for a walk in the garden and a stroll by the river. What harm can there be in that?"

"What indeed?" Lionel agreed, glancing at Bernardina. "There, madam, I told you there was nothing to worry about."

Bernardina saw that whatever support she might have gained from Don Ashton was now gone. He was palpably relieved at Luisa's reappearance and clearly only too happy to accept her innocent explanation, one that Bernardina herself didn't believe for a moment.

"There is mud on your shoes and on the hem of your gown." She pointed to the offending dirt with a moue of distaste. "That is most indecorous, Luisa."

"I explained that I was walking along the river," Luisa said with a sharp edge to her voice. " 'Tis muddy there."

Bernardina tried one more shot before Don Ashton could make his escape. "Did you meet with anyone while you were walking?"

Luisa shook her head. She modified her tone, saying

reasonably, "I don't believe so, Bernardina. Oh, I may have exchanged a word with the gardener, and I believe I passed a fisherman or two along the bank." She shrugged. "Is there anything wrong in that?"

Bernardina was defeated. She could see it in Don Ashton's expression.

He said cheerfully, attempting to dispel the strained atmosphere, "Well, I will leave you two ladies to enjoy your afternoon. If I can I will sup with you this evening."

"Perhaps you could bring a guest?" Luisa suggested, gazing up at him with wide-eyed innocence. "It would be so enlivening to see a fresh face and have someone new to talk to."

Bernardina drew a sharp breath and Lionel's eyes narrowed. It was not Luisa's place to make such a suggestion and she certainly wouldn't have done so at home in her parents' house. He looked at her more closely. There *was* something different about her. An air of self-possession that he hadn't noticed before. And her deep blue eyes were particularly bright and shiny, as if something had pleased and excited her.

He was about to dismiss her request when it occurred to him that there really was nothing objectionable to the idea. It would salve his conscience a little if he could give her some outside entertainment, and since the guests would be chosen by him Dona Bernardina could not really protest.

He turned to the duenna. "Would it put the household out too much if I invited a couple of guests for supper this evening, madam? It is short notice, I know."

Bernardina bridled. "Why, of course there would be no difficulty, Don Ashton. I ensure that the household is provisioned and run well enough to accommodate twenty people at table at the shortest of notice."

He offered a placatory bow. "I know your talents, madam, and appreciate them every day."

Bernardina smiled for the first time in the interview. Indeed the prospect of guests pleased her almost as much as it did Luisa. She would enjoy organizing the supper party, something she had done often in Seville. Her mind was already turning to menus.

"How many guests should we expect, Don Ashton?"

Lionel considered. An idea had come to him. He could see a way to make this supper party both pleasurable and also useful.

"No more than two, I believe," he replied. "But I cannot guarantee that at such short notice the guests I have in mind will be free, so you mustn't be too disappointed, Luisa, if it can't be managed today. If not I will arrange it for another day."

Luisa lowered her eyes as she curtsied, murmuring, "You are so kind, Don Ashton. I know I plague you unmercifully."

"Not quite unmercifully," he said dryly. "But it does seem that you cause your duenna some concern. It would please me if you would be a little more considerate."

Dona Bernardina looked gratified and Luisa swallowed the reproof without visible annoyance, although inside she seethed. It seemed that the more often she escaped for a few hours with Robin the harder it was to return to the confines and constraints of the house and Bernardina's stolid, predictable company.

This afternoon they had merely walked a little along the river. In that she had not lied. Robin had told her of his childhood, of the mother he could no longer remember, of his stepmother and his stepsisters, whom he adored. The description of their lives, their childhood freedom, had made Luisa ache with envy.

Robin had had only an hour to spare to walk with her that afternoon but he had promised that the next time they met he would tell her the story of his sister Pen's first marriage, and the excitement and adventure of her second to the French spy Owen d'Arcy. For Luisa these stories were as entrancing and fascinating as anything she could read in a book. More so, she amended, since the *Lives of the Saints* was her main source of reading material.

Robin had also promised to take her to a real gaming house one night very soon. Luisa lived on these promises and stories, hoarding them, taking them out and examining them whenever the tedium of her daily life became too oppressive. Now, as the door closed behind her guardian, she sat down with her tambour frame and returned in her head to her walk and talk with Robin. There had been a moment when he had held her hand. So easily, so naturally. He had only released it when they'd come under the observation of the fishermen on the bank.

Luisa hugged the memory to her and when Bernardina began to discuss the dishes that should be served at supper she was able to respond with an enthusiasm that gratified her duenna.

LIONEL LEFT THE HOUSE HALF AN HOUR LATER dressed for an audience with the king. In the stable yard he met Malcolm, who had just returned from the city.

"Sir." Malcolm greeted his master with a bow. He reached inside his doublet and handed Lionel a slim leather-wrapped packet. "Captain Olson gave me this for you."

"Good. He had a quiet voyage from Bruges?"

"Aye, sir. He said he would be returning on Saturday's high tide, so will take any dispatches you have."

"I will have several. You may take them to the dock for me first thing Saturday morning." Lionel tucked the packet into his inside pocket. "Tell me, Malcolm, how are your rides with Dona Luisa?"

Malcolm frowned slightly. "Without incident, sir. The lady rides well and likes to gallop."

Lionel nodded. "Where do you ride?"

"Along the river mostly, sir. Wherever she can let Crema have her head." Malcolm coughed into his closed fist before remarking, "I have the feeling that the lady feels very constrained, sir. Riding gets the fidgets out of her."

Lionel raised his eyebrows. "You may well be right. Just as long as that is all she is doing."

Malcolm shrugged. "She enjoys watching people, sir. On occasion she will exchange greetings. But she has never in my company dismounted."

"Good. See that she doesn't. In her country, the reputation of a lady of her lineage cannot be compromised even by a whisper."

"She is safe with me, sir."

"I know it. Otherwise I would not have entrusted her to you." Lionel smiled, slapped the man's shoulder in easy camaraderie, and mounted his own horse.

He rode back towards Whitehall, the packet of letters burning a hole in his shirt. He had no time to look at them now but they were enough to have him executed for treason. His sister Margaret had been active in the Reformation and had died for her beliefs. Lionel had little commitment to his sister's choice of worship, but he loathed the regime that had killed her. He loathed the fanaticism that led to the hideous persecution of those who chose another way of worship. Flanders and the Netherlands suffered most dreadfully beneath the Catholic yoke and it was among those who fought Spain's dominion there that Lionel drew his support for the defense of England.

There would be promissory notes in the letters in his pocket for funds to be drawn on local bankers and promises of ships and armaments from the Flemish burghers if England should rise up against Philip and Mary. In return, he would supply information about the anti-Catholic movement in England, about how those who worked to undermine Mary planned to proceed. The news of Mary's pregnancy would not yet have reached Flanders, but it would cause an uproar. Lionel had not divulged the Spanish insurance plan should Mary fail to produce an heir, and he had no intention of doing so.

Pippa was now his concern. His alone. And he would guard her safety jealously. He had helped to make her Philip's victim, he would do everything in his power now to undo the damage. It had become almost a sacred duty, an absolute obligation. Only by fulfilling it would he be able to live with himself.

He left his horse in the massive stable complex of the palace, and made his leisurely way towards Philip's private office. As he expected, Renard and Ruy Gomez were in attendance.

Philip laid down his quill and looked up from the parchment on his desk. He had a weary air, as if he was short of sleep. He sanded the sheet of parchment as he said, "Lionel, we bid you welcome."

"Sire." Lionel bowed to the king, then offered a courteous greeting to the other two men. "You wished to see me?"

"The woman." Philip's nose twitched, his mouth turned down as if the very mention of the woman he had violated was repugnant.

His next words confirmed the impression. "We don't care to see her every day. My wife finds it very difficult, very distressing . . . and of course nothing must be allowed to upset the queen in her present condition."

"Of course not," Lionel agreed smoothly. "What do you suggest we do about Lady Nielson?" He spoke her name with quiet deliberation, compelling the men in the office to affix a face and a personality to their tool.

An expression of fastidious distaste crossed Philip's face. Whenever he debauched a woman he would confess and do penance and was then disgusted by his victim, as if her violation and his own fall from grace had been her fault. He did not answer Lionel's question. It was Ruy Gomez who spoke.

"The husband cannot be trusted to care for her. And her family are too powerful, their allegiance too uncertain, for us to permit them to take her under their roof until her pregnancy is resolved. Fortunately they are still in Derbyshire and we have already sent a messenger with the order that they remain there. Owing to their daughter's disloyalty to the queen her family are not welcome at court or even in London. Lady Nielson herself must not leave the palace, but she must be taken out of circulation. The king has written an order to that effect."

Philip nodded and folded the parchment on which

he'd been writing, dropped hot wax on the fold, and pressed his signet ring into the wax. "You will take it to her and her husband, Ashton." He held the sheet across the desk.

Lionel took it, held it loosely at his side. He observed thoughtfully, "Everyone knows that the queen holds the lady in disfavor. I see no reason why it should cause undue remark if Lady Nielson is forbidden the queen's presence."

He paused before continuing, "For the sake of appearances her husband should, of course, remain in the queen's favor. Fully occupied in her service, and of course, the king's." He bowed to Philip.

"It will make it easier to keep him under close watch," Philip remarked. "How much contact is he to have with his wife?" He leaned forward over the desk, his hands clasped on the papers in front of him.

"I don't think that should concern us. He spends very little time in her company at present, I see no reason for that to change. But I would suggest, sire, that Lady Nielson continue in Don Ashton's charge." Ruy Gomez made his suggestion softly and Simon Renard nodded.

"Aye, and that should be made clear to the husband," the ambassador declared.

Philip regarded Lionel closely from heavily hooded eyes. " 'Tis an irksome task, I fear, Lionel."

Lionel's expression was customarily impassive. "Not beyond endurance, sire. She will be required to keep to her own chambers, to walk about the palace only where she can be certain of not encountering Her Majesty. I imagine, since her health is of some importance, she would be permitted some freedom to walk about the grounds, to take a gentle ride on a well-mannered horse, to spend a little time on the river, while the weather remains clement."

"Yes . . . yes . . . we cannot risk her health. She is to follow our physicians' orders at all times. They will examine her weekly and she will obey their dictates."

Lionel glanced up at the great court portrait of Henry VIII and his family that hung above Philip's desk. Such a harmonious picture of family life, such a complacent paterfamilias. No one would guess at the innumerable betrayals, the cruel treacheries, the violent denunciations that informed the happy scene. He took his time with his response.

"Lady Nielson is no fool, sire. She will ask questions. Why should she, of all the women of the court fortunate enough to find themselves in her happy condition, be subjected to such close and careful attention from the queen's physicians? A woman, in addition, who's been ostracized by the court at the queen's command."

"It matters not," Philip said with a dismissive gesture. "Let her question how she wishes, she will receive no answers." He swung his head towards Ruy Gomez. "The husband remains compliant?"

"Aye, sire. And will do so for as long as there is threat to his paramour."

"Perhaps the threat should become manifest." Simon Renard spoke now, drawing his black cloak around him as if feeling a chill. "An accident, nothing too serious. Just enough to make sure they don't become complacent."

"The musician is already scared out of his mind," Gomez said. "The love nest Nielson has created in the palace terrifies him. He would prefer the anonymity of the tavern. But you are right, Renard, Nielson could perhaps do with a reminder that his lover is vulnerable."

"I will arrange something," Renard said. "Nothing too serious, just a little accident."

"And you, Ashton, will keep the wife happy."

Lionel bowed. "In as far as it's within my capability, sire."

"And you will find a way to deal with awkward questions?" Renard asked with an intent frown.

"In as far as it is within my capability, sir." The papers in Lionel's doublet seemed suddenly twice the thickness, their bulk easily visible to a sharp-eyed suspicious watcher.

"We have every faith in you, Lionel." Philip rose, his expression amiable, his hand outstretched.

Lionel took the hand, bowed over it. "I am honored, sire. I will do all I can to earn your trust."

"We know it." Philip smiled. "We place our trust in our good servant."

Lionel glanced at the two others in the office. They were both smiling their acquiescence in the king's declaration. "I give you good afternoon, my lords." He bowed once more and left the king's office, the order forbidding Lady Nielson's presence in open court still held loosely at his side.

She would be a virtual prisoner, able to leave the palace only with the permission and in the company of Lionel Ashton, who was to all intents and purposes now her jailer.

And her protector.

Fourteen

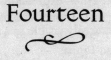

LIONEL WENT IMMEDIATELY TO THE NIELSONS' APART-
ments. His step quickened as he drew closer and he
wondered how he would find her. Would she be wan
and tired? Or bright and sparkling the way he so loved
to see her? Whatever her state of mind it was not going
to be improved by the harsh message he brought her, he
reflected grimly. Her initial reaction was going to be
one of dismay and indignation, but if she would listen to
him, he thought he knew how to soften the blow.

He heard the uproar before he reached her door.
Pippa's voice raised in anger, a hubbub of male voices,
Stuart Nielson's the loudest of them all.

Stuart was saying, "For God's sake, madam, you dare
to countermand the queen's order? To refuse such con-
descension, such consideration?"

"I have no need of either!"

On Pippa's furious rejoinder, Lionel entered the
chamber without attempting to knock. It wouldn't have
been heard anyway.

Pippa was standing at bay, with her back to the bedcurtains, her hand at her throat holding her chamber

robe drawn tightly around her. Three men in black gowns, black hoods with the lappets tied firmly beneath their chins, stood in a half circle facing her. They clutched the leather bags that, with their costume, denoted their profession. They were the queen's physicians.

Stuart Nielson was attempting to take hold of his wife but judging by her expression she would stick a knife in his gullet first. Lionel was unable to suppress a grin. He wouldn't give these four a ghost of a chance against the enraged Pippa.

She saw him first and the look of relief in her eyes made his heart turn over. Through no fault of her own she was beset on all sides, friendless and without the support of her family. Her brother could do some things to aid her, but he could not stand against the might of a royal decree. It was clear from her eyes that Pippa believed the one person who would be able to support her had come to her side.

"What on earth's going on here?" Lionel asked. "You can all be heard from the far end of the corridor."

"I will not have these . . . these leeches . . . these black crows poking and prodding me, even if they are the queen's physicians," Pippa declared in disgust, her eyes bright with anger and conviction. "I will have my mother's physician to examine me if I must be examined. They are saying they have to confirm my pregnancy. God's blood, do they think I don't know my own condition?"

"You cannot dismiss the queen's attendants," Stuart said, a note of desperation in his voice. He too looked at Lionel as if upon a savior. "You must explain that to her, Mr. Ashton."

"We have the queen's orders, sir," one of the black-clad figures declared. "Lady Nielson is to submit to our examination every week."

"God's blood! But I would rather die!" Pippa exclaimed, her voice rising alarmingly. "I will have my mother's physician or none at all, and so I tell you *all*!" She glared at them.

"I think it best if you leave the lady in peace for this afternoon," Lionel stated. "It cannot be good for her health to become so distressed."

"A serene mind is certainly the greatest aid to a successful pregnancy," the same physician said reluctantly, pulling at his neat gray beard. "But what are we to tell the queen?"

"You may tell her that since Lady Nielson was very fatigued and rather emotional you felt it advisable to complete the examination another day." Lionel went to the door and opened it in a gesture that combined invitation with command.

There was a moment's hesitation, while the physicians looked between their furious potential patient and the calm but clearly authoritative man holding open the door. No one took any notice of Lord Nielson, still standing close to his wife.

"Very well, sir. We shall return another time." The spokesman for the group peered at the lady. "Your color is high, madam. I would advise letting a little blood and taking only curds and whey for the next two days."

"Get out!" Pippa demanded, pointing to the door. "If you think I'm going to let you weaken me with your leeches, you may think again. Leave me in peace and my color will return to normal, I promise you!"

Muttering, the three swept from the chamber. Lionel closed the door on them.

Pippa hadn't moved from her spot by the bed, but

she was frowning now. It had occurred to her that something was very wrong with this picture. Lionel had marched into her bedchamber as if he belonged there. He had taken charge of the situation, ignoring Pippa's husband, just as if he had every right. Stuart had offered no remonstrance but had simply stood aside and let Lionel take over.

She was accustomed to, although still puzzled by, her husband's unusual subservience to the Spanish, but why with Lionel Ashton? Was it simply because he was part of the Spanish contingent and stood close to the king, and was therefore due the same deference? She shot a speculative glance at Stuart. He was standing in silence radiating acute discomfort.

"Well, you have my thanks, Mr. Ashton, for dispatching those crows so effectively," she said with a slightly sardonic edge to her voice. "How fortunate that you happened to be passing my door."

"Indeed, Ashton," Stuart said with sudden bluster, hearing implicit criticism of himself in his wife's tone. "Are you in the habit of bursting into private chambers without so much as a knock?"

"You would not have heard one if I had knocked," Lionel said. "As it happens I am on Their Majesties' business. 'Tis convenient that I find you both here."

He tapped Philip's document in the palm of his hand and said deliberately, "My business concerns your wife, Nielson. But you should hear it."

Pippa felt cold trickle down her spine. She was afraid. She told herself that she had no reason to be afraid if Lionel had a hand in whatever this business was, but she couldn't find reassurance.

"Is that for me?" she asked, reaching out a hand for the document.

"It is perhaps better if your husband reads it first."

Pippa's nostrils flared slightly and with a swift gesture she twitched the parchment from his loose hold. "If it concerns me, sir, then I will be the first to read it."

Lionel bowed his acquiescence. His suggestion had been merely form, something that Stuart Nielson would expect. A husband, after all, had dominion over his wife, at least in public.

Pippa broke the seal and unfolded the paper. She read it in silence, then in the same silence handed it to Stuart.

His fingers quivered a little as he read the contents. He looked up and across at Lionel, who wore his usual air of quiet detachment. "So you are to ensure that my wife obeys these instructions?"

"That is the king's wish."

" 'Tis a task that should surely fall to her husband's hand." Stuart's voice shook. This seemed to him the final insult. He could not imagine how to explain it to Pippa, who was looking at him now with raised eyebrows.

"One would think so," she said. Her banishment from court caused her no pain, indeed it would be a relief. Enduring Mary's open hostility on a daily basis was wearing. But it was still puzzling. She had done nothing new to deserve it. "Presumably Stuart is not to be banished?"

"No, his services are required by Their Majesties. I imagine that is why they have given me the task of overseeing you." He offered the sop to Stuart's pride. The man was on the rack, his anguish so palpable Lionel could not help but relieve it, however much he despised Lord Nielson. It wasn't as if his own hands were clean.

Pippa's frown deepened. "I do not understand any of

this. Why would the queen insist that I receive the attentions of her own physicians? Why would she congratulate me on my pregnancy and say that we would carry our children together, and then banish me from her sight? I do not understand it at all."

She moved away from her defensive position by the bed and sat on the window seat, her head turned sideways so that she could look out at the bright day that seemed somehow to emphasize the terms of her imprisonment.

Lionel suggested casually, "The queen is overjoyed at her own pregnancy. Perhaps she feels that yours will draw attention away from her own. She is not one to yield the center of attention. Not one to tolerate a rival. But perhaps she also feels that she owes you some compensation, so providing you with the same medical attentions as she receives herself will salve her conscience."

There was just enough truth in this to make some kind of twisted sense to Pippa. She would accept the queen's ruling, not that she had any choice, but she would accept it on her own terms.

She said firmly, "If I'm to be exiled from court, then I will go to my parents. They will be returning to Holborn any week now."

"That won't be possible," Lionel said quietly. He knew the force of the blow he was about to deliver. "Lord and Lady Kendal have been informed that they too are persona non grata at court, or even within the city limits."

Pippa whitened. To be deprived of her mother at such a time. It was unthinkable. She could not go through pregnancy and childbirth without her mother's support.

She shook her head. "No . . . no, they cannot be so cruel. That is not possible. What have I *done* that they should treat me so barbarously?" Angry tears glittered in her eyes but she refused to shed them. Lionel now seemed to her the instrument of her torment. He was the messenger and the enforcer and she felt only betrayal.

She stared at him as if seeing him for the first time. Then she turned to look at her husband, angry challenge in her eyes. Surely he would not stand aside at this injustice without a word of protest.

Stuart wrung his hands. What could he do? What could he say? They would never let Pippa out of their sight with the child she carried. And they would never let her family anywhere near her until all was done. But he *had* to say something under the glare of her accusation.

"Pippa's sister Pen, could she not be invited to stay with her? Lady Pen is a great friend of the queen's. The queen owes her much."

Lionel heard the man's desperate attempt to cast himself in a good light by offering some comfort with a solution that he knew was spurious. He was aware of the reality and it did only more harm to Pippa to raise false hopes even for a second.

"It is for love of your wife's sister that the queen has treated your wife as leniently as she has done," he pointed out sharply.

"Nevertheless, I will go and ask if Pen might be invited to court." Stuart went to the door, knowing he would never ask such a thing, but desperate to get away from a pain he could do nothing to alleviate.

"Why will they not permit me to share the Lady Elizabeth's imprisonment again?" Pippa rose to her feet, her agitation setting her skirts swirling violently around her. "I will be well out of Mary's sight in Woodstock."

"There is no point even asking such a favor," Lionel said. "It will only anger the queen further."

Stuart opened the door. "I will seek audience with the queen." The door closed behind his hasty departure.

"Pen is supposed to be in England for Christmas," Pippa said dully. "If they will not permit me to see her, I don't know how I shall bear it." She sat down again, her hands clasped loosely in her lap. "Why would they do this to me?"

Lionel came over to her and knelt before her. "Listen to me now, Pippa. You must trust me." He took her hands, unfolding them so that they lay small and thin in his own square grip.

"Why?" she asked simply. "You are to enforce the rules of my banishment. Why should I trust you? Your loyalty is to them. You would oppress me at their behest."

"No," he said. "That is not so. I play my own deep games, Pippa. I can tell you no more than that, but you *can* trust me. I will make this right."

She looked at him closely. "Whose side are you on?"

He shook his head. " 'Tis not as simple as sides, love. Your brother plays the same games. You trust him."

"I have had good reason to do so," she returned. "Forgive me, but I have seen nothing to encourage my trust in you. We have loved each other, lusted after each other, enjoyed each other. And I would dearly wish to feel that that was sufficient for trust. But I do not think that it is." She shrugged, a little helpless gesture that made him want to weep.

"Think now, Pippa. This will not be so bad." He held her cold hands to his face, blew warmly on her fingertips. "I will look after you. I will always be at your side. Is that so bad?" He cradled her hands in his and smiled up at her, the smile that always swept her with warmth and reassurance.

"There will be no prying eyes, and not even an inconvenient husband can object to the time we spend together."

"But why is Stuart so willing to agree to such a humiliating situation?"

Lionel chose his words carefully. "He is in a very vulnerable position, Pippa. You discovered his secret, what if someone else did? I would guess he's terrified and will do nothing to rock the boat."

Pippa nodded slowly. The consequences for Stuart and his lover if their secret was ever discovered were too hideous to imagine. "I had not thought him a coward," she said in quiet acceptance of this change in her husband.

She leaned forward suddenly and switched the subject. "And you will tell me nothing of these games you talk about?"

"Not yet."

"But sometime?"

The prospect of telling her the truth was so dreadful to him that he could not contemplate it. He would find a way to get her and her child to safety without revealing the horror of what had been done to her. He *had* to.

Pippa scrutinized his expression and could read nothing there. It was wiped clean, as so often when he was physically present, but absent in mind or spirit. "Where are you?" she demanded. "Where have you gone?"

He shook his head. "Nowhere, love. I am here, with you."

Pippa leaned back against the window, her hands loose now in his. They all had dark places. They all had secrets. Was it unreasonable to expect Lionel to reveal his dark places and his secrets in order to gain her trust? They had known each other such a short time. They knew so little of each other. Maybe knowledge and trust went hand in hand. And they could have neither without some struggle, some effort, some compromise.

"You are and you aren't," she said with a tiny smile. "Do you think, since we are to spend so much perfectly legitimate time in each other's company, that we might spend some of it without clothes?"

He laughed, his relief sharp in his eyes, spreading through his body. "I am certain of it." He released her hands and stood up. "I have a suggestion, one that I hope will please you."

"Tell me." Life seemed to have come back to her. Her skin felt warm, her hands hot where he'd held them, the blood pulsed strong once more in her veins.

"This evening, would you care to come and sup with me?" He regarded her closely. "My ward is desperate for company and I thought perhaps it might please you to learn a little more of me. For us both to spend time together in a more ordinary situation."

"Your ward?" Pippa was astonished.

"Dona Luisa de los Velez of the house of Mendoza," he supplied. "I knew her parents well in Seville. She refused a marriage contracted for her, and to divert Luisa and any possible scandal I brought her with her duenna to England. She's a sweet-tempered girl on the whole, but she's bored to tears, and I have sadly neglected her entertainment—" A knock at the door interrupted him and he frowned with annoyance.

"Who is it?" Pippa called, rising from the window seat.

"Robin."

She glanced at Lionel, who said almost to himself, "How convenient."

Pippa had no idea what he meant but she went swiftly to the door to open it.

Robin wrapped her in his arms and hugged her. "I've just met Stuart. What is this tale he's telling me?" He stepped into the chamber and his eye fell on Lionel.

"I didn't realize you were still here," he said coldly, keeping one arm around Pippa. "I rather assumed that having delivered your message you would have had the decency to leave my sister alone."

"That would be rather difficult, Lord Robin," Lionel said gently. "Since I am charged by Their Majesties with your sister's care and well-being, I expect to be often in her company."

Robin looked askance at Pippa. To his surprise she didn't seem either angry or resentful at Ashton's calm statement.

" 'Tis true enough, Robin," she said. "See for yourself." She handed him Philip's document and moved away from the protective circle of his arm.

Robin perused the parchment, then he tossed it disgustedly onto the table. "Why would they do this to you?" He addressed the question more to Lionel than to his sister.

Pippa shrugged. "Lionel . . . Mr. Ashton . . . thinks it's possible that Mary's afraid my pregnancy will draw attention away from her own."

She gave a short laugh. " 'Tis an absurd fear. She

bears the heir to the throne, after all, while I carry no more than a viscount's babe. But Mary has her megrims, as we well know. And I fear she's been looking for a chance to punish me further for my loyalty to Elizabeth."

Robin absorbed this. He looked at Lionel. "Is that what's behind this?"

"It could well be," Lionel responded. He stood beside the empty grate, one arm resting along the mantelpiece, one booted foot on the fender. His free hand was tucked inside his doublet, his fingers feeling the presence of the slim packet of letters from Flanders that as yet he had not had time to examine.

"But that does not explain why my father and his family are forbidden to come to London . . . why my sister is denied the comfort of her mother at this time." Robin stood foursquare, his cheeks flushed with anger and distress for Pippa, his puzzlement clear in his bright blue eyes. "That is surely simply punitive."

"It may be," Lionel agreed. "But perhaps together, we can give your sister the care and protection she needs."

"And what of her husband?" Robin demanded. "Why is he not charged with his wife's care?"

"I believe Philip and Mary think he will be kept too busy on their concerns to have time for mine," Pippa said with undisguised sarcasm. She returned to her seat in the window, tapping out a rhythm with the ivory sticks of her fan against the stone sill.

Robin looked at her. He knew that obdurate set of her mouth, the defiant light behind her hazel eyes. There had been no improvement, it seemed, in Pippa's relations with her husband.

He glanced at Lionel Ashton, then again at Pippa.

He remembered her earlier interest in the man. He hadn't known they were acquainted beyond that vague interest, and yet it struck him now that there was some connection between them. Pippa seemed remarkably at ease in the company of the man who had been designated her jailer, as if his presence in her bedchamber was perfectly natural.

"I was hoping, Lord Robin, that you would join with me in taking care of Pippa," Lionel said, reverting to his earlier statement. "There is little restriction on her movements, so long as they meet with my approval and she avoids the public rooms of the palace. If we put our minds to it, I am sure we can make the months of her pregnancy neither lonely nor tedious."

Robin frowned. He had no inclination to align himself with a man who was a member of Philip's cohort, and yet he could not refuse Ashton his help in a matter that concerned Pippa. But it was all too smooth and simple sounding. Something felt awry.

Pippa's unnatural acquiescence, for instance. The ease that seemed to flow between her and Lionel Ashton, the informal, comfortable manner in which he used her name. Surely she should be fighting this? Resisting Ashton in some way? And surely Ashton should be playing the part of jailer and not comforter and friend?

But Robin could feel himself drawn to the man. He could detect no insincerity in his relaxed and friendly manner, or in his suggestion that they should join forces to help ease the harshness of Mary's edict. He began to wonder if Lionel Ashton was not exactly what he made himself out to be.

The insistent, monotonous tapping of the ivory fan on the stonework was filling his head, making it impossible to think clearly. "God's bones, Pippa, stop that! 'Tis driving me crazy."

Pippa looked surprised; she hadn't been aware of her musical diversion. "Your pardon." She folded her hands into her lap.

Lionel spoke into the sudden silence. "I have invited Pippa to sup with me at my house this evening. I think it might divert her to leave the palace for a few hours. I hope you will do me the honor of joining us too, Lord Robin. If you have no pressing engagements, of course." He raised an interrogative eyebrow.

Robin was dumbstruck. Luisa's lively countenance swam into his internal vision. *Dear God, how could he have forgotten her so completely?*

Pippa glanced at him curiously. "Is there a difficulty, Robin? I cannot visit a single man alone, even if I am ostracized at court, and he is in some sort my jailer."

"Even a single man with a ward and her fearsome duenna." Lionel laughed. "As I was explaining to Pippa, my ward is in sore need of diversion. You would be doing me a great favor by escorting your sister to sup with us this evening."

Luisa! In need of diversion! Oh, didn't he know it! Robin struggled to gather his thoughts. He wanted to laugh at the absurdity of such an invitation. How on earth would Luisa react? Was she clever enough to dissemble? Would Ashton tell her ahead of time who his guests were to be? Would she be prepared for him?

What a deliciously absurd tangle.

"Robin?" Pippa prompted, puzzled at his continued silence. "Will you come?"

He could not possibly refuse even if he wished to. "Yes . . . yes, of course," he said hastily, a choke of laughter in his voice. Pippa would be immensely diverted by this situation but he could hardly share his secret at the moment.

He composed his features into a thoughtful gravity. "I was just thinking of what I must rearrange. But there will be no difficulty, I am sure."

He turned solemnly to Lionel. "I had not realized, Ashton, that you had a domestic establishment in London. A ward, no less. From Spain?"

"Aye," Lionel said. "Her parents were close friends of mine. I have known her since early childhood."

Robin nodded with the same solemnity, observing, "I fear my command of the Spanish tongue is not sufficient to conduct much of a supper-table conversation."

"Dona Luisa's English is very accomplished. Dona Bernardina, her duenna, however, speaks little, but Luisa and I will act as interpreter for her."

"What time should we come?" Pippa asked. The prospect of the evening had diverted her. She was aware of a very female curiosity that demanded satisfaction. There was a whole side to Lionel that would be revealed in his domestic situation. Was he as distant and remote a guardian as he was a courtier?

"Eight o'clock, if that will suit you. My house is close to the Savoy Palace, about thirty minutes by water. You will recognize the steps by the iron gate leading into the garden. Two cressets will be hung from the gateposts, and someone from the house will be waiting for you."

He had no need of signposts, Robin thought with an inner chuckle.

Pippa glanced at Robin, who said without a hint of his amusement, "Then I will come for you here at seven-fifteen, Pippa."

She nodded. He hesitated, waiting for Lionel to take his leave, but the man had not moved from his position by the fireplace. Robin could see no alternative but to make his own departure.

"Until later." He bowed to Ashton, bent to kiss Pippa, and strode from the chamber to rearrange his evening's plans.

"How strange that you should have a ward, and a house, and a whole life that I know nothing of," Pippa mused. "A life filled with people who know you so differently from the way I know you."

"I am an open book, my love," he said with a smile. "Step into my parlor at eight o'clock tonight and read what you may."

He took her hands and brought them to his lips, kissing her fingertips. "The more you know about me, the more you will know that you can trust me."

"But you will not tell me of the deep games you play?"

He shook his head. "That I cannot . . . not yet."

She sighed. "Well then, I will be satisfied with what I can glean for myself."

He left her then and Pippa rang for Martha. An evening away from the palace, conducting herself with perfect propriety in her lover's company, promised only the most delicious, clandestine diversion.

She would put aside her doubts and confusions for this evening and enjoy herself. There were perhaps compensations to be had from Mary's harsh orders. And no one had said she might not write to her mother. Seven months was a long time. Perhaps things would change and her mother could at least be beside her for the birth.

LIONEL DID NOT IMMEDIATELY RETURN HOME. HE would not deal under his own roof with the letters he carried and always took the most elaborate precautions to protect Luisa from the consequences of her guardian's true loyalties.

He walked through the narrow alleys towards Charing Cross, taking his time, ears and eyes on the alert for the possibility of a follower. Certain he was not being watched he ducked beneath the low lintel of a tavern. A man behind the counter looked up briefly, then without catching Lionel's eye returned to drawing ale for a customer.

Lionel made his way across the floor thick with clotted sawdust towards a narrow staircase at the rear of the taproom. No one appeared to notice him, certainly no one acknowledged him. He climbed the stairs swiftly and entered a small loft under low eaves. It was hot with the trapped stale air of a summer just ending, but he resisted the urge to open the small shuttered casement that looked over the street below.

He threw the heavy bar across the door and lit the stub of a candle on a rickety table that together with a three-legged stool offered the only furniture in the place.

He laid the packet of letters on the table, drawing the candle closer, and bent over them as he untied the string that held them together. He read in silence. War was brewing between France and the Hapsburg empire. The emperor was terrified that if Mary died childless then her cousin Mary, Queen of Scots, betrothed to the French dauphin, would be the natural Catholic heir to the English throne. France and England would be united against the Hapsburgs. Lionel's informants had learned that to avoid such an outcome the emperor was prepared in the event of Mary's premature death to support the claims of Elizabeth to the throne. On condition that she marry her sister's childless widower, Philip.

A cynical smile flickered across Lionel's mouth. A papal annulment was easily arranged in the name of political expediency. But would Elizabeth be prepared to accept such an arrangement? She would have to abdicate her own independence, and then accept the Catholic faith. Lionel thought she would have no objection to the latter, the lady was the ultimate pragmatist, but he rather doubted she would accept the former.

It was his task, however, to inform her that in the right circumstances she would have support from an unlikely quarter. That implicit support could only strengthen her hand at present and provide stronger safeguards against the threat of assassination. Once Philip was aware of his father's second-string planning, he could begin to put pressure on Mary to receive Elizabeth at court once more.

But they would probably await the outcome of the queen's pregnancy before making any such move, Lionel decided. In the meantime he would work on Robin of Beaucaire. The man had already established communication with the imprisoned Elizabeth and he would make a sound accomplice . . . once he had accepted that Lionel Ashton was in the right court. At the moment, Lionel was aware that Robin disliked him, and deeply distrusted whatever influence he seemed to have with his sister. Lionel would have to change his mind, and a friendly domestic supper was one good way to start. And Pippa would influence her brother. Robin would come to trust Lionel if his sister did.

He pushed the parchment aside and opened another. It was of a more personal nature. His brother-in-law wrote of his children, Lionel's nephews and nieces, Margaret's children.

They had burned Margaret the day after she had given birth to Judith, who was now three. It was Philip, on a mission to Flanders for his emperor father, who had personally denied her respite from the interrogators of the Inquisition. They had stretched her on the rack during her labor, in one last vile attempt to save her soul with a recantation. Margaret had not given it to them.

Lionel folded the letter, no expression on his countenance now. The rest of the correspondence was as he expected. Promissory notes and promises of arms and men in the event of an uprising in favor of Elizabeth. He held the documents over the candle flame and watched as the ends curled and the fire consumed them. A small pile of ashes lay on the table.

He brushed them into his cupped palm and cast them into the grate. The information, the code words, were now in his head. He would send his replies to Bruges on Captain Olson's trading vessel.

He left the tavern as unremarked as he had entered it. The evening air cleared his head, but he had retrieved his horse and ridden most of the way to his house before the darkness of memory had lifted sufficiently for him to face his guests.

Fifteen

PIPPA WAS READY AND WAITING FOR ROBIN BY SEVEN o'clock. She paced her bedchamber, listening for sounds from Stuart's chamber, but there was only silence. She guessed that he had not gone to Mary with the request that Pen should be invited to court to visit his wife. She didn't really blame him, it would have been a futile errand that probably would have irritated the queen. But still, he might have made some effort to stand up for her, it was the least he could do in the circumstances.

Robin's knock made her heart jump and she realized how impatiently she'd been waiting for him. She grabbed up her cloak from the chest at the foot of the bed as Martha hurried to open the door.

"Are you ready?" Robin asked unnecessarily as she came across the chamber, clasping her cloak at her throat.

"Yes, I've been ready this age." She made one final check of her appearance and could find no fault, then she turned back to Robin. Her eyebrows rose in surprise. "You look very tidy. Almost elegant."

Robin was annoyed to feel his cheeks warm. "That's a backhanded compliment if ever I heard one."

Pippa laughed. "It was not meant to be. It was sincerely meant. I was just a little surprised, you have no interest in sartorial matters."

"Not in the way you and Stuart have, certainly," he declared. "To hear the two of you chatter on about dress one would think it was the most important consideration in the world."

"Well, sometimes it is," Pippa retorted. "Thank you, Martha." She took her gloves and fan from the maid. "I doubt I shall be late, but go to bed if you wish. If I need you I will ring when I return."

"Yes, m'lady." Martha curtsied. "I'll wait up for you. The nights are turning chilly, I'll have a fire kindled against your return."

Pippa smiled her thanks and went out on Robin's arm. In the corridor she looked around her. The usual crowd of people were milling about, spilling into the wide hallway at the far end, clustered in arched doorways.

"Is it only Mary I'm forbidden to show myself to, or must I behave as if I'm invisible the minute I stick my nose out of my chamber?" Pippa murmured with a sarcastic smile.

Robin didn't know the answer, and it was a legitimate question. "Let's see if anyone acknowledges you," he said, keeping his voice as low as hers. "As far as I know, there's been no general decree to ignore you."

"Not yet," Pippa returned. She walked with her head up, smiling slightly when she saw an acquaintance, but offering no verbal greeting. Her nods and smiles were acknowledged but she detected a certain stiffness to them. Not that she cared.

It was Stuart who would suffer the most. He would be showered with false sympathy, conversations would stop abruptly as he approached, he would overhear her name whispered. For a man whose currying favor with the Spaniards had already lost him friends and respect, it would rub salt into the wounds.

And for some reason she could find it in her heart to feel sorry for him.

Robin made a point of greeting acquaintances effusively, calling out to people, waving with cheerful insouciance, as they progressed out of the palace and down to the water steps.

"You'll find yourself in bad odor with the queen if you go on like that in my company," Pippa remonstrated. "She'll see it as defiance."

"I care not," Robin said. "Ah, there's Jem. I sent him to hail a wherry for us."

The page loped across the quay to his master. "I've found a nice clean one, sir."

"Good lad." Robin escorted Pippa to the steps. He ran a critical eye over the wherry that bobbed at the bottom of the steps. So many of the craft for hire were filthy, soiled with whatever cargo they had last carried, be it bloody carcasses, broken ale casks, or a crate of chickens or piglets. This one was swept, the decking dry, and the benches were covered with relatively clean sacking.

"This will do."

He thought as he jumped down into the boat that it would have been nice if Ashton had offered to send his own barge to fetch them. Luisa, while trying to persuade him to take her downriver to Richmond one night, had waxed most eloquent on the barge's elegance and commodious seating. She had not taken kindly to his refusal to attempt such a journey in the dark of night, on a part of the river that was unfamiliar and known for its unpredictable currents and eddies. A stream of Spanish insults had fallen upon his head. Only to be as fervently withdrawn with a flood of apology.

Robin grinned slightly at the memory and wondered again how Luisa would manage herself this evening. It would be an interesting test of her resourcefulness, something in which he placed considerable faith.

"What's amusing you?" Pippa demanded, taking his proffered hand and stepping down beside him.

"Oh, just a passing thought," he said airily. "The sacking seems clean enough." He gestured to the thwart.

Pippa brushed it with her hand, then spread out the skirts of her cloak before she sat down. She regarded Robin closely. "Just a passing thought?"

"Aye." He took the seat opposite her. Jem took his place in the stern with the boatman, who began to pull for midstream.

Robin didn't hesitate to deflect the conversation from his own thoughts. "What is it that you like so much about Lionel Ashton?" he asked directly. He was no more inclined than Pippa to tread lightly when it came to the welfare of those he loved.

"Who said I liked anything about him?"

" 'Tis obvious, Pippa. The man is charged with overseeing your every move and you don't seem to resent it in the least. That's not like you."

He paused, and when Pippa said nothing, continued a little diffidently. "It seems to me that there's something between you. This afternoon I noticed it. I would almost call it a closeness."

He scrutinized her expression in the dusky gloom.

He had a sense, a premonition almost, that Pippa was in some danger. He didn't know where it would come from or what it would be, but he could almost smell it in the air, and he had spent enough years living on his wits to know that smell as clearly as if it were the devil's sulphur.

"I do like him," Pippa said. She could see little point denying it. There was no need to admit to anything else. "I don't know why. He seems to like me too."

"I can understand that." Robin leaned over, covering her gloved hands with his own. "But . . . but, Pippa, you must be careful. You're already out of favor at court. You are carrying your husband's child—"

"My husband is unfaithful to me." Pippa interrupted him, sliding her hands free of his light grasp.

"You cannot be sure—"

"I am *certain*." She stared at him, her eyes fixed, daring him to disagree with her.

In the face of that conviction Robin could only believe her. "I am sorry," he said after a minute. "Truly sorry, Pippa." Then, still hesitantly, he said, "But you know what they say about two wrongs?"

"Don't lecture me, Robin. You know nothing about it." She looked up into the sky where the evening star was bright and a gibbous moon was rising over the trees lining the river.

He sighed. "Maybe not. But when it comes to family I'm all you've got for now, Pippa. I can't watch you do something that will ruin you."

Pippa laughed suddenly. "Oh, how dramatic, Robin. I'm not going to be ruined! Surely it's good that I find my jailer a pleasant companion. You would not begrudge me some pleasure in his forced company?"

"No . . . no, of course not." *Just not too much*. But

Robin kept the addendum to himself. "When is the babe due?"

"I'm a little uncertain, but I would guess in late April or very early May," she said. "I do appreciate your concern, Robin, but you must see that there's no need. Lionel has as much a care for my reputation as do you. You would not else have been here with me now. What could tongues find to wag about in a quiet supper party with a child and her duenna and me accompanied by my brother?"

Child?

Immediately diverted, Robin reached up to adjust the set of the plume on his flat velvet cap. He would gain nothing from Pippa with further questioning . . . at least not tonight. He flicked at the small ruff at his neck, lifting the lace edging with a fingertip. "You approve of my dress then?"

"Certainly. I am always telling you that you should wear blue. With eyes like yours it would be foolish to wear any other color."

Robin shuffled his feet. "There is nothing special about my eyes."

"Oh, yes, there is," Pippa crowed. "They are the very twins of your father's. I doubt my mother would have fallen so readily for Lord Hugh if it hadn't been for his eyes."

"Sometimes, for a sensible woman, you talk arrant nonsense," Robin declared roundly.

"Oh, I am not always sensible," Pippa said with a mischievous gleam in her eye. "But believe me, brother dear, you are not the only one to notice things about people. You are very different these days with your newfound interest in cleanliness and clothes. I would wager that you are courting."

"More arrant nonsense!" Robin exclaimed. *He was not courting. Of course he was not.*

"Those must be Ashton's water steps," he called out a little too loudly. Pointing to the bank, he stood up too soon in his eagerness to have an end to this conversation, and the wherry rocked violently. He fell back heavily onto the thwart and his hat flew off.

Jem leaped for it, catching it the instant it was about to fall into the water.

"Oh, well done, Jem." Pippa applauded. "That would have been a sad loss."

Robin picked himself up and retrieved his cap if not his dignity. The wherry bumped the water steps and the man waiting for them above took the painter and made the boat fast.

Robin climbed up onto the quay, straightening his doublet, dusting off his cloak and hose. Pippa came up the steps lightly and joined him. She looked around her with interest.

The mansion threw light from its many windows across the sweep of lawn to the iron gate that separated the garden from the river. It was a substantial house, with a wide stone terrace and parapets. A beautifully outfitted barge was tied up at the steps.

Pippa nodded thoughtfully. Lionel Ashton, it seemed, was a wealthy man. Not that that was surprising. Most of the Spaniards who had come with Philip were rich. But as far as she knew none of them had London houses.

But then how many of them had wards to house?

"This way, my lady . . . my lord." The man who had been waiting for them held a lantern high and preceded them through the iron gates. He wore a resplendent livery of green and silver. Robin sent Jem back with the wherry and followed Pippa and their guide. The grounds were familiar to him, but he had never entered the house, so it was easy for him to appear as unfamiliar and curious as Pippa.

LUISA TURNED AROUND IN FRONT OF HER MIRROR OF silvered glass. "Oh, Bernardina, do you think this mantilla goes with this gown? Should I not wear the green silk? See, there are threads of green in the embroidery here." She picked at the embroidered flowers on her orange damask underskirt.

"My dear child, there is no need to get so excited," Bernardina said, but with a fond smile. Luisa looked particularly well this evening. The gown of ivory velvet over the vibrant underskirt set off the warm pink glow of her complexion. She could well understand the girl's exhilaration, indeed felt some herself. They had been so long out of society.

It had been so long since there had been a truly lively conversation at the supper table. And she was looking forward to demonstrating her skills as chatelaine to Don Ashton. He would find that she had provided a most delectable repast for his guests, and he would see how perfectly his ward conducted herself in company.

"Did Don Ashton give you the names of his guests?" Luisa asked, unpinning the virginal white mantilla that she wore and reaching for the green silk.

"No, I had barely time to exchange a word with him. He was in a hurry on his way to dress." Bernardina took pins from the dresser and began to arrange Luisa's mantilla to her satisfaction. The green against her black hair was very striking.

"But he did say they were brother and sister. There

could be no objection from your dear mother to a family party."

Luisa made a small moue of dismay. A brother and sister sounded like poor company. An elderly pair who kept house together, presumably. Don Ashton would, of course, go out of his way to find the most boring and respectable guests.

But even a brother and sister would be more enlivening company than dear Bernardina and her embroidery frame for an interminable evening. And if they were truly respectable enough even for Bernardina then a reciprocal invitation could be accepted. And maybe she would meet other people there.

Luisa's spirits, never down for long, rose on a surge of optimism. She would charm this dull and elderly pair with her wit, her sweet Spanish docility, and her music, and they would open the doors for her.

She flicked at the mantilla that Bernardina had pinned to her looped braids. "I do think it is better. Do you not?"

"Certainly," the duenna agreed. "You have impeccable taste, my dear. You get it from your mother."

Luisa's eyebrows flickered a little at this. Her mother, for as long as she could remember, had dressed in unrelieved black. She was certainly a graceful figure, with the perfect poise dictated by her rigid adherence to society's rules of conduct, but it was hard to see where taste came into an endless succession of black gowns and mantillas.

However, Luisa reflected that when it came to her daughter's clothes her mother had shown no such restraint. She had made certain that Luisa was always dressed beautifully, although with perfect decorum. So perhaps Bernardina was right. Luisa felt a flash of sympathy for her mother, wondering if she might have enjoyed a more varied wardrobe if the role of wife and constantly bereaved mother and then widow hadn't dictated otherwise.

"Your fan, my dear." Bernardina handed Luisa a painted black silk fan. "You will have little need of it tonight, 'tis cool enough, but the correct gestures can be so graceful."

Luisa smiled and demonstrated with a flick of her wrist. She looked at her duenna over the top of the fan and Bernardina gave a little gasp. "You must not flirt, child! Indeed you must not."

"Oh, 'tis just a game, dearest." Luisa kissed her faded cheek. "I will not disgrace you, I promise."

"Of course you will not." Bernardina tutted and patted her shoulder.

Luisa glanced towards the unshuttered casement. "Oh, they are coming. See the lights." She flew to the window, then, hearing another gasp of remonstrance from her duenna, stood against the wall, hidden by the curtain, watching the wavering light of the torch on the path below. Two cloaked figures followed the liveried watchman.

"Come . . . come . . . we must be in the hall to greet them," Bernardina said urgently.

Luisa let the curtain fall and followed Bernardina. At the head of the stairs she heard her guardian in the hall below.

"Lord Robin . . . Lady Nielson . . . I bid you welcome."

"Our thanks for your hospitality, Mr. Ashton," Robin of Beaucaire said easily.

Luisa's slippered foot, extended to touch down on the top step, hung immobile. Her breath stopped in her chest. *Robin.* Her breath returned in a great swoosh. Robin and his sister. How she had longed to meet this Pippa who had defied the queen, who had been imprisoned in the Tower, and yet had managed to live the life she chose.

She was gripped with a thrill of near unbearable excitement that mingled with a delicious twinge of fear. *What could possibly have possessed him?* Was he teasing her? Testing her? Or had it simply been an accident that brought him here? He would not invite discovery . . . surely he would not?

Her chin lifted, her mouth curved in a confident smile. Either way he would see that she could handle herself in any situation. And if he *had* hoped to discompose her, he would discover that Luisa de los Velez of the house of Mendoza could play any game he could.

She flipped open her fan and followed her duenna down the stairs.

Sixteen

LIONEL MOVED FORWARD AS HIS WARD AND HER duenna descended to the hall. "Lady Nielson, allow me to present Dona Bernardina de Cardenas."

Bernardina swept a stately curtsy that Pippa reciprocated with a friendly smile.

"And my ward, Dona Luisa de los Velez." He took Luisa's hand and drew her forward.

Pippa smiled at the girl. "I'm delighted to make your acquaintance, Dona Luisa." Lionel's ward was not quite the child she had expected, she reflected. And she was certainly beautiful with those amazing dark eyes, creamy skin, and that glossy black hair. A little plump, perhaps, but many men considered that an asset in a woman. She cast Lionel a quick glance and wondered if he did.

Lionel introduced Robin to the two women. Robin bowed with great ceremony to Dona Bernardina and with rather less formality to the younger lady. His eyes skimmed over her and she kept her own gaze demurely on her feet.

"My lord," she murmured from behind her fan. "I bid you welcome."

"My thanks, Dona Luisa. And how do you find this country of ours? I trust you're enjoying your stay."

" 'Tis very quiet, sir," Luisa said, peeping at him over her fan. "I find there are fewer diversions here than in Seville."

"Well, that is a fault to be laid at my door," Lionel declared, ushering his guests into the parlor at the rear of the hall. "I have been so occupied with affairs of state that there has been little time to introduce Dona Luisa to court society."

"If the truth be told, Dona Luisa, you are missing very little," Pippa said. "Most of the so-called entertainments are terminally dull."

"But there must be dancing ... music ..." Luisa protested. "Pray take the chair, Lady Nielson." She indicated a straight-backed chair with carved arms and sat herself on a stool beside it.

Pippa took the chair, thinking with a little shock of surprise that this girl was treating her with all the respect due an elder. Which, of course, in Luisa's eyes she was ... a respectably married matron. Pregnant into the bargain, although Luisa couldn't know that. It was a novel position in which to find herself, and Pippa wasn't entirely sure that she enjoyed it.

Robin declined a seat, preferring to follow Ashton's lead and remain standing beside the hearth where a small fire had been kindled against the gathering chill of an autumn night.

Dona Bernardina, her stiff black skirts standing around her as if on their own legs, perched elegantly on the very edge of a chair cushioned in green velvet.

She offered an observation in Spanish. Luisa was

quick to translate. "My duenna asks if you are well, Lady Nielson."

"Very well, I thank you." Pippa bowed her head in the duenna's direction. "I trust you are well also."

A quick exchange and Luisa said, "Dona Bernardina is very well, she thanks you for your consideration."

Dear God, was this going to go on all evening? Pippa searched for some other platitudinous courtesy and suddenly met Lionel's gaze. It was so full of comprehending laughter she choked on her carefully constructed sentence.

Dona Bernardina issued a stream of incomprehensible words and Luisa jumped to her feet, offering wine to the stricken guest.

Pippa waved it away, managing between violent fits of coughing to say, "No . . . no, I thank you. I don't care for wine."

"Lady Nielson prefers mead," Lionel said, going to the sideboard where reposed a silver jug and a decanter of Venetian crystal. He poured from the jug into a chased silver goblet and brought it to Pippa.

Bernardina plied her fan in a vigorous attempt to cool her guest's overheated complexion, while Pippa tried politely to dispense with her ministrations, all the time acutely aware of the concern lurking beneath Lionel's blandly social countenance as he waited for her paroxysm to cease before handing her the mead.

Robin remained beside the fire, judging that Pippa had no need of his attentions. How had Ashton known she preferred mead these days? Robin had only just discovered it himself.

"Lord Robin, may I offer you wine?" Luisa was at his side. A fragrance of orange blossom and jasmine surrounded her. It was exotic. English women had no such perfume. It was exotic and yet somehow natural, as if it was embedded in her skin and hair.

"My thanks, Dona Luisa." He took the proffered goblet and her fingers brushed his hand in a fleeting gesture that could have been accidental, except that it wasn't.

"A pastry," Dona Bernardina said in halting English. "We have made some Spanish delicacy for our guests." She fetched a silver tray from the sideboard and presented it to Pippa, who was now gratefully drinking from her goblet, Lionel still at her side.

Pippa looked for the most innocuous-seeming of the sweetmeats. Her childhood sweet tooth had diminished over the years and these days seemed to have disappeared almost completely.

Lionel took a pair of silver tongs and lifted a tartlet from the tray. He placed it on a tiny silver dish on the low table beside her chair. "This is filled with goat's cheese and a little honey. I think you will like it."

"If you say so, sir," Pippa murmured, taking a delicate bite. It was delicious. Her mouth curved, and despite the formality of the occasion she could not help observing sotto voce, "Once again your knowledge of what would appeal to a pregnant woman amazes me."

He was clearly not amused. A frown crossed his eyes. "Spanish ladies of rank do not discuss such matters in the company of men," he reproved in a low voice, glancing first towards Dona Bernardina, who was occupied with the platter of sweetmeats as she earnestly made her own choice, then to Luisa.

"They are not listening," Pippa pointed out, smiling, quite unaffected by the reproof. "Luisa seems to find Robin's company more amusing than mine. Not that I would blame her for that."

She took another appreciative bite of the tartlet. "And her duenna is rather more interested in sweets than she is in our conversation at the moment. Not that I would blame her for that. These are quite delicious."

Her smile was so infectious, her tone so lightly mischievous that Lionel felt as stuffy as a pedantic uncle. "Spanish manners are different from English," he said somewhat defensively.

"Oh, don't I know it!" Pippa chuckled. "There are some similarities, however, in the way we conduct certain activities. Wouldn't you say, sir?" An eyebrow lifted suggestively.

Pippa was taking an inordinate delight in this charade, Lionel reflected. He had hoped to give her pleasure, take her mind off her troubles, and it seemed he had succeeded. His supper invitation had tapped into some vein of mischief that he had glimpsed but rarely. It enchanted him and made him want to throw caution to the winds. And as a result was very dangerous.

"Luisa has led a very sheltered life," he stated in repressive tones, but then amusement got the better of him and he couldn't keep the smile from his face.

"That's better," Pippa said. "Now, tell me something of Seville and I'll offer no more provocation . . . although," she added with a considering frown, "that might be a pity."

Luisa, blithely unaware of her guardian's concerns for her maidenly sensibilities, was offering the tray of sweetmeats to Robin. "Those with the dates are very good," she advised solemnly. "I expect you like sweet things, Lord Robin."

"And why would you think that, Dona Luisa?" He took the tongs she held out to him and helped himself to a stuffed date.

"Oh, sometimes I know things about people," she said with an airy wave. "I have the . . . how do you call it . . . the second sight."

Dona Bernardina bustled over before Robin could answer. She smiled at Robin but her dark eyes were sharp and suspicious. She began a slow and solemn discourse.

Robin understood that he was being headed off. Luisa's duenna was not about to allow a tête-à-tête of any kind. He nodded politely, ate his almond-stuffed date, pretended to understand, and tried to ignore Luisa's scented presence so close to him. He knew she was laughing although her expression was one of docile attention to what her duenna was saying. Periodically she would offer a translation.

It seemed Dona Bernardina was talking of wild flowers. Robin knew nothing of wild flowers. He muttered about ragged robin, and Solomon's seal, and wild violets, names dredged from his boyhood. Luisa solemnly translated. Dona Bernardina waxed ever more eloquent on the subject.

Robin rolled his eyes desperately in Pippa's direction, but she was occupied, talking intently with Lionel Ashton. A conversation that probably had nothing whatsoever to do with wild flowers, he thought resentfully. He could not look directly at Luisa, but he was certain she was deriving great amusement from his predicament. There would be an accounting later, he promised himself.

Relief came in the shape of a servant who ceremoniously threw open double doors that led into a commodious dining hall. A long table was set with candles, flowers, and delicate porcelain. Nothing rough and ready in Lionel Ashton's establishment.

"Dona Bernardina wishes me to say that this is a supper in the true Spanish style. It is what we eat at home in Seville," Luisa stated as she took her seat at the table.

Bernardina said something, her hands moving fluidly as she spoke. Luisa leaned closer to Pippa, who sat beside her, and whispered, "Lady Nielson, my duenna is apologizing that she cannot conduct a truly edifying conversation with her guests when you do not speak her language. It is customary for duennas to be accomplished at edifying conversations."

Pippa glanced at her and saw the mischievous glint in Luisa's eyes, the uptilt of her mouth. She couldn't help returning the conspiratorial smile and Luisa's smile immediately became wide and confident. She reminded Pippa of herself before the world's black dog had jumped on her shoulder. She was suddenly fiercely reminded of times when she and Pen would conduct just such sotto voce observations in company. Pen, most of the time, would try to be reproving, but then her eyes would sparkle and she wouldn't be able to keep the grin from forming.

She looked across the table at Robin and surprised an intent stare. His gaze was fixed on Luisa. And there was something in his eyes that Pippa didn't think she'd ever seen there before. Her spine jumped as if she'd been alerted to some as yet unknown situation.

She looked again at Luisa and caught the unmistakable droop of one eyelid in Robin's direction. *Just what was going on here?* Robin abruptly dropped his gaze to his platter and Luisa with a demure smile asked her duenna a question about the preparation of the dish in front of her.

Pippa's lips pursed in a silent whistle. Did Lionel have no eyes? He was concerned that she raise no topic of conversation that might shock his ward's Spanish modesty, but he couldn't see that Luisa was flirting, albeit silently, with Robin.

The duenna was a different matter, Pippa decided. The woman's eyes were ever watchful, moving between Luisa and Robin. Had she seen that surreptitious wink? She must surely be aware of the way the atmosphere around the table had a lightning crackle to it; it made the fine hair on Pippa's arms stand on end. How could Lionel be unaware of it? And yet he seemed oblivious. He kept up a stream of unimpeachable small talk, touching on music, poetry, the latest dances. Luisa's responses were soft and slightly distracted, Robin on the other hand kept his end up with fluid ease. Pippa, highly amused and intrigued, did her part.

It seemed impossible that Robin and Luisa could have met before. Perhaps this was just an instant attraction. And why not? She had felt that same spark the first moment she had laid eyes on Lionel. Why not Robin and Luisa? But Luisa was a little young for Robin, she caught herself thinking. And the cultural divide was vast. Robin could not seriously court a Spaniard.

Besides, he was already courting. She was convinced of that and his denials had not changed her mind. Perhaps one woman had opened his eyes to the beauty of others. And Luisa was certainly a beauty. But she *was* a little young for Robin, nevertheless.

She was certainly too young for Lionel, and she could detect no particular closeness between ward and guardian. Pippa noted this with a degree of satisfaction that made her wonder if she had been the tiniest bit jealous. She had certainly been very curious to see this domestic situation . . . more than ordinarily curious. But Lionel's blindness in the face of whatever game his ward was playing with Robin was evidence that he had little time to notice his charge or to spend on her concerns.

A neglect that could well prove a mistake, Pippa reflected. Not that Robin would do anything dishonorable, but if Luisa was already feeling her wings it was going to be very hard to clip them. Should she mention it to Lionel? Alert him? Or would that be assuming too great an intimacy? Pippa had a feeling that it might. Lionel was so private and reticent about his own concerns, although he had no such hesitation about hers.

If this relationship was going to go anywhere it would have to be a two-way street. Pippa surprised herself with the decision. It seemed to allow the possibility of a future for them, which of course was absurd in her circumstances.

As if aware that he was the focus of her thoughts, Lionel turned suddenly towards her. "What do you think of our *zarzuela*, Lady Nielson?" He indicated the bowl of fish stew before her. "You are not eating very much."

"The flavors are most unusual," she said, toying with her spoon.

He leaned closer and forked a piece of succulent eel from her bowl. "Try this?"

His plain gold signet ring glowed dully in the candlelight as he raised the laden fork. Almost absently Pippa realized as she took the offering that in general he wore very few jewels. Most unlike his Spanish friends, or even the majority of the English court. Tonight, for instance, he wore, apart from his signet ring, only one other piece.

She put the fork in her mouth, her gaze for the moment fixed to the strange serpent brooch of blackest jet that nestled in the ruff at his throat. He leaned forward to her bowl again and the candlelight caught the blue-white diamonds at the forked tips of the serpent's tongue. Two brilliant emeralds in the eye sockets blazed.

"A strange brooch," Pippa said, aware of a thickening at the back of her throat.

" 'Tis a family heirloom," he replied. "I think *zarzuela* may not suit you tonight. I will carve you a little chicken? I believe 'tis cooked in almond milk. You might find it soothing to the stomach." The prosaic statement was an acknowledgment of her moment of weakness. Once again she wondered how he could divine such moments in the very instant she was aware of them herself.

"Thank you." She looked down as he placed a piece of white breast meat on her plate. "The brooch . . . did it belong to your father?"

"Yes," he said. "And his father before him. Lord Robin, do you hunt?"

The conversation was turned but Pippa barely noticed. She was aware now only of an acute and unfocused unease. She could not take her eyes away from the sinuous jet-black shape, the diamond sparkle, the fire of emeralds at Lionel's throat.

Suddenly she had to get away, out of this house. She touched fingertips to her throat, aware of a mist of perspiration, a cold chill on her back. Her fingers quivered. Unease became panic. She fought it down, forced herself to keep her seat, toyed with the chicken, let the conversation flow around her, and slowly the terror faded.

"Pippa . . . Pippa, are you unwell?"

She became aware of Robin's insistent voice, and then of Lionel's hand warm over hers.

"I felt a little faint," she said, withdrawing her hand swiftly and without knowing why. "Perhaps I should return to the palace."

Dona Bernardina looked stricken at such an abrupt end to her elegant repast, and Pippa explained directly, "Dona Bernardina, forgive me, but I am with child, in the early months."

She resisted a glance in Lionel's direction to gauge his reaction to her frankness, and was rewarded after a shocked instant by the duenna's response. "Don Ashton, my lord . . . pray take your wine into the parlor." She waved her hands at them imperiously, sure of her ground here. This was women's territory and she had trodden it often with Dona Maria.

Meekly the two men took up their goblets and left.

Pippa endured the hand chafing, the fanning, the outpouring of sympathy and congratulation. An outpouring that came from the duenna not from Luisa, who could not imagine, after watching her mother endure one ill-fated pregnancy after another until she was worn to the bone, how anyone could empathize with Robin's sister's condition.

Pippa, strong again and as impatient now with Bernardina's attentions as she was with her own infuriating moments of weakness, rose from her chair. "You have been so kind, but I think I am best in my bed now, madam. . . . If a servant could be sent to summon my brother."

She turned to Luisa as Bernardina, having rung a handbell with all the vigor of a fire alarm, hastened from the chamber when it was not immediately answered. "Luisa, I hope you will visit me in the palace one day. If Mr. Ashton can spare the time to bring you to see me."

"Oh, that would be delightful." Luisa met her gaze directly. "I would dearly love to be presented to the queen."

Pippa grimaced. "Then you need someone other than myself. I am persona non grata with Queen Mary."

"But why then is my guardian your friend?" The words fell from Luisa's lips before she had a minute to reflect.

"He is my brother's friend," Pippa improvised. "I made a useful chaperone." She watched Luisa and caught the blush. It was faint but there was no mistake. However, she had to applaud the girl's general composure.

"I am not averse to the role," she said easily, aware but untroubled that she was trampling on Lionel's private daisy patch. Luisa would come to no harm with Robin, but there were predators and the most alert duenna could not compensate for a mentally absent guardian.

Not coincidentally it occurred to Pippa that she could repay some of Lionel's devotion to her own well-being by keeping an eye out for his ward's. It would be a pleasing quid pro quo.

A bustle in the doorway heralded the return of Lionel and Robin. "I have ordered my barge to take you back to Whitehall," Lionel said.

Robin had Pippa's cloak over his arm. Immediately she felt a tension between the two men and guessed regretfully that they had passed an awkward time together. Robin had made no secret of his dislike and distrust of Lionel Ashton, both of which were based upon Lionel's Spanish affiliation, but Pippa had hoped that he was beginning to overcome his prejudice and see some of what she saw in the man. A fond hope it seemed at present.

Robin draped the cloak over Pippa's shoulders. She drew on her gloves. Robin made his bows to Dona Bernardina and Dona Luisa, who received hers with a tilt to her chin that threw back the green folds of her mantilla to reveal the dark coils of her hair.

Very pretty, Pippa thought appreciatively. She put her hand on Don Ashton's proffered arm and they walked down the garden to the quay.

Lionel stepped into the barge and held up his hand for Pippa, who took it and stepped beside him. He squeezed her fingers, said quietly, "I will visit you tomorrow," and returned to the quay.

"Lord Robin, I look forward to continuing our talk. The scarab is a fascinating creature." His voice was soft and conversational. A smile flickered over his mouth, but his gray eyes were sharp and cold and calculating.

Robin felt as though they were reading his very soul. It took all his years of experience to keep his own expression bland, his own eyes calm. It was Ashton's second reference to the scarab. The first when they were alone in the parlor could have been accidental, the second was not. Robin's thoughts were in turmoil. Was Ashton attempting to ensnare him? Were the codes now known to the Spanish ambassador and his spies? If he showed any recognition, would he be betraying himself to Spain? And if the codes weren't known to Simon Renard then who and what exactly was Lionel Ashton?

"I daresay we shall meet at my sister's side, Mr. Ashton," he said with a formal bow. "Since I assume you will be there in your position as jailer."

"I would prefer not to call it that," Lionel said with

the same smile. But his eyes had not ceased their intense scrutiny. "Companion, perhaps?"

"Robin, it grows chill," Pippa called from the barge, puzzled by this inaudible yet clearly strained conversation between the two men.

"I'm coming now." Robin bowed to his host. "A most pleasant evening, Ashton. I thank you."

"And I thank you." Lionel returned the bow.

Robin joined Pippa. The boatmen pulled away from the quay and Pippa huddled into her cloak.

"What were you two talking about on the quay?"

"Nothing of any importance," Robin replied. "Just the courtesies."

Pippa looked at him closely in the swinging light from the cresset. "There seemed little of courtesy in your manner, at least to an observer."

Robin stroked the silky plume of his hat that he now held in his lap. "I wonder if your friend is what he seems?" he said, watching her now as closely as she was watching him.

"Which of us is?" Pippa said without batting an eyelid. "I find myself questioning everyone these days. 'Tis too dangerous to be honest, Robin. We must all dissemble . . . adapt to whatever company we find ourselves in."

Robin did not respond, merely sat staring over the black water, stroking the plume of his hat.

After a minute, Pippa said casually, "I invited Dona Luisa to visit me at Whitehall if her guardian would escort her."

Robin turned to look at her. "Did you now."

"You seemed to enjoy her company."

He shrugged.

"You don't think she's too young for you?"

"Pippa, what nonsense is this?" he demanded, stung finally.

"Sauce for the gander," she replied with a grin. "You questioned me about Lionel earlier, making all kind of assumptions. I am merely giving you your own again."

Robin had been debating whether to let Pippa into his secret, but now decided irritably that she didn't deserve the confidence, however much it would amuse her. He would save it for some other time when he wasn't so preoccupied.

He went over in his mind the conversation with Ashton in the parlor. Looking for a topic of conversation he had commented on an unusual chess set where the ivory carved pieces were all insects. He had been fascinated by the queen, a wonderfully whimsical bee, and the king, a giant stag beetle. It was Ashton who had drawn his attention to the pawns, ordinary beetles to Robin's eye, but his host had described them with great deliberation as scarabs. Egyptian scarabs.

It was the one identifying word known only to Elizabeth's supporters. Or it had been. But now maybe it was known to the enemy, who could use it to identify traitors to the queen.

He had been very careful to show no reaction, Robin was sure of it. The answering identifier had not come close to his lips. But he needed to talk with de Noailles without delay. If there was a traitor in their midst then Elizabeth and Thomas Parry must be warned.

"Do you mind returning alone to the palace?" he asked abruptly.

"Why?" Pippa leaned forward, her eyes now serious, no hint of teasing in her manner. "Is something wrong?"

"I don't know. But I must talk with de Noailles. His

water steps are before Whitehall. I would like to get out there."

"Is this to do with this evening?" she pressed.

Robin hesitated. Pippa was as loyal to Elizabeth as anyone was, and had risked as much as anyone in that lady's cause, but now she was entangled in some way with Lionel Ashton. Now Robin didn't know what he could tell her.

"You think Lionel is not what he seems?" she prodded, still leaning forward with a penetrating gaze.

"I don't know. What do you think?"

Pippa sat back. Would she be betraying Lionel's confidence if she told Robin that Lionel himself had said he played a deep game?

She sighed. "I believe he is not what he seems. But I do not know what he is."

Robin nodded. Whatever was between Pippa and Lionel Ashton, it had not affected her essential honesty. "That's where I stand too. But I need to talk to de Noailles without delay."

"I believe Lionel can be trusted," she said after a minute, her voice now very low. "But don't ask me why I believe that."

"I must make up my own mind on that score," Robin responded soberly.

"Yes," Pippa agreed. "In that case I wonder if it would be wise to have Lionel's own boatmen leave you off at the French ambassador's water steps."

Robin whistled through his teeth, cursing himself for such an elementary mistake. Lionel Ashton had thrown him completely off course with his scarab talk. "You're right. I'll take you to your bed, and make my own way after."

Pippa sat in frowning silence for the remainder of the journey. It was unheard of for Robin to make such a tyro's error. Whatever had disturbed him about this evening must be very serious. It had certainly taken his mind off the fair Luisa.

Seventeen

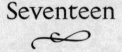

GABRIEL ADJUSTED THE LEATHER STRAP AROUND HIS neck. The lyre was heavy and the strap that held it was too tight, cutting into his shoulder. In his haste to make his rendezvous he had not taken the time to position it properly.

The evening star showed bright above the glistening gray river at the end of the lane. Gabriel hummed softly to himself, a melody that he had composed for Stuart. Tonight he would play it for him in the welcome anonymity of the tavern.

Stuart had agreed to spend tonight in the tavern instead of in the little chamber in the palace. Gabriel could not relax there. Even though Stuart had installed a strong lock and a heavy bar across the door he was jumpy and afraid, hearing footsteps in the corridor outside when there were none, imagining ears pressed to the door, eyes that could pierce the heavy oak. In the tavern there were no spies, everyone had their own secrets and kept them.

They would sup in the chamber under the eaves that Gabriel considered their very own. Unlike Stuart he did not allow himself to think of all the other couples who also used the chamber. He knew it troubled Stuart but for him it was an irrelevancy. There would be a fire in the grate, wine in the flask, wax candles in the sconces. And Gabriel would play the music of his soul.

Something struck him in the middle of his back. The melody died on his lips. He spun around, bewildered. A group of men stood about twenty feet from him. They stared at him with hard, red-rimmed eyes from beneath pulled-down caps. Their mouths were twisted, their faces rough. One of them raised a hand and a stone flew through the air, hitting Gabriel in the shoulder.

He cried out at the pain. A second man raised his hand; the stone this time hit Gabriel on the cheek. He felt warm blood trickle. But for a moment he could not move. He could not understand what was happening. Other men emerging from doorways and alleys along the lane converged on the group as if drawn by invisible string. They stared at Gabriel with the hungry eyes of a predator. Some bent to pick up stones from the muddy lane.

Another missile flew, striking Gabriel's lyre. He heard the gilded wood crack. And the sound brought him to his senses. He turned and ran. He knew there would be no help. This was London, where the mob ruled the streets. Even if one of the rare city watchmen happened upon the scene he would look the other way and hurry past lest he too become the focus of the rabble's violence.

Gabriel heard them behind him, a steady trot of booted feet on the cobbles. Another stone hit him in the back, winding him. He tripped, fell to his knees in a muddy puddle, and they were upon him. He covered his head with his hands and waited for the blows, but none came. Instead a low vicious chant of obscenity beat down upon him. In the vile language of the gutter they called him what he knew himself to be in their eyes, a perverted, unnatural beast. Someone bent over him, pushing him down onto his back. He spat into Gabriel's face.

Gabriel closed his eyes against the leering hateful faces staring down at him. The stale, fetid odor of their clothes and bodies and breath was overpowering. Gobbets of saliva soaked his face, spattered his clothes as they chanted their obscenities. A boot made contact with his ribs and as if from a great distance he heard himself moan. Now it would begin . . .

But it didn't. The chanting ceased. They still stood over him, but he felt them move back a little, giving him room. He could hear them breathing. He didn't dare to open his eyes and yet his body moved of its own accord, like an injured mouse who thinks the cat has forgotten about it and tries to crawl away.

He staggered to his feet, and they let him. He opened his eyes a slit, just enough to see how to push his way through them. And they let him go.

Once free he broke into a stumbling run. Behind him the chorus of obscenities began again, but his tormentors didn't follow him and the mocking chant faded away as he reached the end of the lane and turned the corner.

Two men in black cloaks, black caps pulled low over their foreheads, moved away from the upstairs window of a house that hung over the narrow lane.

"Good enough," one of them observed.

"Aye," agreed the other, picking up a pile of coins from the table. "Not a message to be ignored." He returned to the window and leaned out. "Here," he called down to the street, and dropped the coins in a shower of copper and silver.

The rabble fell upon them, and then upon each other. The man above shrugged and stepped away from the window. "Animals."

"They have their uses," his companion commented with an indifferent shrug of his own. "Let us make our report to Renard."

GABRIEL STAGGERED IN THROUGH THE DOORWAY OF the Black Bear and fell to his knees in the passage. His body ached, a deep throbbing pain that was as much mental as physical. He was soiled with saliva and the filth of the kennel where he had fallen. His clothes were torn, his lyre cracked beyond repair. In his ears rang still the vile chanting of the mob.

But he was safe here. He would just rest here in the dim passage until he had the strength to climb the stairs to the chamber where Stuart would be waiting.

The landlord emerged from the taproom and nearly tripped over the huddled figure in the shadows. "Eh, what's this then? What d'ye think y'are doin' 'ere. Get out!" He raised a foot to kick the disreputable, filthy beggar back into the street.

"No . . . no . . . wait!" Gabriel straightened himself against the wall and the landlord recognized him.

He whistled. "What 'appened to you, sir?"

"An accident," Gabriel said.

"I'll fetch Mr. Brown to ye." The landlord hurried away upstairs in search of Stuart, who was known to him only as Mr. Brown.

Gabriel stood leaning against the wall. His face felt swollen and when he put his fingertips to it he felt the jagged edge of the cut crusted with blood. And then Stuart was beside him.

After one shocked oath, Stuart moved swiftly, issuing a stream of orders to the landlord as he helped Gabriel up the stairs. Hot water appeared, bandages, arnica and witch hazel. Within half an hour, Gabriel, his filthy garments consigned to the midden at the rear of the tavern, sat by the fire wrapped in a blanket, a tankard of mulled wine between his hands.

"Now tell me what happened," Stuart pressed gently. Now that the urgency of action had passed he was filled with shock and horror at his lover's condition.

At the end of Gabriel's halting narrative, Stuart's shock and horror had yielded to a deep cold rage. He knew what this was about. He had been given a warning. There would be no reprieve. Regardless of Pippa's pregnancy, they still held him in a noose. He would not be permitted any leeway. Put a toe wrong, and Gabriel would suffer.

"I don't know how they could have known, Stuart," Gabriel said, stretching his cold bare feet to the fire. "Those obscenities they screamed at me . . . how could street rabble have known what I am? Is it apparent just by looking at me?"

"No, of course not," Stuart said, turning away to hide his expression. He poured more wine for himself. "You fell foul of a mob, love. They were looking for trouble and you came along. What they shouted meant nothing. It was just words to them."

Gabriel bent down and picked up his lyre. "I was going to play for you tonight." He plucked a string and the instrument's note was harsh and discordant.

"I will get you another, the finest lyre in London." Stuart knelt down in front of him. He rested his head on

Gabriel's knees and the musician stroked his hair with his long, delicate fingers.

He could not go on like this. Stuart knew that he had reached the watershed. He had been a coward too long. He would find a way out of this . . . whatever it took to obtain their freedom, he would do it.

ANTOINE DE NOAILLES REGARDED ROBIN WITH A considering frown. "We have to change the code," he said. "We cannot wait to discover whether Ashton is with us or against us. You must go to Woodstock with the message. Go by Sir William of Thame and take it also to Sir William Stafford. They will know how to disseminate it from there. I will alert our people in London."

"I will go as soon as may be," Robin agreed. "But how are we to discover Ashton's purpose? You have heard nothing about him . . . about his inclinations?"

The ambassador shook his head, looking chagrined. "I would have sworn that if he was playing some deep game I would know of it. But I am not infallible, Robin. My network is not infallible."

He pulled at his beard, wrinkling his nose. It had a rather comic effect but Robin, who would ordinarily have been amused, was not so now. "It pains me to admit it," de Noailles said with a heavy sigh.

"I cannot imagine that Ashton could be one of Elizabeth's supporters," Robin stated robustly. "He is so close to Philip and his advisors. He has a Spanish ward. He has been put in charge of my sister at Philip's behest."

"Does Lady Pippa have an opinion on Mr. Ashton?"

It was Robin's turn to frown. "She appears to like him," he said.

"That displeases you?"

"It troubles me."

There was silence for a long moment as the ambassador absorbed the implications of this. "You think she may be in some danger?" he asked delicately.

"I don't know," Robin replied. He didn't wish to talk about Pippa's private affairs or his concern for her with anyone. It smacked of disloyalty and gossip although he knew the ambassador had a purely business interest in the question.

The Frenchman accepted this without a murmur. He rose from his chair and went to the sideboard. "Wine?"

"Thank you." Robin threw another log on the fire. It was late and he had roused de Noailles from his bed. He rubbed his eyes with a weary gesture and yawned.

"I will compose a letter for the Lady Elizabeth and change the identifying code word," the ambassador said, handing Robin a goblet.

"Before you leave for Woodstock, talk with your sister. She is ever loyal to Elizabeth and I believe her to be a shrewd judge of character. Discover if she and Ashton ever talk politics. Perhaps he has revealed something of importance to her, but maybe she is unaware of its significance."

"She told me that she believes he is not what he seems," Robin said, gazing into the ruby contents of his goblet. "But she also said that she doesn't know what he is."

"I see." De Noailles shook his head. "Press her a little deeper. She must have some reason for believing that."

"Aye," Robin agreed. "She must have some reason."

"In the meantime I will set my own people to looking more closely into Mr. Ashton's circumstances. We investigated when he arrived, of course, but no one knew anything of him. He had spent time in Flanders, was an intimate of Philip's, but appeared to have no history, no past that we could look into. He seemed to be exactly what he presented himself to be. A friend and ally of the Spaniards and a shrewdly clever arbitrator and mediator."

Antoine sighed again in disgust. "We saw an opponent; we thought that by knowing him we had defanged him, and instead he turns out to be a damnably clever spy for the Spaniards, or a supporter of Elizabeth buried so deep no one could guess at his secret."

He drained his goblet. "My masters will not be pleased."

Robin made no comment. He knew that de Noailles was out of favor in France as well as at Mary's court. He hated England, this "nasty island" as he called it, and longed to return home. Pen's husband had hoped to succeed him as French ambassador to Mary's court, a position that would have brought his wife back close to her family, but the French king had not approved the transfer. Owen d'Arcy was too valuable in France, at least at present.

"Owen d'Arcy might be able to discover something," he suggested on the thought. "He has men in Flanders as well as in Spain."

The ambassador nodded slowly. Owen ran his spies rather differently from de Noailles, and was more prepared to get his own hands dirty in the pursuit of information.

"I do not know that we have the time to ask for the

chevalier's assistance," he said. "A message will take at least a week to reach him, then he will need time to make his own inquiries, and then another week to send us information."

"Nevertheless, I think we should ask him," Robin said. "We don't have to wait for his results, though. In the meantime, we do what we can here."

Antoine sighed once more. "Yes . . . yes . . . I suppose you're right. But if I ask the chevalier's help it makes me look inefficient, incompetent."

"There is no need for anyone to know that you sought his help," Robin pointed out. "Owen is an old friend. He will do you a favor without broadcasting that you asked it."

The ambassador considered this, then nodded again. "Yes, indeed. I will have a letter off to him on the morning's tide. Go you to your rest now, and as soon as you are able discover what you can from your sister, and then return here for the letters I would have you carry to Woodstock."

Robin set down his goblet, stifling another yawn. "I'll gladly take my leave, sir, if you've no further need of me this night."

Antoine waved him away with a friendly smile, and when the door had closed on his visitor he sat down at his writing table and sharpened his pens. He would get no sleep tonight.

PIPPA AWOKE SOON AFTER DAWN. SHE LAY WARM AND relaxed under the heavy covers, listening to the cheerful crackle of the fire that some anonymous servant had lit in the hearth at the first peep of day. It was good to feel a chill in the air after the exhausting heat of the long summer. Good to look forward to a breakfast of porridge and mulled ale. And then she would ride.

A burst of energy surprised her. It had been weeks since she had awoken feeling energetic and full of the day's promise. She sat up. She was not in the least sick. Instead she was starving.

She saw the dry bread that Martha had left for her and laughed out loud. She couldn't imagine ever wanting to eat anything so unappetizing. She slid to the floor and rang the handbell for her maid.

Her eye fell on the folded parchment that contained King Philip's orders for her restricted existence. She picked it up with a grimace of distaste and reread it. It seemed fairly clear that without Lionel's permission she couldn't leave her chamber, let alone the palace on a riding jaunt.

Pippa refolded the paper and tapped it thoughtfully against the palm of one hand. Lionel had said last night that he would visit her this morning, but she had no idea what time. A host of things could delay him, one of their interminable council meetings for instance. She was expected to sit here and wait for him.

But maybe not. If she was very careful to avoid being seen by any member of the court, she could leave the palace secretly for an hour. It was still very early, few people would be up and about in the public rooms. Her groom would be escort enough, he always had been before.

She went to the window and stood looking out, tapping the paper now against the glass. She didn't want to stir up an ant's nest, things were bad enough as they were, but surely she could slip out just for an hour. One hour in the crisp fresh air of early morning to celebrate how well she felt.

She would go, Pippa decided . . . and to the devil with the consequences. "Martha, bring me porridge and mulled ale," she instructed the maid almost before she had fully entered the chamber. "I am going riding."

"Yes, m'lady. You're feeling well, then?"

"Very," Pippa stated, stretching luxuriously. "Hurry now. I'm famished . . . oh, and send a page with a message to the stables. Fred should meet me with the horses in the blacksmiths' court in a half hour." She would take a leaf out of Lionel's book when it came to clandestine excursions and use the parts of the palace frequented almost exclusively by servants. No one would notice her or her horse in the bustle of the blacksmiths' courtyard.

Pippa ate her breakfast with relish and then chose the most sober costume in the linen press. A dove-gray velvet gown with a dark brown silk hood would not attract attention. She would take the back stairs and corridors just as she had done before when meeting Lionel at the kitchen water steps.

She could not be accused of disobeying the spirit of the royal edict even if she was defying the letter, she reflected as she slipped from her chamber. She would not offend the queen's sight, or Philip's.

Her lip curled slightly but her mood was too buoyant this morning to be downcast for more than an instant. She hurried down the stone stairs that gave onto the blacksmiths' court through an arched entranceway.

The court was crowded with servants and grooms leading horses towards the blazing braziers where the smiths in their leather aprons worked at the anvils, apprentice boys plying the bellows with desperate vigor. It was hot and noisy despite the freshness of the morning.

Pippa saw Fred holding her sorrel mare and his own cob at the far side of the court. He had a rather puzzled air as he looked around him, clearly wondering why his mistress had chosen this as a rendezvous. Pippa stepped out into the court and then stopped, frozen in her tracks.

From the stone arch opposite her three men strode into the smiths' court. Philip, Ruy Gomez, and Lionel Ashton.

She stepped back into the shadows of the gateway but it was too late. They had seen her. Her mind whirled. She could turn tail and run, hoping that it would never be mentioned, or she could brazen it out.

As she looked at Philip she was filled with a great loathing for that short, slight man. He reminded her of an evil gnome with misshapen legs and a receding hairline, the supercilious coldness of his expression, and the dark circles of dissipation under his eyes.

What possible right did he have to banish her? Mary had that right, but Pippa could not believe that it was Mary who had decreed her exile for something as trivial as a rival pregnancy. Her husband must have prompted her, somehow convinced her that Lady Nielson's loyalty to Elizabeth was a stronger threat than they had thought.

And they were quite right about that. Pippa thought of her correspondence with Elizabeth and a glitter of defiance lit her hazel eyes.

She stepped out of the shadows and glided into the open court. Her head high she approached the three men and with a swirl of her skirts curtsied deeply.

"Forgive me, Highness. Mr. Ashton bade me fetch my horse here if I wished to ride this morning. He did not think, I am sure, that Your Highness would find a reason to come to such an unlikely place as the smiths'

court. I would not have offended your sight intention-
ally."

She rose from her curtsy although the king had not
bidden her do so, and stood holding her whip against
her skirts, her eyes fixed without expression on a stone
in the wall behind Philip's head.

Philip said nothing, merely stared stonily right
through her.

Lionel stepped between them as if to shield one or
both of them from the sight of the other. "The error
was mine," he said in his calm remote tones. He laid a
hand on Pippa's shoulder and turned her away, swinging
out the folds of his cloak to envelop and hide her as he
stepped behind her.

Only then did the king move. He spun on his heel,
Ruy Gomez following, and they returned from whence
they'd come, whatever had brought the king to the
smiths' court forgotten or dismissed.

"My horse is the sorrel." Pippa pointed with her
whip. "Will you ride with me, Mr. Ashton?" She tried
to sound cool and collected but she was aware of a slight
tremor in her voice now that the confrontation was
done.

"I will ride with you," he said as distantly as before.

"I could not have known Philip would come here,"
she said with soft vehemence. "Of all the ill luck!"

Lionel made no response. He waited until she had
mounted the sorrel with her groom's assistance then
took the reins of the cob. He spoke to Fred. "I'll escort
Lady Nielson. You may return to the stables."

Fred loped off and Lionel in calm silence mounted
the sturdy brown cob.

"That's a most inelegant mount for a courtier,"
Pippa observed with a tiny smile.

"It will serve the purpose," Lionel said indifferently. He nudged the cob's flanks, directing him out of the court.

Pippa drew up beside him. "Where will we ride?"

"In the park."

Silence fell between them until they reached a broad grassy ride beneath the trees. Fallen leaves crunched under the horses' hooves and a cascade of gold and orange and yellow fell around them from the branches above.

"What more could Philip do to me?" Pippa demanded, unnerved by Lionel's continued silence. "Send me to the Tower?"

"I doubt that, but he's a bad man to anger. You would be advised not to do it again." He sounded so detached, so matter-of-fact, so unsympathetic.

"It was not intentional," she repeated. "But I had such an urge to ride and I didn't know when you would come to me."

He turned his head and regarded her closely. "You look different this morning."

"I feel different. Full of life . . . but how true that is." She laughed but Lionel did not smile and she wondered if she had angered him despite his seemingly matter-of-fact attitude.

"I've upset you," she stated.

"No," he denied. Pippa had not upset him, but seeing her there facing down Philip with that proud set to her head, the defiant glitter in her eyes . . . that had distressed him beyond words. The contrast between the conscious, courageous young woman who would not bow to the king's will, and the insensible, fragile body that he had nightly carried from Philip's presence filled him with a rage so powerful it nauseated him.

"You *are* angry with me," she insisted.

He drew rein abruptly. *"No!"* he stated fiercely. "No, Pippa, I am not." He leaned across and took her face between his hands. "Believe me." He kissed her mouth and the horses shifted beneath them.

"God's blood!" he muttered. "Let us dismount." He swung from the cob and Pippa, more than happy to accept this change of mood, slid to the ground before he could come round to help her.

"We seem destined to make love in the open air," she observed, going readily into his arms, resting her head on his shoulder as she looked up into the gray eyes where urgent desire mingled with something else that disturbed her. Something distressful.

She touched his face with her fingertips. Gently, tentatively brushed his eyelids. She stood on tiptoe and kissed the corner of his mouth, wanting to banish whatever it was, wanting to see in his gaze only passion, the same passion that burned in her loins.

He caught her to him, kissed her deeply, sliding down with her to the carpet of leaves that crunched and crackled beneath them as they loved one another in a hasty scramble of tangled clothes and limbs.

Pippa pressed herself upwards into him. His hipbones were sharp against her soft flesh as each thrust drove him deeper and deeper inside her. Their eyes were open, fixed upon each other. She saw the moment when the tide would take him, and he saw the same in her face. He held back for an instant, not breathing, and then as the wonder spread into her eyes he thrust once more.

Pippa cried out, biting her lip till she tasted blood, and held him against her, pressing her hands into his back as if she could fix him forever against her, live forever in this glorious incandescent instant of bodily joy.

But it passed as it always did, leaving her feeling for a moment bereft. Lionel rolled sideways and lay on his back, his hand over his eyes, his chest heaving as if he'd run a marathon.

She leaned over him, propped on one elbow, and kissed him again. Laughing he caught her against him and rolled with her until she lay on her back again and he hung above her.

A calm mouth, gray eyes, where she read both compassion and distress. An expression so familiar and yet unknown, so terrible and yet reassuring. She had never seen him look like this before. But she had. Somewhere in the shadows of her mind, she had seen that expression on his face. A darkness gathered around her. She stared up at him, then her eyes found the serpent brooch at his throat. It had disturbed her last night. Now it terrified her.

She sat up, pushing him away, dashing a hand across her mouth as if to get rid of some vile taste.

"What is it?" he said, sitting up beside her. "Pippa, what's the matter? Are you sick?"

"I don't know," she said in a voice that didn't sound like her own. "Who are you? What are you?"

"What do you mean?" He tried to smile, to laugh even, but he knew, a cold shaft in his heart, that the time had come.

"Something bad has happened," she said, feeling for words. "I know it. I have always known it in some way, but not so certainly as now. And *you* did it." She looked at him with hard, accusing eyes filled with horror.

"No," he said. "No, I didn't, Pippa." The denial sounded feeble to his ears, unconvincing, because it was not rendered with conviction. He blamed himself for what had been done to her as much as he blamed Philip.

She stood up slowly, straightening her skirts automatically. Lionel rose with her. She leaned against a tree, instinctively needing its support, and faced him. "You will tell me now, Lionel. You will tell me what this bad thing is."

The same hard, accusing, horror-filled eyes forced him to look at her, forced him to face what had to be done.

"Yes, I will tell you," he said as a great calm came over him. "But you must listen to the end."

She nodded but her eyes never left his face as he began speaking. And they stared there unwavering until he had fallen silent.

She touched her belly. "This child is Philip's," she said as if confirming it to herself. Her voice was flat, expressionless, and her eyes were now vacant, without any emotion, as if she was no longer capable of feeling. And it filled Lionel with terror as her horror and anger could not do.

"This child is Philip's," she repeated. "And you helped to put it there. You and my husband."

This time she almost spat the words at him and he flinched. He had given her no explanation, no excuse, just the plain unvarnished facts. To excuse himself had seemed impossible. But now he knew he had to do or say something to lessen her unutterable disgust and contempt.

"Your husband," he said. "You must understand that they threatened him with exposure, but more than that they threatened the life of his lover."

"And I counted as nothing when compared to his lover," she stated, cold and bitter as the grave. "My husband is of no further interest to me. But what of you, Lionel? What did they know about you that would compel your so willing assistance?"

"Nothing," he said. "I gave my assistance in my sister's name . . . and for England's security."

"Oh, what unimpeachable, unselfish aims!" she scoffed. "What's the sacrifice of one woman when set against such worthy goals?"

"I didn't know you," he said, hearing how pathetic a defense it was when set against such an outrage, such an atrocity. "I thought . . ." He tried again. "I thought I could ignore the person and see only the goal. I found I could not."

"Oh?" She raised her eyebrows. "You found you could not. Once Philip's seed was securely planted you found you could indulge the luxury of remorse. Is that it?"

"No."

But she brushed right past his denial. "And what twisted goal gave you the idea to make love . . . no, to have sex with this tool of the Spanish? Remorse? Pity? Or just the desire to experience what your king had had?" The words flew at him, poisoned darts that found their mark, each and every one of them.

"You came to me," he said in barely a whisper. "You came to me, Pippa, and I could only give you what you needed . . . what we both needed."

She shook her head at him in wordless disgust and pushed herself away from the tree. The recognition of this evil had given her a strength she didn't know she possessed. She brushed past him and with the same steely determination mounted her horse unaided.

"Pippa . . . Pippa . . ." He came up to her, put a hand

on her bridle. "There is something else you must hear—"

"Get out of my way!" She slashed at his hand with her whip. "I would not hear another word out of your mouth." She struck the sorrel's flanks with her whip and the horse leaped forward, crashing down the ride towards the palace.

Lionel watched her go. He was empty, no feeling, no emotion left. He had not told her of Margaret. But now he thought that to use his sister's tragedy as an excuse for his own dreadful violation would be but another violation.

But Pippa *had* to listen to him. He had to save her and her child, and he could not do that without her trust. But how could she ever trust him again?

Eighteen

"Pretty flowers, sir," Jem observed, regarding his master slyly as he folded shirts and clean linen into the leather traveling bag.

"Aye," Robin agreed, tying the stems of his carefully selected bouquet with a yellow silk ribbon from his little sister Anna's ribbon box.

"I daresay the lady will be pleased," Jem observed with the same sly grin.

"Damn your impudence," Robin said, but without heat.

He surveyed his bouquet with complacency. Lovely late roses, their heads heavy with the night's dew, milky ox-eye daisies, and vivid yellow and orange marigolds. All the very best of the autumn garden at Holborn. Informal, bold, yet graceful and full of sunshine, it was a selection that suited Luisa. Of course, it would be presented to Dona Bernardina, his official hostess of the night before, but Luisa would know she was the intended recipient and the charade would amuse her.

It was still very early, a beautiful crisp autumnal morning. He had had no more than two hours' sleep but he had a lot to accomplish. After his courtesy visit to Luisa and her duenna, designed to enable him to tell Luisa he would be going away for a few days, he would go to Whitehall to talk with Pippa, then return to de Noailles to pick up the ambassador's letters and instructions.

"Meet me at Aldgate at noon," he instructed Jem. "I want to get to Thame tonight so we must ride hard." He pulled a wooden comb through his nut-brown curls, grimacing at the way they sprang back into the same unruly tangle just as if they had a life of their own.

"Aye, sir. Should I pack another suit of clothes?"

Robin considered the matter with a thoroughness he would not have accorded it a few weeks ago. "Yes, you had better," he said.

"We'll be gone a good while then, sir?"

"Not more than a week, but I'll need a change of clothes for visiting. I can't show myself in public with travel-stained garments."

"No, sir." Jem nodded solemnly. "Of course not, sir."

Robin shot him a suspicious glance. "You find something to amuse you, lad?"

Jem shook his head. "No, sir . . . not in the least, sir."

Robin suppressed a smile and reached for his doublet. "Just make sure you're at Aldgate by noon," he said with an attempt at severity. He caught up his short cloak and slung it around his shoulders, then armed with his bouquet left the house.

He reached Lionel Ashton's mansion just before eight o'clock and rode around the back into the stable yard to leave his horse. Luisa, attended by a very businesslike-looking groom, was about to mount an elegant, cream-colored mare just as Robin rode into the yard.

A tiny gasp of surprise and pleasure escaped her, to be swiftly swallowed. She stepped away from Malcolm, who had been about to boost her onto her horse. "Why, Lord Robin, what an unexpected visit," she said in dignified accents. "I was about to go for a ride."

"Then don't let me hold you up, Dona Luisa," he said, swinging down from his own horse. "I came merely to thank Dona Bernardina for her hospitality last even."

"And to give her flowers, I see." Luisa eyed the bouquet. "What a pretty bunch. Shall I take them for you?"

He bowed with a flourish and handed her the bouquet. She smiled up at him as she smelled the roses. "What a heavenly scent."

Robin did not say what he had thought, that the fragrance had reminded him of Luisa's own the previous night. He merely bowed again.

"Malcolm, I will ride later," Luisa said. "I must take Lord Robin to Dona Bernardina."

"Very well, madam." Malcolm took the mare's reins just above the bit. His examination of the visitor was automatic, swift, thorough, and covert, and ensured that he would always recognize Robin of Beaucaire at any time and in any guise. It was one of Malcolm's many skills that made him particularly useful to his employer.

"Come, Lord Robin. I don't know if Dona Bernardina has left her chamber as yet. She does not in general come down before midmorning, but I will arrange the flowers and you may give me a pretty message for her."

"That will do very well," Robin agreed. "Is your guardian at home?"

"I don't know . . . I don't believe so," she said with a

cheerful little skip. "He usually attends the king at day-break, when His Majesty reviews the day's business."

It was the answer Robin had hoped to hear. He was not yet prepared to engage Ashton in further conversation on the subject of scarabs.

It was to be hoped Ashton would visit Pippa early too, Robin reflected. She would not take kindly to being confined the entire morning awaiting her jailer's permission to leave her chamber. But then perhaps she would no more mind that than she seemed to mind the royal edict, he amended acidly. Maybe Lionel Ashton could do no wrong. Pippa had certainly given that impression yesterday.

He returned his attention to Luisa just as they entered the house. She was skillfully engaged in innocuous small talk that required little concentration but would draw no remark.

She addressed the steward who had admitted them. "Senor Diaz, would you send a message to Dona Bernardina's chamber and tell her that Lord Robin is here to pay her a visit? Oh, and bring . . . bring . . ." She turned to Robin. "What do you eat and drink at this time of day in this country?"

"Ale, meat, cheese, bread," he said. "What do you eat in Spain?"

"Just bread and preserves, and we drink watered wine."

"Then you should offer me what you would eat yourself."

Luisa looked a little doubtful and Robin laughed. "As it happens I have already broken my fast," he told her. "I have no need of refreshment and indeed have only a few minutes to spare."

"Then I will inform Dona Bernardina immediately."

The steward spoke in thick but fluent English as he executed a stately bow.

"Oh, and send someone with a vase for these flowers," Luisa called after him as she led Robin into a small parlor at the rear of the house.

"We are alone," she said in a meaningful whisper. "Not for long, I fear, but let us take advantage of it." She reached up and kissed him on the cheek.

He smiled. "That may be daring in Spain, dear girl, but in England 'tis a very chilly way to greet one's friends."

"Oh?" She tilted her head on one side. "Demonstrate your way, please."

He caught her chin on the tip of a finger and swiftly, lightly, kissed her on the mouth. "There, that is considered quite acceptable."

Luisa's cheeks pinkened. "Not in Spain," she breathed.

He chuckled and stepped back as the door opened to admit a servant with a pewter vase. "Dona Bernardina, madam, will come down in half an hour." He set down the vase and left.

"That's very swift," Luisa marveled. "It normally takes her at least an hour to dress. Either she wishes to do you signal honor, my lord, or she is desperately anxious for my reputation." She began to arrange the flowers.

"Alas, I cannot wait, so she need have no fears for your reputation," Robin said. "I came really to tell you that I have to go away for a week, maybe a little longer, so do not look for me at our usual times."

Luisa continued with her flower arranging. "Where are you going?" The question sounded simply curious.

"Into Surrey," he said. "To visit some friends."

"Oh, I see." Luisa licked a spot of blood from her finger where a thorn had caught it. "What road do you take out of London to go into Surrey?"

"Out of Aldgate," he told her. " 'Tis one of the main gates out of the city."

"It must be very busy there," she observed, setting the vase on the table where the morning sun set fire to the orange and yellow of the marigolds.

"Aye, busy enough," he agreed. "There are several taverns serving wayfarers. Now, I must go. I have to meet my page at noon."

"At this gate?" She turned from her admiration of the flowers.

"Aye," he agreed again, his mind now moving ahead. "I'll bring my sister to visit you on my return."

"As chaperone?" Luisa inquired with a demure smile. "Or as excuse?"

"Either or both," Robin returned.

"She said she would be happy to play the part of chaperone."

"Oh, did she?" he said with a dry smile. He could well imagine Pippa making such an offer. She had already dropped some heavy hints about his interest in Luisa.

And she'd also said that Luisa was too young for him. *Was she? Too young for what?*

The fact that he could ask himself the question startled him. He wasn't courting this Spanish maid, he was merely enjoying an amusing and slightly flirtatious friendship and giving the girl a taste of freedom and experience at the same time. All perfectly harmless. She would return to Spain and he wouldn't give her a second thought.

"I must take my leave at once," he said abruptly. "I

have much to do this morning. Pray give my respects to Dona Bernardina and ask her to forgive my haste. I will call upon her again on my return."

Luisa's smile was slightly distracted as she curtsied her farewell, but Robin didn't notice anything amiss. He bowed and left the house, hurrying to the stables for his horse.

Luisa went to her own chamber. She sat on the chest at the end of the bed and considered the fantastic idea that had jumped into her head. It was fantastic, impossible, lunatic. But it wasn't impossible. Not really impossible. If she had the courage, she could do it.

But what would happen afterwards? Her reputation would be destroyed. It would kill her mother, not to mention Dona Bernardina. Or . . .

Or, she could find herself a husband. A husband of her own choosing. Or . . .

Or she could just see if she could put such a lunatic idea into practice and then if she succeeded she could back away and return home with no one any the wiser.

Yes, that was what she would do. Luisa hopped off the chest. She should take a few things with her just in case. . . .

No, there was no just in case. She was going to have a tiny little adventure that would hurt no one. She would not take anything with her, and that way there would be no temptation to push her little adventure into a big one with hideous consequences for a lot more people than herself. This was just a test of her ingenuity.

Don Ashton would hear of it, of course, because Malcolm would have to tell him. And he would probably send her straight home on the next ship to Spain.

But maybe he wouldn't. He was not unreasonable,

just unaware. As long as Bernardina didn't find out, there would be no need for Don Ashton to do anything.

TOO YOUNG FOR WHAT? THE QUESTION WOULD NOT leave his mind. It became an internal chant, taunting Robin as he rode back to Whitehall. He had never given Luisa's age a second thought. He had never given the girl herself a serious thought. This was just an interlude that amused them both.

But he was a man of thirty summers and she was a woman of eighteen. No great discrepancy there. A lot smaller than in many marriages. Women married men old enough to be their grandfathers in some cases. Of course, the women's wishes were not in general consulted in such cases. Luisa had refused just such a marriage arranged for her.

But why in the name of Lucifer was he thinking about marriage? Whenever he thought, which wasn't often, about the kind of woman who would suit him, he could think only of Pen, Pippa, and Guinevere, his stepmother. They all had certain qualities that he could not imagine doing without in a wife. They were equal partners in their marriages, heretical though that was. They managed their own affairs, equally heretical, and they were entertaining and clever and no man's fool.

Robin realized rather glumly as he stabled his horse that he hadn't met any women like the women of his own family, which presumably accounted for his lack of interest in marriage. He had never considered it. But now it seemed as if he was.

Luisa.

No, it could never work. He would never get her family's permission even if he asked for it. Presumably

Lionel Ashton was in loco parentis so he would have to be asked. And that was a snake pit if ever he'd come across one.

Who and what was Lionel Ashton? If he was on the right side, a true sympathizer, then maybe he would not be averse to such a proposal. But if he was the devil's own Spanish spy, then he would see Robin hang, or lying in a gutter with his throat cut, before he'd countenance such a proposal. And if indeed that was what Ashton was, then Robin could have nothing to do with anyone or anything that came under his influence, however drawn he was to Luisa.

"Everythin' all right, my lord?"

Robin became aware that he was standing in the middle of the busy yard, swinging his whip against his booted calf, and staring at nothing. The groom who had taken his horse was regarding him curiously.

"Yes . . . yes . . ." Robin said irritably. "I'll need my horse again in half an hour." He strode out of the yard, beneath the arched gateway that led into one of the inner courts of the palace.

He pushed aside all thoughts of Luisa and the extraordinary path down which those thoughts had propelled him, and concentrated on what he would say to Pippa.

He decided that he needed to be honest with her, tell her of Lionel's approach. She would then tell him whatever she knew or suspected or guessed. If he avoided any hints about her strange and to him dangerous intimacy with Ashton, then they could keep the discussion on a matter-of-fact footing.

If she was in some way involved with Ashton, then hearing that he probably was a Spanish spy and not just a plain member of Philip's retinue would be hard for

her, but Pippa knew the world they lived in too well not
to be able to handle such knowledge. She had said herself that everyone had to dissemble, that honesty was
too dangerous to be practiced. She had no illusions. She
would be able to reconcile herself to such a blow. To the
knowledge that Lionel was using her.

Robin hoped fervently that his sister had done no
more than flirt with the man. He prayed that she had
really had her eyes open, that she understood and accepted that the man was the enemy even if she was attracted to him. Surely she had protected herself from
too much intimacy?

He hurried up the staircase, tapestries whispering in
the breeze of his passing. He ignored the crowds of
people now thronging the corridors. At Pippa's door he
knocked sharply and tried the latch. It was locked from
the inside.

"Pippa, 'tis me."

There was silence from beyond the door. He rattled
the latch again. "Pippa, are you still asleep? I have to
talk to you now. I'm going on a journey in a couple of
hours." He couldn't say more than that while shouting
at a closed door in a public corridor.

He knocked again.

The door opened. He stepped in, speaking as he did
so. "I'm sorry if I woke you but 'tis urgent that I . . ."
His voice died as he looked at her. "Good God!" he
whispered. "What has happened? What's the matter,
Pippa?"

She was so white he could see the blue veins along
her forehead, beneath her jaw, standing out in her neck.
There was a wildness in her eyes, and she seemed to be
holding herself together, as if afraid that if she relaxed
her posture her body would fly apart.

"Is it the baby?" he demanded when she didn't respond. "Are you sick? For God's sake, Pippa, answer me!" He took her upper arms and shook her, desperate to get a response from her. Then he put his arms around her and held her as tightly as he could because he could think of nothing else to do.

Pippa let him hold her, let his warmth and his familiar smell and the feel of his body cut through the dreadful black trance that had enveloped her since she'd returned to the palace. She knew what she had to do, had known from the first moment of that ghastly revelation, but a paralysis had crept over her once she had locked herself into her chamber and she had not been able to think, let alone plan.

"Are you sick?" Robin repeated after a minute, still holding her tightly. "Is it the baby?"

Pippa pushed herself away from his comforting arms. "No, I am not sick, Robin. But I have to leave here now . . . right now. And you must help me."

Her voice was strangely flat, colorless, as pallid, Robin thought, as her complexion. He was aware of an anxiety so powerful that it bordered on fear. He dreaded what she was going to tell him but he knew he had to hear it.

"Tell me," he said.

She told him, standing still in the center of the chamber, holding her elbows across her body, her voice as flat as a millpond, the only expression in her eyes, where green fires burned in the hazel depths. Only by keeping all emotion from her voice could she put words to the horror. She was degraded by what had been done to her; she felt filthy. It was agony to tell the facts of her degradation, but she kept to herself the hideous sense of her own worthlessness. A feeling that made her want to scream and tear at her hair, to rip at her skin with her nails.

But she showed none of this.

Robin listened in appalled horror. There was much evil in his world, he had come to grips with that knowledge many times over in his thirty years, but the cold-blooded viciousness of this violation was beyond his comprehension. And yet he knew it to be true. It was beyond comprehension but it entirely fitted with Philip's reputation for vice, his fanatical Catholicism, and his hunger for power.

It put all questions about Lionel Ashton to rest. The man was as evil as his master. And he would pay. Robin would see to it.

But *Stuart* . . . Stuart had sold his wife to save his own skin. "Stuart," he said at last in a voice where hurt and bewilderment mingled. "How . . . ?"

"They threatened his lover," Pippa said as flatly as before. Stuart's betrayal no longer meant anything to her. Not beside Lionel's. "I do not think he was so worried about his own life."

She moved finally from her statuelike pose in the middle of the chamber and sat down on the end of the bed, one hand absently cradling her stomach.

"I have to get away from here, Robin. I cannot let them do what they want with me and this child. And I must go now, today. I cannot endure to stay another hour under the same roof as any of those men. So you must help me." It was a clear statement of a fact that would admit no negotiation.

It did not occur to Robin to offer any. It was simply a matter of how she was to leave and where she was to go.

"I am supposed to leave on a mission to Woodstock

for the ambassador," he said. He debated for only a second whether to tell her that the sudden mission was necessary because of Lionel Ashton. He couldn't bring himself to speak the man's name to her. And yet why had Ashton told her this truth? What possible goal would it serve? Surely they needed Pippa unaware and compliant.

"Why did he tell you?" he blurted without volition. "What did he hope to gain by that?"

It was a question Pippa didn't want to examine. She had demanded the truth from Lionel and he had given it to her in all its brutality. In some tiny recess of her brain where shock and horror had not penetrated, she knew that he had not told her simply to cause her unimaginable distress. But she could not think about that, about reasons for Lionel's actions . . . any of them.

She shook her head. "I don't know. We had just made love and—" She waved a dismissive hand at Robin's exclamation. "Spare me the prudery, Robin. My husband prefers men to women. My preferences are my own." *And I live with their consequences.* The recognition hovered, unspoken.

Robin nodded and kept a grim silence.

"I don't imagine he would have told me if I hadn't known that something bad had happened to me and that he had a part in it."

With an involuntary movement she crossed her arms over her body again in a defensive hug. "How does one know these things, Robin? Did some unconscious memory, like a nightmare that haunts you even if you can't describe it, lodge itself in my mind?"

"I don't know," he said, his heart aching for her. He knelt beside the bed and took her cold body in his arms and rubbed her back.

She stayed in his embrace for a few minutes, more to ease Robin's distress than for any real comfort it brought her, then she straightened her shoulders and stood up. "It matters not, Robin. I have to deal with what is and what will be. I will go with you to Woodstock."

Robin jumped to his feet, sure here at least of his ground. "Pippa, you cannot go to Elizabeth. There's no safety for you there. If you join her openly you will be accused of treason. And there's no way you can take refuge with her without Bedingfield's finding out."

"Then I will not go to Elizabeth," she said with an icy calm. "But I will go with you out of this place. I cannot stay here. If you won't help me, then I must go alone."

Robin put his hands on her shoulders. He almost shook her in a desperate need to break her icy detachment. He could barely recognize her. The bright, laughing, devil-may-care Pippa on whom the sun always shone was now this cold shadow.

"Don't be ridiculous, Pippa. Of course you won't go alone. We'll go to Woodstock and then I'll take you into Derbyshire."

Pippa was surprised that she had already made her plans. She shook her head. "No, I won't be safe in England. You will have to help me get to France, to Pen and Owen."

"Yes . . . yes . . . that would be best," Robin agreed, his mind once more working freely. "But then what?" What future would she have running with an infant from the long arm of Spain?

"I can't think of the future," she stated. "I can only deal with the present. I have to get myself and this child to safety."

Her voice was steady, her tone firm as if she was stating the obvious, and Robin could only accept her need to focus on the immediate issues. He pushed his bleak question to the back of his mind. It was fruitless to dwell upon the answer now.

He spoke his thoughts as they came to him. "How can we keep your escape a secret for a day or two . . . you had best be ill and keep to your chamber. Your maid . . . what's her name? . . . Martha . . . can she be trusted?"

"I doubt it," Pippa said with a wry twist to her mouth. "She has already betrayed my confidence once to Stuart."

"Then you'll have to be rid of her," he said matter-of-factly. "Send her away. Pretend that she has offended you in some way and—"

"No, I cannot be so unjust," Pippa interrupted him. "But I will send her to Holborn. I will say that my mother has requested that she assist the housekeeper there for a few days and that I will use a palace servant until she returns at the end of the week."

"That will serve." Robin paced the chamber. "I will attend on de Noailles now and return here for you within the hour. Make your preparations and see to the maid."

He stopped in midstride. It was a relief to be making plans, to be dealing with the situation not crying over it, but he could not imagine how Pippa was managing to maintain her calm focus when the ever-present reminder of the hideous thing that had been done to her was growing inside her. He wanted to talk to her about it, but he could find no words.

He had to be content with the recognition that beneath the happy-go-lucky, flirtatious facade, she was and had always been a woman of the same ilk as her mother and sister. She would manage to do what had to be done. And yet his silence made him feel like a coward.

He reached for her, wanting to take her in his arms again, but instead she merely reached up and kissed his cheek. " 'Tis all right, Robin. I will get through. Just help me to get out of this vile place."

"Yes," he said. "I'll return within the hour."

"I'll be ready."

The door closed behind him and Pippa locked it. Then she locked the connecting door to Stuart's chamber. She sat down at the table, mixed ink powder with water in the inkwell, and dipped her quill.

She thought for a minute. Thought of how Stuart, her husband, had used her, had betrayed her. And she felt nothing. Stuart had deemed her unworthy of his love and loyalty and she deemed him unworthy of any emotion of her own. Why should she waste words and energy on accusations and recriminations?

She began to write. She told him simply that she knew what had been done to her and why he had lent his support. And she told him she was leaving him. Their marriage was not valid in her eyes or those of the church. She would not expose him, but in return he must keep her disappearance a secret for two days and make no attempt to find her, or to claim her as his wife.

She signed the parchment, sanded it, folded it, and sealed it. She wrote his name on the front.

She tapped the folded sheet against the palm of her hand. It was the end of her marriage. The end of her life as she had known it. The end of all expectations of what her life would be.

A curious thought. Strangely detached from her self, from the physical presence of her self in this so familiar chamber.

Pippa unlocked the door to Stuart's chamber and entered. It was empty as she had known it would be. She didn't think her husband had slept in his own bed for close on a week.

She put the letter on the mantelpiece above the brightly burning fire. He would find it when he returned from wherever he was, to change his clothes for the day.

She left, locked the door again, and rang for Martha.

Nineteen

❦

"I think I would like to ride in the city this morning, Malcolm," Luisa stated as she arranged her skirts in graceful folds across the saddle.

"Not much chance for a gallop in the streets, m'lady," Malcolm pointed out, mounting his own horse.

"Maybe not, but I'm tired of the river and the park. I've seen little enough of the city and I would like to ride towards the city walls. Isn't there a place called Aldergate?"

"Aldgate," Malcolm corrected.

"I understand it's very busy, with crowds of people, a lot to see," Luisa said with an eager and disarming smile.

"That's true enough. But it'll be noisy and dirty. Can't hear yourself think, like as not."

"Oh, I would like to hear some noise and see some dirt," Luisa declared. "You cannot imagine how tame life is, Malcolm."

"Reckon I can at that," Malcolm replied. "But Crema won't like it."

"Oh, she'll be good as gold." Luisa leaned over and stroked the mare's neck. "It's good for her to learn to handle crowds."

"She'll handle them well enough," Malcolm said. "But she won't like it, is what I said."

"Then perhaps I should use another horse. Don Ashton has others, surely one would suit me."

Malcolm shook his head. "Mr. Ashton doesn't keep ladies' horses in his stables . . . none but Crema."

"So what should we do?" She raised an inquiring eyebrow.

"Reckon we'll take to the streets," the groom said phlegmatically. He headed for the gate out of the yard and onto the street.

Luisa smiled and followed, her heart skipping a little with excitement. It was a challenge, to see if she could outsmart the sharp Malcolm. It would only be a momentary triumph, but she needed something to keep her wits honed.

Thanks to her excursions with Robin the street scenes were not as unfamiliar to her as she would have Malcolm believe. She averted her eyes from a bearbaiting, glanced with a shudder of sympathy at a vagrant whose ears had been pinned to the pillory, and guided with an expert hand Crema's delicate high-stepping across filthy cobbles and through the running sewage of the kennels.

Malcolm kept his eye on her in his usual relaxed fashion. He had some sympathy for the lady's need for a change of scene. They left the Royal Exchange behind and rode along Lombard Street. Luisa could see the city walls up ahead. All around her the throng ebbed and flowed going into and out of London. Aldgate was very close now.

Luisa drew rein suddenly. "Malcolm, I would like to look in that silversmith's shop." She pointed with her whip to the dark interior of a shop whose wares were indicated by a silver hammer hung above the lintel. " 'Tis Dona Bernardina's birthday next week and I had it in mind to buy her a silver thimble."

She gave him her smile again. "I cannot buy anything if I cannot visit the shops and markets."

That was certainly true, Malcolm reflected. He dismounted and went to help Luisa from her horse.

"There's no need to accompany me," she said, covering her face with her discreet black mantilla. "I would not wish to leave Crema in the hands of a street urchin."

Malcolm looked into the gloom of the silversmith's shop. He could see nothing out of the way there. There were no other customers, and the smith himself was polishing a pair of candlesticks.

He took the reins of both horses. "Very well, m'lady. I'll wait here with the horses."

"Thank you, Malcolm."

Her smile was concealed beneath the silk of her mantilla but he could hear its warmth in her voice. He nodded with a half smile in return and turned to survey the street.

Luisa stepped over the threshold of the shop. The silversmith came forward, rubbing his hands expectantly. "What can I show you, m'lady?"

"Thimbles," she said, her gaze darting around the dim, dusty room. She saw what she had hoped to see at the rear. "Could you assemble what wares you have and I will return in five minutes to make a selection."

The smith beamed his agreement and disappeared through an archway to the right of the table where he'd been working.

Luisa darted towards the door she'd seen at the rear of the shop. If it did what she expected of it after her excursions with Robin, it would open onto a back alley. The back alleys were all connected, a whole warren of lanes that snaked through the city keeping vaguely to parallel paths with the main thoroughfares.

She stepped out into sunshine. It was close to noon. A couple of very small half-naked children toddled out of a noxious courtyard into the lane. Luisa hurried past them. She knew where Aldgate was from Lombard Street, all she had to do was follow the same basic direction along the backways. No more than three or four minutes.

She half ran, her skirts held high to protect them as much as possible from the muddy, unpaved ground. To her surprise she felt no fear. It was reckless even at high noon for a woman dressed as she was to go alone through these parts of the city and yet she felt ridiculously invulnerable. And maybe she gave off some aura of invincibility because apart from a few curious glances no one made any attempt to impede her progress.

The lane twisted and turned and debouched into Aldgate at the very top of Lombard Street. Luisa stopped to catch her breath. She wondered how she would see Robin in this throng. He would be heading for the gate, of course.

She pushed her way towards the gate, where a constant shoving, shouting procession pressed in both directions. Watchmen stood idly by. Outside curfew the gate was open to all unless they received orders to close the city. Luisa found a spot against the wall, close to the gate, and waited, searching the throng, her heart beating fast. If Robin didn't appear soon, she would have to go back to Malcolm.

And then she saw him. He was riding beside a closed carriage and his expression made her stare. Her excitement vanished like a flame under a bucket of sand. She had never seen him look so bleak, so angry, and yet so cold. She was used to his laughter, his teasing, his light flirtation, and sometimes to an intensity in his gaze that made her heart sing. But this was not a man she knew.

She stepped out almost without thinking, right into his path. "Robin?"

He looked down at her, so astonished that for a moment it was as if he didn't recognize her. "Luisa?"

The carriage had halted and a lad of about thirteen jumped down. "Are we to go through, sir?" He stared at the veiled woman in frank curiosity.

"Just a minute, Jem." Robin dismounted. "What on earth are you doing here, Luisa?"

"It was a little adventure. I wanted to see if I could slip away from . . . Oh, never mind that! What is the matter, Robin? What has happened?" She laid a hand on his arm, her voice a thrum of anxiety and sympathy.

The carriage door opened and Pippa stepped down. "Why have we stopped?"

" 'Tis just me," Luisa said, tossing back her veil. "I was having a little fun but I see that I have been foolish." She came to Pippa, reaching a hand for hers. "You look so dreadful. Both of you. Please tell me what has happened. How can I help you?"

Pippa's first reaction was impatient annoyance. They had no time to stand in the street having a pointless discussion with an importunate girl who didn't understand anything of reality.

"You cannot, Luisa," she said with a dismissive gesture, turning back to the carriage. And then came a sudden overwhelming desire for the company of another woman, for the familiar comforts female companionship would offer after the dreadful betrayals of men.

But she needed her mother or sister, not Luisa. Luisa was too sweet and too young to understand life's evils. And she should be sheltered from them.

She said peremptorily over her shoulder as she climbed into the carriage, "Come, Robin, we have no time to waste."

Before she could close the door, however, Luisa scrambled in after her. "You may think I can be of no help, Lady Nielson, but I think I can," she said with a stubborn twist to her mouth. "I intended to turn back as soon as I had met with Robin, but now I know that that is not what I am supposed to do."

Robin's head appeared in the doorway. "God's blood, Luisa, get out! What are you doing here alone?"

"Never mind," she said. "I'm going with you. Lady Nielson is my chaperone, so there will be no damage to my reputation, and I can see that she needs my help."

They had no time for this, Pippa thought. But she felt a certain admiration for Luisa's persistence, and a sympathy with her relish for adventure. Both traits she recognized in herself. She wondered fleetingly if she still possessed them. Or had they been stamped out of her by the heavy boots of horror?

And then she thought that maybe Luisa could help her to find that part of her old resilient self that would enable her to lift her head above the mud. At the very least her bubbling companionship would be a diversion.

She threw scruple to the devil. If the girl wanted to find herself hip deep in this mire, then so be it. "Let her come, Robin."

Robin shook his head. "For God's sake, Luisa, Dona

Bernardina ... your guardian ... they will be frantic with worry."

"I will find a way to send them a message." She threw a shrewd glance between the two of them. "When it is safe to do so."

No fool, this Dona Luisa, Pippa thought. She said with something approaching a smile, "Robin, if you are not prepared to wrestle Luisa from this carriage, I think she must accompany us. Indeed, I would think it discourteous of you to send her home alone through the city streets and you know that we dare not tarry another minute."

Robin realized he could dispute neither of these statements. Luisa had settled herself firmly on the seat opposite Pippa and it would take more than a mere man to wrestle her down. He threw up his hands, slammed the carriage door, and remounted.

LIONEL BARELY HEARD THE CONVERSATION AROUND Philip's council table. His fingers stroked the narrow stem of his wine goblet, his gaze rested unseeing on a patch of sunlight on the oak surface of the table.

"Don Ashton, how did it happen that Lady Nielson flouted the king's edict this morning?" Gomez leaned across the table towards him.

Lionel forced his attention back to the chamber. "That was my error. Last even I had given her permission to ride this morning and told her to depart from the smiths' court. When His Majesty decided to visit the court himself I did not think that Lady Nielson would have ventured forth so early in the morning."

He shrugged and drank from his goblet. "It was

barely past dawn. Ladies of the court are not in general early risers."

"Unless, of course, they are attendant upon the queen," Renard declared piously. "Her Majesty is at her prayers well before dawn and dealing with matters of state soon after."

Lionel made no response to this admiring observation. He drank again and leaned back as a page hastily refilled his goblet. The wine seemed to be having little effect on him although he was drinking more deeply than was his habit.

"You appear distracted, Don Ashton," Philip remarked, leaning one elbow on the wide carved arm of his chair, reflectively rubbing his chin with his forefinger.

"No, sire. I am not in the least distracted." Lionel set down his goblet.

"I am considering whether it would not be better for all concerned if Lady Nielson were to be removed to my house. My ward and her duenna are already in residence, so there would be no hint of impropriety. It will be much easier to control her movements there. 'Tis impossible in the palace unless she is kept under lock and key and I don't think that would be wise. We don't wish to draw yet more attention to the situation. Her obvious imprisonment in the palace would stir up anger and resentment from Elizabeth's supporters and we need to keep them quiescent."

"And what of her husband?"

"Lord Nielson, I am certain, will offer no objections. He can be told to explain that since he's so busy himself he cannot care adequately for his wife, and she would benefit from close female companionship since her own family are absent from court."

"Nielson will do as he's told after last night's little incident with his lover," Renard said, his thin mouth tight. "My men tell me it went off very well."

"Well, I think you should do as you think fit, Don Ashton," Philip stated. "The queen and I have no wish to think of the matter again."

Unless it becomes necessary. It was the unspoken thought of every man at the table, but no one would venture to cast doubts on the successful conclusion of the queen's pregnancy.

Lionel pushed back his chair. "I will put this matter in train immediately."

He bowed to the table and left the chamber.

Removing Pippa from the palace was essential to securing her safety. He had had this suggestion in mind for several weeks, guessing that it would be well received, particularly by Pippa, but that had been before this morning's dreadful revelation. Now he had to coerce her cooperation. His shame and remorse were so powerful he could not imagine how he was to face her, how to talk to her. But it had to be done.

He rapped sharply on her chamber door. Silence answered his knock. He rapped again. Usually her maid was with her. Still silence. He tried to lift the latch but it was locked. He hesitated for a minute, then strode to the door of the adjoining apartment.

His knock there was also received in silence but he could hear someone moving around and without hesitation he opened the door.

Stuart whirled from the fireplace, a letter in his hand. "What are you doing here?" he demanded, white-faced.

"I was in search of your wife," Lionel said calmly. "Her door is locked and there is no answer to my knock."

"Perhaps she's asleep," Stuart said. His hand trembled and he let it drop to his side, concealing the parchment in the folds of the cloak he still wore. He had found Pippa's letter as soon as he'd entered his chamber.

Lionel frowned. He went to the connecting door and tried it. It was locked. "You have a key presumably."

"Yes . . . uh . . . no," Stuart stammered. He had had no time to absorb the shock of Pippa's letter, of the realization that she now knew every horror that was to be known, before Ashton had burst in upon him. And even in the best of circumstances the other man somehow managed to reduce him to a cowardly stumbling idiot.

"Yes? Or no?" Lionel inquired in the same detached tone that Stuart hated. The man was a cipher, his remote air masking his thoughts and feelings.

"No." He shook his head vigorously.

"Come now, man. I find it impossible to believe that you have no key to your wife's chamber." Lionel held out his hand. "Give it to me."

How had Pippa imagined he could keep her disappearance a secret for two days from the man who was charged with watching over her? Stuart thought desperately. A stronger man than he was could not withstand Ashton's hard-eyed stare, the imperatively extended hand.

His gaze darted involuntarily towards the chest by the window. Lionel followed his eyes and quietly crossed the chamber and picked up the brass key that lay openly on the chest.

He inserted it in the lock and opened the door to Pippa's empty chamber.

"Do you know where she is?" he asked, his voice unchanging.

"No." That much was true.

Lionel turned back to Stuart. "I think you had better let me see that letter." He gestured to the hand that Stuart still held at his side.

Helplessly and in silence Stuart handed it to him.

Lionel read the letter, crumpled it in his hand, and threw it into the fire. "Do you have any idea how much danger she's in?" he demanded, and the anger now was clear in his voice.

It stung Stuart. "Of course I do! And do you think I don't know why Gabriel was attacked last night? I am many things, Ashton, but I'm not a blind fool."

For this moment Lionel could find none of his usual disdain for Stuart Nielson, he himself was tarred too thickly with the same brush. "I would imagine Pippa's with her brother. There's no one else she would turn to, is there?"

"Not that I'm aware of."

"Very well. As it happens, we can keep her disappearance a secret for a while. I have the king's permission to remove her to my roof, where she will have the companionship of my ward and her duenna. They will assume that that's where she is."

"And you will go in search of her?"

"Of course." The affirmative was sharp. "If she's not with her brother then I'm certain he will know how to find her. I'll find *him* through the French ambassador."

"How did she discover this?" Stuart's question was both bewildered and resentful. "How could she have found out?"

Lionel hesitated, then said, "She discovered your secret by accident. She's known about it for some weeks. For the rest . . ." He shook his head. "It seems that she retained some confused memory of what happened to her on those nights with Philip. She insisted on knowing the truth."

"And you simply *told* her?" Stuart was aghast.

"She deserved the truth," Lionel said curtly. "It was the least she deserved after what had been done to her."

"Then why not let her go with her brother . . . now that she knows everything?" Stuart spoke with surprising power and determination.

"And you really imagine Philip and his cohorts will shrug their shoulders and wish her well?" Lionel demanded impatiently. "If I don't find her before they do, her life will not be worth a sou. You know that as well as I do. And you know damn well that only I can protect her."

Stuart's complexion grew even paler. He turned aside from the other man's hard and angry stare. "I have had enough, Ashton. I will not play this part any longer. I will not be blackmailed any longer."

"And how do you intend to stop it?" Sarcasm edged his voice. He no longer felt pity for Stuart. His own actions were despicable, but he had not known Pippa, he had owed her no loyalty, he had betrayed no trust.

Stuart simply shrugged. He would not tell the enemy what he intended to do.

"For your wife's sake, do nothing foolish," Lionel demanded harshly. "Let no one know of her disappearance." He turned on his heel and left Stuart, the door banging shut behind him.

Stuart slowly unclenched his fists. Pippa was out of his hands. She was Ashton's responsibility. His own responsibility lay in undoing as much as possible of the damage he'd done her.

The Bishop of Winchester would hear a full confession of Lord Nielson's relationship with Gabriel. The bishop would have to keep the secrets of the confessional but he would have to agree to annul the Nielsons' marriage. With that achieved, Stuart would send notice of the annulment and the reason for it to Lord and Lady Kendal. At least Pippa would be free of him. And she would never have to lay eyes upon him again.

Once he'd made what reparations he could he would take Gabriel and they would flee the country. He would have to work quickly to ensure the advantage of surprise. They were watching him closely but they thought he was still afraid of them, and they need never know otherwise until he and Gabriel were on the high seas.

LIONEL WAS ADMITTED IMMEDIATELY INTO THE PRESence of the French ambassador.

Antoine de Noailles concealed his surprise and his intense curiosity with a diplomat's expertise. "Mr. Ashton, an unexpected pleasure. May I offer you wine?"

"Let us not beat about the bush, de Noailles. I need to know where Robin of Beaucaire has gone. I had some conversation with him last evening . . . perhaps he mentioned it."

The ambassador poured wine and handed his guest a goblet. "Pray take a seat, sir."

"No, I thank you. I prefer to remain on my feet." He regarded de Noailles over the lip of his goblet and spoke crisply. "Come, let us not play games, man. There is no time. I have reason to believe that Lord Robin is escorting his sister. She is in very grave danger and, although Lord Robin may be an accomplished courier and an experienced spy, he cannot protect the lady unaided."

"He is not in your league, I grant you," the ambassador said with a tiny shrug. "I would wonder why you would wish to protect her when you were so intimately involved in putting her in this danger."

A muscle twitched in Lionel's cheek but other than that his face remained without expression. He reached into the inside pocket of his doublet and drew out a small box. "This may speed up our conversation." He laid it on the table beside the ambassador.

De Noailles picked it up. He shot his visitor a quick comprehending glance before lifting the lid. A seal in the shape of a scarab lay on a piece of velvet. "Your credentials?" he inquired, taking the seal gently in his hand.

"If you would have them," Lionel returned with a dry smile. "I would have you understand that only the direst circumstances would force me to reveal them."

"Yes, I'm sure that's true." He returned the scarab to its box and handed it back to Lionel. "Even I do not have the seal. How many are there?"

Lionel shook his head. "You know as well as I that there are three. Only three."

"And do you know who holds the other two?" Antoine's eyes were greedy with curiosity.

"No," Lionel said. He laughed slightly. "We are a select group, my dear sir. And I have just compromised myself. Now, tell me where I may find Lord Robin."

"I think first you must tell me how you intend to prevent the Spaniards getting their hands on the child Lady Pippa is carrying without breaking your cover."

"I have no choice but to break my cover," Lionel said. "It was always going to be a necessity in the end. I had hoped to preserve it until close to the end but . . ." He shrugged. "Needs must when the devil drives, *mon ami.*"

He tossed the scarab box from hand to hand. "If I can succeed in preventing Spain taking over English sovereignty then a lost cover is worth it." He tucked the box back into the inner pocket of his doublet.

"Tell me . . ." De Noailles eyed him shrewdly. "What do you hear about Mary's pregnancy?"

"Probably what you hear. That it is false . . . that it exists only in her mind . . . a product of wishful thinking." He raised an inquiring eyebrow.

The ambassador nodded. "I hear that 'tis said among her women that she has had a similar condition before, some kind of strangulation of the womb."

"But her physicians give her hope."

"They wish to remain in her favor."

"And who can blame them," Lionel said with a sardonic shake of his head. "Are you going to tell me what I wish to know, sir?"

"I suppose I must, although you have not given me any guarantees of the lady's safety."

Lionel's mouth took a grim turn. "I swear to you on my sister's grave that I will keep her and her unborn child safe."

The ambassador sat in silence for a minute. The soft menace in his visitor's voice chilled him. Only a fool would run afoul of Lionel Ashton.

He said finally, "Robin has gone to Woodstock, stopping to visit Sir William of Thame on the way. You put the cat among our pigeons last even, sir, with your talk of scarabs. I have changed the identifier and Robin has gone to inform Parry and thus Elizabeth that there may be a spy in their midst."

"There certainly is one, if not half a dozen," Lionel said with a dismissive shrug. "But as it happens, sir, 'tis not I. You have no need to change the identifier."

"No," the ambassador agreed. "If you will wait but a minute I will give you a letter for Lord Robin that will explain that . . . and in addition I hope will enable him to see you in a new light." The latter statement was accompanied by an ironically raised eyebrow.

Lionel merely inclined his head in acknowledgment and set down his glass with a chink on the table. The ambassador wrote rapidly, waxed and sealed the paper, and handed it to Lionel.

"My thanks," Lionel said shortly, thrusting it inside his doublet. "I will take the road to Thame then. For the moment, the Spanish council believes that Pippa is under my roof, keeping company with my ward and her duenna. We have a head start."

"I will ensure that everyone knows that and nothing else," the ambassador said. "God go with you, Mr. Ashton."

"I'll settle for luck," Lionel replied. "I have little truck with any god. Too much evil is done in that name."

MALCOLM WAS A PATIENT MAN. HE HELD THE HORSES' reins in the sunshine outside the silversmith's shop, watching the passersby and giving no particular thought to the time. He understood that women enjoyed shopping, and Dona Luisa had little enough opportunity for it. If it took her half an hour to choose a thimble he would not object.

Finally, however, it struck him that she was taking a very long time. He tethered the reins to the iron ring set into the wall of the shop and entered the gloomy interior.

The silversmith came in from the back with a swift

and eager step at the sound of footsteps in his shop. "Ah, y'are back, m'lady, I've—" His welcoming voice died as he saw that the newcomer was not the young lady for the thimbles.

"Oh, begging your pardon. I thought you were another customer."

"Where's the young lady who came in here a short while ago?" Malcolm looked around the empty shop, a sinking feeling in his belly as premonition loomed.

"She asked me to get out some thimbles for her to look at. Said she'd be back in five minutes." He glanced at the watch on his belt. "That was close on half an hour ago."

"Hell and the devil!" Malcolm muttered. Dona Luisa for some reason had given him the slip. How had he let himself be fooled by that sweetly innocent smile?

He strode to the rear door and stepped out into the alley. Two half-naked grubby toddlers were playing in a mud puddle. "You seen a lady go past here?" he asked them.

They gazed up at him in wide-eyed incomprehension. He muttered another oath and ducked back into the shop.

"She coming back then, sir?" The silversmith was rather disconsolately examining his tray of thimbles.

"I doubt it," Malcolm said on his way out of the front door. He retrieved the horses, mounted his own, and then leading Crema he went around the side of the shop to the alley behind.

She had been interested in Aldgate, and clearly she'd found the back way there. A woman hanging washing on a line told him that she had seen a veiled woman run by her cottage.

"In summat of an 'urry, she was," she observed

placidly, shaking out a shirt. "Thought it were strange. We don't get such folks around 'ere."

Malcolm thanked her and pressed on towards Aldgate. With something akin to despair he examined the throng, the shrieking barrow boys and street vendors. It was a lively enough scene and would satisfy anyone's thirst for variety, but there was no sign of Dona Luisa. He tried the three taverns, although he could not imagine that such a sheltered creature would venture into their sour-smelling taprooms.

He asked a straw-sucking watchman if a young lady with a black veil had passed through the gate. The man shook his head and spat on the ground at his feet. "Nah, seen no lady 'ere. Leastwise, not on foot."

"On horseback?"

"Nah. In a carriage."

"How long ago?"

The watchman took another straw from behind his ear and sucked on it as he considered the question. " 'Alf an hour, mebbe. Mebbe more. There was a gennelman ridin' alongside the carriage."

"Describe him."

The man shrugged. "Didn't take much notice. Regular kind of gennelman. Wearin' a green cloak. And he were on a black 'orse."

A gentleman in a green cloak and riding a black horse had visited the Ashton mansion that morning. Dona Luisa had seemed more than ordinarily pleased to see the visitor. Malcolm had heard her hastily swallowed exclamation of pleasure at the sight of Robin of Beaucaire.

He could go after them himself, but he didn't know what road they had taken, and if he missed them, or if the lady was not Dona Luisa, then he would have wasted critical time. It was possible that she had been snatched out of the lanes when she'd left the silversmith's, although he didn't think that likely. The cottage of the woman who had seen her was situated at the very point where the lane opened onto Aldgate.

No. Malcolm made up his mind. Dona Luisa had gone of her own accord, so she was in no immediate danger. It was for Mr. Ashton to decide what to do. He had to avert a scandal and if Malcolm was involved in a scene on the highway a scandal would definitely result. There were maybe things Mr. Ashton knew about Lord Robin of which Malcolm was unaware. He could not afford to waste another minute.

He put his horse to the gallop, and, leading Crema, forced his way through the crowds.

Twenty

"I THINK THEY HAVE BEEN GONE FOR FAR TOO LONG, Don Ashton," Bernardina announced. "It has been well over an hour."

"That is hardly a long ride," Lionel said, one hand on the newel post. The duenna had arrested him on his way upstairs to gather necessary articles for his journey and he could not conceal his impatience. "You worry overmuch, madam. As long as she's with Malcolm, there's nothing to fear."

Bernardina opened her mouth to protest just as the front door was flung open behind them. She turned with a gasp as Malcolm hurried in.

"*Madre de dios!*" she cried. "I knew it! Where is she? Where is my baby?"

Malcolm didn't understand the Spanish but the gist was perfectly clear. He brushed her aside, however, and addressed Lionel. "She gave me the slip," he said without preamble. "Said she wanted to go into a silversmith's shop to buy a thimble for the duenna and went out the back way."

"*What?*" Lionel stared at him in disbelief. "Luisa?"

"Yes, sir. I'm trying to tell you. She wanted to go to Aldgate for some reason, but now I think she was meeting someone there. The watchman saw a lady in a coach pass through the gate."

"There must be dozens of ladies in coaches going through the gate!"

"Aye, sir, but the gentleman riding alongside sounded from his description like Lord Robin of Beaucaire," Malcolm said stolidly.

Dona Bernardina had understood nothing but she knew that name. She gave a little shriek and sank down on a bench against the wall. "I knew it," she moaned. "I knew when they came to supper that no good would come of it."

Lionel turned to her. "What do you mean? Luisa had never met the man before. She has never met anyone outside this house."

"I told you . . . I warned you. . . ." Bernardina was weeping now. "What will her dear mother say? I told you there was something suspicious about the way she keeps slipping out of the house when I'm asleep. I told you, Don Ashton, that there was a *man*."

Lionel stood in frowning thought. Malcolm said, "I'm right sorry, sir. She didn't have anything with her . . . for a journey, like. She just seemed like her usual self. A bit lively, but then she always is when we go out."

"I should have found some outlet for that liveliness," Lionel said acidly. "She fooled me, Malcolm, there's no reason for you to feel guilty."

Malcolm did not look absolved. "I didn't know whether to go after them, sir, but I didn't want to waste any time just in case."

"No, you did the right thing to come straight to me. What a wretched little minx she is." He sounded annoyed, but there was none of the shock and anger that Malcolm had expected.

"What is it?" Bernardina demanded. "Do you know where she is?"

"I believe I do, madam." He tapped his palm against the shiny round knob of the newel post. He had a much more urgent matter to attend to than worrying about Luisa.

What on earth had possessed the girl? If he was right, she was with Robin and Pippa. He had to get Pippa on a boat to France, and he had to be on the boat with her. He could not leave her until she was ensconced in the safe house he had prepared. Now he would have Luisa to worry about. He could hardly send her home alone, and certainly not with Beaucaire's escort. And he couldn't be hampered by Bernardina.

"Damn the girl!" he muttered. "There's no need to fall into a swoon, madam, she has a chaperone. No harm will come of this adventure. No one need know of it and if there are questions she has simply gone on an excursion in the company of Lady Nielson and her brother."

"She has eloped," Bernardina said tragically. "It will be the death of her mother."

"She has not eloped. Beaucaire is not such a fool, in fact I strongly suspect he had no idea what she was planning. Her mother will not know of it unless you tell her." His voice was a snap. "Go to her chamber and pack up a few necessities for her. Malcolm says she has nothing with her. There must be things she will need."

"You're going after her?"

"Of course I am, woman! I'll catch up with them before nightfall. Malcolm, you'll accompany me. Have the chestnut saddled, he'll be fresh."

He took the stairs two at a time. Of all the ridiculous complications. Getting Pippa to safety was a matter of life and death. For her sake he had sacrificed his cover and would never be able to retrieve it. Antoine de Noailles would inform his masters of Lionel Ashton's true affiliation and Spain's network would hear of it in no time. They would hunt him down; he knew far too many of their dirty secrets.

And until he could safely send Luisa back with Malcolm, he would be encumbered with an eighteen-year-old maiden with stars in her eyes.

He opened a locked drawer in the armoire and lifted the bottom. He took the papers from the secret space and inserted them under the false bottom of a small leather traveling bag. He put two neat sacks of doubloons and the box containing the scarab seal on top of them.

He took clean linen, hose, and shirts, and laid them carefully in the bag. A money pouch went into the inside pocket of his doublet where reposed the French ambassador's letter to Beaucaire. He moved with smooth efficiency. He was in a hurry, but not a desperate one. He knew where Beaucaire's little party was going, and he could catch them up on the road to Thame easily enough. The carriage would slow them up considerably. But it would keep Pippa from prying eyes.

Malcolm was waiting for him in the hall, still with an air of discomfort. "Horses are ready, sir."

"Good. Have this strapped to my saddle." He handed over his bag. "Ah, Dona Bernardina, is that Luisa's bag?"

"Yes, Don Ashton." Bernardina was looking both dignified and disapproving as she handed him the embroidered tapestry bag. "But I think I should accompany you."

"If I could take you, I would, believe me," he said with heartfelt sincerity. "But you will not be able to keep up."

Bernardina knew this to be true. She gave a heavy sigh. "I feel that it is my fault."

" 'Tis no one's fault but mine," Lionel said briskly. "You'll have her back in no time."

Bernardina crossed herself and her fingers moved restlessly over her rosary. Lionel hesitated for a second and then shook his head and strode from the house, Malcolm on his heels.

"OH, BUT CARRIAGES ARE VILE THINGS," PIPPA SAID with a sigh, trying to ease her backside on the hard thinly cushioned wooden bench as the iron wheels jolted in the uneven ruts of the road. "I would much prefer to ride."

"So would I," Luisa agreed. She regarded her companion curiously. "Is there a reason why you do not, Lady Nielson?"

"I think we can dispense with the formalities, Luisa. I am usually called Pippa."

"Then I will call you that too if you wish it." Luisa smiled a little shyly. "We are very formal in Spain. 'Tis difficult to feel comfortable with your English informality."

Pippa raised her eyebrows. "Do not tell me you are formal with Robin, Luisa."

Luisa blushed. "No . . . not exactly. But then we have had adventures together."

Pippa found the idea of Robin's taking an innocent maid adventuring too delicious to resist.

"I scent truth!" she said with something approaching a grin. She leaned over to roll up the strip of leather that covered the window. " 'Tis too stuffy in here, we'll put up with the dust."

She sat back again and stretched the tight muscles in her neck. "Come, tell me all. It will divert us a little."

She listened with incredulous amusement as Luisa told her of all her excursions with Robin.

Luisa embellished her stories a little as she saw how life seemed to return to Pippa's eyes and a little color crept into her cheeks. Luisa didn't know what had happened, why they were bouncing around in this uncomfortable carriage, or even where they were going, but it was clear as day to anyone with a smidgeon of sensitivity that some disaster lay behind this precipitous journey and Luisa was certain that Pippa needed her.

She had never been needed before. She had been cossetted and confined, surrounded by people for whom her comfort and wishes were their main concern, and it was a novel sensation to know that it was her turn to provide the comfort and the cossetting.

Pippa laughed aloud at Luisa's description of the gaming tables from where, in her guise as servant girl no better than she should be, she had risen the night's winner to the chagrin of her male competitors.

Robin leaned sideways on his horse and stuck his head in the window. "What has amused you?"

"I've been hearing how you've been leading this poor girl astray," Pippa said. "Fancy encouraging her to behave like a whore!"

Robin grinned. "She came to no harm."

"No, indeed I did not," Luisa agreed with a touch of indignation.

"I doubt you'd be here now if you hadn't felt your wings," Pippa commented.

"I am here because something bad has happened and I think I can help," Luisa stated, fire in her eyes. "I was only intending to have a little adventure, to test my wits against Malcolm's vigilance, and give Robin a surprise. But then it seemed that you needed me." She looked between them, her eyes bright now with challenge.

The moment of diversion had passed. For a short while Pippa's spirits had lifted but now the knowledge of her misery came back with renewed force. The black cloud enveloped her once more and she felt her unhappiness like a physical weight that had settled on her heart.

She said bleakly, "I am glad of your company, Luisa. Robin, let us break our journey for half an hour soon. I am awearied of this carriage and ache from top to toe."

"High Wycombe," he said. " 'Tis the next village. Do not show yourself unveiled though."

"How should I?" Pippa demanded. She wanted to snap at Robin for making such a stupidly obvious comment, but she controlled the urge. He was struggling so hard to do and say the right things. It was not his fault that nothing would ever be right again.

"Why must you not be seen?" Luisa inquired.

Pippa shook her head. "I cannot tell you. 'Tis dangerous knowledge."

"I see." Luisa nodded. "Then I will ask no more questions."

Pippa closed her eyes again. While she found Luisa's presence a comforting distraction she couldn't begin to think what they were to do with the girl. Lionel would be searching frantically for her.

And once he realized she herself had escaped he would also be searching for the king of Spain's whore.

The wretchedly familiar metallic taste was in her mouth and the nausea that had not troubled her so far today rose thick and acid in her throat. She leaned towards the window. "Stop the carriage!"

She stumbled out the minute it had halted. Luisa was behind her. She held her veiled hood back as Pippa vomited into the hedge. "My mother was always sick," she said. "With all her pregnancies."

Pippa straightened slowly, telling herself that one day this would stop. "There is lavender water in my bag, and spearmint. Bring them, will you? I will stay here in the air for a minute."

Robin was standing a few feet away, trying to appear as if he hadn't noticed his sister's distress, but concern was writ large on his face.

How soon would her disappearance be discovered? He prayed that their plan would work and they had at least two days' start on the pursuit. And there would be pursuit. They wanted the child she carried, but Pippa now knew too much to be left at large. He guessed that if they got her in their hands they would keep her alive only until after the child's birth, or until Mary gave birth to a healthy heir.

Perhaps she would be safe in France with her brother-in-law. Owen d'Arcy knew how to hide people as well as to discover them. Once she was beyond Spain's reach they might let sleeping dogs lie, although she would always be at risk. Philip's reputation for vice was so well known that Pippa's tale of her violation, if she chose to tell it, would barely stir the waters.

Robin wondered if she would keep quiet for the child's sake. The lands under Spanish hegemony were littered with Philip's bastards but this one would bear Stuart Nielson's name. The truth of its parentage could easily be kept secret and the child would suffer no stigma. But Pippa would not be able to risk a return to England, not in Mary's lifetime. Only if Elizabeth inherited the crown would Pippa be truly safe.

How Pippa herself would react to the child once it was born was a question of such magnitude that Robin didn't want to explore it. Time enough when they had her safe.

Pippa came back to the carriage, pale but composed. She saw Robin's dark expression, the shadows clouding his eyes, and she touched his hand as if to offer comfort, absurd really when she had none to give herself. "I'm ready to continue, Robin," she said simply.

He nodded. "We'll stop in High Wycombe and get some refreshment . . . perhaps we should stay there for the rest of the day?"

Pippa shook her head in vigorous denial. "No, we must press on . . . put as many miles between us and London as we can. As soon as you've done your work in Thame and Woodstock, we'll make our way to the coast."

"Are we to go on a voyage?" Luisa inquired.

"You aren't," Robin stated flatly. "As soon as Pippa is safe, Jem will escort you back to London."

Luisa made no comment, merely climbed back into the coach. She leaned back in her corner and regarded Pippa anxiously. "Feeling better?"

"Yes, I thank you." Pippa closed her eyes, thinking that if she could just sleep for a little, brief unconsciousness would give her both respite and strength.

Luisa closed her own eyes, the better to think. She had planned to suggest that Jem take a message of her own to her guardian, its gist that her reputation was quite safe with Lady Nielson, who had need of a female companion on her present journey.

It was of course possible that Don Ashton wouldn't see the matter the way she did. In fact it was more than likely that he was already searching for her. But he wouldn't know where to start. He knew nothing of her friendship with Robin, no one knew of it. He would think for the time being that she had been abducted from the streets. They would be desperately anxious and for that she was sorry, but she couldn't see what else to do.

There was one thing of which she was certain. She was going to see this mysterious adventure through to the end. The idea of returning to her previous existence was impossible to contemplate.

LIONEL AND MALCOLM RODE AS IF THE DEVIL'S hounds were on their heels. They reached High Wycombe late in the afternoon and split up to make inquiry of the town's three inns. It was the most obvious place for the travelers to have stopped for refreshment and Lionel was not surprised when Malcolm reported that the White Hart had served a gentleman and his page, and had sent refreshments out to the two ladies who had remained in the carriage except for a few minutes stretching their legs.

Lionel drank a tankard of ale at the ale bench outside the inn and considered. Robin had to carry his now unnecessary message to Lord William of Thame, but he could not risk taking Pippa there with him. Philip and

Mary's spies were everywhere and buzzed with particular vigor around Elizabeth's avowed supporters. The ladies would have to be left in an inn somewhere while Robin completed his business.

He guessed that they would stop well before nightfall, and Robin would probably plan to ride on to Thame tonight and continue to Woodstock in the morning, leaving his companions in hiding. Unencumbered he would be able to ride hard and deliver his messages quickly, so he had to be intercepted tonight, before he reached Lord William at Thame.

Lionel frowned into his ale. He had no illusions. His hardest task would be to convince Robin of Beaucaire to put his sister in his safekeeping. It could prove an impossible task.

He carried with him de Noailles's instructions that Robin cancel his present mission and accept Lionel Ashton as a trustworthy colleague, loyal to their own causes. But would that be sufficient to get Beaucaire to listen to him despite what he must now know about his part in what had been done to Pippa?

Pippa. Even if he succeeded with Robin, how was he to regain Pippa's trust? He was no closer to an answer.

He tossed back the contents of his tankard. "Let's be on our way, Malcolm. We'll need to ask in the villages if they've been seen. I'm certain they'll deviate from the road as we get closer to Thame."

"Right y'are, sir."

They followed the carriage's progress as far as Princes Risborough, and then learned from a cottager that the gentleman riding alongside the carriage had asked for the name of a nearby inn off the main Oxford road that had beds for travelers.

"The Black Cock in Chinnor's as good as it gets in

these parts, and so I told him," the old man said, leaning on his fork over the compost heap he was turning. "Not up to much for gentry folks, but as good as it gets."

"We have them," Lionel stated. His outward demeanor was as calm and detached as always, but his heart felt squeezed and apprehension lay sick and heavy in his belly. He had to persuade Pippa to trust him enough for him to get her to safety. He had to persuade her to endure his unendurable company until she was safely on French soil. He would bear any humiliation, sacrifice every iota of his pride, to achieve this. And he would swear to her that once she was safe he would leave her life forever.

And he didn't know how he could do that.

He turned his horse across the field indicated by the cottager and they rode in silence as the last pink rays of the setting sun faded in the western sky.

PIPPA LOOKED AROUND THE SMALL CHAMBER IN THE Black Cock with a grimace. "I would rather sleep in a tent," she said. "This is filthy. I'm certain there must be fleas."

Robin held up the tallow candle provided by their surly landlord and surveyed the accommodations as unhappily as she. There was but one guest room in the inn and the four of them would have to share it.

"Well, we must make the best of it," Pippa said in resolute tones. She reflected that if this miserable hovel was the worst thing that happened on their flight they could count themselves fortunate.

She made disposition briskly. "Luisa and I will take the bed. Robin, you won't mind the truckle bed, and Jem, I'm afraid you will have to make do with the floor."

She gave the page an apologetic smile. "We'll find a blanket for you."

Luisa tried to conceal her horror at the smell of damp and mildew and dirt. At the unglazed window and the filthy straw on the floor. Pippa's matter-of-fact acceptance of the conditions astonished her. But she had never been exposed to the rough living of a traveler, unlike Pippa, who as a child had traveled in the company of a troop of soldiers the many miles from Derbyshire to London when Lord Hugh of Beaucaire, Robin's father, had arrested her mother and taken her to appear before King Henry VIII and his Star Chamber.

Robin set the candle on the shelf above the cheerless hearth. He regarded Luisa in the dim light and saw her consternation. "You should have stayed at home," he observed.

Luisa flushed angrily. "I do not mind this," she denied. "Pippa will need my help all the more in these conditions."

Pippa gave her an appreciative smile. "That is a very kindly thought, Luisa," she said. "I'm sure we can do something to improve this. I shall go and confront Goodman Brown. He must sweep up this straw and replace it with fresh rushes. A fire would help the dampness, and he must supply fresh herbs to sprinkle on the mattress."

Pippa was aware of a welcome surge of energy at the prospect of something concrete to deal with. Moping with unhappiness sapped one's energy and drive quite dreadfully, she reflected.

Robin followed her into the narrow passage outside. "Pippa, I must leave you here," he said, pulling the door closed behind him so that Luisa could not hear.

"Yes, I know what you have to do," Pippa replied quickly. "Will you return this night?"

"Yes, of course. My errand will not take long."

She tried to hide her relief that they would not be alone overnight. "Then go to it, love. I'll have enough to do trying to make this place habitable and finding something halfway palatable for supper."

"I will leave Jem with you."

Pippa nodded. "Yes, that would be wise. We shall put him to work." She smiled at Jem, who had accompanied his master. "A poor exchange, I know, Jem, but I would not wish to be left here without a man's company."

Jem was so gratified by this elevation in status that he forgot his disgruntlement and returned readily to Luisa and the bedchamber when Robin waved him away.

Robin said uncertainly, "I hate to leave you."

"The sooner you're gone the sooner you'll be back," Pippa replied, heading for the stairs.

"This may cure Luisa of the wish to go adventuring," he said with a sigh as they reached the cramped hallway at the bottom of the stairs.

"Would you wish her cured?" Pippa regarded him with narrowed eyes.

"She's Ashton's ward. She can mean nothing to me," he returned with sudden harshness.

The surge of energy that had buoyed her faded as abruptly as it had come. "She's not tarred with her guardian's brush. I sense only goodness in her." Her voice was low and bitter and she averted her eyes so that he did not see the pain in them. But he felt it nevertheless.

"Pippa, I—"

"No, don't say anything. There's nothing to be said.

I will manage this." She touched his hand. "Go, Robin. We have but two days before they discover I'm gone."

Again he hesitated, but now she met his gaze steadily. "Go," she repeated.

He nodded, and strode out into the gathering dusk.

Pippa stood for a minute, wrestling with the pain that threatened to sap her resolution completely. She knew that she must not see herself as a victim. If she did so she would see no point in going on. She had been touched by an evil, but it was not her *self* that had been touched. She had to hold on to that.

With a little encouraging nod to herself she turned towards the kitchen, prepared to do battle with Goodman Brown and his slatternly wife.

She heard Lionel's voice from the yard before she had taken a step. It came so suddenly it seemed to have sprung from her thoughts. She stood immobile in the shadows of the hall, terror icing her veins. He would take her back.

But she would not go. She would die rather.

Robin's voice, raised in anger and alarm, reached her, drowning out Lionel's more measured tones. She crept farther into the shadows as if they would somehow protect her from discovery.

Had he come after Luisa or herself? Not that it mattered. Once he saw her he would try to take her back.

She moved at last, forcing herself to go to the door that opened on the yard. She could not, *would* not, be found cowering.

Lionel and a man she didn't know had dismounted from their horses and were facing Robin, who had his hand on his sword hilt.

"Don't draw on me, Beaucaire," Lionel said. "I will not fight you and it will do no one any good if you run me through. I have something from the French ambassador for you ... something that may make matters clearer." He put his hand inside his doublet.

Robin kept his hand on his sword but made no move to draw it. With his free hand he took the sealed document. The seal was authentic, unless Ashton had stolen it, or had access to an exact replica. Doubts swirled as he read the message. He knew the ambassador's handwriting and this was certainly it.

He handed the paper back, saying dismissively, "That is all very well, Ashton, but your true colors matter little to me. Your ward is above stairs. My sister is my business, and I may do it all the faster now that my mission is canceled."

"No, I'm afraid she's mine." Lionel took the letter, folded it, and put it back in his pocket. "You must forgive me, but I can get her to safety more effectively than you, Beaucaire."

"As effectively as you used her," Robin said, his hand still on his sword. "You must forgive *me*, Ashton, but I would not trust my sister to you if I were on my deathbed."

"It is for Pippa to make that decision. 'Tis her life at stake," Lionel declared, still quietly. "I believe I can save her life, where you will fail."

Pippa struggled to make sense of the exchange. *What was he saying? What did Robin mean about true colors?*

The sight of Lionel filled her with such rage and sorrow that it took her breath away. She had expected never to lay eyes upon him again and was utterly unprepared for the effect his presence had upon her. It made it impossible for her to think clearly, to make sense of what was going on.

She heard Robin's sword rasp in the sheath as he

drew it. And she knew that good swordsman though he was he would be no match for Lionel.

She stepped out into the yard, her voice carrying through the gloom. "No . . . no, Robin, sheath your sword."

Pippa looked directly at Lionel with eyes so cold he felt they would turn him to stone.

"So, Mr. Ashton, am I to understand that your deep games were all in the right cause? I should be grateful that you would save my life, it seems. How nice for us all to have you on our side."

Her lip curled in a sardonic travesty of a smile. "You will understand, I'm sure, that I prefer to take my chances with my brother. Luisa, however, is above stairs. You will be glad to know that she is quite safe, her reputation untarnished."

"I never doubted that," he said, knowing he must not waver, must not allow Pippa to turn him away however much icy scorn she poured upon his head. "She will return home with Malcolm as soon as 'tis light. But you *must* hear me out, Pippa. Beaucaire cannot do for you what I can."

He looked across at Robin. "I doubt you would dispute that, would you?"

Robin said nothing, his lips set tight and thin in his taut face.

"That may be so," Pippa returned, repeating flatly, "but I will take my chances with my brother."

"You should hear him out." Robin spoke with obvious difficulty, but there were facts he could not deny. It was clear as day that Lionel Ashton had skills he could not begin to match. A mole who could bury himself so deeply in enemy territory would have tricks way beyond Robin's experience.

He put a hand on his sister's arm. "There is so much at stake here, love. At least listen to him."

Common sense told Pippa to take her brother's advice, but it was a bitter pill. Without a word or a gesture she turned back to the inn.

Robin regarded Lionel in bleak silence. Lionel inclined his head in acknowledgment of all that lay beneath the silence, and followed Pippa.

Twenty-one

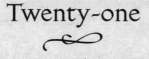

LIONEL FOLLOWED PIPPA UPSTAIRS. SHE DIDN'T AC-knowledge him as she flung open the door of the bed-chamber and entered the room, but she didn't slam the door in his face either.

Luisa gave a little gasp when she saw him and then faced him with the air of a hare at bay. "How did you know how to find me?" she demanded.

" 'Tis unwise to underestimate Malcolm," he said dryly. "I'll talk with you later but for the moment my business lies with Lady Nielson and her brother. Go downstairs and remain with Malcolm until I come to you."

Luisa looked at Pippa in confusion. Instinctively she took a step closer to her.

Pippa touched her shoulder briefly. " 'Tis a compli-cated situation, Luisa, but you need have no fear."

She glanced towards the door where Robin now stood bristling like a terrier. She could hardly endure the prospect of being alone with Lionel, but she could endure even less the prospect of an audience to what-ever was going to be said.

"Robin, will you take Luisa downstairs? See if we can get a fire in here and fresh rushes and some kind of supper."

Robin frowned. "I think I need to hear what Ashton has to say. Do you not wish me to stay with you?"

Pippa shook her head. "No. This lies between him and me."

Robin hesitated before saying reluctantly, "Very well. But I shall be just downstairs. You are to call if you need me."

"I doubt Mr. Ashton means me any further harm."

Lionel winced at the acid remark but he said nothing, merely stood waiting until Robin and Luisa with the intrigued Jem had left them alone.

"What a miserable pigsty," he observed, glancing around the chamber.

"I don't imagine you're here to make small talk," Pippa stated.

She clasped her hands tightly against her skirts, aware that her fingers were trembling a little. She told herself she had nothing more to fear from this man. He had done everything he could to her, but she was afraid that he would say or do something that would weaken her. He had always had such power to move her, to draw her to him. She needed to be armored against him.

"No," he agreed. He looked at her. "I need to tell you something I have never revealed to another person. I tell it to you not as excuse for what I have done, I understand that for you there can be no excuse, but as a simple reason, a matter of fact. Will you hear me out?"

Pippa saw the pain in his steady gaze, heard the desperation beneath the calm tones. She knew she was going to hear something she didn't want to hear, that she was going to be touched with some other evil, and her spirit shrank from it.

"I will hear you." She shivered in the cold dankness of the chamber and drew her cloak more tightly around her.

"I believe I told you that I had five sisters," he began, looking straight at her, but she realized with an inner shudder that he wasn't seeing her, he was inhabiting some other place, some other time.

"Margaret was my twin. She married a Flemish merchant when she was fifteen. Her own choice of husband."

"You lived in Flanders?" Pippa crossed her arms over her breast, hugging herself beneath the cloak. Simple factual questions would be her armor, they would keep all feeling at bay.

"Our father had a fleet of merchant ships that sailed out of the port of London. Pieter Verspoor was one of the traders in Ghent who did business with him. He came to stay one summer. We had a house on the river at Chiswick. He stayed for several months."

The sentences came clipped and short. The tallow candle flickered on the shelf above the hearth and his face was in deep shadow.

"Margaret and Pieter fell in love. It was wonderful to see them together. My sister never did anything by halves. She saw the world in black and white and when she committed herself to something it was with all her heart and mind. She would entertain no criticism, no doubts, once she had given her loyalty to a person or to a cause. She and Pieter were married in Chiswick and sailed to Ghent on one of my father's ships the next day. It seemed their marriage was idyllic. There were two

children in quick succession. Healthy children and un-
complicated births."

He paused for a heartbeat and then said, "In the
spring of 1549 they went to Geneva, where Pieter had
some business, and there Margaret heard John Calvin
preach."

Lionel turned away from Pippa and she could only
see his deeply shadowed profile. He didn't speak again
for a long time and she didn't prompt him. The cold
was now in her bones. And it had little to do with the
ambient temperature in the chamber.

When he spoke again she started. His voice sounded
hollow, as if it was coming from some deep pit.

"You know of course of the emperor's Edicts against
the Reformation. You know how harshly they are ad-
ministered in the Netherlands. You know that it is a
crime punishable by death for a man to know of his
neighbor's heretical beliefs and fail to report them to
the authorities. You know of the Edict of Blood that
makes it a capital crime for any layperson to discuss the
Bible and for anyone who has not studied theology at a
university even to *read* the Bible."

Pippa managed a half nod of comprehension. Her
tongue was thick in her throat. She knew of these things
in the abstract. Everyone did. But she had never had to
confront their reality. The armor was being stripped
from her shred by shred as the horror that would end
Lionel's story began to take life and form.

"Margaret became a passionate Calvinist. Pieter
pleaded with her for the sake of her children to keep her
beliefs to herself. We all pleaded with her." His voice
dropped as if he were talking to himself.

"I still don't understand why she wouldn't listen to
reason. Why she refused to keep her religious beliefs

within the walls of her own house. But Margaret displayed her Calvinism to the world. She would not stoop to clandestine hedge preaching. She preached it in the marketplace. There was no need for a neighbor's tale-telling, although there were many who did. She spoke for all to hear.

"She was three months pregnant with her third child when she was arrested. Because her husband was a respected and powerful citizen, she was treated with consideration, allowed to receive visitors, housed in some degree of comfort. Until Philip arrived in Ghent, sent by his father to sharpen the teeth of the Edicts. The emperor Charles had heard that too many heretics were escaping the stake."

Lionel turned back to Pippa. His expression in the gloom was as twisted and bitter as his voice. "Philip visited my sister in jail. Margaret was a very beautiful woman. She had a fire in her eyes that could inflame a man. Philip offered to overlook her heresy if she would become his mistress. Margaret laughed in his face.

"He took my sister's case under his own personal judgment. She was delivered to the Inquisition in Brussels, who for the remaining months of her pregnancy strove for her immortal soul."

His face twisted with pain and contempt. "They allowed us to see her after five months. They offered us the chance to plead with her to recant. According to the Edicts if she recanted they would bury her alive. If she refused she would be burned. The child was still alive in her womb, God alone knows how. Margaret was unrecognizable, an old and broken woman, but they would not send her to the death she chose until after the birth."

Pippa felt that she had supped full of horror that day.

Horrors that all began and ended with Philip of Spain. She kept her eyes on Lionel and despite everything her heart went out to him. She had tried to shield herself from emotion but there was no shield or buckler proof against the anguish she saw in his eyes.

He continued, his voice now without expression, his face closed. "She would not recant. They racked her during her labor and she still managed to deliver a healthy girl child. They took the child and burned Margaret the next day in the public square. They used green wood. I could do nothing to help her. I had to stand and watch my twin sister, half dead already after months of torture, die a slow and agonizing death.

"I could do nothing!"

It was a dreadful low cry wrenched from the depths of his soul. Pippa was aware that she was weeping soundless tears and she made no attempt to stop their fall. She could not drag her eyes from his tortured countenance. Sick and weak, she sat abruptly on the bed.

When he spoke again, the desperation had left his voice but it was infused with passion of another kind. His gray eyes glittered like liquid mercury.

"I swore then, in the moment of her death, that I would be avenged upon Philip, upon his father, upon Catholicism. I would find ways to frustrate Spanish interests wherever they lay. To do that I had to work from within. I had to get close to the man, become an intimate in his retinue. And I had to lose all emotion, all moral scruple, and pursue just one goal."

He looked at Pippa and for the first time since this had begun she thought that he was really seeing her again, that he had returned to this chill and shadowed chamber. "I do not expect you to forgive me, or even to understand."

He opened his palms in an unconscious gesture of futility. "I did not know you. I could not stop what happened to you, but I could stop their plan from coming to fruition. To do that I had to be a part of it. I intended to take you to safety just before the birth."

He shook his head and turned away from her again as if he could not bear to look at her any longer.

"I did not know you," he repeated softly, "but I realized after that first dreadful night that I had not succeeded in quelling all emotion. I could not distance myself from you as a person, as a *woman*. I found myself needing to get close to you, to help you somehow. When you came to me after you'd discovered your husband's secret, I could not hold back. I gave you what I felt you needed and in the giving received in return a gift more precious than any I could ever have imagined."

He turned slowly back to her. "Since that moment I have been true to you, and to that gift. And now you must let me get you to safety. My plans are laid, although I had not expected to implement them so soon. I have revealed my hand to Philip and am no further use to the people I work for, indeed my life like yours is in danger. So you must bear my company until we reach France. I will not intrude upon you, I swear it, and once you are safe you need never lay eyes upon me again."

Pippa took a deep, shuddering breath. She could find no words. He had drawn her to him with the tale of his agony, just as she had feared, but he was still the man who had taken part in her violation. She told herself this fiercely as if it would thus tear apart the connection he had spun between them. But there was another fact that held tight the silken thread. He was still the man she had loved.

Had? Or *did?*

The hurt was still too great for her to see the answer clearly, but she would have to discover it. Just as she would have to discover if she could forgive.

"What happened to Margaret's child?" Once again she sought distance in facts.

"Judith was given to her father. She's now three years old."

Silence fell between them. Lionel had bared his soul. He could do nothing now but await Pippa's judgment. He stood unmoving, watching her as she remained sitting on the bed, her hands clasped in her lap, her eyes on the floor.

Feet on the stairs, a sharp rapping on the door broke their mutual reverie.

"Pippa!" It was Robin's voice, loud, imperative, infused with anxiety.

Pippa was aware only of relief. "Come in, Robin." She turned her head to the door as it opened.

Robin stood in the doorway suddenly awkward. He didn't know what he'd expected to find, but when at last he couldn't endure the waiting he had raced upstairs in a fever of concern and a sweeping resurgence of his deep anger and distrust of Lionel Ashton. He couldn't understand how he had agreed to leave Ashton alone with the woman whom he had so devastatingly betrayed.

What he found was Pippa sitting quietly on the bed, Ashton standing by the window, and an atmosphere so heavy and portentous that Robin felt that he had intruded upon something that was absolutely none of his business.

"Jem is bringing up hot coals to make a fire and the goodwife is sending a girl to clean the floor and lay fresh rushes," he said as if this was his excuse for intruding. "There's a decent fire in the taproom, we can sit in there until this chamber is prepared."

Pippa felt his discomfort as if it were her own. "Did you contrive supper?" she asked, managing a reassuring smile with difficulty, trying to return some normality, some ordinariness to their situation. "I am famished."

"Oxtail soup," Robin said, a little comforted by the smile. His eyes darted to Ashton by the window. "Are you intending to stay under this roof tonight?"

Lionel said quietly, "That is up to your sister."

Robin looked at Pippa. She rose from the bed. There was no real decision to be made. She could not fall again into Philip's hands, and her best chance of escape lay with Lionel. What lay between them must be ignored. *If it could be.* But that rider she firmly put from her.

"I'm willing to take your advice, Robin. It seems Lionel made plans for my escape long ago."

She came up to him, putting a hand on his arm. "You should not compromise your own position further, love. If you return to London no one will suspect you had anything to do with my disappearance."

"No," he said flatly. "That I will not do. I'm willing to leave the management of this to Ashton, but I am staying with you, Pippa."

"And I'm staying with you too." They had not noticed Luisa, who had followed Robin up the stairs with a much quieter tread and now stood behind him in the doorway.

"You will return to Dona Bernardina with Malcolm first thing in the morning," Lionel declared.

"Forgive me, Don Ashton, but I think Lady Nielson

needs a woman at her side." Luisa stepped past Robin to confront her guardian.

"I do not know what is going on, or why you have to escape, or even where you are all going, but I am going to stay with Pippa. She is with child and it will be most uncomfortable for her to make this journey with only men." She gave Lionel a little nod that was both defiant and confident.

"You would wish me to be with you, Pippa, wouldn't you?"

Pippa could almost find it in her to laugh. Lionel looked astounded; Robin looked as if he didn't know whether to embrace the prospect of Luisa's company or to run from it in terror.

It was clear to Pippa, at least, that Luisa, whether she had acknowledged it or not, had made her choice of husband and was not going to give up without a fight. It was high time Robin found himself a wife, and Luisa, for all her youth, would do very well, she now decided. She had a strong spirit and an unconventional view of the world that would appeal to Guinevere and her daughters. Luisa would feel right at home in Robin's family. Maybe something good would come out of this horror. Maybe she could play matchmaker. It would be a welcome diversion.

"I'll be glad of your companionship," she said. "I can't see how there could be any objections, since I would be your chaperone and you would be traveling with your guardian's escort."

Luisa's answering smile was grateful but the look she gave Robin was triumphant.

Lionel frowned. He didn't need another distraction on this journey but he did need Malcolm to ride ahead to Southampton to organize the ship to take them to

France. He had been trying to think of an alternative since Malcolm would have to take charge of Luisa, but if the girl came with them then he could revert to the original plan. It would save precious time. And a pursuit would not be looking for a party of four.

He looked thoughtfully at Robin and wondered if he realized that Dona Luisa de los Velez of the house of Mendoza had elected him her life's companion. As soon as he could, Lionel decided, he would get out of Luisa exactly what she'd been up to with Lord Robin of Beaucaire under her duenna's nose. In the meantime her intended could take charge of her. He seemed more than capable of doing so, and if wedding bells rang when this nightmare was over, so much the better. It would be the only way to mollify Bernardina.

Dona Bernardina. She would be out of her mind with worry. But he could not reassure her until they reached Southampton.

"Don't make me regret it," he said curtly to Luisa, who gave him a radiant smile that he had difficulty resisting.

He changed the subject. "We must make all speed. The carriage is too slow. Malcolm will ride ahead at dawn to organize the ship. Beaucaire, I trust you can spare your page to take the carriage back to London. We must cover our tracks."

Robin's nod was terse.

"And if you will take Luisa on your pillion, I will take Lady Nielson."

Again Robin nodded.

"I will ride alone," Pippa said. She detested pillion-riding and she did not relish the prospect of clinging to Lionel's belt for long hours.

"No, you must ride with me. We cannot buy horses

and thus leave a trail," Lionel pointed out. All diffidence had left him; he held the authority here now and the decisions were his to make. "If there is any pursuit, and I don't expect any, then we will split up and go our separate ways to Southampton."

"So much for Luisa's reputation," Pippa murmured.

"You're remarkably flippant," Robin said, flushing.

" 'Tis that or weep," Pippa returned smartly, sounding much more like herself. The die was cast, nothing would be gained by a show of resentment. She would think up some alternative to the pillion pad on the morrow.

"I have every faith that Luisa's reputation will be safe in your brother's hands. It appears to have been so hitherto," Lionel observed, dry as dust. It was Luisa's turn to flush.

Pippa stepped in. "If we've settled the mechanics of this, could we please go in search of oxtail soup?" She headed to the door, the others on her heels.

Lionel followed them downstairs. Malcolm stood by the open front door, chewing reflectively on a straw as he gazed out into the star-filled night. He turned at his master's approach. "So what now, sir?"

"You'll leave for Southampton at dawn." Lionel spoke briskly. "I believe *Sea Dream* is taking on a cargo of cloth and raw wool and expects to sail to Calais in two days' time. If all goes well and we ride hard we should reach Southampton by then, but tell her captain to be prepared to postpone his departure in case we're delayed."

"Aye, sir."

"Then meet us at the usual house in Chandler's Ford. I'll need you to escort Dona Luisa back home. She can't travel alone with Lord Robin."

"No, sir," Malcolm agreed. "And I'll make sure she doesn't give me the slip this time."

Lionel nodded. "Go to your supper then, I have some arrangements to make with mine host."

He found Goodman Brown in the kitchen nursing a tankard of strong ale while his good lady bustled red-faced over her cook pots. "Fresh rushes indeed!" she grumbled. "An' dried 'erbs on the mattress. Jest who do they think they are? Too good for the likes of ordinary folk."

Her husband offered no opinion and regarded Lionel's sudden appearance in the kitchen with hostility and apprehension. "What would you be wantin' in 'ere, sir?"

"I need another guest chamber," Lionel explained. As he saw Goodman Brown about to shake his head, he said sharply, "You'll be well paid for it."

"There's the chamber over the wash'ouse," the goodwife said at last, her tone grudging.

"Show it to me, if you please."

The woman wiped her hands on a grimy cloth, took up a lantern, and headed for the kitchen door. The air outside was pleasantly cool after the heat of the kitchen but it was not particularly fresh.

The washhouse was a small building attached to the main house. The smell of soap and lye permeated the air as Lionel followed the woman up a rickety set of stairs and into a small chamber. Moonlight fell onto the dusty floor from an unglazed round window high on the wall. The only furniture was a narrow cot.

Lionel inspected the straw mattress. It seemed cleaner than the one in the main house. He guessed it was rarely used. The inn didn't attract many wayfarers.

There were no fleas that he could discover. And the washhouse had an important strategic advantage.

"This will do. Fetch sheets of some kind and blankets, and make up another bed of straw and blankets on the floor. Your maid will share the bed in the other chamber with my ward. Supply both chambers with jugs of hot water and a lamp, the ladies will be retiring within a half hour."

He didn't wait for an acknowledgment but strode immediately down the stairs and back to the inn. He found the rest of the party in the taproom, dipping spoons and chunks of dark barley bread into a communal bowl. A much-eroded wheel of golden cheese sat in the middle of the stained deal table.

"This soup is surprisingly good," Pippa said. She was amazed at her own hunger, at the pleasure she was taking in its satisfaction. She felt healthy and energetic, as if some burden had been taken from her. Which was absurd, because all her burdens were as heavy as ever.

" 'Tis good if you're not too fastidious about its container," she continued on the same cheerful note. "I doubt the pot has been washed since it was on the wheel." She slid up on the bench to give Lionel room and passed him a thick crust of bread.

"My thanks." He wondered what she was really thinking. She was behaving as if nothing momentous had occurred; her manner to him was courteous and friendly; there was no special warmth, however, and she barely looked at him.

If she had chosen this approach as the least awkward for their companions, he would simply follow suit. He sampled the soup with his bread, and drank from the pitcher of ale that was circulating among them.

It surprised him that Luisa appeared to have no

reservations about this rough-and-ready communal supper. It was almost as if she was accustomed to an inn's taproom and had supped in this manner before. Perhaps she had, presumably in Beaucaire's company.

He glanced at Robin. The man was wound taut as a lute string but his concerns tonight were clearly all for his sister. He was watching her like a hawk. She, in her turn, responded to his anxious glances with reassuring smiles.

"There's a small chamber over the washhouse with a separate entrance from the kitchen yard. Pippa will sleep there and I'll keep guard at her door so that if we have any unwelcome visitors I can get her away without having to come through the inn. Malcolm will keep watch in the inn throughout the night. Robin and Luisa will take the upstairs chamber. I have arranged for the girl, Nell, to sleep with Luisa."

He glanced around the table with an interrogatively raised eyebrow but no one offered any objections to his arrangements. He swung off the bench. "Luisa, Dona Bernardina packed a bag for you with some necessities; 'tis in the hallway. I'll escort you to the washhouse now, Pippa. There should be a jug of hot water in both chambers. Then I'm going to make a reconnaissance. Beaucaire, will you accompany me?"

"Yes . . . yes, of course." Robin scrambled off the bench. Luisa would be safely in bed with the curtains drawn by the time they returned.

"How beautifully organized," Pippa murmured, unable to resist it. "You seem to have thought of everything, sir."

He responded in kind. "I try. I presume you have a bag?"

"In the chamber above. Jem, will you fetch it?" She

nodded to the page, who ran from the taproom still eating his bread and cheese, and returned within a minute with Pippa's leather bag.

Lionel took the satchel and slung it over his shoulder. He turned to Luisa. "I bid you good night, my ward. When I have a moment to think, we shall have a little talk, you and I."

"Yes, Don Ashton," Luisa murmured with downcast eyes. Her meek demeanor didn't fool anyone.

"Robin, you will see her safe upstairs. Come, Pippa." He went to the door.

Pippa threw her cloak around her shoulders and followed him in silence. Only a potboy was in the kitchen, sitting on the hard wooden bench in front of the range, yawning deeply. It was his job to keep the range on overnight but the warmth of his sleeping place more than made up for its lack of softness.

"You will not bolt this door tonight," Lionel instructed him as he opened the kitchen door.

"Oh, but missus—"

"Forget your mistress for the moment," Lionel interrupted him. "For tonight, I am your master and you will obey my instructions, is that clear?"

The boy nodded, his sleepy eyes widening. "You'll 'ave to make it right wi' the missus."

"I'll make it right, rest assured," Lionel said in softened tones. He stepped out into the unpaved yard.

Pippa looked around, wrinkling her nose. There was a strong smell coming from the midden at the rear of the yard, and the dirt beneath her feet was slimy with kitchen garbage that had been tossed from the back door.

"I need the outhouse," she said doubtfully. "I wish I didn't."

"I'll wait here for you."

She trod resolutely to the shack that stood next to the midden. She opened the door then retreated. Some things were possible, some were not.

"That bad?" Lionel inquired.

"That bad."

"Try the bushes." He indicated a scrappy group of red currant and gooseberry bushes bordering the kitchen garden.

Pippa sighed but could see no alternative. Lionel turned his back on the bushes and she hurried behind them reflecting with a mixture of surprise and dismay that the intimacy of this dilemma didn't trouble her as it should.

She returned within minutes, grimacing as she straightened her skirts. "I trust our next resting place will be a little more salubrious."

"I wouldn't make a wager on it," Lionel responded. "We need to travel off the beaten track." He climbed the rickety stairs to the washhouse, Pippa on his heels.

A lantern burned low on the floor beside a jug of water and a makeshift bed of straw covered with blankets.

Pippa dipped her finger in the jug. " 'Tis not what I would call hot, but it will do." She glanced inadvertently at the improvised bed.

"I'll leave you then."

There was no help for it unless she wanted to sleep in her gown. She said as neutrally as she could, "Before you go, would you unlace me? I don't wish to sleep in my gown and 'tis awkward to do myself." Without waiting for an answer she gave him her back so that he had no chance to see her face.

Lionel said nothing as he swiftly unlaced her stomacher, making sure that his fingers made no contact with the thin shift beneath. Her warmed flesh had a scent of cut grass, of newly turned earth, and it sent his senses whirling.

"My thanks," Pippa said, her voice thick. The proximity of his body, the feel of his fingers so close to her skin, made her want to weep anew, but this time with pure contrary desire that could never be fulfilled. The irony of their present situation was like the torture of Tantalus. They had never been naked together when they'd made love; something she had frequently lamented. Now it would be so easy.

"Is there anything else I can do? I am a passable lady's maid." Lionel too was aware of the supreme irony of this moment, just as he was aware of the swift beating of his heart, the deep-rooted passion he felt for this woman.

She shook her head and put her hands at her waist, forcing the conversation into a path that would douse desire. "How soon do you think it will it be before I have to put panels in my gowns?"

He shrugged. "Another month perhaps, maybe more. Women are very different in the way they carry their children."

She took a deep breath, then spoke the thought that she had not dared to articulate even in her mind. "There are ways to rid oneself of an unwanted child, are there not?"

"So I believe, but I don't know them." He kept his voice as calm and neutral as hers.

"No, neither do I." It was spoken at last, and now perhaps it could be forgotten.

"Is that what you would wish?" He asked the question with difficulty.

Silence stretched taut between them, swarming with

a hive of impossible considerations, impossible possibilities. Then eventually Pippa said, "I don't know. What of you?"

She looked at him with a clear, direct gaze. "Would you wish to rid the world of this child . . . the child of the man who tortured your sister to death?"

"How can I answer that?" he said in a low voice. "If you cannot answer it, Pippa, how can I?" He opened his hands in a helpless gesture.

She gave a little shrug, a gesture as helpless as his own, and turned her gaze from him. He wanted to hold her but he didn't dare, so he hurried away, leaving her alone in the little chamber above the washhouse.

Twenty-two

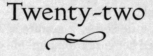

THE SOLEMN PARTY OF FOUR BLACK-CLAD GENTLE-
men climbed down from their open carriage before the
door of Lionel Ashton's mansion. They carried their
black bags and the lappets of their caps were tied firmly
beneath their chins. Their gowns flapped at their ankles.

A man at the head of the troop of horsemen who had
accompanied the queen's physicians strode to the door
and rapped sharply with the hilt of his dagger.

The door opened slowly and Senor Diaz, the steward, surveyed his visitors with a mixture of curiosity and
hauteur. "Mr. Ashton is not within," he pronounced,
the English fluent but the Spanish accent heavy.

"No matter. He understands our business. We are
come to see Lady Nielson," the visitor stated. "I bring
the queen's physicians to attend her."

The steward gave him a blank stare. "Lady
Nielson?"

"Aye, Lady Nielson. She is at present residing under
Mr. Ashton's roof," the other said impatiently.

"I don't believe so," Senor Diaz stated, his not inconsiderable bulk barring the door. "But if you will remain here a moment, I will consult with the lady of the house, Dona Bernardina." He stepped back and firmly closed the door.

The steward was not in his master's complete confidence, but he was aware that something concerning the suddenly absent Dona Luisa had caused Mr. Ashton's present journey. Dona Bernardina's long face and frequent sighs merely added to his suspicions.

He found the duenna in the small parlor where she was accustomed to sitting with her charge.

"Was that someone knocking?" She rose eagerly from her chair, setting aside her tambour frame. "Is Don Ashton returned?"

"No, madam. 'Tis a troop of the queen's horse escorting the queen's physicians. They say they are come to attend upon Lady Nielson."

"Lady Nielson?" Bernardina gazed blankly at him. "How could that be?" She smoothed down her skirts with anxious little pats of her plump white hands. "Why would they expect to find Lady Nielson here?"

"I do not know, madam. I understood the gentleman in charge of the troop to say that she was residing at present under Mr. Ashton's roof."

"What a silly mistake to have made. Send him in to me."

The steward bowed and returned to the door just as a series of imperative knocks rattled the oak.

He swung open the door. "My lady will speak with you, sir." He offered a half bow to the leader of the troop. "Who shall I say is calling?"

"Sir Anthony Crosse," the man said, brushing past the steward. "And I do not care to be kept cooling my heels on the doorstep."

"No, sir. Forgive me, but in Mr. Ashton's absence I am instructed to keep the ladies from any disturbance." The steward opened the door to the parlor. "Madam, Sir Anthony Crosse."

Bernardina had resumed her seat and now kept it, offering her visitor a calm but cold smile. She spoke in Spanish and waited for the steward to translate for her. "We are not accustomed to visitors in Don Ashton's absence, senor. How can I help you?"

Sir Anthony stepped into the parlor and felt the first stirring of discomfort. He was on the king's business, bearing His Majesty's writ. He had been told to expect some resistance from Lady Nielson but that he was to overcome it however necessary. He had not been told to expect a confrontation with a stately, jewel-encrusted, mantilla-swathed lady who spoke no English.

He bowed deeply. "Forgive the intrusion, madam, but I am on the king's business. I bring the queen's physicians to attend upon Lady Nielson, who, I understand, is at present a guest under Mr. Ashton's roof." He glanced expectantly at the steward, who provided the translation in a monotone.

Bernardina was so astonished, so anxious to correct such a misapprehension, that she felt the need to speak directly to the visitor and searched her sparse English vocabulary.

"No . . . no . . . indeed not so. Such a stupid notion, senor. Lady Nielson was here for . . . for supper, yes . . . yes, but no . . . no she does not live here. I can tell you that she is with Dona Luisa de los Velez of the house of Mendoza . . . as chaperone. Dona Luisa will be back anytime now, yes . . . yes, she will, but Lady Nielson . . . no, I do not think." Her expressive shrug filled in the blanks.

Sir Anthony stared at her. None of it made any sense to him. He opted for a simple route. "Where may I find Mr. Ashton, madam?"

For the first time some of Bernardina's confused anxiety showed. Flustered, she stammered, "I . . . I do not know . . . I am not party to Don Ashton's business."

"I see. I must ask you to forgive me, but my orders are explicit. If you cannot produce Lady Nielson then I must search the house to find her. Pray remain in the parlor, madam, and you will not be molested in any way."

Sir Anthony strode from the chamber. He flung open the front door and stood in the doorway, preventing anyone from closing it, while he bellowed his orders to his men.

Bernardina listened to the booted feet tramping through the house. Her heart was beating so fast she thought she would swoon. She had no idea what was happening but she had only one thought, to protect Luisa's reputation. Don Ashton was not here to do it so it was up to her. It might seem as if these men were not interested in Luisa, but since Don Ashton had told her the girl was with Lady Nielson then any business that involved the one would inevitably involve the other.

After what seemed an eternity the booted feet crossed the hall again and the great front door opened and slammed. Only then did Bernardina rise from her chair.

The steward entered the parlor. "Forgive me, madam. They wouldn't let me come to you."

"What did they want?"

He spread his hands in incomprehension. "They seemed convinced that Lady Nielson was in residence. I told them only you were here and that Don Ashton has gone on a journey and so has Dona Luisa."

"You did not imply that Dona Luisa had gone alone?"

"Hardly, madam. You had already told Sir Anthony that she has gone somewhere with Lady Nielson. I would not contradict you."

Bernardina waved him away and returned to her seat. She could do nothing but wait and pray. She took up her rosary.

"So it seems all our birds have flown the coop," Philip said in a low voice that throbbed with rage. With a sudden violent movement he drove the blade of a silver paper knife into the table. The blade bent and he hurled the knife to the floor.

"How did it happen?" He glared at his two companions.

Ruy Gomez steepled his fingers. "Our men lost Nielson and his lover when they attended mass at Southwark Cathedral this afternoon. But they are sure to pick them up again within the hour. They cannot have gone far." His tone was smooth and soothing.

"They are of no importance with the woman gone," Philip declared. "But by the mass, when they're caught they will die a hard, unshriven death." He took up a silver chalice and drained its contents.

Simon Renard pushed back his chair with an impatient movement, his customary poise disintegrated. "Where would the woman go? And where in the name of grace is Ashton?"

"He has gone after her, I imagine," Gomez said.

"Why would he not tell us then?" Renard demanded.

He stood up and began to pace the council chamber like a caged panther.

The question remained unanswered as its incredible implications dawned for the first time. Ruy Gomez stared down at the table. "He cannot be working against us," he said finally, almost in an undertone. " 'Tis not possible."

The sound of Westminster's bells ringing the six o'clock curfew penetrated the closed windows of the chamber. Philip stood up abruptly. "Send to the gates and question the watchmen. If Ashton left the city . . . if the woman left the city . . . someone must have seen them. I go to the queen." He stalked from the room, slamming the door at his back.

"Please God, the queen comes to full term and a healthy delivery," Renard muttered.

Ruy Gomez looked across the table at him. "You would do better to pray that we lay hold of Lady Nielson and her bastard."

THE HOLD OF THE BOAT REEKED OF FISH OIL AND WAS slippery with blood and silvery scales. Gabriel and Stuart were barely aware of their uncomfortable, malodorous surroundings as they waited for the rattle of an anchor chain, the sound of creaking sails that would tell them they were on their way from Southwark docks downriver to the English Channel.

They had entered Southwark Cathedral boldly through the main doors. Stuart had made confession to the Bishop of Winchester, Gabriel to a lesser priest, but they had both departed the confessional clothed in the robes of novices, hoods drawn low to hide their untonsured skulls. They had left the cathedral through a side door from the sacristy.

Stuart knew he was an able man, only blackmail and terror had robbed him of the ability to think and plan with the natural wit and wisdom that had attracted Pippa back in the days when the sun shone. Now, as he heard the anchor rattle, the feet on the deck turning the capstan, as he felt the first swing of the boat's hull beneath him, he knew again the stirrings of his old pride and self-confidence. He had defeated the spies. He was taking Gabriel to safety. Pippa was in Lionel Ashton's hands, in the care of a man who had sworn to protect her. And she was now free of her betrayer. Her husband was no longer her husband.

He reached over and lightly brushed Gabriel's hands, tightly clenched across his lyre. They would sail first to the island of Jersey while the fisherman trawled the deep waters of the Channel for its rich catches, which they would salt in the barrels behind Stuart's head. And from there they would find a small boat to take them to the French coast. They would go overland from there to Italy. No one could touch them now.

PIPPA WOKE FROM A DISTURBED SLEEP AS THE MOON fell across her face. She was disoriented for a moment, aware of that same deep unnameable fear that had dogged her for so long. And then she remembered that the fear had a name. A face. She knew all about it and so it was no longer a fear. It was a matter of fact.

She touched her belly. It felt the same. Flat. Concave, actually, as she lay on her back. But there was a life in there. A life that had been put there without her consent . . . without her knowledge.

She tried to force herself to bring Philip's face into her mind's eye but her mind slipped away from the image whenever it began to take on structure.

She heard a sound from the floor beside the cot and softly turned her head. Lionel was sitting up on his pile of straw and blankets. She held her breath, not knowing why she didn't wish to let him know that she was awake. Just that she didn't.

He stood up carefully, and she knew he didn't wish to wake her. He trod softly to the puddle of moonlight on the floor beneath the unglazed round window high on the wall. He was fully dressed except for his cloak.

She watched him, watched his rigid back, the set of his strong neck, the line of his profile as he turned his head up to the moon as if seeking warmth from the pale silver light. She knew that he was thinking of his sister. Reliving his helplessness in the agony of her death.

She wanted to go to him, to hold him and comfort him as he had once comforted her. But she was as wounded as he and while he had been helpless to prevent his sister's torment, he had not been helpless to prevent her own.

She lay with her head turned on the cot, looking at him as he continued to stand in the moonlight. Was forgiveness ever possible? Even if it wasn't was there some comfort they could give each other?

Without conscious decision she slid from the cot and trod softly towards him. He didn't turn, whether because he wasn't aware of her or chose not to be, she couldn't tell. She stood behind him and silently put her arms around his waist, resting her head against his back.

A slight shiver went through him but he made no other move. He felt himself suddenly devoid of will. The strength of his authority had evaporated up here in

the little moonlit chamber. He was stripped to his frail-
ties, the ordinary human weaknesses that he had not allowed himself to admit lest they interfere with a
purpose that transcended all things ordinary. And now,
as he felt Pippa's body against his, he knew that he had
misunderstood the importance of ordinary things. A
misunderstanding that was going to cost him all hope of
happiness.

"You're thinking of Margaret." Her voice was low
and he could feel the warmth of her breath on the back
of his neck.

"Aye."

"Of how you could do nothing to help her."

He made no reply and she stood there, encircling
him with her arms, her bare feet chill on the wooden
floor, the night air cold on her nape. But his body was
warm against hers as she pressed herself into him with a
hungry, urgent need for contact in her own hurt and
loneliness.

"They all just stood there watching as she died.
Hundreds of them. Blank-faced, silent, unmoved, and
unmoving." He spoke suddenly, his voice a harsh rasp in
the moonlight.

"And like them I stood there and watched as Philip
violated you . . . But I *swear* to you, Pippa, on
Margaret's grave, that while I kept silence I was not unmoved."

" 'Tis possible that that faceless crowd were also
moved but unable to speak," she said, her hold loosen-
ing a little.

"I did not keep silence through fear," he said.

"No," she agreed, her arms dropping to her sides.
"In the interests of a greater good."

He turned slowly towards her. "I will not defend myself, Pippa. Your accusations stand true."

Silently she gazed up into his face. He held her gaze, his gray eyes clear and steady. Then he took her face in both his hands and kissed her, a hesitant, questioning kiss.

She held herself very still, her eyes still fixed upon his, as his lips pressed lightly, warmly against her mouth. Was there something perverse in this need she had for this kind of contact, the reassurance of another loving body? The reassurance of *Lionel's* body? But she felt through the hands on her face his own need for the same thing.

He drew her backwards to the bed. He touched her breasts through her shift and she felt their new tenderness. He opened the shift and kissed her breasts. Every movement was hesitant, as if he waited for permission. She ran her hands through his hair, pressing his head to her bosom. She kissed the top of his head, her hands moving to his shoulders as she fell back on the narrow cot.

And later he shifted himself on the narrow cot so that he held her in the crook of his arm, and she slept like an exhausted child with her head in the hollow of his shoulder.

Lionel did not sleep. He kept vigil, watching over her, filled with such a fierce need to protect her he couldn't imagine ever sleeping again.

Twenty-three

MALCOLM LEFT AS DAWN'S GRAY LIGHT ENCROACHED upon the night. A sleepy Jem harnessed the horses to the carriage a few minutes later and took the London road. Within the inn the kitchen boy bent to poke the embers in the range and throw on kindling to create a burst of flame that would satisfy Goodman Brown and his wife when they came down yawning from their chamber above the kitchen.

Luisa, who had lain awake most of the night beside Nell, who had slept the sleep of the truly exhausted, wondered how she was to get out of bed with any decency when Robin lay on the truckle bed beyond the curtains.

She leaned over and twitched aside the curtains. Nell grunted in her sleep. Groaned and sat up.

"Lord'a'mercy! Missus'll be 'ollerin' to raise the devil!" She tumbled through the bedcurtains, hauling down her petticoats. "I'll be up in a minute wi' fresh coals." And then she was gone.

Robin was on his feet, straightening his doublet, rubbing his beard, which seemed to have grown to unruly proportions during the short night.

"I'll be in the taproom," he mumbled to Luisa's tousled head, showing between the bedcurtains like an autumn daisy.

She waited for the door to close then got to her feet. She was in chemise and petticoat and her bare feet immediately took the chill from the floor. Her farthingale and stomacher and gown lay where she had discarded them with Nell's help on the chest at the foot of the bed. Without Nell's help she would have difficulty putting them on again.

Pippa, too, would have difficulty dressing for the morning. They would have to help each other.

Luisa wrapped herself in her cloak and gathered up her outer garments and the embroidered bag containing her other necessities. Don Ashton had said the washhouse was outside the inn beyond the kitchen.

She found the back way to the kitchen, was ignored by yawning folk tending fires and bacon just as she ignored them, broke out into the kitchen yard and identified the washhouse by its smells of lye and pig-fat soap.

She climbed the rickety stairs and a heartbeat after she knocked on the door remembered that Don Ashton was sharing this chamber with Pippa.

Her knock sounded like Gabriel's trumpet.

"Who is it?" It was Don Ashton's voice but Luisa couldn't retrace her steps. Not with an armful of lace and bone and silk and the steps creaking beneath her.

" 'Tis Luisa," she tried, her voice quavering.

"In the name of grace!" The door was flung open.

Don Ashton stood there in his hose and shirt, his boots in his hand. His shirt was unbuttoned, and Luisa found her eyes riveted to the broad expanse of chest thus revealed. His nipples were hard and small and brown. She had never seen a man's bare chest before.

Lionel stared at her for a minute as if he didn't know her, then realized what she was gazing at with her mouth slightly open, her deep blue eyes wide as platters. He dropped his boots with a clunk to the floor and buttoned his shirt, fumbling with the tiny pearl studs in his haste.

"What in the devil are you doing here?" he demanded, trying to take command of the situation with a show of impatient annoyance.

Luisa did not immediately reply. Her fascinated gaze drifted downwards and Lionel was acutely conscious of the prominence of his sex in the tight hose. The image of Dona Maria, Luisa's mother, rose in his mind. If she witnessed this scene she would have hysterics. And Dona Bernardina . . . God's blood, it didn't bear thinking of. He fought the urge to cover his genitals with his hands, it would only draw yet more attention to this ludicrous and inappropriate situation.

Instead he said with an assumption of haughty dignity, "What is it you want, Luisa? You have no business here."

"I . . . I . . . thought that I did have," Luisa said, her eyes still wide, still riveted on her guardian's pronounced dishabille. "I thought Pippa and I could help each other dress."

She glanced quickly at the intimate bundle of clothes in her arms, then unable to help herself returned her eyes to the overwhelming evidence of her guardian's maleness. Had he thought nothing of revealing himself in this way to Pippa?

"But perhaps . . ." she stammered. "Perhaps she doesn't need me. Perhaps you are helping her." The thought flashed that someone must have helped Pippa undress the previous evening. And Nell had been with Luisa.

Lionel decided it would be best to ignore this. Any attempt at an answer would lead only into a quagmire that made him shudder.

Pippa, who had woken at the sound of the knock and was now blearily blinking sleep from her eyes, realized that the situation required intervention. Lionel seemed for once at a loss for words. She swung herself off the cot and went to the door. She smiled reassuringly at Luisa over Lionel's shoulder.

"Come in, Luisa. Laces are the very devil. Mr. Ashton can repair to the taproom and finish dressing with Robin."

"Oh, I wouldn't wish to drive Don Ashton from his chamber," Luisa said on a mischievous impulse. She had never seen her guardian at a disadvantage before, and he most definitely was at this moment. "I didn't mean to interrupt."

"You are not interrupting anything," Pippa stated, hearing Lionel's quick indrawn breath. "Mr. Ashton was repairing to the taproom anyway." She gave Lionel a little punch in the small of his back.

Lionel shook his head like a dog shaking off water. "Yes . . . yes . . . I was . . . so I was." He hopped first on one foot then on the other as he pulled on his boots, then stepped away from the door, holding his doublet and cloak modestly against him.

He brushed past Luisa in the doorway and his descent of the rickety stairs was loud and rapid.

Luisa turned her wide-eyed gaze on Pippa. She took in her state of undress. She wore only a crumpled shift that was unlaced almost to her waist, and there was something shockingly intimate about the length of bare leg revealed below the hem of the thin white garment. It was as clear as day to her that Pippa and Don Ashton were a great deal more familiar to and with each other than they had hitherto indicated.

A fact that Luisa found very interesting. Her guardian always backed up Dona Bernardina's strictures, prated about his ward's reputation, the need to keep her in seclusion to maintain her maidenly modesty, and here he was enjoying a liaison with a woman married to another man. She wondered if Robin knew and decided that she would ask him at the earliest opportunity.

"No one will ever tell me what 'tis like to lose one's maidenhead," she said. "Of course Dona Bernardina still has hers, at least I can't believe that she doesn't, and my mother could never bring herself to talk of such indelicate matters. But I think I should know, don't you, Pippa?"

"I think for the moment you should be satisfied with reducing your guardian to a state of utter discomposure," Pippa replied, but she couldn't help a chuckle.

"I didn't mean to be indiscreet," Luisa said primly.

"Oh, spare me the piety!" Pippa exclaimed. "You knew exactly what you were doing." She grinned. "And I don't blame you in the least. I would have enjoyed the same game in your shoes. Come, let me lace you."

Luisa breathed in deeply as Pippa tightened her laces. She reached for the farthingale but Pippa said, "No, don't bother with that. Petticoats will have to do. We don't need any more encumbrances than we already have. Fasten me now, but not too tightly."

Luisa, emboldened by Pippa's evident amusement,

tried for some more information. "Are you running away with Don Ashton . . . leaving your husband?"

Pippa twisted her hair into a silk snood at the nape of her neck. Luisa was entitled to some explanation. "Well, I am running away, and I am leaving my husband. But I am not running away with Lionel in the way you mean."

Luisa nodded thoughtfully. "I did wonder why Robin would be helping you to do such a thing. 'Tis a grave sin to leave one's husband."

"Now, that piece of piety I can also do without," Pippa stated with an edge to her voice. "You should bear in mind that sometimes one sin cancels out another."

She gathered up her bag and made for the door. "Come, we must hurry. We need to be on the road soon after first light."

Luisa, now a little discomfited herself by Pippa's remark and puzzled by the edge in her voice, followed in a more subdued frame of mind.

The four of them stood in the taproom making a hasty breakfast of bread and fried bacon, washed down with ale. No one said much, the atmosphere was taut in the dim light of a single tallow candle, and Luisa watched her guardian and Pippa with a covert eye. They stood apart, not even exchanging a glance, but she knew what she knew. She shot a quick sideways glance at Robin, who stood with his back to the window and the gray square of light, and she wondered again if he knew the true nature of his sister's relationship with Don Ashton.

If he did, he presumably condoned it. Luisa decided it was past time she discovered some of these mysteries that were so well known to her companions. And as she thought that, she was aware of a most peculiar sensation. A curious tingling in her lower body, a sudden clutching in her belly. She watched Robin's mouth and knew that she had to feel his mouth on hers. Not the light brushing, almost teasing kisses he had hitherto bestowed, but something else entirely. She had to feel his hands on her body.

Her cheeks flooded with color and she had the horrid feeling that one of her companions might be able to read her innermost thoughts. She choked on a crust of bread and turned away, hiding her embarrassment in a fit of coughing.

It was Robin who thumped her back. "Eating too quickly," he observed. "And the bread's stale into the bargain."

Lionel set down the ale pot. "Let's be on our way. We must get beyond Newbury by nightfall."

"More than forty miles," Robin said, casting Luisa a doubtful glance. He knew Pippa's strengths but he was not so sure of Luisa's.

"We have no choice" was the curt response. "I'll settle up with the innkeeper. Robin, make sure the horses have pillion pads."

Robin went out into the gloomy morning. Their horses were saddled and waiting in the stable yard, horse-hair pillion pads attached to the rear of the saddles. Pippa was not going to be happy slummocking along in such an undignified fashion, he reflected, and the horses were going to be exhausted carrying a double load for more than forty miles. The latter issue concerned him more than the former.

"We'll have to change horses," he said when Lionel appeared.

"Aye, and 'tis the very devil. We'll have to stop at an inn on a well-traveled road to get decent beasts and if we're pursued they'll be asking for us at every inn on every major roadway between here and Penzance."

"Then perhaps we should steal horses," Pippa said from behind Lionel. "Find a field with a couple of good, sturdy animals and make an exchange. Philip's men can't make inquiry at every farmer's house we pass."

"I hadn't realized you had a criminal mind as well as a resourceful one," Lionel remarked.

"You don't know her," Robin said, wishing as he said it that he had bitten his tongue. It had been intended as a little inside joke with Pippa but it hadn't come out in the least jesting.

"Not as well as you, I'm sure," Lionel agreed without expression. "Let me put you up, Pippa." He lifted her onto the pillion. For a moment he kept his hands at her waist, asking with soft concern, "How are you feeling? Not sick?"

"No." She was aware of the bristling Robin, and Luisa's inquisitive gaze. She shook her head, swiftly dismissing Lionel's question, brushing away the intimate touch of his hands. For better or worse, last night had happened, but she was not prepared to make public proclamation of the fact.

She changed the subject. "Do you think the pursuit has started already?"

He replied in a similarly brisk tone. "I hope not. But we have to be prepared. At least they won't be looking for a party of four."

He mounted in front of her and walked the horse out of the yard, Robin and Luisa following.

IT WAS THE DEEPEST HOUR OF THE NIGHT BUT THE council chamber blazed with light from the wheels of candles hanging from the delicately painted molding of the plaster ceiling.

"Who is Ashton? In the name of the Holy Mother, *what* is he?"

Philip's question was the cry of a screech owl in the night. He swiveled his hollow-eyed stare around the room. A vein throbbed in his temple. His face was drawn with fatigue.

"We know that he and his manservant passed through Aldgate yesterday afternoon and took the Oxford road. We also know that Robin of Beaucaire, escorting a carriage, passed through on the same route about an hour earlier." Renard paced the chamber as he spoke, his hands clasped at his back.

He was trying to deflect the king's questions because the answers were impossible for him to articulate. The fault for this catastrophe lay entirely at the Spanish ambassador's door. So far no one had skewered him with the blame, but it would come. Oh, yes, it would come.

Philip pushed back his heavy carved chair with such violence that it fell backwards. "You will get him," he declared. "I care not how. You will get me Ashton, and by the bones of Christ, when he's on the rack I will turn the wheel myself."

"Sire, I have sent men on the road to Oxford, and also as a precaution there are patrols covering all the major highways leading from Aldgate. He cannot have had more than a two-hour start. He will not escape us."

Philip crossed the chamber to where Renard stood against a bookcase. He pushed his face close to the ambassador's. "If you value your head, Renard, you will see that he doesn't."

Flecks of the king's spittle glistened on Renard's cheek but he didn't dare to wipe them off in the charged silence. Then finally Ruy Gomez spoke. "Where we find Ashton we will also find the woman."

Renard sidled along the bookcase away from Philip. "I have also sent men to cover the major ports," he said. "They will not be able to leave the country by ship. Not the woman, not her brother, not Ashton."

"And Ashton's ward. She's missing too. We have to assume she's with them."

"Four people are more easily tracked than one, or even two," Gomez pointed out. "There is the carriage, for a start, and with the women they would have had to stop for the night. They will be asleep in some inn somewhere and by dawn or soon after we shall take them."

Philip gave him a bleak stare, then strode from the council chamber.

Renard at last wiped the spittle from his cheek. "How did we miss it, Gomez? What did we miss? We suspected nothing." His tone was almost pleading as he threw up his hands in a gesture of bewilderment and despair.

"My spies found nothing in their investigation. Ashton was a friend of the Mendozas; his credentials were impeccable. He loves Spain; he's a devout Catholic; his dearest wish is to see his own country return to the old religion."

"Or so he *said*," Gomez pointed out with careful emphasis. "I don't know how he deceived us, Renard. But the king will not soon forget."

"I suppose 'tis not possible that we are mistaken now. That he has gone in search of the woman to bring her back?"

Gomez gave him a pitying look. In the face of the unthinkable the arrogant, ruthless diplomat was a mere shadow of his former self. "You know that is not so, Renard. We do not know who or what he is, but we can be certain he is no friend to Philip or to Spain."

Renard nodded slowly with an air of defeat. In a lifetime of service to the Holy Roman Emperor, his family, and his religion, he had now made an error that would wipe out that career, destroy its manifold successes, and tar him permanently with the brush of failure.

LIONEL SET A PUNISHING PACE AND BY NOON THE horses' flanks were dark with sweat, their breathing labored. Pippa had ridden easily for the first four hours, but it was harder to ride pillion at speed than in the saddle; she couldn't adapt her body to the animal's gait in anything like the same way.

She used Lionel's back for support and made no complaint. She concentrated on the one blessing: despite the jolting she had no nausea.

Lionel kept a grim silence. He felt her weight sagging against his back and knew how fatigued she must be. But she had to hang on and endure until they were forced to stop and change the horses.

Robin kept his own horse up with Lionel's except when the path became too narrow, then he fell back a few feet. Luisa clung on, pale, frightened now by an adventure that had taken on a deadly seriousness, and terrified that she would lose her grip on Robin as fatigue threatened to overwhelm her.

There was a cold wind, and the skies were overcast, the fields brown with stubble. Crows circled in the pine trees, and pheasants started in the hedgerows as the horses thundered past. They kept to the byways and met few people.

At noon Pippa shouted into the wind that snatched her words, "Lionel, I have to stop for a few minutes."

"What? I can't hear you." He didn't slacken his pace and his voice was impatient.

She twisted sideways until she could yell into his ear. "You have to stop. I have to get down for a few minutes."

"I know you're tired," he yelled back at her. "We all are. But we can't stop yet. Just hold on for another hour, then we'll stop to change horses."

"For God's sake, I can't wait that long!" she cried in some desperation. "It's not that I'm tired, but my bladder is bursting. I think it's pregnancy, but all this jolting is agony."

Lionel could see no alternative. He swore under his breath but he slowed his horse and veered off into a small spinney beside the cart track.

He swung down and reached up to lift Pippa down. Her knees almost buckled as her feet touched ground. "I thought I was stronger than this," she muttered crossly as she hung on to his arm for a minute.

"Just be as quick as you can. Robin and I will water the horses. There's a stream over yonder."

Luisa, stumbling a little when her feet touched ground, followed Pippa into the seclusion of the trees. "I wish we could get horses of our own," she called from behind her own bush.

"We're going to," Pippa stated, emerging from concealment. "I have no intention of riding pillion any farther than I have to."

Pippa spoke with such confidence that Luisa had no

doubt at all that she would arrange matters to their joint satisfaction.

Lionel was pacing the stream bank while Robin held the horses as they drank. Lionel regarded the women with an impatient concern as they rejoined them.

"Ready now?"

"Yes," Pippa responded, a little taken aback by the sharpness of the inquiry. She put her hands into the small of her back and stretched her shoulders. "How soon before we change horses?"

Lionel wearily pressed his fingertips into his eyes. It was a reasonable enough question but for some reason it exasperated him, as if she was somehow questioning his decisions.

"I haven't decided," he snapped.

"I doubt they can go on much longer with a double load," Pippa pointed out, annoyed now by this dismissive impatience.

Lionel took a deep breath. "We'll go on to the next hamlet. I don't suppose we'll find an alehouse, but there'll be a farm or cottage that will give us some food. Then we'll head across the fields in search of a horse exchange. With fresh beasts we should get at least to Whitchurch by nightfall. And with luck and a rest they'll take us to Southampton tomorrow, where Malcolm will be waiting. Now let me put you up." He lifted her onto the pillion pad without ceremony and Pippa wisely held her tongue.

Lionel regretted his ill-temper as soon as they were once more on the road. He was finding it hard to maintain his usual calm in the face of his growing anxiety. He told himself that they would not yet be missed, but he could think of any number of ways in which their flight could have been discovered and the pursuit hard on their heels.

And he knew with grim certainty that he would have to use his knife on them all and then turn it on himself before they were taken by Philip's men.

Twenty-four

THEY RODE ON FOR ANOTHER FIVE MILES UNTIL THEY came to the tiny hamlet of Beedon Hill. A humble alehouse stood at a rudimentary crossroads just outside the hamlet.

Lionel dismounted and with a nod to Robin that he should keep his place in the saddle ducked beneath the low lintel into the dark interior.

"Anyone at home?" he called into the recesses of what seemed to be a single ground-floor chamber.

"Who wants to know?" An elderly man shuffled into view from the inglenook. "Nuthin' but visitors these days. Can't think what's goin' on." He peered at Lionel from beneath an ancient wool bonnet.

"Have you no candle, man?" Lionel demanded impatiently. " 'Tis black as pitch in here."

"Ain't got money to burn," the man said, not moving. "Who be you an' what's it ye wants?"

"Who I am is none of your business. What I want is food and ale for four travelers. You'll be well paid." He clinked the pouch of coins in his doublet.

"Four is it?" The old man scratched his head, bald

beneath the bonnet. His rheumy little eyes glittered in the dimness.

"That's what I said." Lionel examined him closely. "What d'you mean, nothing but visitors?"

The man shrugged and his eyes slid around Lionel. "Nuthin'," he said with a shrug. He bent and spat in the sawdust at his feet. "Don't get no passersby 'ere, 'tis all I meant. Locals come in fer a drop o' October ale now an' agin', and a bowl o' punch when I've the makin's."

He looked up at Lionel again. "So what was it ye said ye wanted?"

Lionel was aware of a vague unease. "Ale, bread, cheese, anything like that. Can you provide it? If not I'll be on my way." Again the coins clinked in the pouch.

The gaze shifted into a far corner of the room and Lionel controlled the urge to follow it. If there was one of Renard's spies crouching spiderlike in the dark waiting for a fly he would not betray himself. He slid a hand down towards his boot and the dagger it held. One move from the corner and the dagger would find its mark so quickly no one would see it coming.

"Eh, Betsy, show a leg there," the old man shouted with surprising force from such a bent and decrepit figure.

Now Lionel turned seemingly casual to the corner and made out what looked like a bundle of rags. The bundle wheezed and took on the shape of a woman of indeterminate age.

"Fetch provisions fer the gennelman. What we got?"

"Cold tripe, morsel o' pig's 'ead."

"Bread," Lionel demanded brusquely. "Bread and cheese. Don't tell me you don't have that, woman."

"Aye, might 'ave." She shuffled off into the dark

recesses of the room and the old man returned to his inglenook.

Lionel stood foursquare in the center of the room, every nerve stretched, his ears straining to catch any untoward sound.

The crone shuffled back and pushed at him half a wheel of thickly rinded cheese and a rather ancient loaf of wheaten bread. Lionel examined the offerings with a grimace but it was the best they were going to get in this miserable hovel. They would have to scrape off the mold, both on the bread and the cheese.

He looked around and spied a flitch of smoked bacon hanging from the rafters. "I'll take some of that." He took his knife from his belt and cut off a third of the flitch.

The woman whimpered but produced no words.

"Ale?" Lionel demanded. "I need a pitcher of ale, and I need to fill water flasks at the well."

"Ale's in the butt out front."

"I'll fill a flagon on my way out."

"Well's in the village. 'Ave to get yer water there."

Lionel threw a handful of coins in the general direction of the old man. "That should more than cover your generosity, my friend."

Wrapping his prizes in his cloak, he hurried outside again, nearly banging his head on the lintel in his haste.

"Where the hell is Pippa?" he demanded, seeing his riderless horse.

"She went in search of the privy," Luisa told him.

"What, *again*?"

Robin answered him, staring straight ahead between his horse's ears. "She said that in present circumstances and in her present condition she was not going to pass up an opportunity when it arose."

"She'll be back in a minute," Luisa offered, seeing that her usually imperturbable guardian looked about to explode.

Pippa at that moment was standing at the corner of the hovel, staring towards the door to what she assumed was the privy at the rear of a small weed-infested yard. A man had gone into the privy just as she was about to hurry across the yard. Instinctively she stepped back into the shadow of the cottage's mud-plastered wall.

She saw now that there were three other men in the yard. They were eating apples. They were dressed in the buff leather jerkin so often worn by soldiers, and carried sword and dagger at their hips. There were four unsaddled horses with nose bags in a lean-to shed. The man emerged from the privy lacing his hose and an old man came out of the house, limping across the yard towards them.

Pippa could not put her finger on what was wrong, but she could smell the danger like a rotten carcass. She turned and ran to the front.

Lionel had just finished loading the food into his saddlebag and was thrusting the stopper back into the neck of the refilled flagon of ale. "God's bones, Pippa! Where the hell have you been?"

"Men," she said succinctly. "Four of them. Armed. Some old man's talking to them."

Lionel wasted no words. He caught her up, almost threw her onto the pillion pad, and mounted before her, shoving the flagon into a saddlebag. Robin was already galloping onto the narrow lane and Lionel whipped his horse into pursuit.

Neither Lionel nor Robin spared the whip on their tired mounts and the animals pounded down the lane, raising clouds of dust. A shout came from behind them, and then the dull pop of a flintlock pistol. Lionel did not concern himself with the gun. He had little time for the newfangled weapons. They were impossible to aim and far too clumsy unless they were almost pressed against their target. But it told him that these had to be Philip's men. The Spaniards favored firearms and they would probably ensure that anyone working for them carried one.

"Their horses," gasped Pippa. "Their horses are stabled. They'll have to saddle them."

Lionel nodded his comprehension. He knew they could not outrun this pursuit, not with weary horses carrying a double load, and he didn't fancy the odds of four against two in a fight. But they had a few minutes. He drew rein abruptly and flung himself from the saddle.

Robin followed suit. "What are we doing?"

"Unsaddle them and send 'em on," Lionel instructed even as he tore at the buckles of his own tack. "With luck they'll follow the tracks for a mile or two."

Pippa was already hauling the saddlebags off and Luisa followed her example.

"Get in the field!"

Pippa obeyed Lionel's instruction, using the saddlebags to push her way through a small gap in the bramble hedge into the field beyond. The bags protected her face from the thorns, but her hands were scratched.

Luisa was behind her, breathless, white, terrified, yet determined. Blood oozed from a long scratch on her cheek.

Robin scrambled through the hedge with saddle and bridle and Luisa's embroidered bag. In the lane, Lionel cut both animals across the flanks with his whip and they took off thundering down the lane, snorting with fear. He joined the others in the field, laden with his own tack and Pippa's leather bag.

He looked around. They had no time to run. "In the ditch." He gestured to a deep ditch that ran the length of the field just below the hedge. "Get in, quick."

Robin threw his burdens in and jumped down. He lifted up his hands for Luisa and she jumped down beside him. Pippa threw the saddlebags down after her and slid into the ditch on her own.

Lionel drew his dagger and began to slash long grasses and weeds from the edge of the ditch, great handfuls of them. Cow parsley, ragged robin, yarrow all mingled with the grasses. He threw these down and no one needed instruction. They lay down on the bed of the ditch and covered themselves with the grass and weeds. The ditch was narrow, the ground damp, but there was no standing water.

Lionel slid down after them. He took Pippa in his arms and held her sideways against his body so that they could squeeze together into the narrow space, then he covered them both. He held his drawn dagger tucked into his sleeve.

And they waited. Pippa could hear her heart, or was it Lionel's? Perhaps it was both. The pounding was so loud in her ears she was sure it would be like a signal, drawing anyone nearby to the ditch.

And then they heard the sound of hooves. Galloping. The crack of a whip. Lionel put a hand over Pippa's mouth. She tasted the salt sweat of his palm.

The hooves stopped abruptly, the other side of the fence. "Looks like they stopped here," a voice declared. "See the tracks. Horses were stopped right there."

"Aye, but they've gone on again. See the tracks," a

second voice said. "Galloping like all the devils in hell were on 'em."

"Aye, and so they are." There was a humorless laugh. "What's up ahead?"

"Nothing much. We'll catch 'em soon enough. There's nowhere to go."

"Let's just have a look-see over here."

They heard booted feet on the dried mud of the lane. A whip thrashed at the bramble hedge.

"Can't see anything here." The voice was almost on top of them. One of the men had entered the field. Pippa opened her eyes in the greenish light beneath the weed coverlet and could make out a pair of boots standing at the very edge of the ditch. Her heart seemed stuck in her throat.

Luisa bit back a sob of terror. Robin's arms held her tightly, her head pressed into his chest. She closed her eyes and prayed with all the fervor of Bernardina with her rosary.

"Let's go on now, George. Time's a-wasting and they're putting miles between us." The first voice sounded impatient.

"All right, all right. Just making sure, that's all."

"In a bramble hedge!" one of his companions scoffed. "Anyone would think we were out here picking blackberries."

And then the horses started up again and the sound of their hooves receded into the distance.

Lionel released Pippa and climbed to his feet, grass clinging to his shoulder.

Pippa stood up beside him. "I was not about to make any noise," she said, referring to the hand across her mouth. She reached up and plucked a yellow yarrow stalk from his hair.

"Pure reflex," he said without apology. He addressed Robin. "Once they catch up with the horses they'll come back here and start looking properly."

"Then we need fresh horses at once." Pippa gazed around the empty field as if she could somehow conjure up the necessary beasts. She was surprisingly calm now, her head clear, her heart once more beating steadily.

"We have maybe ten minutes. We can't stand in the middle of this field." Lionel picked up the tack and the bags at his feet. "Let's get into those trees. They'll give some kind of concealment."

He gave Luisa a long, appraising look. She was white and shaking, but her eyes were steady, no hint of terror or wildness in them. It reassured him but it did not surprise him. Luisa was a Mendoza, in whose veins ran the pure courageous blood of Castile.

He spoke rapidly, giving voice to his decisions as they were made. "We can't risk an inn from now on, they'll be in every village and hamlet from here to Southampton. We'll have to sleep in the open tonight."

"Surely they'll be watching all the ports," Pippa said, voicing a fear she had hitherto managed to suppress.

"No doubt," Lionel agreed, starting off across the field.

He sounded to Pippa completely unconcerned and she found it both heartening and annoying to have her legitimate fears dismissed so casually. It was one thing to have a cool head in a crisis, quite another to behave as if they had nothing really to worry about. With a troop of pistol-wielding ruffians out for their blood and on their heels, it seemed a little optimistic, to say the least.

She hitched the saddlebags onto her shoulder and set off after him, half running in an effort to keep up with his long stride. Luisa trotted beside her and Robin brought up the rear, every few seconds glancing over his shoulder towards the lane.

They reached the small stand of birch trees. It offered scant concealment but they could probably mount a defense here if they had to, Lionel decided. In extremis and with adequate warning, he and Robin could take on four men, although he didn't care for the odds. But they could pause here and take stock, knowing they would not be taken unawares.

Luisa sank down on a tuffet of moss among the roots of a spreading birch. Lionel regarded her thoughtfully. If Renard's men knew she was with him, she could never again pick up the threads of her previous innocent existence. She was now in as much danger as the rest of them.

He cast a glance towards Robin, who stood staring fixedly in the direction of the lane, his hand resting on the hilt of his sword. It struck him that he didn't have to worry too much about Luisa's future, just as long as he could ensure she stayed alive to have one.

"We could stand and fight," Robin said.

"Aye, but I'd rather run. Fighting takes time and dead men are hard to hide. But let's plan a defense just in case." They moved a little away, conferring in hushed tones.

Pippa nudged Luisa and gestured with a jerk of her head. She put a finger to her lips and Luisa, intrigued, scrambled up and followed Pippa to the other side of the coppice.

"What is it?" she whispered.

"See that smoke." Pippa pointed to a plume of smoke against the gray sky. "If 'tis a farm, we might find horses. Come. We'll see better from the top of that little hill." Pippa gathered up her skirts and half ran, half walked to the top of the small rise.

"Well, now," she said with satisfaction. "Would you look at that."

Luisa looked down into an unfenced meadow where six horses grazed placidly.

Pippa produced the two rope halters that she had been carrying against her skirts. "One for you and one for me."

Luisa took the proffered halter uncertainly.

"Let's go and get ourselves a pair of mounts." Pippa started down the hill, swinging the halter. Luisa, after a second's pause, followed her.

"I fancy the sorrel myself," Pippa said. "Why don't you try for the piebald gelding. He looks about the right size for you." She glanced at Luisa, seeing her hesitation. "Have you never caught a horse before?"

Luisa shook her head.

"Well, we don't want to set them running by missing the first time, so I'll catch the piebald and you can hold him while I catch the sorrel." Pippa advanced into the field, clicking her tongue invitingly.

The horses looked up, then resumed their grazing. Pippa bent and picked up a couple of windfalls from a stunted apple tree. She approached the piebald, murmuring softly. He let her reach him, then raised his head again with a nervous whinny. She laid a hand on his neck and offered him the windfall on the palm of her other hand. He took it and almost in the same movement she had the halter over his neck.

"Hold him, Luisa. Just keep talking to him so he doesn't startle the others."

"You've done this before," Luisa said admiringly. She

took the halter and stroked the piebald's neck while he stood perfectly calm and listened to her.

The sorrel was jumpier, watching Pippa's approach, then sidling away when she got close enough to touch her. Pippa showed no agitation, no sense of haste although her mouth was dry with the need to be done with this. She talked to the filly as she had done with the piebald and offered her the apple. The horse poked her nose into Pippa's palm but when Pippa caught at her mane she reared her head and stepped back again.

"Wretched creature," Pippa muttered in a voice like honey. "You're just playing games." She turned her back on the horse, holding the apple loosely by her side, and feigned indifference.

As she had hoped, the sorrel's curiosity was piqued. She approached Pippa and nudged at the hand that held the apple.

"So you want it now," Pippa murmured, opening her palm as she turned sideways to the horse. The sorrel let her stroke her neck and took the halter peacefully, as if to say that she had had every intention of doing so when she was good and ready.

Pippa led her to a tree stump and clambered onto her bare back. "Can you mount with this, Luisa?"

"Yes, of course," Luisa declared, anxious not to fall short again. She managed to scramble onto the piebald and took a firm hold of the halter. She had ridden bareback secretly once or twice on her family's hacienda under the aegis of a young horse trainer who had not been able to resist the entreaties or the large blue eyes of the daughter of the house. Now, seeing how at home Pippa seemed on the back of the sorrel, Luisa was glad of that clandestine experience as they rode the animals up the hill to the coppice.

"God's bones!" Lionel muttered when he noticed that he and Robin were alone in the trees. "I suppose I must understand your sister's need for these frequent trips into the bushes, but why in hell can't she say when she's going?" He spoke in an undertone; there was no knowing who might hear if he called out.

"I'd go in search of them except that I don't want to come upon them in the middle of—" He allowed an expressive shrug to complete the sentence.

"Wait. What's that?" Robin laid a hand on Lionel's arm. "Horses."

They turned as one in the direction of the unmistakable sound of hooves breaking through bracken, and then stared as Luisa and Pippa rode up to them.

"We have our horses," Pippa announced, sliding to the ground. "There are a pair of chestnuts who will do nicely for you two. You'll find them just at the bottom of the hill." She didn't wait for a response but slid the rope harness over the sorrel's neck and handed it to Lionel.

"Luisa and I will saddle up with the regular tack while you catch your mounts." She picked up the bridle that Lionel had used and swiftly began to harness the horse.

Lionel swung the rope halter against the palm of his hand, looking at her back as she went about her task with deft efficiency. He glanced at Robin and caught a glimmer of amusement in the vivid blue eyes.

"We'll take our instructions from you then, madam," he said, unable to hide his own amusement.

Pippa glanced at him over her shoulder and for a moment a glow showed deep in the hazel eyes. It was a light he had seen so often in the early days of their union and to see it again now lifted his spirits, gave him a sense of renewed hope. Hope that she would eventually regain her lightness of spirit, her optimism, her firm hold on the world.

She turned back to her task, but not before he'd seen the tiny mischievous smile touch her mouth. He raised an eyebrow at Robin, who grinned, took the other halter from Luisa, and loped off through the trees. Lionel followed.

When they returned, mounted on the chestnuts, Luisa and Pippa were standing beside the saddled horses, the saddlebags already in place.

"I've been watching the lane but I haven't seen any sign of anyone," Pippa told them.

Lionel nodded and swung down from the chestnut. He saw that Luisa was competently adjusting the stirrup leathers on her piebald and he reflected that this sheltered aristocrat certainly knew the basics of livery. Clearly neither of these women should be underestimated.

"We'll strike out across those fields, but steer clear of the source of the smoke," he said, boosting Pippa onto the sorrel before remounting his chestnut, leaving Robin to help Luisa.

Lionel glanced up at the overcast sky. "We have about four hours to nightfall. We'll make camp then."

He reached over and took Pippa's bridle. "Will you be able to ride that long?"

"Yes, of course." She twitched her bridle from his hand. "I'm not going to break, Lionel. I'm only pregnant."

"Perhaps I should rephrase that," he remarked. "Given that very condition, are you going to be able to ride that long without stopping every fifteen minutes?"

Pippa gave an exaggerated sigh. "Let's hope so," she said. "But 'tis the very devil of an inconvenience."

He laughed and moved his horse in front of hers as they threaded their way through the trees.

Only pregnant. As the afternoon wore on the two words settled in Pippa's head like the line of a song that kept repeating itself so that she couldn't think of anything else. It kept time with the horse's cantering hooves on the ground. *Only pregnant.*

Only pregnant and running for her life, and the life of the child she carried. A child of a hateful abomination of a union.

And yet still *her* child.

Twenty-five

THE FUGITIVES STOPPED FOR THE NIGHT UNDER A line of trees edging a broad strip of water. They had seen almost no one during the long afternoon's ride and Lionel's choice of campground was well clear of the narrow lanes and byways that would take them to Southampton on the morrow.

Pippa slid to the ground with an involuntary groan. "I could sleep for a week, but I could also eat a horse."

"Unfortunately I can satisfy neither of those needs," Lionel said. "But if trout will stave off the pangs and a bracken bed will cushion you sufficiently for sleep, then I see some hope."

He took the ale flagon from the saddlebag and handed it to her, together with what was left of the bread and cheese. "Get started on that while Robin and I make camp."

"No, we'll help," she said, after taking a long drink and handing the flagon to Luisa. "Tell us what to do. We are your willing foot soldiers, general." Her tone was light in an effort to mask her leaden fatigue.

Lionel was not deceived but he followed her lead.

He said as lightly as she, "If you want fish for your supper, my dear, you'll have to mind your tongue."

And for one wonderful moment there was no hint of tension between them. She smiled, he returned the smile, and all the warmth and intimacy that they had ever shared ran in a current deep and swift between them.

Then Pippa blinked, feeling oddly as if she were staring into a too bright light. She turned away and began to root through the saddlebags searching for something . . . anything . . . just to interrupt that current, to dim that light.

Lionel hesitated for a second, then he too turned away, saying with cheerful authority, "Robin, I'll leave you to set up camp while I see about some supper." He strode off to the river.

Robin and Luisa went off deeper into the trees in search of kindling and Pippa set about caring for the horses. When they were unsaddled, watered, baited, and tethered where the grass was rich, she listened for sounds of Robin and Luisa, but could hear nothing. It was truly dark now in the trees, but the evening star had pierced the overcast. She trod softly to the river and spied Lionel lying on his belly some fifty feet along the bank.

She knew better than to disturb a fisherman, let alone a poacher, so tiptoed across the dew-wet grass until she was standing behind him.

"Don't move." The whisper was so low it was barely uttered. His hand darted into the water and emerged, a speckled brown trout thrashing in his hold.

"Got you!" he said with a triumphant little chuckle. "Pass me that stone."

Pippa saw the stone that lay behind three other inert

fish glistening on the grass. She gave it to him. He killed the trout with one neat blow, then with his knife swiftly and cleanly gutted all four of them.

"You have the skills of a countryman," she observed. "Did you learn them in your childhood, in Chiswick?"

"No. They were learned through necessity," he replied. "I fished as a child, but with a rod." He leaned over the bank and scrubbed his hands in the clean water, then rose, drying them on his britches.

They stood quietly in the near-darkness. The evening star glittered on the river where not a breeze ruffled its surface. Lionel raised his hands and lightly clasped Pippa's face. His hands were cold from the river and a shiver ran through her. He bent his head and kissed her, lightly at first, then with increasing pressure. She didn't move, offering neither encouragement nor resistance.

He raised his head and still clasping her face looked down into her eyes. "My error," he said, his voice as dry as dust. "I had thought perhaps, after last night—"

She interrupted him. "We both had needs last night. We both were lonely. It had no more significance than that."

Lionel winced. His hands fell to his sides. "As I said, my error."

Pippa gazed down at the grass, crushed beneath her feet. The scent of wild thyme and pennyroyal and camomile rose on the soft air. She wanted to tell him that she had not wanted to hurt him. That she loved him but she didn't know how to reconcile that love with the overwhelming truth of his betrayal, and so everything she said to him somehow came out twisted and bitter.

"I wish I could let it go," she murmured after a minute. "I *must* let it go, Lionel. I must forgive."

"I do not expect you to," he said.

"No, but I cannot live unless I do. I will shrivel in hatred and bitterness and I cannot be like that.

"For the child I cannot be like that." She raised her head once more to look at him.

He said quietly, "The child is Philip's."

"The child has no father," she said with finality. "This child has only its mother and its mother's family. It will bear no taint but will grow safe in love and it will know *nothing* of its father."

She bent suddenly to pick a handful of thyme, thinking absently that it would season the trout, but it was really an excuse to take her eyes from his steady pain-filled gaze.

"I will go from here to my sister. To Pen and her husband," she said. "Owen d'Arcy is well able to keep me and the child safe from Philip's bloodhounds."

"Owen d'Arcy," Lionel said. "Yes, I am sure he is well able. But he is known to be your brother-in-law. Don't you think Philip and his bloodhounds might suspect that would be your first move?"

Pippa looked up in surprise. "Are you acquainted with my brother-in-law?"

"We are in the same business."

"Ah." She nodded, wondering why she had not made that connection herself.

"I think even your brother-in-law would agree that for the moment you are best with me."

"But I need my sister," Pippa whispered. "I cannot have my mother. I need my sister."

He heard her loneliness and his heart ached because he couldn't give her what she needed. There was no substitute, not even her brother, for the companionship of a mother or a sister. And he was filled with sorrow at the knowledge that he himself could never be all and everything to her. Even if they overcame this misery that lay between them, there would always be a need for a type of companionship and support that he could not fill.

"Later," he said. It was all the comfort he could offer her and she merely nodded and left him on the riverbank, taking her bunch of wild thyme to the fire.

Lionel gathered up his fish. He had lied to de Noailles when he had said he didn't know the identities of the others who held the scarab seal. Owen d'Arcy was one of the two men. Their mission was simple and intensely personal. They worked against Spain and the persecution of the Inquisition. As such they held no specific loyalty to a sovereign or a country, but lent their aid where their interests were served. France, in her present struggle with Spain, was more than happy to accept the anonymous assistance of the scarab holders.

Lionel had been forced to reveal his identity and allegiance to the French ambassador and was now no use to his colleagues or their cause. He wondered how Owen d'Arcy would judge his decision. Would d'Arcy have done the same to save his wife's sister?

He would discover soon enough.

AFTER THEIR SUPPER LIONEL TOOK THE FIRST WATCH and Pippa fell asleep on her bracken bed as soundly as if she had sunk into deep pillowy feathers.

Not so Luisa. She was filled with an overwhelming sense that the time had come for her to make some definitive move. In the quiet stillness of the trees, where only the murmuring of the river against its banks and the soft rustlings of night creatures disturbed the peace, she was actuely conscious of her body, of her senses, of the strange excitement that had filled her since the beginning of this frightening journey.

Robin was tending the fire and she hitched herself onto an elbow among the bracken. "Robin?" Her whisper was imperative although soft enough not to wake Pippa. "Come over here."

He trod carefully around the fire and knelt beside her. "What is it? Do you need something?"

"I wish to talk to you." She patted the bracken beside her. "You can lie here beside me and then we won't disturb Pippa."

Her black eyes glimmered in the firelight and her mouth had a most inviting curve to it. Robin tossed aside irrelevant scruples.

"Move over then." He lay down beside her as Luisa obligingly shifted herself and then with solicitous little pats settled his cloak over him.

"You could kiss me good night," she suggested.

"I could," he agreed, but made no move to do so.

"Don Ashton and your sister are lovers. Why shouldn't we be?"

Robin was not surprised that Luisa had guessed at this truth. He said only, "Pippa is no Spanish maiden."

"No. But she's married."

Robin leaned on an elbow and looked down into her face. He touched her cheek, the line of her mouth. "No," he said. "I will take you to wife, Luisa de los Velez of the house of Mendoza, but I will not take your honor. You will remain chaste until our wedding night."

"I had not thought you such a prude," she said in disgust.

"I am. Just ask my sisters." He leaned over and kissed her lightly. "Go to sleep now. 'Tis too cold and drear for lovemaking anyway."

"I had thought it might make one warm."

He slid an arm beneath her and rolled her against him. "We may sleep in this fashion. It will warm you. Bundling is a perfectly acceptable way of sleeping."

She chuckled into his shoulder and eased her body comfortably against him. "I still think you a prude."

"Now would not be a good moment to defend myself against your guardian."

"I shall talk to him," Luisa said. "Since he has no such scruples, I shall ask him why I should." She put an exploratory hand on his belly.

Robin removed it. "For God's sake, Luisa, this is torment enough. Go to sleep. We must be on the road by dawn."

" 'Tis truly torment?" she whispered against his neck.

"Truly."

"Good." She curled up tightly against him. "Then I will wait."

Twenty-six

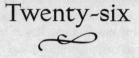

Malcolm leaned against the seawall on the Southampton docks and gazed ahead down the narrow crowded Southampton Water towards the Solent. It was high tide and merchant ships loaded with cargo were leaving the docks as others waited in the roads to take their places. *Sea Dream* swung at anchor with three other trading vessels in midchannel.

Malcolm could make out two small figures on the deck. One of them held something to his face. The sun caught the glitter of an eyeglass. Casually Malcolm untied the bright scarf he wore at his neck and shook it out as if getting rid of a fly among the folds, and then retied it. Immediately a dinghy was lowered from *Sea Dream* and a man descended the swinging rope ladder to drop neatly into the bow. Two oarsmen took up their oars and pulled strongly against the wind towards the docks.

Malcolm waited until the dinghy was close in, then he turned, whistling between his teeth, and strolled casually towards a warehouse to the right of the docks. He was dressed in woolen britches and a buff jerkin, a plain cap pulled low over his forehead. Only the red scarf gave him any color.

He entered the warehouse purposefully, the door swinging half closed behind him. Then he stepped to the side of the door and looked out through two strategically placed small holes in the wooden wall. The scene on the dock was as it had been when he'd left it. No one was looking towards the warehouse, no one was coming towards it.

He nodded his satisfaction. It was as he had hoped. His presence in Southampton was not known to Renard's spies, although the bastards were crawling all over the town and the docks. But while he could smell them from fifty yards they had no idea who he was. If they saw him, they'd take no notice of a dockhand who looked like every other. Not that he was taking any risks.

He hurried to the rear of the warehouse and slipped out through a narrow door into a small yard crowded with crates and bundles of cloth and wool awaiting loading onto *Sea Dream*. Behind a small mountain of cloth bundles, he waited until he heard the door open followed by a low musical whistle. He answered in kind and the master of *Sea Dream* stepped into the hiding place. He gave Malcolm a terse nod. Captain Longton was a man of few words.

"You'll be ready to leave on tomorrow evening's tide?" Malcolm asked.

"Aye. High tide's at ten o'clock. Will I be takin' a passenger?" His voice was as low as Malcolm's.

"Two," Malcolm said. "The master and one other. But be prepared to postpone your departure in case they're delayed."

"Trouble?" the captain inquired laconically.

Malcolm shrugged. "The town and docks are crawling with it. If you had to pick 'em up somewhere quieter could you do it?"

"*Sea Dream* has a deep draught. We could ride out in deep water if they could get to us by dinghy," Longton said, but he sounded doubtful. "We'd need a rendezvous time, can't be hangin' around in the Solent for too long."

Malcolm frowned and the two men stood in thoughtful silence.

Malcolm spoke finally. "We'll see what the master has to say. With luck I'll meet them by midafternoon tomorrow. Look for us here at six tomorrow evening."

Longton nodded. "We'll be loadin' cargo all day, but we'll take our time, leave some bales to load for evenin', so the yard here'll still be busy." He gave a nod of farewell and disappeared.

Malcolm waited for a few minutes, then left by a back gate into a narrow dark lane that ran behind the docks. He made his way to an evil-smelling hovel and ducked beneath the lintel. Some twenty minutes later he emerged, an old bent creature with a pronounced hump, dressed in filthy rags, his hands and face encrusted with grime.

Thus attired he went back to the docks to do some eavesdropping.

LUISA SLEPT ONLY FITFULLY. THE WARMTH OF ROBIN'S body, the earthy scent of him as he held her, filled her with a burgeoning excitement, but she was also frightened. The knowledge that she had found her future with this man, that he loved her as she loved him, was tainted by the knowledge that a danger that hadn't been explained to her could wipe it all away.

She had been given no explanation but it would have been clear to a village idiot that her companions were engaged in a treasonous flight. Treason meant death of the worst kind. For all her sheltered existence, Luisa knew the facts of her world. And she feared the Inquisition as all rational people did. It came out of nowhere, fed on whispers, and took the innocent and the guilty alike into agonizing darkness.

Finally she slipped out from under Robin's arm without waking him and rose to her feet, gathering her cloak around her. She stood looking down at Robin for a moment. He was sleeping deeply, trustfully, as if nothing threatened him. She looked across the fire to Pippa's bracken bed and wondered if she slept in the same manner, or if she too was wakeful and fearful.

Trying not to crack twigs that would awaken the sleepers, Luisa crept towards the tree line where she guessed she would find her guardian keeping his watch. She saw him standing against a tree trunk, looking across the field towards the lane from whence she assumed unwelcome visitors would come.

"Don Ashton?" she whispered.

He didn't start at her voice, merely said, "Luisa? Why aren't you asleep?"

"I'm too restless." She stood beside him. It was still dark, but there was a hint of gray in the sky.

"Frightened?"

"Yes. Maybe you think that's my own fault. I shouldn't be here at all."

"That thought had crossed my mind."

"I have to be here." She crossed her arms over her breast beneath her cloak and stared into the lightening sky. "I love Robin. He loves me. I'm of an age for marriage. If I weren't here now, then I would have given up all hopes of happiness. Whatever this treason is, it would have separated us. Is that not so?"

"Aye, 'tis so."

"You and Pippa are lovers." She said it directly, without rushing but praying that there was no tremor in her voice.

He looked down at her then. His instinct was to see impudence and quell it with a guardian's sharp authority. But two days in his ward's close company had opened his eyes to her character.

He said mildly, "I wonder if that's any of your business, Luisa."

"Yes, it is. Because we are all in this danger together, and I am not prepared to die without knowing what it is to . . . to experience that. If 'tis all right for you and Pippa to have such a liaison, then I see no reason why it should not be all right for Robin and me."

"There is one difference," he observed. "Pippa is no maid."

"No, and the child she carries is not her husband's. Is that not so?"

"Aye." A roughness entered his voice and Luisa half wished she had not begun this. But she said nothing, refusing to offer the retraction and apology that rose instantly, defensively, to her lips. In the silence that followed she fought hard to keep her own and at last he spoke again.

"I can tell you only that much rests on that fact. Our own lives mean little against what's truly at stake." He could tell her no more because Pippa had already decreed that her child had no father. If she had this child in safety then no one but those who had to must know who sired it.

"I understand that," Luisa said, somber but confident. "Robin says he will take me to wife but he will not take my honor. Because of what you have told me, I would change his mind."

She looked up at him, her expression grave. "I wish to know these things, sir. I wish to know what it is to be a woman."

Lionel ran his fingertips over his mouth. "I would not deny you that knowledge. But I think, if you have a little more faith in my ability to get us all out of danger, that you might garner the knowledge on your wedding night."

"And if I choose not to wait?"

Lionel laughed suddenly. "I can assure you, Luisa, that there will be no opportunity for experiments in love before we take ship from Southampton. But once at sea, you may try your persuasion on Robin. As soon as we land in France, you will be married."

"And you promise me that that will happen?"

"I don't deal in promises." Once again the roughness entered his voice. "I deal in possibilities, Luisa. Trust those. I can promise you nothing else."

With a tiny accepting nod, she turned away. He laid a hand on her shoulder. "Wake Pippa and Robin. I'll gather the horses."

Luisa returned to the fire immediately. She was not comforted by her discussion with her guardian, far from it, but she knew a great sense of release, as if the burdens of her upbringing had somehow been lifted. She could make her own decisions, test her own strengths, find her own self.

Pippa was already awake, warming her hands at the fire's embers. She smiled at Luisa and glanced across to where Robin was stirring under his cloak. She raised her eyebrows.

Luisa smiled back, delighted that she didn't blush. "Don Ashton is getting the horses. He says we must go at once."

Pippa got to her feet, stretched, yawned, gathered up the water flasks, and headed for the riverbank. Lionel was already there, splashing his face with cold water. He gave her a swift appraising look as she knelt beside him.

"Sleep well?"

"Surprisingly," she replied. "What is this ship *Sea Dream*? How did you know it would be at Southampton?"

" 'Tis one of my own fleet. When my father died I inherited everything. I keep the merchant trade going."

Pippa filled the water flasks. "In addition to spying and the like," she observed.

"Aye, in addition to that," he responded without expression. "I have exceptional managers and captains."

"I suppose that explains the London mansion," Pippa said, pushing the stoppers back into the flagons. "I wondered where you acquired your wealth."

"I am rich."

"But never sought a title?" She gave him a curious glance. "For a family with wealth, titles are easily bought."

"My father had no interest in buttering up to sovereigns or their acolytes, and nor do I." There was unmistakable contempt in his voice. He stood up and lifted the full water flagons. "Hurry now. We have to reach

Chandler's Ford by midafternoon. We must ride without respite."

"We'll have to stop," Pippa declared. "Or, I will have to."

"I did not mean it quite so literally," Lionel responded. He gave her a quick smile and her answering shrug was wry.

They rode through the breaking dawn, again keeping to byways and field paths. Pippa was only faintly surprised that Lionel seemed to know where he was going across this uncharted land. He was the owner of a merchant fleet, had a family home in Chiswick. Only in another life was he an habitue of the Spanish court, a trusted confidant of Philip of Spain. Nothing he could do or be would surprise her anymore.

Late in the afternoon they rode across a meadow thick with dandelions and daisies. Ahead lay the tiny hamlet of Chandler's Ford that straddled a narrow tributary of the River Itchen.

Lionel dismounted and took the halter off his exhausted horse. "We'll turn them loose here," he said. "Malcolm will have a care for them when he has time. Until then they'll rest comfortably here."

Pippa dismounted and stood leaning wearily against her mount, for the moment unable to make her limbs work. She wondered if her own total exhaustion could harm the child she carried.

Lionel looked at her. Her white, thickly freckled countenance had a grayish cast, purple shadows lay beneath her eyes, every line of her angular features stood out. Her thinness that had once given the attractive impression of wiry strength was now that of a dying flower, the sap running out of it as its thin stalk drooped towards the earth.

It was not simply physical exhaustion, it was a deep emotional draining that was leaching the life from her.

A surge of frustration and anger washed through him. And he welcomed its cleansing flow. He had promised he would not intrude upon her; he would accept her judgment and suffer his own guilt. But now he was going to break that promise. It was time to set aside his guilt, his self-disgust, his remorse. They weakened him.

He went over to her where she still drooped against her horse. He put his arms around her, kissed her mouth as she raised her head in surprise, then lifted her up, holding her securely against him.

"What are you doing?" she exclaimed. "Put me down, Lionel."

"No," he said. "I am going to carry you across this meadow and into the cottage at the ford. There you will rest by the fire and the goodwife will make you an infusion. Then you will eat and drink, before we move on again."

"I am not an invalid," she protested, even as her body sank into the powerful cradle of his hold. "And I am perfectly capable of deciding when I need to rest . . . or anything else, for that matter."

"Quite possibly, but you're going to let me make those decisions for you for the moment," he said calmly as he strode with her across the meadow. "It will be much simpler and easier for both of us."

"And why would that be?" she demanded.

"This is one instance when one head is better than two," he responded. "Let it be mine."

"What's Don Ashton doing with Pippa?" Luisa asked, staring after them.

"I have no idea. I only hope he does," Robin said. "Help me unsaddle the horses."

*   *   *

PIPPA, DECIDING SHE WOULD SAVE HER STRENGTH FOR
more important bones of contention, offered no further
protest. They went through a kissing gate and into a
narrow lane that led to a ford, no more than a path of
stones wide enough for a cart to cross the stream. A
small lime-washed cottage stood beside the ford.

Lionel rapped with his knuckles on the door in a
quick rhythm and it was opened instantly.

Pippa stared at the bent old man in his ragged garments.

"Malcolm?" she said after an instant.

He grinned through his grime. "Aye, Lady Nielson,
the very same. Come you in."

Lionel set Pippa down on the rough wooden settle
beside the fire. "Put your feet up."

She did so without demur, resting her back against
the high side of the settle, her face towards the fire. He
rolled his cloak into a thick bundle and pushed it behind
her shoulders.

"Where's Goodwife Abbot?"

"In the back," Malcolm said. He regarded Pippa with
ill-concealed concern. "I'll fetch her."

Lionel stood warming his backside at the fire. Pippa
looked at him. He seemed very much at his ease, as if all
the urgency of their mad dash across the countryside
was now dissipated. And yet surely, she thought, they
had arrived at the most dangerous moments of their
flight.

"You have a question?" he asked, feeling the searching intensity of her regard.

She shook her head. "Not really." She could detect
now the taut resolve behind the composed facade. It
was in his eyes that had a touch of iron to the gray, and

in the line of his mouth and jaw. He was rock solid, as steady and unflinching as any deep-rooted oak tree in a gale, and she too now felt confident that his will *would* prevail. He would save her and her child. He would defeat Philip; in this he would defeat Spain.

Her limbs became heavy and relaxed, her head resting against the bundled velvet at her back, and for a moment her eyelids drooped.

"What can I do fer ye, sir?" A woman stepped into the firelight, but her gaze turned instantly from Lionel to Pippa. "Eh, what 'ave we 'ere," she said, bending over Pippa. "Be you ill, madam?"

"No," Pippa said, managing a smile. "Just very tired and with child."

"Can you make her ladyship an infusion, goodwife?" Lionel asked. "Something to strengthen her."

"Oh, aye, that I can." The woman chafed Pippa's hands for a minute then straightened. "Peppermint, valerian, a touch o' milk thistle, in an elder-flower cordial. That'll put 'eart in ye, m'dear."

She moved around the small room, selecting herbs from the ceiling racks where they were dried. She took an earthenware jar from a shelf, poured some of its contents into a pewter cup, added the herbs, then added hot water from the steaming kettle on the trivet in the fireplace. She stirred the mixture, added a large dollop of honey, and brought it to Pippa.

"There y'are, m'dear. Drink it down."

Pippa clasped the cup in both hands. The steam was fragrant and reminded her suddenly of her old nurse, Tilly. It was just the kind of soothing medicine that Tilly would have mixed. She glanced up at Lionel, but saw that he was now deep in a low-voiced conversation with Malcolm.

She took a sip of the infusion and watched them through half-closed eyes, trying to gauge the tenor of their conversation although she could hear no more than a word or two.

Robin and Luisa arrived soon after and Pippa hitched herself up on the settle, drawing up her feet so that there was room for Luisa to squeeze herself near the fire.

Robin joined Malcolm and Lionel, and the goodwife after an appraising glance at Luisa brought her a large cup of buttermilk and a piece of gingerbread.

"You are something of a physician, goodwife," Pippa said with an appreciative smile. "Your diagnostic skills are remarkably accurate."

The woman smiled back and took Pippa's empty cup. "Anythin' else I can get you, madam?"

Pippa shook her head. "No, I thank you." She looked over at the men. "I think Luisa and I should be a part of this conversation, sirs. We have been pampered sufficiently, our poor weak spirits given enough of a rest."

Lionel turned to her. "It would do you more good to close your eyes for an hour. We have no need to move until five."

"And maybe I will do that," she said steadily. "But I will sleep better, sir, if I know what lies ahead."

"She will," Robin murmured. "I applaud your efforts, Ashton, but she'll only go along with you so far."

"If you say so." Lionel came over to the settle. "Very well. At five, you, Malcolm, and I will ride into Southampton. You and I will be rather differently attired . . . more in Malcolm's fashion."

He glanced at the other man, who gestured significantly to a bag on the floor beneath the window.

"We shall go aboard *Sea Dream* at Southampton Dock. Robin and Luisa will make their way to Bucklers Hard, a hamlet on the Beaulieu River. Goodwife Abbot's son has a dinghy there. He will sail them to the mouth of the river, where they will wait. *Sea Dream* will sail on the tide and sometime after midnight she will drop anchor in the Solent in deep water on a line with the mouth of the river. Robin and Luisa will then join us on board and we will sail for France."

"Why does that sound so simple, yet fill me with such dread?" Pippa inquired with a mildness quite at odds with her racing blood. She sat up, swinging her legs to the floor. "Why can we not all go aboard the ship in Southampton?"

Lionel leaned over her, brushing her lank hair from her forehead. " 'Tis safer thus. Malcolm has been doing some spying of his own. Renard's men are posted at every entrance to the town and they're patrolling the docks. Four people are more conspicuous than two."

"There is more," she said steadily, fixing him with a direct gaze.

It was Robin who answered her. "Your safety is paramount, Pippa. You and your child must get away tonight. It will be much easier to spirit just you and Lionel aboard. If there is a difficulty in picking up Luisa and me . . . the current may be too strong, or the wind . . . or there may be excise men on the watch in the Solent . . . then I will find another way for us to cross the Channel. They won't be looking too hard for the two of us."

Lionel took her hands. "I will make this all right, Pippa. You will trust me to do that." The clear gray eyes held hers. There was such an intensity of determination, of passion, of promise there that she felt as if she would be consumed by the sheer power of his will. She could only try to match her courage with his.

"Yes," she agreed. Her voice was suddenly stronger. "And can I trust also that there will be hot water on board this *Sea Dream*? I for one have slept in my clothes and not changed my linen in three days."

Lionel smiled, knowing the courage it had cost her to make the jesting demand.

"That much I can promise you, my love," he said softly, and touched his fingers to her lips in a brief caress.

Twenty-seven

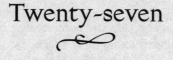

PIPPA WAS GLAD SHE HAD NO MIRROR TO SEE HER REflection once she was dressed in the ghastly garments Malcolm had brought for her. A tattered skirt that had once been yellow but was now so dirty it was a dull beige and an equally grimy bodice with an edge of torn lace. She pushed her feet into the wooden sabots that were so large they were like boats.

She tried unsuccessfully to push her toes to the very end of the clogs. "I hope I don't have to walk too far in these."

"I hope you won't have to walk at all," Lionel remarked. He looked her over critically. "Pull the shawl up over your head and cover your face as much as possible."

Grimacing, Pippa swathed her head in the mustysmelling folds of red wool.

"You don't look in the least like yourself," Luisa pronounced.

"Good," Pippa said. "Neither does Lionel."

Lionel did look particularly disreputable with his face darkened with burnt cork and an artistically drawn scar lifting the corner of his upper lip. He wore stained leather britches and jerkin, and his hands were the calloused hands of a laborer, the nails broken and filthy.

Lionel smiled, showing crumbling teeth. It was a disguise he had assumed on many occasions and he was well aware of its effectiveness.

Pippa turned to Robin, asking anxiously, "You are content with this plan, Robin? What happens if they're watching that river?"

"They won't be," he said confidently. "But anyway I understand that the dinghy is beached out of sight of the main quay. We should be able to launch it without detection."

He put his arms around her and hugged her. "Once we're in the dinghy they won't be able to touch us. Don't worry. We'll see you on board *Sea Dream*."

She nodded, refusing to admit the slightest doubt in her mind, the slightest tremor of fear. "I know you will. God go with you." She kissed him, kissed Luisa, who hugged her convulsively, and then she said to Lionel, "I am ready. Should we go?"

"We should." He put a hand on her shoulder and steered her out of the cottage. He could feel the tension of her body beneath his hand but he could also sense her steadiness of purpose. Of course she was afraid, who wouldn't be? But she was not going to let it show. He knew her sister Pen's history and he had heard some story about her mother, Lady Guinevere Mallory, and her battle with the old King Henry VIII. Mallory women, he thought, were not cut from ordinary cloth.

Malcolm was already seated on the driving board of the farm cart. He jumped down to help Pippa into the back. It was full of recently cured sheepskins and bales of raw uncarded wool.

"What a dreadful stench!" she exclaimed.

"Aye, people don't realize that the finished product has unsavory beginnings," Lionel said.

Pippa sat on a pile of sheepskins. "I stink myself," she observed. "So I'll blend in nicely."

Lionel laughed. "It's going to be worse, I'm afraid. You can stay there until we get close to the city walls, but then we're going to cover you with the skins and a bale of wool."

"How disgusting," she muttered. "I shall probably be sick, I warn you."

He accepted the remark in the spirit it was intended and said cheerfully, "I hope not. It will only be for a short while, just until we get beyond the walls and into the warehouse. Then you can breathe fresh air for a few minutes, before we wrap you up again."

He jumped onto the bench, beside Malcolm. "Let's go."

Malcolm cracked his whip and the cart horse lumbered forward.

"Wrap me up why?"

"You know the story of Cleopatra and the rug?"

"Yes."

"Same principle. You'll go aboard wrapped in a bale of cloth."

"Oh." Pippa grabbed the side of the cart as it jolted in a particularly deep rut. "This disguise seems a little pointless if I'm not ever to be seen."

" 'Tis merely added insurance."

Which made perfect sense, of course. "How will you go aboard?"

"As a dockhand loading bales of cloth. One of which will be you."

Pippa nodded and fell silent. She could find no fault

with the plan but that did nothing to assuage her fears. The autumn dusk was gathering and flocks of rooks circled noisily above the treetops before settling for the night. Cows lowed from the fields, waiting for milking time. The countryside was so calm, so ordinary, and she wondered, if she should escape tonight, whether she would ever be able to return to the land of her birth. And what of her mother? Would she ever see her mother again?

Her breath caught in her throat and to her horror it came out like a sob. She swiftly turned it into a yawn as Lionel twisted around on the bench in immediate response to the tiny sound.

"Just sleepy," she mumbled.

He was unconvinced but judged it better not to push her for the truth. It would do no good for her to put doubts and fears into words, not at this juncture.

Instead he asked Malcolm, "What time do they close the gates?"

"At six. We should get through just a minute or two before."

"Good timing. With luck they'll be in too much of a hurry to get home to their own firesides to give us more than a cursory glance."

The walls of the city were visible in the dusk when Malcolm drew the cart aside under a hedge and Lionel climbed into the back. He spread a sheepskin on the floor. "Quickly, Pippa."

She lay down, holding her breath at the reek of urine that had been used for the tanning process. Lionel threw another skin over her and then swiftly piled bundles of wool on top.

"Can you breathe?"

"I'm trying not to."

"Keep as still as you can."

He went back to Malcolm and the cart started up again.

Pippa lay rigid; wool tickled her nose and she tried desperately not to sneeze even as she breathed lightly through her mouth. The floor of the cart was hard and uneven and something pressed fiercely between her shoulder blades. But worse than anything was her inability to see what was happening.

The cart came to a halt and she heard Malcolm call to someone. "Headin' for the docks, sir. Got a cargo of skins and wool."

They must be at the gate. She felt something hit the side of the cart and she stopped breathing altogether. Something hard poked at her. She imagined it to be a pitchfork and now she was convinced the wool and skins would be tossed aside and she would lie there exposed. She needed to breathe but she didn't dare. She waited in a terror surpassing anything she would have believed possible. And then the cart lurched forward again and she took a deep gulp of the foul air and sneezed violently.

"Jest a minute there!" There was an imperative shout and the cart came to a stop. She heard the sound of running feet.

Dear God! She had sneezed while they were going through the gate.

Lionel gazed blandly at the watchman who came running up. He sneezed and blew his nose between his fingers, wiping them on his britches. "What's up, mate?" He sneezed again. "Damn wool," he said. "Gets up me nose."

The man stared at him suspiciously. He leaned over the side of the cart and looked inside, bending his head close to the pile of wool. Then he sneezed suddenly himself.

"Yer right at that," he said, wiping his nose on his sleeve. "Foul stuff." He slapped the side of the cart and returned to help his colleague heave the great iron gates closed for the night.

Lionel whistled casually between his teeth as he exchanged a significant glance with Malcolm. Neither of them spoke or looked once behind them to the interior of the cart.

Pippa fought waves of nausea, brought on, she knew, by panic. It had nothing to do with pregnancy. It was sheer terror. The cart lumbered over stones now, the wooden wheels clattering. She concentrated on the sounds around her, to take her mind off her nausea. There were voices close by, rough, grumbling tones, grunts, and heavy breathing. A creaking sound like straining ropes, and the flapping of heavy cloth.

They must be at the docks.

The cart came to a halt once more and after what seemed hours the vile coverings were flung aside and she was staring up at a clear night sky, breathing salt air, feeling a cold wind on her heated cheeks. Her unruly stomach settled down once more.

Lionel leaned in, taking her hands to pull her to her feet.

"Forgive me, I don't know why that happened . . . I couldn't help it," she gasped as she staggered upright.

"All's well that ends well. Come here." He reached up to take her waist and swung her down to the cobbles. They were in a small enclosed yard, empty except for a few bales of cloth.

Pippa looked around. "Where's Malcolm?"

"He's gone. He has to get Dona Bernardina on a ship

back to Spain. Then he will journey into Derbyshire to tell your family what has happened and reassure them that you're safe. You and Robin."

Pippa looked at him incredulously. "You thought of that!"

"I imagine it's been preying on your mind some-what."

Somewhat! Pippa thought. The prospect of her mother's frantic anxiety when she heard of her disap-pearance had been almost more than she could bear. So much so that she had pushed it to the back of her mind, trying to quell her misery by telling herself that it would be many weeks before the news traveled to Derbyshire, and maybe by then she would be able to send a message from France.

But Lionel had found time to think of this and plan for it.

"Thank you," she said. She reached up a hand to touch his face in a fleeting grateful caress and he grasped her wrist tightly for a moment, looking down into her eyes, holding her gaze, intense and yet with the same compassionate sweetness that had so drawn her to him from their first real meeting.

Once again all the warmth and intimacy that they had ever shared ran deep and swift between them. It was almost as if what had been destroyed was now growing back. As if the roots themselves had never been torn from the ground and were now putting forth tender lit-tle shoots of possibility.

"You have no need to thank me, Pippa."

He let go her wrist. "At least wait until we're safely on the high seas," he said with a wry smile. "Then maybe we'll have this conversation again, when I can in-dulge my gratification."

At that moment a stocky man with a rolling gait and a distinct air of authority came over to them. He gave Pippa only a cursory glance. "They'll be givin' us the evil eye soon, sir, if we don't finish loadin'. We have to catch the tide."

"Right," Lionel said, all briskness again. "We're ready. Help me unroll the cloth."

The two men attacked a large bale of unbleached cloth, spreading it across the cobbles. Pippa obeyed Lionel's beckoning finger and lay down in the middle of the material. She found she was no longer capable of fear. Everything had taken on such an air of unreality that she felt she was existing in a dream, a sensation that was only accentuated when the cloth covered her head and bound her arms tightly to her sides.

Carefully they rolled her over until the cloth was wound mummylike around her and she resembled nothing more than a column of material.

Lionel hoisted her up over his shoulder, placing a steadying hand on her backside as she dangled down his back. "Just hang limp, Pippa," he murmured.

As if she had any choice, Pippa reflected, swathed as she was. It was damnably uncomfortable, the blood had rushed to her head and she felt quite dizzy. But again, to her astonishment, her earlier terror had quite dissipated.

Lionel moved out of the courtyard, through the empty warehouse, and onto the dock. He kept his head lowered but his eyes darted left and right as he walked steadily to *Sea Dream*'s gangplank.

"Eh, you not done yet?" A rough voice hailed him just as he approached the gangplank.

He turned slowly, his mouth drooping, his lower lip hanging open. He looked at his interlocutor with the vacant stare of a half-wit. The man was dressed in the buff jerkin of a soldier, armed with sword and dagger, and he had the air of one spoiling for a fight.

"You, I'm talkin' to you!" The soldier jabbed Lionel in the chest with his forefinger. "They've been loadin' this ship all day. There's others waitin' for the berth."

Lionel continued to offer his loose-lipped stare. "T' maister," he mumbled. "I dunno nuthin', sir. T' maister knows."

Captain Longton, who had gone ahead, yelled from the top of the gangplank. "Get up here with that load, you half-witted bugger! We're ready to cast off."

"T' maister," Lionel mumbled again. He hitched his burden higher on his shoulder as if it was particularly heavy.

Pippa felt the wooden shoe slip. Desperately she tried to catch it on her toe, but the cloth made it impossible to bend her feet. She felt the sabot slide off her toe, and through the racing blood in her ears she heard the clatter as it hit the cobbles of the quay.

The soldier stared at the shoe, then up at the bundle, and comprehension dawned. Someone was being smuggled aboard. It was what he'd been told to look for. He gave a triumphant shout and lunged forward, his sword in his hand.

Lionel dropped Pippa unceremoniously to the cobbles just a second before the sword reached its target. His own knife now glittered in his hand as he dodged the thrusts of his opponent, looking for an opening.

Pippa kicked and fought her way out of her bindings. She sprang to her feet in one movement, not thinking, not feeling, reduced to an animal state of pure muscle and impulse.

A heavy oiled chain lying on the cobbles caught her

eye and she grabbed it up without thought or even an act of will, staggering under its weight as she swung it wildly at the soldier, who was shouting for assistance. His sword caught Lionel a glancing blow on the arm and at the sight of his bright blood dripping to the ground, Pippa became enraged.

With a gigantic effort she hurled the entire chain at the soldier's head. It struck him on the ear and he staggered. She bent, took up the loose cloth, and flung it over him, tangling his limbs. He went down on one knee. Light spilled over the quay as the door to the tavern on the docks was flung wide and men surged out drunk and eager for a melee.

"Run!" Lionel yelled, grabbing her hand.

She saw then with a sickening jolt to her stomach that *Sea Dream* had taken up her gangplank and was already moving away from the dock. She was being rowed away, twelve pairs of oars pulling to a chanted rhythm while men swarmed over her rigging, hoisting her foresail.

"They're going!" she gasped.

"Just run!" He hauled her after him towards a long jetty that stretched out into the water at the far end of the quay. She ran. Her tattered skirts streaming behind her, her now bare feet torn by the rough stones. But she felt no discomfort. Behind them came the sounds of pursuit. Shouts, pounding feet. A stone flew past her ear.

They were abreast of *Sea Dream* as they reached the very end of the jetty. A rope flew through the air and Lionel caught it in one hand. He grabbed Pippa against him with his free arm and jumped for the deck. His foot slipped on the rail and he fell, still clutching both rope and Pippa, banging against the side of the ship, which was now picking up speed as the wind from the open water caught the sail. The wound in his arm opened further under the pressure and hot blood soaked Pippa's bodice.

She reached up and seized hold of the rope above Lionel's head, so that it could take her weight and free Lionel of the need to hold her.

"Climb!" he instructed, giving her an almighty boost with his free hand. And she did so, hand over hand, aware of Lionel dangling beneath her, bleeding into the water that now slipped rapidly by.

Hands reached over the rail and grabbed her, yanking her up and over to fall in a heap on the decking. Lionel was seconds behind her. Willing hands pulled him over the rail and he fell across Pippa's body, knocking the breath from her.

For a moment they both lay dazed and unmoving, then Lionel hitched himself up onto his elbows and leaned over Pippa.

"Lucifer and all his angels!" he said. "Where in the name of God's good grace did you learn to fight like that?"

"I have no idea," she said. "It just happened. I was so *angry*, Lionel. Not frightened, just filled with rage. He was going to kill you." She gave him a rather bewildered smile that nonetheless managed to be a little smug.

He kissed her, on her nose, on her eyes, then on her mouth. She put her arms around his neck and kissed him in her turn with a sudden wild hunger. She had nearly lost him. They had so nearly been lost to each other. And she now knew that she could bear anything but that.

A loud cough from above brought them back to the reality of the ship's deck, the cold wind, the creaking rigging. Lionel pulled himself to his feet. Blood still dripped from his arm.

"Thought it best to set sail," Longton said, sounding somewhat anxious. "Reckon you needed to make a quick getaway."

Lionel ran a hand through his disheveled hair. "Aye, that we did. Although I'd not be here now if it weren't for my warrior friend." He laughed, and it felt like the first time since he could remember that he had laughed with genuine amusement.

Pippa scrambled to her feet and leaned against the deck rail. She looked back to the receding dock. A group of men still stood at the end of the jetty, staring after them. "Are we safe? Truly safe?"

Lionel glanced at the captain. "Can they come after us?"

"They could try." He shrugged. "But they'd have to find a ship, and far as I know there's none in Southampton Water at the moment ready to sail. Besides, the tide'll turn in a quarter hour. We'll be out in the Solent by then and nothing can catch *Sea Dream* in full sail with a good wind behind."

"But we have to pick up Robin and Luisa," Pippa said urgently. "We can't leave them."

The captain looked up at the sky. "There'll be a good overcast within the hour. You look like you need some medical attention, sir. And the lady, too."

Lionel examined Pippa. "There's blood on your bodice."

" 'Tis yours," she said, lifting his arm where his shirt was ripped to reveal a long bleeding gash. "Where can we go to tend to this?"

"My cabin, madam. Mr. Ashton will have the use of it

on the voyage. You should find all you need." The captain nodded and returned to his quarterdeck.

"I don't understand," Pippa said. "He didn't say he would pick up Robin and Luisa, he just said the sky would be overcast."

"He's a man of few words," Lionel said. "But he meant that a dark sky will favor us. Come, let's go below."

Pippa let her hand curl small and unresisting into his palm. That burst of violent energy still infused her and she still felt the imprint of Lionel's mouth on hers. A strange euphoria filled her, so that she didn't notice that she was leaving bloody footprints on the immaculate decking.

Lionel noticed, however, as they reached the companionway. He looked at the trail she had made. "Your feet must be cut to ribbons."

"Yes, I think they are," she said happily. "But they'll heal."

Lionel looked at her askance. If he hadn't known better he would have said she'd had one tankard too many of strong ale. She gave him a beatific smile, and he laughed aloud at the contrast of the deep, glowing hazel eyes with her filthy face and the tangled dirty mess of her cinnamon curls. In a convulsive hug he caught her against him with his good arm.

She rested her head on his chest. "So much to talk about," she said, her voice serious once more. "So much time wasted in anger and bitterness."

It was as if all the pent-up bitterness that had been constricting her very soul had been consumed in that wild outburst of animal rage. It was as if that scorching heat of fear and fury had somehow purified her. She could see clearly again and her spirit felt green and fresh and welcoming, like the earth warmed by the spring sun.

He stroked her hair, knowing instinctively that now was not the time for him to speak. Then he gently released her, pushing her towards the companionway.

Pippa looked around the captain's small but well-appointed cabin. "How neat this is," she said. "And how clever to have a bed that comes out of the wall like that. It takes up no floor space."

"Get out of those filthy clothes," he directed, knotting his scarf with his teeth around the wound in his arm before lifting a large, lidded wooden pail. "There's water aplenty. I promised you that, I believe."

"Let me wash and bandage your arm first," Pippa said, hunting for bandages in one of the lockers fitted into the bulwark.

"It can wait. 'Tis only a flesh wound. Let me wash you first and look at your feet. And then you may return the ministrations." He set a round wooden tub in the middle of the floor. "Strip off those disgusting garments and stand in here."

"You mean," Pippa said slowly, "that we are at last to be naked together?"

"Yes, but for purely practical purposes," he replied with a grin. "Should I help you with those clothes?"

"I can probably do it more quickly, since you have only one workable arm." She stripped to her skin with swift careless movements and then stood suddenly and absurdly shy under the swaying lantern that hung from the ceiling.

Lionel ran his eyes over her in a lingering caress before indicating the tub with a jerk of his head.

Pippa stepped over the edge. She closed her eyes tightly as water cascaded over her head. Then his hands were all over her, warm and soapy, rubbing her hair, her body, lingering on her breasts so that her nipples rose small and hard, sliding between her thighs so that she gave a little murmur of suspended pleasure. He knelt to wash her feet, his fingers gentle on the cuts. She winced nevertheless, her body once more alive to sensation both pleasurable and painful.

He stood up and lifted the pail of water again. "Keep your eyes closed." The water poured over her and she protested faintly that there wouldn't be enough for him.

"There will be. Step out now." He wrapped a linen towel around her, then sat on a low stool. "Kneel down and I'll dry your hair."

She did so, resting her forehead against his knees as he worked on her hair. "Clothes," she murmured. "I have no clothes."

"I thought you wished to dispense with such burdensome articles," he said, rubbing briskly.

"I can hardly go on deck naked," she pointed out.

"True. But we have no need to go anywhere at present. It will be another hour before we can expect to see Luisa and Robin."

He took the towel from her head. "There, 'tis so thick that's the best I can do."

Pippa shook her hair loose around her face and down her back. It smelled wonderful. Damp but clean. She let the towel fall from her body, no longer shy. "Your turn, sir." She reached for his belt.

She washed him as he had washed her, her hands moving over his body in the same way, lingering where it would please them both. His penis rose and hardened between her hands and she laughed softly as he stood with his hands on his hips, his eyes closed.

"You're like some pasha in a harem," she accused,

standing on tiptoe to kiss his mouth. "What else does my master desire?"

"A towel first," he replied with a languid gesture.

Playfully she threw a fresh linen towel at him, and then perched on the stool watching him dry himself. The sight of his naked body thrilled her. He was so spare, pared to the bone, all sinew and muscle. She was deeply aroused and yet willing to wait, relishing the anticipation. Once Luisa and Robin were safely aboard, then there would be no reason why they shouldn't bolt the cabin door and stay there until they reached France.

Her tongue touched her lips in a lascivious gesture of which she was not in the least conscious, but it made Lionel catch his breath.

"I think perhaps you *should* put some clothes on," he said a little unsteadily. "Now is not the time."

"I am aware," Pippa said. "But what shall I put on?" She opened her palms in a helpless gesture.

Lionel wrapped the towel around his loins and padded to the bulkhead. "Malcolm should have ensured the necessaries were stowed in here."

He handed her hose, chemise, petticoat, and a simple gown of pale green linen. "No farthingale, no hood," he commented. "But there's this." He held out an embroidered silk shawl. "And a pair of slippers." Plain kid slippers followed.

"What more could I ask? You seem to have planned for everything." She dropped the chemise over her head and sat down to pull on the hose.

"That surprises you? How very disappointing. I thought you knew me better than that." He had opened another locker, which contained clothes for himself.

"I suppose it doesn't really surprise me," Pippa conceded, shaking out the skirts of the linen gown. "Let me dress your arm before you put on the shirt. I saw some witch hazel and bandages in that locker."

He allowed her to wash and dress the wound, and fasten a clean bandage around it. Her hair fell forward over her face as she bent to her task, and his fingers trolled idly but pleasurably through the damp curls. He traced the curve of her neck, marveling at its delicacy, and the tight whorls of her ears.

"I feel as if I'm discovering you anew," he said in soft wonder. "As if I had not known you before, had not known what it is to love you and desire you."

She raised her head. "I feel it too. But without urgency. 'Tis as if we must wait until everything comes together as it was always supposed to."

Lionel nodded, running a fingertip over the line of her mouth.

"This is a time, this hour that we have when we must wait, when things are being renewed." She spoke hesitantly, feeling for the words. "Like buds waiting for the earth to warm."

She shook her head. "That is so fanciful and I am not in the least a fanciful person, as Robin will tell you."

"On which subject, let us go on deck. We have been at anchor this last half hour."

"We have?" She scrambled to her feet. "I didn't notice."

"I did." He pulled on his shirt, tucking it into the waistband of a pair of plain britches.

"I don't think I can bear to put these slippers on," Pippa said, grimacing. "My feet hurt so when I put them to the ground."

"Easily remedied." He bent to put his shoulder against her belly and hoisted her up. "Forgive me, but this is the only way I can manage with one arm."

"Just don't drop me this time. Once in an evening is quite enough."

They emerged on deck into a profound and silent darkness. The ship showed no light but rocked gently at anchor. Lionel set Pippa down and she thought at first that the deck was deserted, but when her eyes adjusted she saw men grouped around the capstan, ready to bring up the anchor, and when she looked up she could see shapes in the rigging. *Sea Dream* would be under way in a matter of minutes once her passengers were aboard.

She looked towards the coast but could see nothing in the dark. "Is it time for them to be here?" she whispered to Lionel. Fear was once more her companion. It sat on her chest like a rock, and filled her throat.

"Soon," he said. He left her and climbed to the quarterdeck, where Longton stood at the wheel, staring out towards the coastline.

"How long can you give them?"

"No more than half an hour. There's navy ships patrolling the Solent. After the fracas at Southampton they'll soon be lookin' for us."

Pippa climbed the ladder to join them. The pain in her feet was sharp but it had ceased to trouble her. She stood silently beside Lionel, staring into the darkness.

There came a low whistle from way up in the crow's nest and Longton nodded. "They've spotted 'em. Unless 'tis someone we don't want."

Pippa clutched Lionel's hand, her heart jumping erratically. She thought she could see a gray triangular shape in the blackness. A sail . . . surely a sail. A seagull mewed, and was answered by another, and then another. But she was certain no bird made those calls.

"Is it them?"

"I believe so." He had shown not a hint of his own anxiety but now he moved swiftly, following Longton to the main deck. Pippa waited where she was, where she could see the gray triangle grow more distinct as it came closer.

Men scurried soundlessly on the deck below. The small sailing dinghy was now clearly revealed and Pippa could see three figures. One at the helm, one on the prow, taking down the jib, and one huddled in the bottom of the boat.

Robin. Her heart lifted, its beat though still fast became rhythmic again. He rolled the jib deftly as it came down. The little boat knocked against the side of *Sea Dream* and was made fast.

Luisa came up the rope ladder first, tumbling over the rail. Lionel lifted her up and held her for a minute. And then Robin jumped to the deck and Pippa was there, hugging him, silent tears pouring down her face.

DAWN BROKE SOON AFTER THEY ROUNDED THE Needle Rocks and *Sea Dream* danced over the lively waters of the English Channel. Pippa lay in the crook of Lionel's arm on the captain's strange suspended bed looking out through the porthole at the rosy tinged waves swelling and slapping against the side of the ship.

Their loins were still joined as they had been when they fell into a deep sleep an hour or so before. She moved her hips against him and felt him stirring within her.

"I love you," she whispered as he opened his eyes to look into her face on the pillow beside him.

"I love you. I have always loved you. Even before I knew you, I loved you," he said.

She smiled and gave herself to a gentle loving that seemed almost as much a part of her as her own breathing.

But even through the joy of this declared love, the delight she took in his body, there ran a current of sadness, a premonition of loss.

Twenty-eight

PIPPA STOOD AT THE DECK RAIL WATCHING THE FOR-
bidding Breton coast slide past in the early evening of
their third day on the *Sea Dream*. They had left pink-
walled Cherbourg behind in the sun and once they had
rounded the point at Brest the waters of the Bay of
Biscay became choppy and the coastline was a series of
rocky indentations in towering cliffs.

"These waves make me feel sick," Luisa said. "Do
they not you?"

"Surprisingly not," Pippa responded, regarding her
companion at the rail with some concern. Luisa's pale
complexion had a greenish tinge.

"I think we are to go ashore soon," Luisa said with a
valiant smile. "But I cannot imagine how we could land
in those rocks."

Pippa had been wondering the same thing. As the
green waves swelled towards the shore they crashed
upon great jagged reefs of rock, sending plumes of angry white-tipped water high into the sky.

She turned to look up at the quarterdeck as the captain began to call out orders. Feet pounded on the deck,

voices called from the rigging as men swarmed up the lines. The rattle of the anchor chain drowned out the insistent cries of the seabirds.

Lionel was standing beside Longton watching the maneuver with a critical frown. It had come as no surprise to Pippa that he counted seamanship among his survival skills. As the only son of a large merchant shipping house he had spent much of his youth learning the craft.

She turned back to the rail, afraid her expression would give her thoughts away. For three days they had barely left the captain's cabin. They had made love in every possible way, sometimes gentle, sometimes gloriously wild and rough. Every inch of her body felt satiated, used to the full, its most intimate secrets revealed. And throughout they had spoken not one word of the future and not one word of the past, lest such a word should diminish the wonder of their union.

But the time had come now. She knew without asking him that Lionel would not be staying with her in the safe house. He could not simply drop out of his world; he had obligations to his colleagues, who could be endangered by ignorance of his new situation. He had information to disseminate.

Pippa still could not shape her own future even in her mind. She was still a married woman in the eyes of the church and the law. Her child would bear Stuart's name. But it would grow up in exile. She must live shut away from the world until it was safe. But would it ever be safe for her to emerge from the shadows?

She heard Lionel's step behind her and forced a smile to her lips as she turned to greet him. But she could not force her eyes to smile and he read the bleakness of her thoughts in their depths. He knew she was thinking of their separation, of the lonely months that lay ahead for her. In truth, he could barely endure to think of it himself. But it must be endured. It would not last forever, and she would be safe.

He would not talk of it now. Time enough tonight when they were alone. "We go ashore here," he said, bending to kiss her upturned face.

"But how will you get through the rocks?"

He laughed as if the question was absurd. "Oh ye of little faith. I've done it many times, my love. But the way is open only for half an hour at this point of the tide, so we must go at once."

Robin came up to them. His expression was grave and Pippa wondered if he too had some doubts about their success at this landing. "The boat's in the water. Should I take Luisa down first?"

"Aye. Have her sit on the bottom of the boat close to the mast. We need to keep the prow high."

He put an arm at Pippa's waist and eased her towards the rope ladder that hung over the rail.

She peered down at the small sailboat that rocked violently with the rough swell. It looked as tiny and fragile as an eggshell.

Robin went first and stood holding the ladder steady as Luisa, tight-lipped, climbed down. She huddled on the bottom of the little boat where Robin indicated.

"You now," Lionel said. "Sit with Luisa."

Pippa climbed over the side; her feet found the first rung and she climbed down quickly, refusing to think of the green and unfriendly water churning below. Robin held the ladder steady and gave her his hand as she reached the bottom.

It was cold and the light was fading in the gray sky. The sides of *Sea Dream* stretched like a mountain above her and she felt she was abandoning a safe refuge for the uncertainty of this threatening sea.

Lionel jumped down and unfastened the line that tethered the dinghy to its mother. He sat in the stern, his hand on the tiller, as the boat began to drift. Robin needed no instruction and was hoisting the small mainsail, which was all the boat carried.

Lionel swung the tiller and the dinghy came up into the wind, then swung on the port tack and her sail filled. She rode the waves easily and Lionel hummed to himself with the insouciance that never failed to reassure Pippa even as it sometimes annoyed her. He was incapable of carrying a tune, that much she had learned.

He glanced at her as she sat with her knees drawn up, her back against the mast, and he winked. "Not your idea of entertainment?"

"No," she agreed.

"Do you see that handle in the bottom of the boat, by your right hand?"

"Yes."

"When I give the order I want you to pull on it hard to bring up the center board. 'Tis vital that you do it instantly, otherwise we'll go aground on the rocks."

Pippa nodded. Somehow the knowledge of having a task to perform lessened her anxiety. She had a part to play and was no longer a helpless bundle of nerves. She waited, alert, watching the rocky reef as it grew closer. It looked impermeable. And then she saw it. A tiny opening. Through the opening she caught a glimpse of quiet water, a sliver of sandy beach.

Lionel brought the boat into the wind. Her sail flapped. "On my command, Robin."

"Aye." Robin was standing ready to lower the sail. Lionel watched the water, waiting for the moment when a wave would carry them towards the opening. He swung onto the starboard tack and aimed straight for it. "Now!" Robin hauled on the sheet.

"Pippa!"

She yanked up the handle and the shaft of wood came up with it. The little boat sailed smoothly through the vent in the reef and they were bobbing quietly on the smooth waters of a tiny cove.

Lionel smiled his satisfaction and steered the boat on the carrying wave to beach gently on the small strip of sand. "Welcome to Finistere."

"Miraculous," Pippa breathed, looking back. It seemed as if the reef had closed behind them.

Lionel had jumped out and with Robin's help was hauling the dinghy farther up the beach. He held out his arms for Pippa. "I don't think you'll get your feet wet."

She allowed him to lift her clear and set her down on the damp sand. Robin brought Luisa to join her and the three of them stood looking up at the cliff towering over them.

Lionel had dropped the mast of the little dinghy and hauled it high up the beach out of the reach of the tide.

"Will you leave it there?" Pippa asked.

"I'll need it tomorrow afternoon to return to *Sea Dream.*"

It had been said at last. He would be leaving her to-morrow. But that was so soon. She had not thought it would be so soon.

"Of course," she said. "How do we get up this cliff?"

Lionel wanted to take her in his arms, kiss that dull neutral acceptance from her eyes and lips. But he could not do that here. They had deliberately chosen not to talk of the future during the last idyllic days. The discussion would be all the more significant for its postponement but it had to take place in private.

He replied in his usual dispassionate tones, "There's a path. Not much of one, I grant you, but it serves." He set off along the beach and they followed him up a steep and narrow trail that twisted its way up the cliff to a wide stretch of wild wind-torn clifftop.

Pippa looked out over the churning waters to where *Sea Dream* still sat at anchor, an almost indistinguishable shape in the near-dark. A riding light showed from her masthead, but otherwise she was in darkness.

"Come." Lionel took her hand and walked away from the sea. Within five minutes they came to a tiny fishing village. Just a group of cottages clustered around a church. Nets hung to dry on racks between the cottages and the smell of fish mingled with the sharp salt smell and taste of the sea.

Lionel led them to a cottage set a little way back from the others behind the church. A candle shone in a window where a large ginger cat blinked bright green eyes at the night.

Lionel knocked and the door was opened immediately. A tall white-haired man, strong-featured with pale blue eyes that had the distanced look of one who has spent a lifetime earning his living from the sea, stood framed in the doorway. He glanced once at the little party and then back at Lionel.

"Monsieur Ashton, we were not expecting you for another four months."

"Plans change, Gilles."

The man nodded. "You are all welcome at my hearth." He threw the door wide and stepped back.

The cottage was warmed by a fire of kelp and driftwood, pungent oil lamps threw small circles of light. A pair of sheepdogs rose from the hearth and came over to greet the visitors, sniffing suspiciously. At a word from their master they returned to the hearth.

A woman came through a door leading to a rear chamber. She was thin, white-haired beneath a starched muslin headdress of curious design, her eyes a darker blue than her husband's, and her faded complexion showed signs of an earlier beauty. She looked at each one of her visitors as if committing their features to memory.

She came over to Pippa and took her hands. "You are the woman with child."

"I didn't think it was obvious yet," Pippa said, surprised. The woman had a strange accent that made her French difficult to understand.

"I am Berthe. You are perhaps a little over three months now?"

"As best I can calculate."

"Good." The woman nodded. "We shall ensure you bring forth a healthy child. You are too thin. It is good you have come to us sooner than we expected."

Pippa glanced at Lionel for some hint as to how she was to react but he was talking with the man, Gilles, using a strange tongue that bore little relation to French. The woman joined in, and Robin, Luisa, and Pippa stood awkwardly in the middle of the sparsely furnished yet scrupulously clean room.

At last Lionel came over to them. "We will all stay here tonight. Robin and I must go out now with Gilles to talk with someone. We will be back very soon."

"What language are they speaking?" Pippa asked.

"Breton. 'Tis like the Cornish tongue. But Gilles and Berthe also speak French, although their accent will be unfamiliar. But you will become accustomed soon enough."

"I suppose I will." Pippa sat down on the window seat beside the cat, who blinked at her and allowed her to stroke his neck. So this was the safe house where she was to spend at least the next six months. She felt neither pleasure nor dismay at the prospect.

"I don't speak French," Luisa said. "Not any kind of French."

"I'll translate for you." Pippa rose from the window seat as Berthe began to take spoons and bowls from a dresser and place them upon the long rough-hewn table that looked as if it had been made from the trunk of an oak tree.

"May I help you?"

Berthe seemed to hesitate, then she offered a half smile that gave Pippa the impression that her hostess dispensed her smiles thriftily. Berthe said only, "I will stir the soup. You will find bread in the oven."

She left Pippa to set out the cutlery and bowls and find the bread oven set into the brickwork at the side of the fireplace.

The men returned within a very short time and Pippa thought Robin had an air of suppressed excitement as if he was holding some secret, but he ignored her questioning look.

"What have you been doing?" she demanded of Lionel. " 'Tis most discourteous to abandon us like that."

"Ah." He smiled at her and bent his head close to her ear. "We have been arranging a marriage, but Robin wishes to keep it a secret from Luisa until the morning."

"Oh." She forgot her annoyance at once in the pleasure of this prospect. " 'Tis wise I think to waste no time." Her eyes gleamed with amusement. She was well aware that Luisa had been pressing Robin without success to anticipate their wedding night on board *Sea Dream*.

"My thoughts exactly," he said with a dry smile.

They ate potato soup and some strange spiny shell-fish like small lobsters. A jug of cider was passed around and Pippa with a pleasantly full belly felt her eyes grow heavy in the lamplit warmth.

Berthe leaned across the table and spoke to Lionel in her strange tongue. He replied in a few short sentences. She rose from the table and went to a large wooden chest from which she took out an armful of colorful quilts and gave them to Lionel.

"Come, Pippa. Let's to bed." He took her under the arms and lifted her bodily off the bench. "We're going up that ladder." He gestured to a narrow ladder that rose from a corner of the room and disappeared through a hole in the ceiling.

Pippa wondered about Luisa's sleeping arrangement and then decided that Lionel would have taken care of it, as he took care of everything. She climbed the ladder and entered a small chamber under the eaves. There was a straw mattress on the floor and Lionel piled the quilts upon it.

He helped her with her clothes and Pippa waited for the surge of hungry passion that had accompanied their every move in the last three days, but it didn't come, and she could feel in his hands that he too was without desire tonight. It would have been a comfort to make love on this their last night, and until this moment she couldn't have imagined being this close to him without craving his touch.

They lay down beneath the quilts, listening to the

soft murmur of voices in the room below. And then there was silence and the gleam of light that had shone upwards through the uneven floorboards of the attic chamber was extinguished.

"So you are going tomorrow?" Pippa, tense now and no longer heavy with sleep, spoke into the darkness.

"I must. But I will come back."

"When?"

"I don't know. I will try to be back before the child is born."

Could she bear it? Bear to spend the rest of her life waiting? Waiting for Lionel to come back with the smell of the outside world on him, with his mind charged and brimming with the large matters that had always informed her own world, while she lived a shrunken existence with her fatherless child?

"Perhaps it would be best if you did not come back," she said, her voice dull in the darkness. The words came from the dark emptiness of her soul that had come upon her as soon as they had sighted the coast of France. She had not formed the thought then, but now she knew it was the only right thing to say. She could not put that burden upon him.

There was a long silence, then he sat up. "I don't understand. Why would you say such a thing, Pippa?"

"Because eventually you will not want to. You will grow tired of coming back to a woman who has not moved, not changed, not really lived in your absence."

She stared dry-eyed into the darkness. "I would not hold you to blame, but there will come a time when I will wait for you in vain."

And he thought that perhaps she was right. But if he did not come back to her it would not be of his own volition. He said briskly, "There will come a time when you will be able to leave this place, return to your own world." He looked down at her, trying to make out her expression in the darkness.

She laughed, a dry humorless rasp. "Can you promise me that, Lionel?"

And he said what he had said once to Luisa. "No, I cannot promise you. I do not deal in promises, only possibilities."

"Yes," she agreed. "As I thought." She turned on her side away from him and lay staring at the wall as he slid back under the quilts beside her. He put his hand on her hip and she let it rest there.

Lionel told himself that she was tired and naturally dispirited, that her comment revealed not lack of faith in him but a dismal view of the future that the bright morning would dispel. And yet, as he thought of how much had been taken from her, her life as she knew forever lost to her, her faith in herself, in her own worth, battered by betrayals, he could understand that she might now think she should face what lay ahead alone. Yet he felt that her faith in him had slipped and it hurt and angered him to lie beside her, knowing she was wakeful and unhappy, and refusing to turn to him for the simple comfort of his arms.

Pippa slept finally and awoke at dawn to find herself alone under the quilts. Voices rose from below with the clatter of crockery and the smells of cooking. Her nose twitched at the rich and wonderful aroma of baking bread.

She scrambled out from under the mountain of quilts and found a jug of hot water and a crisp linen towel on the floor beside the straw bed.

"Pippa?" Luisa's voice came from the ladder and her head appeared in the hole in the floor. "Oh, you are

awake. Don Ashton sent me to see." She brought the
rest of herself into the attic. "Everyone's very busy. I
think they're preparing for some feast or something,
but I can't understand a word anyone says. Even
Robin's only speaking French."

Pippa remembered that there was to be a wedding
today. Her own griefs must be put aside in her happiness for Robin and Luisa. It seemed that Robin had not
yet shared the happy news with his bride-to-be. In
Luisa's shoes, she would be somewhat annoyed, Pippa
decided, but it was not for her to propose for her
brother, so she only smiled and said cheerfully, "Let me
get dressed and then I'll find out what's going on."

She washed and dressed in the same simple gown
that Lionel had provided on *Sea Dream*. She would have
to get some new clothes from somewhere. But she had
no money. She had brought nothing with her, no jewels,
no coin. She had quite literally gone into penniless exile. She wasn't sure that Robin had much in the way of
money with him. But he would be able to supply her at
some point. And Pen, too, of course. But she couldn't
contact Pen until it was safe. And when would it be safe?

No, today she was not going to think of herself.
Luisa too had only the gown she stood up in and it was
much the worse for wear. Something had to be contrived.

Invigorated by this need, Pippa climbed down to the
main room. A shaft of morning sun fell through the
open door onto the newly swept floor. The long table
was piled with wonderfully painted earthenware crockery and at one end Berthe was rolling pastry.

She greeted Pippa and Luisa with a friendly nod. "If
you wish to break your fast, there is bread and quince
jelly outside."

Pippa thanked her and they went outside where the promised meal was set out on a small table in the sun. There was no sign of either Robin or Lionel, but Gilles was sitting on an upturned log mending a fishing net. He too offered a silent but nevertheless friendly nod.

They would need flowers, Pippa thought as she spread jelly on the warm bread. You couldn't have a bride without a bouquet. There were wild flowers aplenty, so that was easy, but Luisa's gown was a different matter.

She left Luisa with her breakfast and returned to the cottage to consult Berthe.

Luisa was licking jam off her fingers when Robin and Lionel strolled into view from around the corner of the church. They saw her and Lionel said something to Robin, then came on ahead. He kissed the top of Luisa's head as he passed on his way into the house, leaving her openmouthed in surprise at his unprecedented carelessly affectionate gesture.

"Robin, is something happening?"

"Why, yes," he said, with a beam so broad it nearly split his face in two. His eyes danced with joy. "Why, yes. We are to be married this morning."

Luisa just stared at him. "Married?" she said at last.

"Why, yes." He looked at her in mock innocence. "You knew surely that we would be married as soon as we reached France."

"Yes . . . yes . . . but not so suddenly. Not just like this." She glanced down at her well-worn gown. "Without warning. You can't just surprise someone with a wedding, Robin."

Robin looked crestfallen. "You can't? I thought you would like it."

"Oh, men," Luisa exclaimed. "Of course I wish to be married, but there have to be preparations."

"Ah, has he told you at last?" Pippa's amused voice came from the cottage doorway. "I was beginning to think I would have to tell you myself."

She came over to them. "I have been talking with Berthe and she has the most beautiful muslin gown which she would like you to wear. I think 'tis possible it was her own wedding gown but she is not a great one for conversation. Come and look at it."

Luisa looked at the bewildered and still crestfallen Robin. Then suddenly she laughed. "Oh, you are the most absurd creature, but I do so love you, and, yes, I will marry you even though you haven't asked me properly."

She flung her arms around him and he hugged her tightly with a sigh of relief, wondering whether he would ever understand her sex.

They were married in the little church that followed Breton custom with its curious roof of rafters shaped to form the ribs of a fishing boat. The wooden pews were filled with villagers, who seemed to regard the four foreigners at the altar with an almost proprietorial air.

Luisa carried a bunch of wild poppies and golden celandine, and Pippa was filled with sisterly pride in her beauty, so darkly exotic with her black hair and deep blue eyes, and yet so delightfully innocent in Berthe's simple white muslin gown embroidered with tiny knots of flowers.

Lionel pronounced the words that gave Luisa to her bridegroom then stepped back to stand beside Pippa. They had barely exchanged a word in the morning's bustle; she had been far too occupied with preparing the bride to engage in any kind of sustained conversation.

Now he stood close enough for their bodies to touch at shoulder and hip, but after a minute she took a step away, unable to bear the proximity as Robin and Luisa exchanged their vows.

Her marriage to Stuart had been a lavish affair in Southwark Cathedral, attended by the new queen and the Lady Elizabeth. The wedding breakfast had lasted for two days. Pippa had floated above it all enjoying the party as she always did in those carefree days. But she could remember very little of her real feelings about her marriage. She had not been in love with Stuart. And now she wondered why she had then thought that didn't matter. She had spoken these very same words that Luisa and Robin were murmuring with such passionate sincerity, to a man she merely liked, taking on the responsibility of a commitment that was terrifying in its immensity. And she had thought nothing of it.

She loved the man beside her with every fiber of her being but they could never belong to each other in the way that Robin and Luisa now belonged to each other. They could love each other, they could make love to each other, but they could never make these vows to each other. The vows she had once spoken without thought for their meaning.

Lionel looked down at her, at her bent head and the slight droop of her shoulders. He was filled with a fierce tenderness, and an overwhelming sense of possession. He did not want to leave her but he had no choice for now. He knew that Pippa was contrasting her own future with the happiness that lay in store for her brother and his wife.

He was aware of a frustration he had once felt before with her. She had deliberately fractured the glory of their reconciliation, and he didn't know why in the name of God's good grace she had pushed him from her, accusing him of a breach of faith that she had quite simply and quite wrongly decided would happen.

He had not wanted to spoil the joy of their time of rediscovery on *Sea Dream* with the reminder of their inevitable parting, but he had not thought then, not even for a minute, that she would decide that parting had to be permanent.

He would not accept it, and he could not bear to see her so unhappy.

He took her arm above the elbow and walked her out of the church amid the disapproving looks of the congregation as the priest intoned the words of the mass.

Pippa was both surprised and annoyed by her sudden removal from the ceremony. "What's the matter?" she demanded when they stood once more in the sunshine in the deserted village.

"I think you're going to have to tell me," Lionel stated. "You throw a baseless accusation in my face. What have I ever done that you would imagine I would break faith with you, now or at some as yet unknown time? I don't think you understand that you belong to me."

"How can I?" Pippa cried softly. "We can never make the commitment those two have made to each other."

"I have already made that commitment to you," he said, his voice quiet and level. "Can you not make it to me?"

The autumn sun was surprisingly warm on the top of her bare head. She crossed her arms over her breast and stared out towards the green line of the sea. "I would not hold you to it."

"Forgive me, but you have no say in the matter," he

responded, resisting the urge to shake some life into her. "And you did not answer my question."

He caught her chin and turned her face towards him. "Answer me, Pippa. Can you not make that commitment to me?"

"What kind of life could we lead?" she said, meeting his eye.

"Will you answer the question?" His fingers tightened on her jaw and his eyes contained both anger and the fear that he might not win this.

"I love you," she said. "I would commit myself and my life to you. But—"

"There are no buts." He caught her face with both hands and kissed her. It was a kiss of possession, but also of passion that expressed his anger and his hurt. He felt her relax, her lips part beneath his, and he moved his hands from her face to her back, holding her against him with all the strength he possessed as if only thus could he ensure she would not run from him.

When finally he released her, she looked up at him, her lips swollen, her cheeks flushed. "I did not mean to hurt you," she said. "But I thought I was being realistic. I must be strong for this child, I cannot be if I am weakened by my longing and my fear for you."

"I will never leave you. Understand this, Pippa. Even when I am not with you, I will live in your mind, in your heart. You will hear my voice as you go to sleep each night and when you awake in the morning, just as I shall hear yours. This I promise you."

"For a man who does not easily make promises, that is a most powerful one," she said, her eyes blurred with tears.

"I only make the ones I can keep." He took her face

once more and gazed intently down at her. "Will you make me the same promise?"

"Yes," she said. " 'Tis one I too can keep."

"And you will stay here and grow fat and contented and when your time comes Berthe will deliver your child. She is an experienced midwife. And I will promise you that I will move heaven and earth to be with you then."

She smiled. "And now you must go."

"Aye, now I must go. But I leave my self behind."

Later as the evening shadows fell long over the feasting guests, she walked to the clifftop with him. He would not let her come down the cliff path to the beach, so she stood like so many women of this land, watching from the cliff as her man took his tiny boat out through the reef and onto the wild green sea.

Twenty-nine

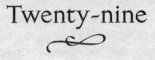

THE FIRST DAY OF MAY DAWNED HOT AND GLORIOUS. Pippa rose with the dawn chorus as she had done every morning of the last six months. She stood in her shift and contemplated the new day as absently she cradled her belly.

The child kicked and she chuckled softly. "You're busy on this May morn, little one." She looked down and smiled ruefully at her inability to see her feet. She had indeed grown fat under Berthe's care. Berthe and Gilles spoke little, in fact none of these Breton folk were quick to give tongue, but they had all watched over her throughout the long, harsh winter months once Robin and Luisa had left to go to the Beaucaire estates in Burgundy.

No strangers ever came to this fishing village. The men fished together, occasionally teaming up with folk from a neighboring hamlet when they ventured far towards Iceland, and when the boats returned safe and laden there would be a mass of thanks and a great feast of celebration, with all the families gathered in the church. Pippa had hesitated to join them the first time but Berthe had come for her and she had been welcomed so naturally that she had never again felt awkward in their company.

She could hear Berthe moving around downstairs and quickly dressed in one of the loose linen gowns that her hostess had fashioned for her. Pippa smiled now to think that she had been concerned about having no money. She had had no need of any. No need of anything at all. At first it had felt strange, frightening almost, to be divested of all possessions, of the power of purchase, but it had not taken long before she had slipped into the rhythm of this life.

The long winter days she had spent curled up with the cat before the fire, sewing for the child growing big within her. Berthe had succeeded in teaching her to enjoy the art of the needle where her mother and her old nurse had signally failed. But now it was spring and Pippa felt herself throwing off the lethargy of winter like a snake sloughing its skin.

She edged down the ladder, an awkward maneuver these days, and greeted Berthe with a few words of Breton that she had managed to master. She took the bowl of new-drawn milk that Berthe insisted she drink every morning, and a chunk of warm crusty bread spread thickly with butter, and went out into the sunshine.

Gilles was whittling a toy for the baby. He had already carved two dolls and a horse with its own little cart. He nodded at Pippa as she came over to him, and showed her the wooden rattle he was carving.

" 'Tis lovely, Gilles. The baby will be quite spoiled with so many beautiful toys."

He cracked a pleased smile and took up his work again. Pippa, still eating her breakfast, continued on her regular morning walk, up to the clifftop where every day, regardless of the weather, she came to gaze out over the cold sea, looking for *Sea Dream*.

She didn't know whether Lionel would come by sea or on horseback over the rough inhospitable landscape of Finistere. She had had no message, but she hadn't expected one. He would come when he would come.

She gazed out across the sea that today was a calm and glittering blue under the soft May sun. The grass at her feet gave off wonderful scents of sea pinks, clover, and lavender. She sat down on the grass to finish her bread and milk and then began idly to make a daisy chain.

The first twinge she ignored. She had had many in the last weeks and Berthe had told her not to be troubled by them. When delivery drew close the womb began to prepare. This twinge seemed no more severe than the others.

The next one, some ten minutes later, was very different. Pippa put her hands on her belly, feeling it harden then relax as the pain, and it was now a pain, not severe but definitely no longer a twinge, diminished.

She was not frightened but she rose to her feet slowly, picked up her empty bowl, and walked back to the village.

Berthe took one look at Pippa when she came into the cottage and said instantly, "Ah, 'tis time."

She put her hand on Pippa's belly and kept it there throughout the next pain. She nodded. " 'Tis good, but not strong yet. Go and sit in the sun. 'Tis too soon to take to the bed."

She began to take herbs from the drying racks as Pippa went back outside, feeling curiously peaceful.

Her body was in charge now and she could only leave it
to do its work.

She sat down on a rough bench that Gilles had put
beneath an oak tree whose branches were just beginning to show pale green foliage and closed her eyes. For
six months she had waited here in what seemed to her
almost a trance, her life suspended, but the waiting
would soon now be over. Her mind turned inward, in-
sulating her from the world around her as another wave
of pain, a little stronger this time, tightened around her
belly.

She didn't hear the horses' hooves on the grassy lane
beyond the cottage. She opened her eyes only when a
shadow fell across the dappled light that warmed her
face.

Lionel stood above her.

"You have come," she said, not moving, just looking
up at him, drinking in the wonderful familiarity of his
countenance. He seemed to have materialized out of
her trance and fleetingly she wondered if he was indeed
a figment of her longing.

He knelt on the grass beside her and touched her
face. "I have missed you so," he whispered. "Every
minute of every day I have longed for you."

"And I for you," she replied as he cupped her cheek
in his palm. "But I knew would come." She parted
her lips for his kiss and tasted the sweetness of his
tongue and his mouth and the long months of separation vanished as if with a magician's wand.

A bubble of energy burst within her and the strange
trance evaporated. She took his hand and placed it on
her belly. "You are come just in time. This babe is anxious to be born."

"Now?" he asked in surprise. "Today?"

"I believe so," she said, and kept her hand over his as her belly hardened again. His expression of confusion and alarm made her smile through the pain. " 'Tis quite normal," she reassured. "I thought you to be the expert on pregnancy."

"I know little or nothing about birth," he replied ruefully. "I was never in a birthing chamber."

"There is a first time for everything." She stood up as the pain receded and placed her hand on his arm. "I think I need to walk a little bit."

"Then let us walk this way," he said. "You must see what I have brought you."

"I have no need of gifts," Pippa replied. "You are all the gift I need."

"Oh, I think you'll find this one pleasing," he said with a complacent grin. "We will walk to the church, if you think you can manage to go that far."

" 'Tis but a few steps," she said scornfully, taking his hand. Energy coursed through her and it was hard to remember her inertia of a few minutes ago. She no longer felt peaceful and passive, but vigorous and eager to resume her life, to be done with this birthing so that she could embrace her child.

She didn't at first believe her eyes when they rounded the corner. A man and a woman stood deep in conversation just outside the church, their tethered horses cropping the grass of the little churchyard.

"Pen?" Pippa breathed. *"Pen!"* She shouted her sister's name in wonder and delight.

"Pippa . . . dearest Pippa." Pen gathered her skirts and came running towards her. "Oh, I am in time. I wanted so much to be with you for the birth. But we could not come before because of the winter and the roads were so bad."

She hugged her sister, laughing and crying at once. "Oh, you're so big. I can't put my arms around you."

Pippa was crying too. "I have had such need of you, Pen. Ever since—"

"Yes, yes, I know." Pen interrupted her, laying her wet cheek against her sister's. "Lionel told us the whole dreadful story. My poor Pippa."

"No, not poor Pippa," Pippa said, smiling through her tears. "I am as happy as 'tis possible for anyone to be. Lionel has come back and he has brought you to me, and this baby is about to be born and—" She broke off with a gasp, a spasm of pain twisting her face.

Lionel rushed over to her, Pen's husband, Owen d'Arcy, on his heels. "You shouldn't have walked," he said. "Let me carry you back."

Pippa merely shook her head and waited for the pain to lose its grip, then she straightened. "Do you remember Philip's birth?" she asked her sister with what was now a wan smile.

" 'Tis all something of a blur," Pen said vaguely. In fact she remembered those long hours of agony all too well. She would not wish such a birth upon her sister and she would not tell her of it. "You must go back to the house."

"Let me carry you," Lionel insisted.

Pippa managed a half laugh. "I am far too heavy. And I can walk the few steps well enough." She turned to her brother-in-law. "Forgive me, Owen, I have neglected to greet you."

"You are a little occupied at the moment," he said in his low melodious voice that held a smile in its depths. "It seems we arrived just in time. Pen was most anxious to be with you."

Pippa opened her mouth to speak and closed it

abruptly. She clutched Lionel's hand, squeezing until the pain released her again.

"We had better go now before the next one," Pen said.

Lionel nodded grimly and without a word lifted Pippa into his arms. He half ran with her, barely noticing the weight in his anxiety to get her back to Berthe.

Berthe regarded his precipitate arrival in the cottage with some surprise. She set down the pot of boiling water that she had just lifted off the fire. "I bid you welcome, Monsieur Ashton," she said calmly.

"Where should I put her? The baby's coming," he said urgently.

"It'll be a while yet," she said with the same calmness. "No need for panic."

"But she's in pain."

"Aye, 'tis always thus. I have prepared the bed in the back. Put her down there and I'll see how she's getting along."

Pippa could almost have laughed at Lionel's total lack of composure. He was always calm and in command of himself and events around him but now he was behaving like a chicken without a head.

The bed in the back was where Berthe and Gilles slept. It was separated from the rest of the cottage by a curtain. It had been stripped and coarse linen sheets spread upon the straw mattress.

Lionel laid Pippa down and stood helplessly as she struggled through another band of pain, beads of sweat standing out on her forehead.

"Go and pace around with Owen," Pippa said when she could breathe again. "I think that's what men are supposed to do at these times. Pen will stay with me."

"Yes, go," Pen said, pushing him towards the curtain. "I don't think you're doing any good here."

Berthe came in with a cup from which curled an aromatic herbal steam. She carried a pile of cloths beneath her arm. She waved Lionel towards the outer chamber, and reluctantly, yet with some relief, he obeyed the instructions and fled to the other side of the curtain.

Owen was pouring cider from a copper jug into two tankards. "I can't find anything stronger," he said, handing one of the tankards to Lionel. "But enough of this should help."

"My thanks." Lionel drank deeply. A muffled cry came from behind the curtain and he paled.

"Outside," Owen said quickly.

Lionel followed him into the noon sunlight.

"She won't die," Owen said, reading his mind. "Mallory women are strong. Strong in mind as well as in body."

Lionel nodded. He spoke softly and yet with a dreadful determination. "I could not bear it, Owen. If I should lose her giving birth to Philip's bastard I will kill him with my bare hands."

"She will not die," Owen repeated. "She will have a healthy child. A child that will be of no use to Philip once it is born out of his reach. There can be no clandestine substitution of a healthy infant for a dead one if he does not have the healthy one in his grasp."

"Mary retired to keep her chamber in Easter week and there has been no news of a birth as yet." Lionel forced himself to contentrate on this conversation when his ears were straining to catch a sound from the cottage.

"Noailles has it on the best authority that Mary is deceived and there is no pregnancy. The swelling of her belly is but a tumor of sorts," Owen said. "But we will await events. Whatever the outcome of Mary's confinement Pippa and her child will no longer be under threat in France. Philip will not pursue them here."

He glanced at his companion for verification and shook his head in sympathy. There was no topic that would distract Lionel.

He tipped up his empty tankard and said, "There has to be something stronger around here."

As if he had heard him Gilles emerged from a shed carrying a stone jar. "Calvados," he said, setting the jar on the ground beside the bench under the oak tree. "My own. This is what we drink at these times. Drink that and, as we say, you will drown the woman's pains." He lifted the jar to his lips, then passed it to Lionel.

The three men sat on the bench under the tree as the afternoon wore on and the level of apple brandy in the stone jar went down. Berthe came out once, told them that everything was going as it should, and hurried into the village, returning within a very few minutes with another woman.

"Why does she need help?" Lionel demanded of Gilles.

Gilles shrugged. "An extra pair of hands is useful at these times."

As the shadows lengthened and the sun began to dip below the horizon, Lionel jumped to his feet. His head was spinning from the calvados. "I cannot sit here any longer." He strode into the cottage.

Owen glanced at Gilles, who gave another phlegmatic shrug and raised the jar to his lips.

Lionel blinked in the dimness of the cottage. He could hear the murmur of voices behind the curtain but it seemed ominously quiet. He found he was holding his breath in absolute terror. And then Pippa yelled and his heart that seemed to have stopped began to beat again. She was swearing, a gasping stream of oaths and obscenities that would have shocked even Lionel in other circumstances.

He burst behind the curtain. Pippa was half sitting, leaning back against Pen's supporting arm. Her eyes were tightly closed, the veins standing out on her neck. The words still poured from her as Berthe and the other woman worked at the end of the bed.

Lionel grabbed Pippa's hand. It was the only way he could help her in this elemental struggle. She clung to his hand with an unbelievable strength, crushing his fingers so fiercely he thought they would break. And then suddenly she relaxed, falling back against Pen, still holding Lionel's hand but loosely now.

He looked towards the end of the bed and gazed in wonder at the slippery, blood-streaked, waxen little body that Berthe held between her hands. She hooked a finger in the baby's mouth and a thin wail pierced the stifling air of this confined space.

"Why, what a fine girl child it is," Berthe said.

"Oh," Pippa said. "Give her to me." She took the child and gazed at her. "Is she not beautiful?"

Lionel thought that was something of an overstatement. The baby's skin was now red and wrinkled, her eyes scrunched up, a waxy film covering her body. But he could count ten fingers and ten toes and a rather fine head of fair curls. Her limbs seemed straight and her cry grew ever lustier. She was, he thought, every ounce her mother's daughter.

"Yes," he said. "Quite beautiful."

Pippa smiled at him, a radiant and utterly complacent smile. And he wanted to laugh aloud with joy. He kissed her and pushed the sweat-soaked hair from her forehead. "How clever you are."

"Yes, aren't I?" she said, yielding the baby to Pen, who hovered, arms outstretched to cradle the newborn.

"Now, Monsieur Ashton, you must leave. We will make Pippa comfortable and see to the babe. Then you may come back." Berthe gave him a little push and Lionel went out.

" 'Tis a girl," he said to Owen and Gilles, who had not moved from the bench.

"Then we must wet her head," Gilles said, heaving himself somewhat unsteadily from the bench and returning to the shed for another jar of calvados.

"You have my felicitations." Owen offered Lionel his hand.

Lionel took it, meeting the intent gaze of the man who had become his friend rather than a distant partner in the last weeks. He was moved by the gesture, for it acknowledged that Lionel had been as responsible for the infant's safe arrival in the world as any blood father.

He sat down with a thump beside Owen and shook his head, dazed and bedazzled.

After a while Pen came out to them. "Pippa wishes you to bring her out here," she said. "Berthe says it will do no harm. She shouldn't walk for a few hours, but the fresh air will be good for her."

Lionel said with concern, "No, it can't be good for her. Surely she must remain in bed."

"Well, if you can persuade her, you have more influence than I." Pen sat down on the bench with a weary but contented smile. "I don't know what's in that jar but I think I would like some."

Lionel went into the cottage and found Pippa sitting

up in the bed in a clean shift with her hair brushed. She cradled the swaddled bundle in her arms.

"You must carry us out," she said. "Berthe says 'tis warm enough for the baby for a few minutes and 'tis so stuffy in here I can barely breathe."

"It can't be good for either of you," Lionel protested.

"Well, if you will not carry us, then I shall walk," Pippa stated. "Berthe tells me it was a very easy birth, although it didn't feel like it at the time," she added. "But I will recover sooner if I don't lie around like a windfallen apple."

Lionel offered no more objections. He lifted Pippa, who still cradled the baby, and carried her outside. Gilles had slung a sailor's hammock between the oak tree and a neighboring birch and Lionel put his burden down carefully in the gently swinging cradle.

Berthe followed them and tucked a quilt over mother and child. "No more than a half hour," she said. "While I do what has to be done within. Gilles, you will help me with the straw." She gave him a significant nod and he followed her into the cottage, leaving their visitors alone.

"I had not thought of girls' names," Pippa said, lightly touching the baby's cheek with her little finger. She looked up at Lionel, who stood beside the hammock. "Will you hold her?"

He had wanted to ask but had not wanted to intrude upon the miraculous closeness of this mother and child. After nine months of sharing the same body they were separated and yet he sensed not yet completely. Now he held out his arms and took the baby.

"Would you wish to call her Margaret?" Pippa asked softly, hesitantly. Afraid that perhaps instead of being the right thing to suggest it was the very worst.

Lionel too touched the child's cheek with his finger-tip, amazed at the softness of her skin and at the extraordinary scent that rose from her. A scent unlike any he had ever known. He thought perhaps it was vanilla but that was too prosaic. It was delicate, flowerlike, and it filled him with such love, such a fierce protectiveness that he didn't think he could let her go.

"Meg," he said, and lifted her to his lips to kiss the top of her head.

"Meg," Pippa said, and held out her arms for her child. Lionel laid his daughter on her mother's breast.

"We came for Meg's birth," Pen said. "But also for your wedding." She stood beside Lionel, her eyes shining. "When you are churched, the priest will marry you."

Pippa looked at her in confusion, wondering if her postpartum daze had affected her understanding. "I cannot be married," she said. "I am married to Stuart Nielson."

"There is a letter from Mama." Pen handed her the letter she had held against her skirts.

Pippa transferred Meg to the crook of one arm and took the letter. Pen and Lionel stepped back as if to give her privacy. She read in silence, absently stroking the baby's cheek as she did so. Malcolm had reached Derbyshire and had told her mother the whole. Reading her mother's words of comfort and advice and understanding, she could hear Guinevere's voice, could almost feel her touch. Tears clogged Pippa's throat, but she read on and suddenly had no desire to weep.

Her mother wrote that although they were still confined to their estates there, they had also received a letter from Stuart Nielson. He had made full confession to the Bishop of Winchester and had enclosed a declaration of the annulment of his marriage to Lady Philippa Hadlow, signed by the bishop.

At the end, Guinevere wrote: *"You may marry as you wish, love. Lord Hugh and I give you our blessing in whatever decision you now make. We put our faith and trust in the man who has pledged himself to your care. You will not be able to return to England unless Elizabeth succeeds Mary, but as soon as we are able we will come to you and Pen. We are anxious to meet your Mr. Ashton, and also Robin's bride. We lament a world that has torn our children from us, but we will contrive. Write to us when you are able."*

Pippa looked at Lionel. "Have you read this?"

"Of course not," he said. "But your sister gave me the gist."

"I hope Stuart and his lover are safe and content," Pippa said almost to herself. She wondered why she was not surprised that Stuart had finally revealed his strength. She could never forgive his betrayal, no one could. But she could wish him well.

She turned her face up to where the evening star and a crescent moon shone through the pale green leaves of the oak tree. Meg began to snuffle at her breast, and then to cry, loud, imperative hungry cries.

ON MIDSUMMER'S EVE PIPPA STOOD AT THE ALTAR of the little church beneath the ceiling that represented the hull of a fishing boat and for the second time made her marriage vows. She remembered how she had stood in this same place listening to Luisa and Robin pledge themselves to each other. Now as she spoke her own pledge, she felt the power of her words as she had not felt them that first time amid all the pomp and panoply of Southwark Cathedral. For better or for worse, she and this man and their child were all and everything to each other.

It was late but the sky on the longest day of the year still held light in it when the feasting was finally done.

"I will take Meg tonight," Pen said. "You are churched and 'tis your wedding night."

"A wedding present that couldn't be more appreciated," Lionel said, taking Pippa firmly by the hand. "Say good night, Pippa."

Pippa kissed Pen and handed over the baby.

"Let us go, wife."

The attic chamber was strewn with wild flowers and lit by a precious, sweet-scented wax candle. The straw mattress was covered with a fine linen sheet with lavender and rosemary threaded into the folds.

It was a bridal chamber and they found themselves strangely hesitant, as if they were indeed a bridal couple who knew nothing of each other's bodies. But when they touched each other in the ways that they knew, then it was as it had always been.

"My wife," Lionel whispered into her ear. "My own."

"My own," Pippa replied, drawing a fingernail down his spine. "My own." She pressed her hands into his buttocks as she lifted her hips to meet his thrust. He slid his hands beneath her, holding her against him, and Pippa gasped at the wonder of it. At the astounding glory of a life that could go so awry and then right itself in such utter perfection.

Afterword

On August 3rd, 1555, after a pregnancy that had been proclaimed for twelve months, Mary finally left her apartments at Hampton Court, where she had waited for four months to be delivered of a child that had never been conceived, and resumed her customary routine. On August 29th, Philip, knowing he would never now have an heir to rule England, left for Flanders, never to return either to his wife or to England. On November 17th, 1558, Mary died and was succeeded by her half sister Elizabeth.

About the Author

JANE FEATHER is the *New York Times* bestselling, award-winning author of *To Kiss a Spy*, *The Widow's Kiss*, *The Least Likely Bride*, *The Accidental Bride*, *The Hostage Bride*, *A Valentine Wedding*, *The Emerald Swan*, and many other historical romances. She was born in Cairo, Egypt, and grew up in the New Forest, in the south of England. She began her writing career after she and her family moved to Washington, D.C., in 1981. She now has over six million copies of her books in print.